INCENTIVE FOR DEATH

INCENTIVE FOR DEATH

A NOVEL

JAMES SPOONHOUR

OCEANVIEW PUBLISHING
SARASOTA, FLORIDA

ISBN 978-1-60809-576-6

Published in the United States of America by Oceanview Publishing

Sarasota, Florida

www.oceanviewpub.com

10 9 8 7 6 5 4 3 2 1

PRINTED IN THE UNITED STATES OF AMERICA

This book is dedicated to Marie Spoonhour
1922–2021

My mother was an Army nurse in WWII, married my father who was in the Army Air Corps but passed away in 1973, raised three sons, and was widowed the last forty-nine years of her life. She was also an avid reader until macular degeneration stole her eyesight late in life and she switched to audible books. She regularly monitored my progress on this book and was hanging on until it was finished. To my regret, she didn't quite make it.

INCENTIVE FOR DEATH

CHAPTER ONE

EARLY APRIL SAW the last of the cherry blossoms drop at the edge of the Tidal Basin. They did not foretell the three homicides that would occur in the District of Columbia over the next twelve hours. Homicides that seemed unrelated—but were actually connected. One of those cases would be assigned to Detective Mac Burke.

* * *

As Monday evening fell, the offices in Northwest D.C. emptied of most employees. Many headed for the Metro stations, while some retrieved their automobiles from the self-contained car parks under their office buildings or walked to public garages where they had monthly spaces reserved.

At Gideon & McCaffery, work wound down a little later. The law firm's fifty-five attorneys occupied two complete floors of the middle-aged Charter Building on L Street NW. By the time the cleaning crew arrived around eight in the evening, most of the staff and all but one of the partners had left. Most of the associates had also departed, except those working on appellate briefs or pleadings with impending deadlines.

Weldon Van Damm, the managing partner of the firm, was in his office in the southeast corner of the 12th floor, the one with the best view of Farragut Square and Lafayette Park. There was a copy of the *Washington Post* laid open next to his desktop computer. Van Damm's office was the largest in the firm, as befit his position.

After a light rap on his door, he looked up to see a young woman in a blue business suit. Gideon & McCaffery was one of the few law firms that did not endorse the trend toward casual dress in the office. The woman could easily have been one of the young attorneys the firm hired each year, worked hard for several years, then decided they were not *partner material* and let them go. He did not recognize her, but he had trouble remembering the names of the annual additions to the associate ranks.

She moved toward his desk and held out a folder containing about a quarter inch of papers. As he reached for the folder, she deftly jabbed something in his neck and just as quickly withdrew the syringe. Van Damm's eyes went wide, and his head and neck shook for several seconds. Then he slumped forward onto his desk. He was dead within twenty seconds of hitting the blotter.

The young woman had touched nothing inside the office. She picked up the folder, and used a knuckle to turn off the lights and depress the lock button on the inside of his office doorknob. Using a tissue, she pulled the door shut and checked to make sure it was locked. She then took the curving internal staircase down to the 11th floor and used the stairs next to the elevator to walk down to the parking decks below street level. Leaving the parking garage, she turned her white car right on L Street and headed toward Georgetown.

CHAPTER TWO

MY NAME IS McDermott Burke. I was named after my mother's father. I currently live in a restored row house in the 700 block of Morris Place NE in a part of the District of Columbia referred to as the Capitol Hill area.

I live with my ex-wife, Maggie Hampton, some three years after we got an amicable divorce, which not even our closest friends know about. We had been married about four years before we mutually agreed on the split.

Maggie has never revealed what she does for a living—not even to me—although I have long assumed that she works for the CIA in some capacity. I call her Mags. She calls me McDermott, my full first name, although nearly everyone else calls me Mac.

Sometimes it is friends with benefits—and sometimes not— when she occupies one of the guest rooms. She still leaves for a month or two, always with no warning that she is departing—or that she is coming home.

The best indicator that she is away is whether her classic 1959 Porsche Speedster is missing from our two-car garage. She had the Speedster convertible when we got married.

*   *   *

On Tuesday morning, I woke up about six thirty.

By seven, I was showered and dressed. I ground a batch of Starbucks Pike Place beans and made a pot of coffee, which I took out to the deck on top of the garage at the back of the house. I sat at the wrought iron table in the shade of a red maple. My guess was that the maple was around a hundred years old, probably about the same age as the house. The sky was clear with a comfortable spring temperature. I was into my second cup and first Marlboro in the dappled shade when my cell rang.

"Mac, Chief Whittaker here. We just got a call—homicide at a law firm in Northwest. Grab Oliver and head over to Gideon & McCaffery at 1817 L Street NW. This could be a big one. Brief me as soon as you clear the scene."

"Yes, sir. Will do."

I speed-dialed my partner, Oliver Shaw. He answered, "What's up so early, Mac?"

"The Chief just called me and gave us a homicide at a law firm on L Street. I'll pick you up in five minutes."

Oliver replied, "Make it ten."

I grabbed my suit coat, headed out the back door and down the steps from the deck to the garage. I hit the garage door opener. I noticed the Speedster was not in residence.

I jumped into my 1991 Jeep Grand Wagoneer and backed into the alley. After lowering the garage door, I headed toward my partner's house, which was only twelve blocks away.

At that point, I had no idea what this case would turn into.

CHAPTER THREE

As I eased down the alley, I reflected on why my thirty-year-old Jeep Grand Wagoneer was still on the road. It was only by my stubbornness that this piece of flawed engineering was still running.

I took Maryland Avenue NE, which was the quickest route to Oliver's house on Holbrook Avenue, not far from Gallaudet University. The curbs were covered with parked cars. As I pulled across the opening to Oliver's driveway, he came out the front door, suit coat draped over his arm.

Oliver climbed into the passenger seat with a big smile and a hearty "What's up?"

"No idea what we've got on this one. Just an address and name of a law firm."

At some point during the thirteen years we had been paired as detectives at MPD, Chief Whittaker started calling me with new assignments, even though Oliver had about five years of seniority on me. I sensed that Oliver never understood why I had become the contact person for the Chief. Candidly, neither did I. It may have had something to do with my being the more verbal partner in our briefings of the Chief on our cases. Oliver never said anything about it, but I sensed that he noticed.

We headed toward Northwest D.C. We took Connecticut Avenue and then turned left on L Street where we saw three blue and white MPD patrol cars in front of a granite and glass office building about fourteen stories tall. The lettering on the marquee identified it as the Charter Building. The medical examiner's white van was also there. I pulled to the curb and slapped an OFFICIAL POLICE BUSINESS placard on the dash. We climbed out and put our suit coats on.

A uniformed sergeant stood at the main entry.

"Morning, Sergeant," Oliver said. "What've we got?"

"We can't shut down the whole building, but we've sealed off the 11th and 12th floors where the law firm is located. We're controlling traffic in and out of those floors. Take the fourth elevator. You'll want to head to the 12th floor. That's the main reception and where you'll find the deceased."

*　　*　　*

A key had been inserted in the control panel so that MPD could control the elevator for the duration. We punched the button for 12 and rose at a slow hydraulic pace.

On 12, we entered a high-end lobby with GIDEON & MCCAFFERY, LLP in 15-inch brass letters on the facing wall, which was covered in taupe-colored linen. At least I assumed that was the color, as I am one of the quarter of males who suffer from red-green color blindness, which means I don't see pastels very well.

To our left was a wall of floor-to-ceiling windows facing toward Georgetown. Near the windows was a spiral staircase about eight feet wide curving down to the 11th floor.

A patrolman stood next to the elevators to control traffic into or out of the firm's offices. We signed his log. He pointed us down a hallway to the right. "Go to the end of the hall by the corner. The crime scene crew and the M.E. are already down there."

We found the crime scene guys in white Tyvek jumpsuits near a small seating area outside the corner office. None of the techs were sitting so as to not cross-contaminate their protective coverings.

Brady Pollard, the lead crime scene technologist, pointed at the dark paneled door, which stood ajar at the entry to the corner office. "The M.E. is inside. After she pronounces, we'll go in and do our thing."

"Thanks, Brady. A secretary or other admin staff?"

"A secretary. We put her in the office next door." He pointed to the closest door adjacent to the seating area.

Oliver and I headed to the door of the corner office and stuck our heads in. Dr. Courtney Vaughan, Assistant Medical Examiner for the District of Columbia, was just straightening up after leaning over the deceased's body, which was sitting in a tall leather desk chair and leaning across the leather blotter inlaid in the top of the large walnut desk. The M.E. was early fifties, about 5'8" tall. Her hair was dark brown with a few gray ones intermingled, likely the result of her eighteen years in the trenches as a D.C. medical examiner.

She held a magnifying glass in her right hand. "Mac and Oliver," she said when she noticed us. "Glad you guys caught this one."

Oliver asked, "What have you got so far, Doc?"

"Only preliminary. I'll need to get him on the table to be more definitive. Quick body temperature, taking into account the residual temp of this office, indicates that he probably died sometime yesterday evening. I'll be more precise after I get a liver temp."

"What's the magnifying glass for, Doc?" I asked. "Kind of Sherlock Holmesian, isn't it?"

"I needed to take a closer look at something—I noticed a small red spot just above his shirt collar on the left side of his neck. Closer inspection with my trusty illuminated magnifying glass— which I always carry in my black case—revealed what looks like an injection puncture mark with a fine needle. I can give you more on that also when I get him on the table. I'll expedite the tox screen to see what turns up. And the magnifying glass used by Sherlock did not have a self-contained source of illumination."

"Good catch," I noted. "So, the method may be fairly easy to determine. It's just a matter of whodunnit."

"Yep. Looks that way. As soon as the crime scene guys are done with the body, we'll get it transported to my shop. The bus is already here. My guys are waiting to bring the stretcher up as soon as they get the 'all clear' from Brady."

"You going to do this autopsy yourself?"

"Yes. As you will find out shortly, the deceased was a mover and shaker in this town of movers and shakers. This case will likely get a lot of attention. So far, no sign of the media. Did you see any when you came in?"

"Nope. But that was a few minutes ago, so the status could easily have changed."

My partner was looking at his phone screen. He looked up at me. "Just checking to see who called it in and the time. The answer is Susanna Wales, the secretary we apparently have ensconced in the office next door. Time of call was 7:15 a.m."

We thanked the M.E. and headed next door. "It's all yours as soon as the M.E. leaves," I told Brady. "She has the bus downstairs when you're finished working around the body."

*   *   *

Oliver knocked on the door of the neighboring office and stepped inside. "Ms. Wales, I'm Detective Oliver Shaw from the Metropolitan Police Department, and this is my partner, Detective McDermott Burke." We both showed her our credentials.

The office showed signs of active use. There were several piles of documents organized on top of the desk with more stacks on the credenza in front of the window. Less than half the size of the corner office where we had just been—I figured it belonged to someone lower in the pecking order.

Susanna Wales was sitting in a chair at the end of the desk. Oliver asked if we could sit and she nodded. We took the two brown leather chairs in front of the desk.

As was our practice, I sat in the chair closest to her and Oliver took the other seat and pulled out his notebook. In our pairing, I was usually the initial interrogator and student of body language, while Shaw was the notetaker and the person who listened to the voices to pick up signals not otherwise visible. It was a system that worked well for us over the thirteen years we had worked as a team.

The woman's red eyes and the wadded-up tissue in her left hand made it clear that she had been crying. She confirmed her name and said that she was Weldon Van Damm's executive secretary. "Actually, they call us legal assistants now, instead of secretaries," she added. She was nicely attired in a gray suit with a white blouse underneath. Other than earrings, she wore no jewelry. No wedding or engagement rings, and she appeared to be in her forties.

I started the discussion. "We understand that you called 911 this morning. Can you tell us what led up to that call?"

"Sure. I work directly for Mr. Van Damm. He's the managing partner here at the firm. He usually gets in around seven thirty in the morning, so I try to get here between seven and seven fifteen. I park in our reserved section of the underground parking garage."

"What time did you get here today?"

"About ten after seven. After parking downstairs, I took the elevator up to 12 and headed for our offices. My office is the cubicle right beside Mr. Van Damm's door."

"Was the law firm already open?"

"There's no door, as such. The elevator that serves our two floors is locked once the last person leaves at night, which is usually the cleaning crew. As usual, the lights were on in the lobby, meaning someone else had already come in. No one was at the reception desk. Never is at that hour. Reception usually staffs up around eight."

I needed to connect some dots. "So, there was somebody in the office before you?"

"I don't know about the 11th floor offices. I usually don't go down there much. The reception lobby lights come on automatically when someone steps off the elevator. The timer is set to stay on all day. So, somebody had come in before me, but I don't know who. That's not unusual. Particularly the associates come in to get an early jump on things."

"Sorry to break your train of thought," I interrupted. "So, you came in and headed toward your office?"

"Yes. I put my purse in the bottom drawer of my desk and retrieved my key to Mr. Van Damm's office to unlock it. He always locked the door when he left at night."

"Was that key locked inside your desk?"

"Yes. I have a key to my desk on my key chain. I unlocked Mr. Van Damm's door and reached in to flick on the lights, as usual. I almost fainted when I saw Weldon asleep at his desk. He never does that. I went over and shook his shoulder a little, but he didn't move. I almost screamed."

I gave her my understanding facial expression and signaled for her to continue.

"I thought he might have had a heart attack. He felt cold when I touched him. I spoke to him a couple more times. I just had a feeling that he had died. I wasn't sure what to do, so I called 911."

"What did you tell the 911 operator?"

"I just told her that I think my boss is dead in his office and could they send someone. She asked me a couple questions and said they would send someone over."

"How soon did the police arrive?"

"About five to ten minutes later, two police officers showed up. Before they got here, I had told our office manager and a couple of the partners that Mr. Van Damm appeared to be dead in his office. They looked inside, but I don't think they went in his office." Shaw asked for their names and noted the three of them in his notebook for a follow-up interview.

When we had finished with our questions, we asked Susanna Wales to stay away from her cubicle, other than to retrieve her purse. Then I asked her to meet us at MPD headquarters so that we could talk to her further. "We won't know until later what the cause of death was, but we need to cover all the bases." She agreed to meet us at two that afternoon. We gave her our cards. We also told her the crime scene techs would want to get her fingerprints for purposes of elimination.

*   *   *

After advising Susanna Wales to notify the office manager that she would be with us during the afternoon, we headed back to Van

Damm's office. I stopped at the doorway, saw no body, and assumed that it had already been transported to the Medical Examiner's morgue.

I asked Brady Pollard if the scene was completed enough for us to enter. "Just don't touch anything yet. We've got a ton of prints still to cover. Otherwise, it's clear."

"His admin is in the office next door," Oliver said. "We asked her to stay put so that you can get her prints for elimination."

Brady asked one of his techs to get her prints and contact information.

Then we entered the corner office for our first good look around. All of the furnishings looked tasteful and expensive. Unlike most lawyers, Van Damm did not have a wall of fame displaying his degrees and other certificates.

I looked closely at the scrimshaw hanging next to his door. It looked to be of excellent quality. "Isn't this stuff illegal these days?"

"I think it's whale bone and not ivory," Brady said. "Probably not illegal to own it."

"So, back to business," I said. "Find anything of interest?"

"Tons of prints and the papers he was working on. Nothing obvious. The inside of the doorknob was wiped clean. There were prints on the outside doorknob, but those are likely to be the secretary's when she unlocked the door this morning and then grabbed the knob again when she closed it after discovering the body. We'll sort out the prints. Bottom line: no smoking gun, no blood, no sign anything had been disturbed."

Brady pointed to the door. "Also doesn't appear to be a robbery. His suit coat is hanging on a wooden hanger on the back of his door. His wallet is in the chest pocket with credit cards and $800 in cash, as well as his identification."

Brady also said that Van Damm was wearing his wristwatch. "It was a classic Phillipe Patek—probably worth $150,000 or $200,000."

"Better bag it all, particularly the wallet."

"Sure."

I looked at the desktop and added, "The M.E. thinks he may have been injected with something. See if you find anything that might support that."

Brady looked at me. "You mean like a half-filled syringe with clear prints on it?"

"Yeah, something like that."

I checked out the desktop again. "Did you get pictures both before and after the body was removed?"

"Yeah. We're going to bag everything you see including the files, computer, and newspaper. The firm will probably squawk about it. We'll get permission later, if needed. Forgiveness is easier to get than permission."

"Did you find his cellphone?"

"Yep. It was on his desk under the newspaper. We already bagged it."

Oliver said, "They probably have direct inward dialing so that callers don't have to go through a receptionist. Brady, can you check with their IT person and, if that's the case, see if we can get a printout of his incoming and outgoing numbers for at least the last month?"

Brady commented: "That'll be another thing they will have a fit about."

"Give it a go and let us know. Thanks, Brady."

CHAPTER FOUR

As we stepped out of Van Damm's office, Oliver pulled his cell-phone and punched one of his speed dial numbers. After a few seconds, the call was answered. "Hey, Doc," he said, "Oliver Shaw here. I know it's early, but any chance of narrowing down the time of death? It will help with what we've got to do here."

Dr. Vaughan replied, "I stuck a thermometer in his liver as soon as he got here. Let me check it." After a pause of about thirty seconds, she came back on the line. "Best guess based on his temp is that he expired around nine p.m., give or take an hour."

"Thanks, Doc. That helps a lot." Oliver ended the call and reported. "About nine p.m.—plus or minus an hour."

"Let's talk to the office manager," I said. "Get a cast of characters and then check with building security."

Oliver nodded in agreement.

We found the office manager, Cornelia Cox, in her office. She was talking with a man with salt and pepper hair who was wearing a blue glen plaid suit. We identified ourselves and showed our credentials. I explained that we needed some information. Ms. Cox introduced us to Ransom Simon, whom she indicated was one of the firm's partners. He offered whatever help he could provide and excused himself.

We closed the door and sat across from a woman of about sixty years with silverish hair and a gray jacket over a black shell and black skirt. She was a small person, probably a little over five feet tall and quite thin. Her face was a little puckered, like she had been sucking on a lemon, which seemed indicative of her general personality.

"What can you tell me about Weldon's death?"

"We don't have a cause of death yet," I replied. "That's what the Medical Examiner will determine for us."

She puckered her lips again, as if that was an unsatisfactory answer. I suspected that repeated puckering is probably what gave her lips deep-seated vertical lines. I asked, "How long have you been with the firm?"

"Since day one when the firm was founded just short of thirty years ago. I came over from the old firm where the five founding partners worked. I've been the office manager the entire time."

"You must have known Mr. Van Damm well."

"I was the first staff employee he hired. For years, my office was two doors down from his."

"Why isn't he part of the firm name?"

"Back then, he was the most junior of the five attorneys who split off to create this firm. Gideon and McCaffery were the most senior back then. And the biggest rainmakers of the bunch."

Oliver asked, "Are Gideon and McCaffery here today?"

Again, with the pucker. "Not hardly. John Gideon died about twenty years ago. He had been a big-time collegiate swimmer at Dartmouth. He was a big guy who lived well and had a problem with his weight. One Saturday morning he went jogging, came back to his house, and had a massive heart attack as he walked through the kitchen. The doctors said he was dead before he hit the floor."

Oliver again: "What about Mr. McCaffery?"

"Well, he's been retired for about ten years. He's eighty-five and lives in Kalorama with his wife."

"Looks like the firm has grown a lot over the years."

She nodded and unpuckered her lips. With an almost proud mama smile, she said, "We're at fifty-five attorneys now with twenty-four partners and thirty-one associates. We have around seventy support staff, including paralegals, secretaries, bookkeeping, et cetera."

"And the firm is on both the 11th and 12th floors?"

"That's right, but the main reception area is on the 12th floor. Clients have to come to the 12th. Anyone can get on the elevator on 11 to leave, both employees and clients."

Oliver asked, "Who's usually here in the evening, say after seven?"

The pucker was back as she thought about it. "Most of the staff is gone by six. Some of the associates work later to score points and possibly be seen burning the midnight oil by Mr. Van Damm. He likes to patrol the offices around eight in the evening to see who is paying their dues. He also comes in on Saturday mornings to do the same, but he never stayed around on Saturday mornings. He would just come in and make a circuit to get a feel for who was working and who wasn't. What he didn't know is that the associates would watch out the windows to see when his car left the garage. Then they mostly all bolted too."

"Playing the game then?" I asked.

She nodded. "He worked the associates hard. When they came up for partnership after eight years, usually only one or two would make partner. If they were passed over for partnership, they were given three months to find a position somewhere else."

I guess I had a querulous expression on my face and she responded. "That process is similar at most firms. Up or out. It's pretty tough for those who don't make the cut."

Oliver asked, "Any way to tell who was here yesterday evening?"

The pucker came back again. "I'm not sure. Our IT guy could probably tell us whose computer was in use at what times, but a lot of the attorneys, both associates and partners, work remotely from home, so that may not tell us much."

"Do you have a cleaning crew come in at night?"

"Yes. Usually at eight. We use Potomac Office Cleaners. I don't know who is on their crews, but the person in charge of our crew is usually Maria Valdez. I'll get you her contact information." Oliver made an entry in his notebook.

At that prompt, I asked if we could get a roster of all the attorneys and staff with their contact information.

The pucker was back again. She looked slightly put out by the request, although I was sure she could just task her computer and we'd have the lists in seconds. We each gave her our business cards and asked that she email the contact information to both of us. She nodded that she would.

I asked where the building security office was. She directed me to an office off the lobby on the ground floor. We thanked her and took our leave. Oliver and I exchanged a look, but said nothing out loud as we headed to the elevator. We each knew what the other was thinking. Oliver did an eye roll and gave his head a slight shake.

* * *

When the elevator doors opened onto the ground-floor lobby, Oliver showed his credentials and asked the security guard at the counter where the main security office was located. We were directed to a glass door just past the bank of elevators. Black lettering on the glass identified it as the office of REPUBLIC SECURITY SERVICES with a telephone number below.

The door was locked but there was a button below a speaker box. Oliver pushed the button and was asked to identify himself.

"MPD Detectives Shaw and Burke."

We were buzzed in and met by a man dressed in highly polished shoes, black trousers, and a starched white shirt with epaulettes bearing a silver bar similar to those worn by first lieutenants in the service. The left shoulder of his shirt had an embroidered black and gold shield with Republic Security Services' name and logo. He held out his hand and identified himself as Lt. Robert Johnson, which we could have figured out from the name tag above the right chest pocket on his shirt.

"I assume you're here about the death on 12?"

We both nodded, shook his hand, and presented our credentials. I asked, "Can we discuss this in your office?"

"Certainly. This way."

His office was neither small nor large. His desk was black, as were his vinyl desk chair and the two chrome and vinyl chairs in front of it. He had a large desktop monitor and keyboard on the left side of his desk. There were two rows of closed-circuit monitors on the wall to his left, all of which appeared to be producing high resolution color pictures from outside the building and various locations inside. Tilting my head at the wall of closed-circuit monitors, I asked, "Where are all the cameras located?"

Lt. Johnson looked at the monitors and pointed while responding. "Outside we have camera one covering the main entry on L Street. Another is above the entry and exit to the underground parking garage, which is this split-screen monitor. A third camera is over the rear service door on the alley, which is primarily used by the cleaning crews and the city trash collection trucks. There is another camera over the elevator doors facing into the parking garage.

"Inside, we have one behind the reception security desk in the main lobby, basically facing the front entry and lobby area. We then have three cameras in elevators 1 through 3. There is no camera in elevator 4. There are also cameras facing the elevators in the landing areas in front of the elevators on all floors except 11 and 12. There is also no camera facing the elevators on 14."

"You didn't mention floor 13."

"There isn't one. The builder was apparently one of those developers who thought it would be hard to rent a thirteenth floor. So there just isn't one. The irony is that the penthouse suite on floor 14 is actually on 13."

"Why no camera in elevator 4?"

"That elevator is a dedicated elevator and goes only to floors 11 and 12, and that law firm has leased those floors since the building first opened about thirty years ago. My understanding is that this building came online in a very down market, and large new tenants could pretty much dictate their terms. I'm told that Gideon and McCaffery came in and agreed to take the two floors, if they got a dedicated elevator. I think elevator 4 was originally planned to be dedicated for the penthouse suite on 14. They also required the builder to install an interior staircase connecting the two floors."

Oliver's brow wrinkled like there was something that did not compute. "But why no camera in elevator 4?"

"I'm told we first put closed-circuit cameras in the elevators about fifteen years ago and upgraded them about five years ago. Both times Gideon and McCaffery asked that no cameras be placed in their elevator or in their lobby. Said it was for client confidentiality."

"Can you burn us copies of all traffic in and out on all cameras from about five p.m. yesterday until midnight?"

"Sure, no problem." He picked up his desk phone and hit a single digit. He said, "Hey, Don, I've got two MPD Detectives with me about the death on 12 last night. Can we burn them a copy of all traffic on all the CC cameras from five to midnight yesterday? Yes, including the elevators. How soon can you have that done?"

Lt. Johnson looked up at us. "We can have those burned for you within about thirty minutes. You want me to send them to your office or will you have them picked up?"

"Can you have them couriered over to our office?"

"Sure." We both gave him our cards.

CHAPTER FIVE

BEFORE WE STARTED talking to a lot of people, I thought we should get some generic information on our decedent. I pulled my cell and called our intern, Kit Cardona.

"Kit, it's Mac. You got time to do some research for Oliver and me? We caught a homicide this morning and need to know something about the guy."

She paused. "I was just headed back to American to do some research on a paper I've got due next week." Kit was a third-year student in the Criminal Justice program at American University. Her goal in life was to be a cop, and she had landed a relatively low-paid internship with MPD and was ecstatic when she got assigned to the homicide division.

I jumped in. "Kind of need this right away. Big-shot lawyer named Weldon Van Damm, the managing partner at Gideon and McCaffery. I gather he may be someone prominent in this town of self-important people."

"Okay, I'll get right on it and leave my initial findings on your desk."

I headed back toward MPD headquarters. Given that it was now lunchtime, we were able to score a space in the parking lot.

CHAPTER SIX

THE METROPOLITAN POLICE Department headquarters is located in the Henry J. Daly Building at the corner of Indiana Avenue NW and C Street NW. Being a history buff, I had read that in his design for the federal city in 1791, Pierre L'Enfant had designated this area as a site for federal courts.

Over time, a variety of municipal buildings had been constructed in the area. During the Depression, plans were made to redevelop the area. Judiciary Square, which is now occupied by the U.S. Courthouse and the D.C. Superior Courthouse, is across the street from MPD's headquarters.

After five years of construction, the Municipal Center was opened in 1941. The six-story building housed multiple city departments, the largest of which has always been the Metropolitan Police Department. The Mayor has since moved to nicer quarters on Pennsylvania Avenue NW near 13th Street.

The building is encased in sandstone in the style of the Pentagon and most other government buildings constructed in the 1930s and 1940s. The outside of the building had become seriously covered in soot and grit over the years and, in my opinion, could use a good pressure washing. The place looks in need of some TLC.

Oliver and I entered the building from the parking lot, bypassed the always slow-moving security screening line, and went through the line reserved for police officers and high-ranking metropolitan officials. We showed our badges and were waved through without the headache of going through a scanner, which would be set off by our pistols.

I only carry my pistol because of department regulations. I have never had to fire it in the line of duty in my thirteen years with MPD and, in fact, the only time I ever fired my pistol in my eight previous years as a Special Agent with the Office of Special Investigations was the monthly firing range qualification required by the Air Force. Back then, we used a Smith & Wesson .38 Special, a 5-shot revolver that had an undersized grip, making them notoriously difficult to use for target shooting. I was a bad shot to start with and always took two of my junior guys to shoot alongside me. They could each qualify with four shots and would each drop one in my target. I never had more than five holes in my target and also qualified.

We rode the escalator to the second floor, and then took the elevator to the fourth floor, home of the homicide division. Like most cop movies ever made, each set of partners had two metal desks facing each other and a single lockable metal four-drawer file cabinet. Ours were near the back of the Homicide room.

We had received three emails from Cornelia Cox, the office manager at Gideon & McCaffery. I sent the lists of attorneys and staff and the cleaning company info to the printer. Oliver confirmed that the closed-circuit footage was on its way to us.

*   *   *

Next up, we took the elevator to five to see our boss, Chief Inspector George Whittaker. Unlike movies and television, his office was not a glass cube at the far end of the floor housing all of the detectives. Given his rank as a Chief Inspector, he was on the 5th floor with all of the other division chiefs and their minions.

Whittaker's assistant, Corporal Beverly Gray, was not at her desk outside his office. We knocked.

"Come in."

After twenty-three years as a detective with MPD, George Whittaker deserved the 12' x 12' office with a window facing Judiciary Square. One wall had a well-worn black leather sofa, and there were two black leather chairs with hobnails in the Chesterfield style in front of his wooden desk.

The wall behind his desk contained bookcases that held awards and citations of significance to his career. The only items not up to the style of the rest of his office were a couple of four-drawer metal cabinets, although they were at least black rather than the usual governmental gray.

George Whittaker had been a detective in nearly all of the divisions, spending the longest period in Homicide. Whittaker is a six-foot African American with a close-trimmed head of hair and a gray brush mustache. He seems taller because he always stands erect and is trim. It doesn't hurt that he is probably the best-dressed person in the entire department.

We both said "Chief" as a greeting and gave a slight nod. He waved us to the chairs in front of his desk. He asked us what we had on the Gideon & McCaffery case.

As was our usual approach, I summarized things first and Oliver followed up with specific details and items for further follow-up. "The decedent was Weldon Van Damm, the managing partner at the firm."

Whittaker exhaled. "I knew him somewhat from events around town."

I continued. "The M.E. found a pinprick on his neck and is suspicious that he was injected with something that killed him. She is running a tox screen and determined TOD as around nine p.m. yesterday. She's doing the autopsy herself this afternoon, and we'll go by to see if anything further shows up to give us a direction to pursue.

"He was sitting in his office chair with his head and shoulders leaning forward on the blotter portion of his desk. Nothing appeared to be stolen. No sign of a struggle."

Oliver joined the conversation. "We've already talked to the office manager who has been there for thirty years. She has provided us with lists of all of the attorneys and the contact for the cleaning service which comes in each evening. Video from all the closed-circuit cameras at the building is being delivered to us within the next hour."

I added, "We did a preliminary interview with his legal assistant—who discovered his body when she came in this morning. She'll be here at two o'clock for us to get a formal statement."

Oliver said, "After talking with her, we probably need to focus on the video to see who was coming and going during the window of seven to midnight. And get those people identified."

"So, preliminarily, it looks to be a homicide, but no ideas on who or why yet?" Whittaker asked.

"No, sir," we both said.

"Keep me posted regularly. This guy was prominent enough that I'll be getting questions from upstairs."

CHAPTER SEVEN

SERENDIPITY HAD PLAYED a significant role in his life, Vincent Morehead reflected. More than once.

After college, he had gotten into Army Intelligence as a second lieutenant. He felt that he had found his niche and excelled in intelligence analysis. What he couldn't stand about the Army, however, were the morons who populated the ranks of majors and lieutenant colonels who were his superior officers. Morehead didn't think they could survive in the real world and their own ineptitude prevented further promotions.

When his four-year tour of duty came to its conclusion, Morehead figured there was a limited shot at advancement with these deadweights occupying the seats above him. He had decided to move on when he was approached by a recruiter for the Special Operations Group of the CIA.

They were seeking people to run intelligence operations disguised as cover businesses owned by the Agency. He saw it as an opportunity to succeed based on merit, contrary to any future in the Army.

After his training, Morehead ran two successful operations in Afghanistan. The first was an import business that brought in weapons and military gear needed by the tribal chiefs in the northern part of the country. In getting that material delivered to the end recipients, he was initially surprised by the extent of shrinkage in the shipments due to theft and black-market sales— mainly by his own staff.

Over the months he ran that operation, he became drinking buddies with Kurt Bardak, the shipping manager where most of the shrinkage occurred. Kind of like the note on cereal boxes that some settling of contents may occur during shipment.

In return for not keeping too close an eye on the shipments, Bardak cut Morehead in on a share of the proceeds from the black-market sales. Morehead started to accumulate money, and he liked it.

Then Langley decided to move Morehead to another front organization. This operation was officially designed to help resettle Afghan refugees displaced by the never-ending war with the Taliban. He asked that Bardak be transferred with him to the new operation. They set up shop in Kabul.

They employed a number of Afghan government people in their new operation and, for a period of time, effectively relocated many refugee families. Their funding from the Agency continued to grow as the volume of dispossessed persons increased. There was virtually no monitoring of the funding, and Morehead developed a system to shrink the funds by keeping two sets of books.

After Morehead had made off with three million dollars from a larger tranche of nearly unaccountable funding, the proverbial shit hit the fan. Morehead had planned well for this eventuality. He had put some of the local government officials in the path of any investigators who came to determine what happened.

After the accounting types gave up and fled back to the safety of the States, the Agency gave up and shut down the relocation operation. Because they couldn't clearly determine who was responsible, the Agency pulled all of its employees back to the Special Operations Group located in the New Headquarters Building in Langley, Virginia. Morehead was transferred out of the Special Operation Group and made the chief of the Financial Analysis Section of the Political Action Group.

Morehead had dodged a major bullet on that one. When he relocated to Virginia, he had a substantial amount stored in three offshore numbered accounts.

Morehead decided he needed to use a more subtle means of growing his wealth. He was not satisfied with the prospect of growth through a wealth manager. Plus, he thought, that led to a paper trail and taxes. He didn't want either.

CHAPTER EIGHT

SUSANNA WALES ARRIVED shortly before two p.m. We had the desk sergeant put her in Interview Room Two. We used to call them *Interrogation Rooms*, but the name was changed to sound less confrontational.

Once inside the interview room, I offered her a bottle of water, and she thanked me.

Oliver took his notebook out to jot down anything that might need follow-up. Everything said would be captured on the automatic audio and video systems for later review if necessary.

I told her that we had an automatic audio and video system. "At the end of our discussion, we have software that converts our discussion into text and then we have you review it, make any changes you want, and sign it."

"Am I a suspect?" she asked.

"Oh no. We do this with all of our interviews. Oliver takes some notes, but he's not fast enough to keep up like a court reporter would." Oliver nodded to that, and she gave a small smile of acknowledgement.

"We figure you knew Mr. Van Damm as well as anyone at the firm. We're looking for background, and any thoughts you have may be helpful, even if they didn't seem important to you at the time."

"Okay. What do you want to know?"

"First, tell us again how long you have worked with Weldon Van Damm."

"For the past fourteen years or so."

"Tell us about Mr. Van Damm."

"Well, he's been the managing partner ever since Mr. McCaffery retired about ten years ago. The other partners elected him the managing partner. He's been running the firm ever since."

"I'm not that familiar with how law firms run. What were his main duties? Did he have problems as the managing partner?"

She said, "Mainly it was overseeing the day-to-day operation of the firm. He also chaired the compensation committee that decided bonuses at the end of the year, which he sometimes got some blowback about. He also oversaw the hiring of new associates and, occasionally, the hiring of a lateral partner from another firm, if they brought in a substantial enough book of business." She paused for a bit, as if she were in thought, and then continued, "About six months ago, the firm was not doing as well as it had been, and he and a couple of other senior partners made the decision to fire five partners and five associates."

"How did they decide who to fire?"

"Well . . . I wasn't privy to those conversations. I did regularly see the monthly partnership books that showed the revenue brought in by each partner and associate. After those ten people had been given their notice, I went through the most recent partnership books, and it looked to me like those ten people were either bringing in less money or working less billable hours than the others. I assumed that is what got them fired."

"Was it a surprise to those people who got fired? I mean . . . did they see it coming?"

"I don't think they saw it coming. The decision was made over the weekend, and the three partners who made the decision dropped the bad news on each of them as soon as they came into the office on Monday."

"So, they were fired on the spot? Uh, did they have to clean out their desks and leave the office right then?"

"Pretty much. I typed the termination letters on Sunday. Those were the letters they were given on Monday morning. The partners got three months' severance pay and the right to officially continue to be part of the firm . . . to help them find a job somewhere else. They were not allowed to come into or use their office after they were terminated. The associates got one month's pay but had to leave immediately. The termination letters came with the severance checks in them. But they only got the severance pay if they agreed on the spot to sign a waiver saying they couldn't sue the firm."

"Did they all sign the waivers?"

"Every one of them did. They were each told, both the partners and associates, that their personal stuff would be boxed and delivered to their homes that afternoon. All of them had to leave immediately so that they couldn't download anything from our computer system. It had to be kind of humiliating, particularly for the partners.

"Mr. Van Damm had a security guard in the office in case anyone had to be walked out to their car. He also had our IT guy ready to immediately cut off all their access to our computer system and the offices."

Oliver spoke up. "Must have been some pretty unhappy campers that morning."

"You got that right. I would say all of the partners and three of the associates were totally shocked. The other two associates were kind of deadbeats and had to know they were never going to make it."

Oliver asked for the ten names. He wrote them down in his notebook.

I asked for the names of the other two partners who participated in the decision on whom to terminate. She gave us those names, and Oliver made a note.

Then I asked, "Did most of them land with another firm?"

"I'm not sure about the associates. I think three of the partners found jobs." She named names. "One decided to start his own practice." Again, she named him. "And one just quit practicing altogether." Again, she identified him. Oliver made annotations in his notebook.

"Did he have any problems with clients? Like disgruntled clients?"

"He was a business attorney. He set up companies and helped them with various corporate issues. He didn't do lawsuits. So, he never lost a case that someone would be upset about. I'm not sure if he ever saw the inside of a courtroom. I think his clients liked him a lot. He socialized with a lot of them—you know, golf, dinners, serving on boards. That sort of thing."

"Was he married?"

"He'd been divorced from his second wife for at least seven years. They didn't have any children. His children by the first marriage are both grown."

"Girlfriends?"

"I think he dated some, but I think it was just people kind of in his own circle. Like friends. Or existing acquaintances. I usually booked his travel, and he hadn't had any seemingly romantic holidays in a long time."

"Had the firm been sued for anything? Malpractice or otherwise?"

"I'm pretty sure that the firm had not been sued for anything in the fourteen years I worked with Mr. Van Damm."

"Are you aware of anyone in the firm or outside the firm who had a hostile relationship with or hard feelings toward Mr. Van Damm?"

"None other than the fired partners. And I think they all got over it."

"Can you think of anyone who had a reason to want him dead?"

"Not really. He was a tough taskmaster with the attorneys. Very demanding. Always trying to squeeze more work out of them. But I think that's the way it is at most firms."

"Okay. We'll hit the print button and the system will have this typed up in ten minutes or so. Then one of us will bring it in for you to review and sign. Sorry about your loss. Will you be staying at the firm?"

"I hadn't even thought about that. Oh my. Guess I'll have to check with the office manager tomorrow and see what happens."

CHAPTER NINE

WHEN WE GOT BACK to our desks, we had received a padded envelope from Lt. Robert Johnson, the head of security at the Charter Building. Inside was a note explaining that they had enclosed a thumb drive covering each of the closed-circuit cameras from five p.m. to midnight the previous day. Each was labeled by the location of the camera.

Someone was going to have to view all the footage and make a list of the times when people entered or left the building and parking garage. As I was reading Lt. Johnson's note, our intern, Kit Cardona, approached my desk with a manila folder, which she said contained her initial background research on Weldon Van Damm.

Kit is five foot eight inches tall and has a tight crown of black hair with a reddish tinge. Her skin is light brown and tinted with freckles across her nose and cheeks. This confident young lady has a total can-do attitude about nearly all requests we make of her. She also has much better computer skills than either Oliver or me.

"Want to make some overtime?" I asked her.

"Whatcha got?"

"Lots of closed-circuit footage from eighteen cameras at the Charter Building. Time span on each is five p.m. yesterday to midnight."

"That'll take forever. What am I looking for?"

"Yeah, it's too much footage. The M.E. thinks the time of death is around nine p.m., so let's initially restrict the search from eight to ten and limit it to the external cameras on the front door, the garage entry, and the rear door, as well as the cameras over the lobby reception desk on the ground floor and in elevators 1 through 3. Also, the camera over the elevators in the garage.

"Maybe also cover the cameras on the elevator landings on floors 9 and 10 for the same time frame," Oliver added.

"For now, ignore the landing cameras at the elevators on floors 2 through 8," I said. "What I'm looking for is a list of the times when people come and go on the cameras. Particularly those leaving between eight thirty and ten so that we can get people at the law firm or building security to try to identify them."

Kit had been taking notes. She held up one finger and said, "Couple of questions. First, aren't there cameras on the law firm's elevator landings on 11 and 12?"

Oliver answered, "Nope, the lawyers didn't want cameras there or in their dedicated elevator, which is number 4, by the way, and only serves those two floors. Supposedly to keep their clients' identities confidential."

Kit scrunched up her right cheek, which partially closed her right eye and compressed the freckles on that side of her face. She always wore this dubious expression when she questioned something that Oliver or I said. "Are there other law firms in the building? I assume none of them are doing the same thing about no cameras."

"You said a couple questions. What are the others?"

Kit did that scrunch-up-the-right-side-of-her-face thing again. "Well," she said, "it is going to be very time-consuming if we make someone sit through hours watching video on ten cameras, with lots of fast-forwarding. They won't be happy about spending that much time. Why don't we make a condensed version that only shows people coming and going, and eliminate all the dead time in between?"

"Good idea. But keep the originals intact. Can you do that?"

"Sure. I'll pick up some clean thumb drives from IT and see if I can sweet talk someone there to help make the duplicates."

"Great. If we're lucky, maybe we get a picture of the person leaving. Probably less likely to catch them coming in because we have no specific time frame to focus on."

Kit: "I'll make sure the compressed videos still have time stamps on them."

I mentally checked that chore off our to-do list.

*   *   *

After detailing Kit Cardona with the package of thumb drives, Oliver looked at me. "What say we get IT looking at his phones and then regroup to figure out our next steps for tomorrow?"

"It's a plan. Let's go talk to Carter Enright." He is head of MPD's Information Technology division. We verified that he was in and we rode down to the third floor to Enright's personal version of the Geek Squad. Their quarters looked more like a college laboratory with long tables covered with every type of desktop and laptop computer, as well as iPads and similar devices. The tables shaded servers beneath.

Enright saw us coming and ushered us into his conference room, which also serves as his office. He was not a conventional sort of guy. He stood about 5'5" with thinning sandy hair. His wardrobe consisted of blue button-down oxford shirts and khaki pants with cuffs. He either wore the same clothes every day or had multiples of the very same items.

On top of that, he had a squeaky, nasal voice. All of this probably contributed to his lack of employability in the private sector—which was a major gift to MPD. Enright could surgically unwrap nearly anything electronic, especially computers, telephones, and digital images.

We had alerted him that we had a request to unravel incoming and outgoing calls on both landlines and a cellphone. Enright brought his best person for the job, Pamela Chenire. She made Carter Enright seem almost normal. While Oliver stood 6'3" and I am right at 6' tall, Pamela is easily 6'6" and wore gray slacks and what looked to be size 12 men's New Balance cross-trainers that made her seem even taller. No wonder she'd been a college basketball star at Dickenson.

Despite all that, the woman could unravel phone data better than anyone I had ever met. We addressed our request to her, as Enright had planned.

I explained what we needed. "This morning we caught what appears to be the homicide of the managing partner of a good-sized law firm in Northwest. His name is Weldon Van Damm. Our preliminary interviews do not indicate any obvious suspects. We have some disgruntled ex-employees, but otherwise we have very little so far.

"What we would like is a list of all incoming and outgoing calls on his cellphone, along with the identity of the person on the other end and their company. Brady Pollard from CSI has the cell.

"Their office also has direct inward dialing, so Brady is supposed to get the history on his desk phone from the firm's IT people. We don't have his home phone as yet but will do a search in the morning."

"We'll need the incoming and outgoing info on all three phones for at least two weeks," Oliver said. "A month would be better."

Pamela made a note of Van Damm's name. "Anything you can get me on his service providers will expedite things."

"How soon can you get it to us?"

"Probably by late tomorrow afternoon if you get me the service providers. I have decent contacts at nearly all of them."

I smiled. "Great. Hopefully, that will help us."

CHAPTER TEN

OLIVER CALLED Dr. Courtney Vaughan. When she answered, he said, "Doc, this is Oliver Shaw. We're wondering if you've come up with a cause of death yet."

"I just got the toxicology report but haven't had a chance to read it. Are you nearby?"

"We're at headquarters but can be there in fifteen minutes."

"Good. Come on by and we can go over what I've got."

We headed to the office of the Chief Medical Examiner on E Street SW, which is catty-corner from NASA's headquarters. After finding a parking place, we went to the reception desk at the M.E.'s office, showed our credentials, and said that Dr. Vaughan was expecting us.

Wearing a thigh-length white lab coat, Courtney Vaughan opened the door a couple minutes later and waved us in without saying a word. We followed her back to her office.

She was not big on social amenities and got right to it. "I did a whole-body exam and didn't find anything obvious, other than the pinprick that I pointed out to you at the scene."

Oliver asked, "Any idea what was injected into him?"

"As I said, I just got the tox report, which I got expedited by calling in some serious chits. The chief toxicologist couldn't find anything specific, other than increased potassium levels, but potassium is naturally released when the muscles relax after death."

I leaned in closer. "So, what's your best guess as to what was injected into his neck?"

"Well—and this is just a guess at this point—possibly succinyl-choline—commonly referred to as 'sux.' It releases potassium. Before you ask—it's a neuromuscular blocker used in small doses to relax the muscles, but in a sufficiently large dosage, it can para-lyze a grown man in thirty seconds or less. That would result in death by asphyxiation and leave potassium behind."

"Is there a test for it?" asked Oliver.

"The complication for us is that potassium dissipates quickly. And then there is the potassium released by the muscles after death. Since we didn't get his body until around twelve hours after death, any potassium from an injection could have been absorbed or covered up by the release from the muscles. We also submitted a biopsy from the area of the injection, but the toxicologist found it to be indeterminate."

"Who has access to this *sux,* or is it readily available?"

"Every operating suite. Succinylcholine is commonly used in small doses by anesthetists to relax the neck muscles to accommo-date intubation. There are other uses, too, but that's one of the most common."

I asked, "So, what's your conclusion as to cause of death?"

"Asphyxiation—consistent with a large injection of sux. The lungs would relax, and breathing would cease in less than a min-ute. That's the best I can give you at this point."

"Oh, for the good old days of gunshot and stab wounds," I added.

Dr. Vaughan shrugged. "Yeah. Sorry. Best I can do for now."

* * *

By the time we returned to the fourth floor, the afternoon was well advanced. Oliver and I looked at each other. He said, "What else do we need to do before we call it a day?"

"We need a search warrant for Weldon Van Damm's house."

He picked up his desk phone and called Beverly Gray, Chief Whittaker's assistant. She handles all subpoena and warrant requests from the detective division, both search and arrest.

"Beverly, Oliver Shaw here. Mac and I caught a homicide this morning. Death of the managing partner of a law firm in Northwest. We need a search warrant for his house." He gave her the name and address. She asked him some follow-up questions. "Thanks, Beverly. How soon do you think you can get it signed by the judge? Late this afternoon or first thing in the morning is perfect."

Oliver turned to me. "She'll run it by her usual friendly judge."

* * *

After a mutual pause, Oliver said, "We need to set up a 'to do' list. Given our dearth of clear suspects, we need to see who inherits." He opened a Word document, headed it *Weldon Van Damm—Next Steps,* and added the date.

Oliver called Lyle Barber, the interim managing partner at the law firm. His legal assistant put Oliver through to Barber. After identifying himself, Oliver said, "Mr. Barber, we need to track down Mr. Van Damm's will. Any idea who might have prepared it for him?"

"Probably Ransom Simon," Barber replied. "He's the main wills and estates guy here at the firm. He does the wills for most of the partners. I'll transfer you over."

Barber conferenced Ransom Simon in on the call. "Ransom, Lyle Barber here. I've got Detective Oliver Shaw from MPD on the line. They're looking for Weldon's will. Did you prepare it?"

"Yes, I did. I've got a copy of the signed will. He last changed it after his divorce about seven years ago."

"Can you email a copy to Detective Shaw, along with any other key estate documents?" Barber asked.

"Sure. It hasn't been probated yet. But it will be a public record once it is." Oliver gave Simon his email address and thanked both of them.

"Back to the list," I said. "We need to see what Kit comes up with from the closed-circuit footage." As our designated scribe, Oliver added that to the list.

"We also need to review the incoming and outgoing call lists that Pamela from IT is assembling for us," Oliver said and added that to the list as well.

I said, "In addition, we need to see what Brady's financial person gleans from Van Damm's records." Oliver noted that as well. "Also, we need Kit's general background info on Van Damm."

"What about a list of his clients?" Oliver said. "Where do we get that?"

"How about the office manager or the new managing partner?" He made a note of that as well.

"We also need to talk to the cleaning crew," I added. "See whether they saw anything. Need to get them before their memories fade."

"And," Oliver said, "what about the two partners involved with Van Damm in the purge?"

We sat thinking for a bit. "Nothing else occurs to me," I said.

"Me neither. What should we do first?"

I smiled. "Well, you've already partially checked off the first item about tracking down the will. Has it come in yet?"

Oliver opened his email. "Yep. Let me print out two copies."

We both sat at our desks reading Van Damm's will, as well as his living will and durable power of attorney.

"Well, his children inherit everything," Oliver began. "He has two children. Both are grown. According to his secretary, they were his children by his first marriage. She said he didn't have any by the second marriage.

"The will says their names are William Van Damm, age thirty-five, and Aurelia Van Damm Perkins, age thirty-two. We need to find out where they live and if they have alibis. Also, need to figure out how big his estate is."

Oliver made another note and added, "Maybe Brady's financial person can help us with that also."

"His living will gives a durable power of attorney to Whitney Van Damm," I noted. "Who is she? He must have trusted her. She had the power to pull the plug if he was a vegetable and to manage his affairs and finances if he was incapacitated. Must be a relative whom he trusted." She went on the list also.

When he was done, Oliver printed two copies of the list. We had ten items to pursue just from day one.

"Ten investigative points, but not a suspect or motive in sight," I summarized. "How about we get an adult beverage and discuss next steps before we call it a day?"

"Capital idea."

We both closed up our desks and grabbed our coats.

*   *   *

After retrieving my Jeep, we headed toward the Capitol Hill neighborhood in Northeast. Not far from Buster's—the gym where we worked out—was an old neighborhood bar called Burton's. We were semi-regulars at the place, which was run by a diminutive lady around sixty years old who inherited it from her late husband. Burton was his first name. Her first name was Shirley.

It was around four thirty when we pushed open the double swinging glass doors. The usual handful of regulars sat at the bar nursing beers. Shirley smiled and called out, "Hey, guys. Business or pleasure?" By which she meant were we working or here to play pool in the adjoining room. Working meant we would take a booth so we could talk in relative privacy.

Simultaneously, we both said, "Business." She spread her arms toward the six vacant booths along the wall opposite the bar. We headed toward the next-to-last booth.

As soon as we were seated, Shirley was standing next to our table. She didn't say anything. She just waited for our order.

"Shirl, you are a breath of fresh air in this depraved world," I said with a smile.

"That kind of day, huh?" She knew what we did for a living, plus we were just about the only people who ever wore suits into her fine establishment—which we had to do to conceal our pistols.

"I would like a very cold Heineken," Oliver said.

"And I'll have a Jack Daniel's Single Barrel on the rocks."

Without a response, Shirley headed to the bar.

"So, Oliver, what did we forget to get set up today?" I said when he pulled out his notebook and started leafing through it.

"After we search Van Damm's house tomorrow, we should start talking to the people at the firm. How about starting with the two partners who helped him decide who to can in the purge?"

"Capital," was my response.

Oliver called Cornelia Cox, the office manager at Gideon &
McCaffery. She was still there. After identifying himself, Oliver
asked her to coordinate an appointment with the two partners
who worked with Van Damm in deciding who to terminate six
months ago.

"That would be Bruce Mills and Lyle Barber. You want to talk
to them separately or together?"

"Together would be fine."

She said, "I'm looking at their online calendars. Looks like
they're open at eleven tomorrow morning. That work?"

"That will be fine. Thanks, Ms. Cox."

Our drinks arrived. After Oliver had a sip of his beer, and I had
savored a chilled sip of Tennessee's finest, I said, "So, now that you've
booked up our morning, what else do we need to do tomorrow?"

"Start figuring out a motive. Who had a reason to want him
gone?" I answered my own question. "Other than the people who
were purged, there must be others. We need to unravel those
threads until something comes up."

Oliver added, "Let's get an idea from those two partners tomorrow whether they think any of those fired had enough anger to
seek revenge."

I suggested, "And see if they can point to any other possibilities." I waved at Shirley for another round. She brought the beverages and a small bowl of shelled peanuts.

"I thought you fellas looked hungry, so I brought some of my
gourmet peanuts from Hub's Peanut Farm over in Virginia. I don't
give those out to just anyone. Only guys wearing suits."

We smiled. Oliver thanked her and grabbed some peanuts.

After finishing our drinks, I drove Oliver to his home. When I
pulled up, his wife, Jewell, was on her knees planting yellow

hyacinths in the narrow bed that ran in front of their porch. She saw us and got up, dusting off her knees and hands.

At 6' tall, Jewell Shaw was my height. She was also a fine-looking woman. She crossed their small front yard and met us as we climbed out of the Jeep. She gave me a hug and a kiss on the cheek. She then hugged Oliver from the side, putting an arm around his waist and smiling up at him. Oliver is 6'3". They make an attractive couple.

"Well, crime fighters, are we safer because you were out there today?" A line she often used when we arrived together.

Oliver slowly shook his head once. "No, but Shirley gave us a bowl of Hub's peanuts, which made the entire day worthwhile."

To which she responded, "If only my cooking was half as appreciated."

I smiled as I climbed back in my chariot and headed home.

CHAPTER ELEVEN

I STOPPED IN the alley outside my garage to turn off the alarm on the house and garage via the remote on my phone, but the screen said it was already disarmed. Then I hit the garage door opener on my key chain. The door on the right-hand side rolled up, and I pulled in.

And what to my wondering eyes should appear? The left side of the garage was occupied by the cream-colored 1959 Porsche Speedster convertible owned by my ex-wife. That meant Mags was in residence.

I took the external stairs to our deck and entered the door to the kitchen. Mags looked up as she slid a casserole dish into the oven. "McDermott." She never calls me Mac. "Good timing. I just put something in the oven."

She walked over and gave me a hug and a kiss. With a smile, I said, "A home-cooked meal? That brightens my day."

"It's just chicken divan with broccoli over rice."

"Didn't know I had the fixings on hand."

"You didn't, idiot. I stopped at the grocery store on the way here."

"That's good. I'm almost out of Cheerios."

"I stocked some other stuff as well. I knew that—other than coffee—there was little likelihood I would duplicate anything you had on hand."

"Safe bet." I still admired this woman. Not a beauty per se, but the overall package was attractive. Mags was about 5'6" with auburn hair. Her face was on the better-than-pleasant side. What makes Mags great is her intelligence and wit.

"You want a glass of wine?" I asked.

"Sure." I know she likes a particular Pinot Noir from the Willamette Valley in Oregon and always keep some in stock for her visits. I pulled a bottle from the rack and uncorked it.

"Need to let it breathe or drink it like a man?"

"Just dump it in a glass. That'll be fine."

I did as instructed and handed her the stemmed balloon, which she took to the breakfast table and sat down. I poured Woodford Reserve bourbon over a single large ice cube and joined her.

"So, what's going on in your world?" I asked, knowing that, at most, I'd get some vague summary of her life.

She gave me that half smile where the right half of her lips curled up, but wasn't matched by the other side. Always a precursor to a fairy tale of some sort.

"I'm in town for a couple weeks. Mostly paperwork." She didn't say for whom. Her academic training at Wharton had been in finance and information technology, which, to my understanding, was not a usual career track for the State Department Security, where she sometimes claimed to work. She certainly hadn't attended the Georgetown School of Foreign Service, from which many State Department employees hail. "Anything new for you?" A quick change of subject from Mags.

"Caught a murder of a lawyer this morning. Managing partner of a mid-sized firm."

"Wife, girlfriend, or partner?" Always perceptive.

"Apparently, no wife or girlfriend on the scene. Oliver and I are still searching for a likely motive, which would help point us in the right direction. May have some disgruntled former employees who were summarily canned in a Saturday Night Massacre about six months ago. We're chasing that rabbit tomorrow."

"You two will figure it out. You guys always do."

She finished off her wine. "Why don't you get us some refills while I get the rice going?" She put an All-Clad pot of water on to boil and retrieved the canvas bag of basmati white rice, which we both liked because the grains grew lengthwise when cooked, and it had a sweeter taste than regular white rice.

I replenished our beverages while she was working on the rice. Before returning to the table, she peeked in the oven to check on the chicken divan. "The timing is going to be just about right."

"You see Jewell lately?" she asked.

"Yeah, I saw her just before coming home. She was planting yellow flowers in the bed in front of their porch."

"Since I'm going to be here for a couple weeks, think we can get together with them for dinner?"

"Sure. Got a preferred day?"

"Let's do it tomorrow night, if that works for them."

"I'll talk to them tomorrow."

"She still at that accounting firm?"

"Think so. Still a CPA doing the exciting stuff accountants do. If you're in town for a while, want to catch a Nationals game?"

"Sure. Too bad it's not football season."

"I'll check the schedule and let you know when the home games are."

"Okay," she said, then moved back to the oven and, using mitts, pulled the casserole out and set it on one of the unused stove burners to settle and cool. She tested the rice, decided it was ready, and drained it through a sieve in the sink.

Mags scooped the basmati rice onto the plates, added a large pat of salted butter, and covered it with a sizable helping of chicken divan, which had a browned cheese crust on top. I've never been a fan of broccoli, but this dish made me reconsider my lifelong aversion to it. I even had seconds.

After we'd eaten, I cleaned up the kitchen and loaded the dishwasher. As usual, when we were both in residence, we then sat down and watched MSNBC or CNN. We each added color commentary to the news stories.

Eventually, we gave up and headed to bed. She didn't even hesitate, and tonight was to be one of those with benefits. It is an unusual relationship, but we both still like each other a great deal. Most of the time.

CHAPTER TWELVE

On Wednesday morning I arose early and showered. Then I went downstairs in my bathrobe, ground the coffee beans, and put on a large pot of coffee. Mags can't start her day without two cups.

I opened the refrigerator to see that Mags had stocked the larder with essentials for a real breakfast: half-and-half—which she has to have with her coffee—bacon, eggs, English muffins.

I heard her stirring upstairs. My signal to start cooking breakfast. I don't do a lot of cooking at home but am quite proficient at making the most important meal of the day, as my mother used to say.

After putting my square cast iron skillet on a burner to warm up, I pulled out the package of thick-sliced bacon and started frying one of life's true delicacies.

Knowing Mags would have coffee before getting ready, I put some half-and-half in a coffee cup and nuked it. I also set out the dish of brown turbinado cane sugar, which she prefers.

The batch of bacon was draining on the paper towel I had placed on a dinner plate when she made her appearance. She nabbed a semi-crisp rasher and rendered a verdict that it was perfectly prepared with a simple, "Mm-hmm."

"Thanks for heating the cream, McDermott." She made her cup of coffee and moved to the breakfast table.

I said, "Morning." A long-standing rule is that Mags doesn't like to respond to questions first thing in the day. Early on, when I would ask her questions in the morning, she would respond with "Why are you torturing me?" So, I learned that simple declarative statements that did not call for answers was the best way to initiate morning conversations.

I dropped two English muffins into the toaster and got out the eggs. While I may not be much of a cook, I had long ago perfected the art of breaking an egg with one hand, which is better at keeping the yolk intact. We both like our eggs over medium with the yolk still runny.

I buttered the muffins and flipped the eggs. Fried eggs cooked in bacon grease do not take very long. After plating the eggs, bacon, and muffins, I set a plate in front of her, which received a nice smile but no verbal comment. After pouring myself a glass of orange juice, I joined her at the table and dug in.

After she had eaten, Mags prepared another cup of coffee. Once she was situated across from me again, she showed a contented grin that meant she had now returned to the human condition. "Springtime in D.C."

"Yep," I added to the non sequitur observation.

"Time to make the donuts," she said.

"Meaning?"

"I need to get going. Need to get ready and head in to work." No details on where "in" was. I didn't even ask anymore.

She finished her coffee, put her cup in the sink, and headed upstairs. I cleaned up the kitchen and then followed her upstairs.

On her way out, she stopped to kiss my cheek and then said, "See if the Shaws want to have dinner tonight."

"Yes, sir," I replied crisply as I clicked my heels and followed her down the stairs from the deck to the garage. She put the top down on her Speedster and cranked the engine, which purred like a contented large cat. She backed out and headed west down the alley, while I then headed east down the alley to pick up my partner.

* * *

Maggie Hampton drove west toward the Capitol Building. The sky was robin's egg blue with only wisps of clouds. She thought it was a perfect day for a convertible. When she reached Independence Avenue SW, she made a right turn along the south end of the Capitol and traveled along the south side of The Mall, savoring having the top down.

At 14th Street SW, she turned left and absorbed the beauty of the Jefferson Memorial and the cherry trees on her right. Maggie crossed what used to be called the 14th Street Bridge, but now was known as the George Mason Memorial Bridge. At the south end of the bridge, she turned the Speedster onto the exit ramp for the George Washington Parkway and headed northwest along the Potomac River. She was now in Northern Virginia between the Pentagon and the river.

Maggie smiled as she cruised up the GW Parkway. She passed Theodore Roosevelt Island in the middle of the Potomac and continued northwest, getting some thumbs-up from other drivers admiring her classic automobile. She rolled past the Francis Scott Key Bridge connecting Virginia to Georgetown.

After that, most of the heavy traffic was headed in the opposite direction toward Arlington and D.C. Once she was past the Chain Bridge Road interchange, she moved to the right lane to prepare for her exit.

In an unincorporated area of Fairfax County known as Langley, Maggie took the exit and curled back under GW Parkway to a smaller roadway with large signs about restricted access. She pulled up to the security gate and presented her identification and authorization to enter the campus of the Central Intelligence Agency. She knew McDermott was curious to know where she worked for certain, but he had never gotten any indication from her directly or otherwise. The guard recognized her and the Speedster, but still gave her papers a close review. A German shepherd sniffer dog on a leash with another guard circled her vehicle.

Eventually, Maggie was waved through and into the 250-acre campus of the CIA. She proceeded to the huge parking lot on the north side of the Original Headquarters Building. Most employees thought OHB stood for Old Headquarters Building. Built during the second term of Eisenhower's presidency, this seven-story structure contained one and a half million square feet of office space.

Maggie put the top up on the Speedster manually and latched it into the windshield frame. Porsche did not make electrical convertible tops until much later than 1959, when her prized vehicle had rolled out of the factory in Stuttgart.

Although she worked in the New Headquarters Building on the south side of the CIA campus, Maggie liked to occasionally enter the impressive main entry of the old headquarters, where she cleared security and crossed the famous lobby mosaic.

The reason she came through the main entry today was both nostalgia and her need for coffee. She stopped at the coffee shop in the food court on the ground floor. Maggie always required a large coffee to take to her desk in the new building. Due to secrecy reasons, the baristas are not allowed to ask for customers' names.

Each person just volunteers a letter or number for the order-taker to put on the cardboard sleeve.

She then took her coffee and traversed the tunnel that connected to the new building. As she walked, Maggie thought back a decade and a half to her first trip through these buildings. Back then, she had also parked in the big surface lot north of the OHB and found her way through the buildings along this same route.

*   *   *

Maggie earned her MBA from the Wharton School of Business fifteen years ago. One of her seminar professors had recommended her for a job, and she was summoned to an interview at The Study Hotel near Penn's campus in Philadelphia.

The well-dressed man who met with her gave a name, which she suspected immediately was not his birth name. He had gray hair and wore a bespoke charcoal suit with a chalk stripe.

He knew her father had been a colonel in the Army who had died in Afghanistan several years earlier. He said that he was meeting with her on behalf of the Political Action Group—PAG—which was a section of the Special Activities Division of the CIA. When she responded that she had no interest in politics, he explained that PAG had nothing to do with politics in the United States.

He told her that the Special Activities Division has two divisions, both of which are clandestine. The largest part of the Special Activities Division, he explained, is referred to as Ground Support or the Special Operations Group. These were the covert paramilitary operations for which the country could deny responsibility, even though it was completely behind those efforts. Maggie pointed out that she had no skills appropriate to that arena.

The gentleman held up his hands. "No, no. That's not why I am here. The much smaller Political Action Group is responsible for covert activities related to political influence, psychological operations, business conspiracies, economic warfare, and cyber warfare. It's the latter areas we want to focus on with you. Business, economic, and cyber."

Maggie paused. "What would I be doing?"

"This will not be a normal desk job. Your missions will vary from day to day, week to week, and month to month. The world is not a static place. We need intelligent people who can tap dance and adjust when the music changes."

"Will I be trained as a spy?"

"Not in the sense of Jason Bourne. But everyone in the Special Activities Division goes through our standard training at Camp Peary in Virginia. Many call it 'The Farm.' There is a more intense program for the paramilitary people coming into the Ground Support operation. They usually come from Delta Forces or Special Ops.

"For the Political Action Group, we have a different program that focuses on tradecraft, firearms, technical support, and skills, such as piercing business and financial transactions, as well as unraveling and tracking money. For those headed for the psychological and political side, there is a somewhat different agenda, which you will not get. We have you in mind for a specific area utilizing your finance and information technology training. You will also receive specialized language training."

She raised her eyebrows. "Kind of sounds like a desk job to me. Probably at a lot lower pay than I can make in the private sector."

"I won't kid you about the pay. It's decent, but not what you can pull down in the business world. But you will never have more of a sense of doing something so worthwhile for the benefit of your country. There will be some travel outside the country or even within the *country. You will be assigned to headquarters in Langley, Virginia. But periodically you will be working with others in the Agency to assemble in-depth analyses and take the steps designed to protect America. You will not be bored."*

They talked for another two hours. He wasn't interviewing anyone else at Wharton. She asked for two days to think it over. At the end of that time, she called the gentleman back and accepted.

Maggie's initial assignment was to the CIA Career Training Program at a large military reservation near Williamsburg, Virginia. She was subjected to polygraph, psychological, drug, and every other type of testing.

She was then transferred to Camp Peary, the CIA's training facility on the same military reservation. In addition to a substantial amount of physical training, she learned a variety of small firearms, self-defense, surveillance detection routes, and tracking. She also had extensive classroom and hands-on probing of financial records at banks, businesses, and other locations. She was educated by the Agency's best hackers in accessing financial and corporate data.

When she finished this course of training, she was issued her final Agency identification and a Glock 19, a small 9-millimeter pistol.

After she finished her language training in Arabic, Farsi, Pashto, and Urdu, she was ordered to report to the Financial Analysis Section of the Political Action Group at the New Headquarters Building in Langley.

* * *

On her first day at the Agency, Maggie had walked this same route through the buildings. Back to today, she thought. She took the elevator to the third floor of the New Headquarters Building where the Political Action Group is housed.

Maggie navigated the hallways toward the southwest corner of the massive building. Like most doors at CIA headquarters, the door bore a number but there was no signage stating what section or division was behind any given door.

She used her smart reader card to enter. Once inside, Maggie approached the two uniformed security officers next to the biometric scanner and metal detector. Even though she knew both of them, she presented her identification, which they scanned. After a second, the guards received a green light followed by yellow text stating "Access Authorized." After passing through the metal detector, which also did a full body scan, the third guard monitoring the screen waved her on.

Maggie then faced two more doors, which each required a smart reader card. The left door only admitted people who worked in the PsyOps part of the PAG. Her smart card unlocked the other door and granted access to the Financial Analysis Section of the PAG. Access to the much larger Special Operations Group was on the other side of the third floor. In all, the Special Activities Division occupied the entire floor.

CHAPTER THIRTEEN

JUST AS I REACHED the end of the alley, my cellphone rang. I stopped at the crosswalk and answered. "Burke here."

"Mac, this is Corporal Beverly Gray." Chief Whittaker's assistant. "I've got your search warrant in hand for the Van Damm residence."

"Thanks for expediting it. I'll swing by and get it, as soon as I pick up Oliver."

"I'll leave it on your desk."

I stayed put at the end of the alley and dialed Brady Pollard, head of our CSI crew. He answered on the second ring.

"Brady, good. You're in early. We just got a search warrant for attorney Van Damm's house. Can you get a crew there in forty-five minutes or so?"

"Oh, sure. I was just sitting here waiting for some detective to call me before my first cup of coffee. And, *voila*, who but Mac Burke should reach out to me? As fate would have it, though, we currently have nothing happening this morning. Give me the address."

I did so and asked him to line up a locksmith as well.

*   *   *

When I pulled up in front of Oliver and Jewell's house, Jewell was just getting in her car to go to work. I did not block their driveway as usual but did hop out and wave them down to convey Maggie's request for dinner. They agreed and suggested Pascal Manales, which they knew Mags liked as well. It is the best New Orleans-style restaurant in D.C. That agreed, Oliver and I boarded my vehicle and headed for MPD headquarters.

On my desk was a 9 x 12 envelope—the search warrant for the Van Damm property. We headed back to the parking lot and drove to Weldon Van Damm's house on Riggs Street NW.

I knew from experience that most of the wealth in D.C. is congregated in the northwest part of the city. Predominantly west of 16th Street NW. There are, however, some pockets of pricey and historical homes east of 16th Street. Van Damm's house was located in the Shaw area—one of the prosperous pockets east of 16th Street—just a little north of Logan Circle, where Rhode Island and Vermont Avenues merged in a roundabout at 13th Street NW.

We took Massachusetts Avenue around Mt. Vernon Square. Just before the start of Embassy Row, we exited onto Vermont Avenue, which took us to Logan Circle. In the center of the circle stands a large bronze statue of General John Logan mounted on horseback atop a substantial granite pediment. I'm sure most people have no idea who Logan was. But I'm a history buff who looked it up. Logan was the Union general in charge of the Army of Tennessee late in the Civil War. Now a park for over a hundred years, the Circle is surrounded by stately row houses, most of which are probably on the Historic Register.

Heading counterclockwise around Logan Circle, we exited onto 13th Street NW, which we followed north for five blocks before turning left on Riggs Street. The street was shaded by sweet gum trees on both sides, which formed a canopy that enveloped the entire street.

We spotted the white and blue crime scene van several houses up Riggs Street. Next to it was a smaller red van with ARMSTRONG LOCKSMITH in gold lettering on the side—Brady Pollard's locksmith of choice when we needed to execute search warrants and have keys made to accommodate the current search and for future reentries.

*   *   *

Van Damm's residence was a three-story row house. The brick had been painted a cream color. The eight metal steps and wrought iron railings leading to the main entry at the second level were painted black.

The short porch landing faced double wrought iron doors adorned with a heavy metal mesh of concentric squares in both the top and bottom panels on each of the doors. The locksmith went to work on the lock that held the heavy metal doors secured. He had them unlocked in less than two minutes.

The locksmith then worked on the lock and dead bolt that secured the double teak doors that were the main entry. Again, within a few minutes, he had both of those locks opened. No alarm sounded because Brady had already notified the alarm company that we were making an authorized entry. He had identified the alarm company by the sticker on the outside doors.

We put on booties and gloves and went inside. The locksmith returned to his red van to make sets of keys for us. The main entry was on the second floor, as was the case with many row houses, including mine.

The entryway was about eight feet across with a red and blue oriental runner on top of an old hardwood floor that had turned dark with age. There was a narrow side table on one wall with a marble top. Next to a vase of slightly wilted agapanthus blooms, there was a small antique dish, which was sitting empty. Probably where he deposited his keys when he came in the front doors.

Brady Pollard and his crew were all suited up in their Tyvek jumpers, which had CSI in black letters on the back, latex gloves, hair coverings, masks, and booties over their shoes. I could tell they didn't know where to begin.

"Guys . . . this is not an actual crime scene in the conventional sense. We are really searching in the dark for a motive as to why someone would kill the late Mr. Van Damm."

"The first thing we need to do is locate all the phones. Landlines, as well as cells. Brady already has Van Damm's cell, which we found at his office. Once we determine the phone numbers, we need to figure out the service providers. Then we can get our IT people to get numbers for all incoming and outgoing calls over the past month."

Brady added, "I already spoke with the law firm's IT person yesterday morning about getting a record of all incoming and outgoing calls on his direct inward dial number. I also have the firm's phone service provider. I should have that info this morning."

I said, "Get that over to Pamela Chenire in IT. She has contacts inside all of the providers and should be able to get the list of in and out calls for us without a hassle over subpoenas."

"Stretch," someone said, but I couldn't tell who, as they all had masks on.

I said, "That would hurt her feelings, if she ever heard that." I don't judge people by appearances, but rather by what they add to my little corner of the world.

Oliver suggested that they also look for Van Damm's home office and find any phone bills. "Those might list calls as well. But, at least, they will give us the service provider information."

"Let's also locate his financial records," I suggested to Brady. "Absent any obvious motive, we need to see if there is anything unusual in his bank records or financials."

"We'll round up anything of interest and give it to our financial analysis lady," Brady replied. "She's good at sniffing out 'items of interest.'" He held up air quotes.

Brady added, "We'll also check any old or new mail, Post-it Notes, and any stray item that would be a clue to Sherlock Holmes."

"We don't have a road map to follow," I said. "We need help. Thanks, guys."

The white-suited spacemen divvied up assignments and got to it.

Oliver and I wandered through the house. The main floor was tastefully decorated with a formal living room and a high-end kitchen to the right side of the house. The kitchen had a Wolf six-burner gas stove and double-wide Viking refrigerator. There was a built-in stack of two ovens with a microwave at the top and a warming drawer at the bottom. Next to the kitchen was a full butler's pantry with workstation and sink. A wine cooler was below the island and held white wines and several bottles of Prosecco. The counters were honed black granite.

I looked in the refrigerator. It looked like mine normally did in terms of contents. Some lemons and limes. All sorts of mixers. A drawer full of micro-brewery beers. Food—not so much. "It doesn't appear that our Mr. Van Damm did much cooking."

Upstairs held three bedrooms plus a master suite. We checked his nightstand drawers. His closet was very organized. He must have twenty bespoke suits. His shirts were all heavily starched and arranged by color. No obvious sign of a safe.

We then went down to the ground floor where we found Brady Pollard in a large home office. He was going through filing cabinets with walnut fronts that matched the paneling. Brady said, "Before he left, I got the locksmith to open all of these and make us keys for them also."

"Find anything yet?"

"Yeah. Found all the invoices for the phones and internet service provider. I'll get those to Pamela in IT as soon as we get back."

"Any notes or correspondence?"

"Not that I've seen so far. He did have a ton of investments though. In fact, he had one whole drawer on a single insurance company, as well as investments in a number of other companies."

"Anything unusual about them?"

"Not at first glance."

"Send me a list of all the companies he invested in. We're meeting with two of his partners later this morning. We'll ask what they know about those companies."

"You know, Brady," Oliver said, "we didn't see a safe in the house. Seems strange for a fairly wealthy neighborhood like this."

"We'll look for a hidden safe," Brady said. "If we find one, we'll get the locksmith back to pop it open."

"Come up with anything of interest from the law office yesterday?" I asked.

Brady shook his head. "Took lots of photographs. Also got some prints on the outside doorknob to his office. Most belonged to his secretary, Susanna Wales, who opened the door and then closed it later. We did turn up three partials on the knob mixed in with her prints."

"Anything turn up on AFIS on the partials?"

"Nope," Brady said. "Came back saying those prints were not in their system."

Oliver glanced at me. "Anything else you can think of for here?"

"Not at this point. Guess we should head over to Gideon & McCaffery to talk to the other two partners who made the decisions on the purge." Oliver and I headed out.

*   *   *

When we got down to my Jeep, it was only ten fifteen. Our appointment at the law firm wasn't until eleven, so I broke out my box of Marlboro 100s and lit up. I stood on the curb and leaned my butt against the front fender. Oliver faced the passenger door, forearms on the roof.

"We haven't got diddly for motive, much less suspects," he observed.

"Maybe the lawyers we're talking to can give us some insight."

When I had finished my smoke, I flicked the ash out with a fingernail and put the butt back in the box. Although I have smoked for a long time, I've never been fond of people who just drop their cigarette butts on the ground.

Van Damm's house was only about a mile from Gideon & McCaffery's office. We entered the underground parking at the Charter Building. I found a space marked for visitors.

We rode the fourth elevator to the 12th floor and entered the reception area of the firm. We identified ourselves to the receptionist. Looking at the calendar on my cellphone, I told her that we had an appointment with Bruce Mills and Lyle Barber.

She lifted a handset. "Mr. Mills, this is reception. Detectives Shaw and Burke are here to see you and Mr. Barber ... Yes, sir. I'll tell them." She looked at us and said, "He'll be right out. Please have a seat."

We thanked her but declined the offer to sit. Always a psychological disadvantage to be sitting when meeting someone for the first time and having to rise to greet them. Kind of a body language thing.

Bruce Mills came out of a door behind the reception desk and introduced himself to us. We identified ourselves and showed him our credentials. Mills was heavyset with dark bags under his eyes. Even though it was only eleven in the morning, he already had signs of a five o'clock shadow on his cheeks.

He led us back through the same door to a conference room with a walnut table about twelve feet long and high-backed leather chairs on either side and at each end. Waiting in the room was a bean pole of a man with a dark blue suit and a comb-over. He was at least five inches taller than Mills, who was about 5'10". He extended a hand to each of us and introduced himself as Lyle Barber. We again showed our credentials to him and gave our names.

Barber took a chair at the head of the table, the power position, and waved us to chairs on his right. Mills sat in the chair to his left.

Barber explained to us that he was the interim managing partner.

I thanked them for meeting with us. "First off, do either of you have any idea who would want to kill Weldon Van Damm?"

They both shook their heads. Barber said, "Weldon wasn't always the easiest guy to work with. In fact, he was pretty darn demanding of the younger partners and the associates."

Mills interjected, "He could be a damned jerk sometimes."

"Who was closest to him here at the firm?"

Mills responded to that one. "I think it is fair to say he had no real friends within the firm. He didn't socialize with anyone here that I know of."

Barber shook his head side to side. "I agree. Maybe occasionally when he was still married, but he's been divorced for several years."

Then I got down to the real purpose of this interview. "We understand that the two of you worked with Mr. Van Damm in determining who would be cut from the firm about six months ago."

Both of them nodded.

"Tell us what that was all about."

Barber initiated the response. "You have to understand that law firms are rated or compared based on the profits per partner. It may be kind of an arbitrary yardstick, but that's how the legal gossip publications, like the *American Lawyer*, rank firms once a year. It affects the quality of whom you can hire or lure away from other firms."

Mills added, "It also tells our own partners how their compensation stacks up against other firms."

"So how did that affect the purge?" I asked.

"Weldon constantly reviewed both partners' and associates' billable hours and fees collected," Barber resumed the explanation. "He was basically looking at who was working hard and who was making rain. In short, he focused on who wasn't pulling their oar."

Mills rejoined the dialogue. "Weldon had decided we needed to cut some deadwood out of the tree. He tapped Lyle and me to join him. Basically, we were just brought on board to ratify the decisions he had already made."

Oliver looked up from his earlier notes. "We understand that five partners and five associates were let go?"

Barber said, "They were the least productive and were a drag on profits per partner."

Oliver ran through the list of names to confirm who had been terminated. Barber confirmed the list was correct.

I asked, "Were any of them surprised by the manner in which they were fired?"

Barber again: "All of the partners were shocked. It was a load of bricks dumped on them on a Monday morning. They were then escorted out of the office immediately. Some of the associates too, although a couple of the associates were never going to cut it here and they knew it. It was just a matter of time for them."

"Were any of them upset enough to seek revenge?"

Barber's face twisted into a grimace. "Three of the partners landed at other firms fairly quickly, although I suspect at a lower salary. Or a lower bonus package. One just quit practicing. The fifth partner was Michael Fitzgerald. He was late fifties and not likely to get picked up by another firm. He hung out a shingle and went solo. How he's doing, I have no idea, but I bet it's not very well. He seemed to live somewhat beyond his means.

"As to the associates, three got hired by other firms. One got a government job. And one just quit practicing law altogether. He was a total deadbeat. He wasn't cut out for private practice."

"Again, were any of them upset to the point where they might want to strike back at Mr. Van Damm or the firm?"

Barber and Mills looked at each other, silently communicating.

Mills spoke first. "Michael Fitzgerald suffered the most, but his nature was such that he isn't one likely to fight back. He had given up a fairly lucrative practice with another firm to join ours. I'm not sure he would be involved, despite probably carrying a heavy grievance against Weldon and the firm."

Oliver said, "We have his contact information and will follow up with him."

My phone pinged at that point. I looked down and saw a list of eight companies that Van Damm had invested in. After reviewing the list, I asked Mills and Barber if they had heard of any of these companies.

Again, they glanced at each other before responding. Barber said, "Those are all companies that Weldon Van Damm set up for clients. They are all still clients of the firm. Why do you ask?"

"It seems Mr. Van Damm was heavily invested in some of them."

"That would be against firm policy." Barber paused. "In fact, our malpractice carrier strongly urges that our attorneys do not invest in their clients' businesses. Just a bad idea in general."

"Is it against legal ethics to invest in a client's business?"

"Not *per se*, but it just raises potential questions about conflicts of interest. In other words, is the attorney giving independent counsel and advice when he's got a piece of the ownership? Just not a good idea."

"Did the firm ever get any complaints from Mr. Van Damm's clients, particularly ones that he had invested in?"

Barber shook his head side to side one time. "Not that I know of. But since Weldon was the managing partner, any complaints would have gone to him."

Oliver jutted his jaw out. "Kind of a fox guarding the hen house situation?"

Barber and Mills looked at each other again, and then both nodded.

CHAPTER FOURTEEN

UNKNOWN TO MAC and Oliver, another homicide had occurred on Monday evening. Eugene Rollins was enjoying the Washington Nationals season opener against the Atlanta Braves at Nationals Park in Southeast D.C., south of the Capitol Building. He had scored three seats in the second deck and taken his two sons, ages twelve and fourteen. They rode the Metro in from Prince Georges County in Maryland to the Navy Yard station, which is one block away from Nationals Park

Each had their Nationals gear on. All three had identical, red-brimmed caps with the red script "W" on the crown. By the end of third inning, the Nationals had three runs to a single score by the Braves. Gene leaned over to his sons and told them to stay put while he hit the head. He then hiked down the steps to access the gallery deck with concessions and restrooms.

He walked through the relatively thin crowd to the men's room about thirty-five feet away. He entered the restroom just ahead of another fan sporting a Nationals cap. Only two of the urinals were in use. Both of the newcomers headed that way.

The second man bumped into Gene slightly. He thought he felt a slight jab in his left butt cheek and turned to the other fellow. "Hey, watch it."

"Sorry, man, I wasn't paying attention." The two of them then proceeded to urinals about fifteen feet apart. Before he was done with his business, Gene Rollins started shaking and collapsed, hitting his forehead on the top edge of the American Standard porcelain and falling to the white tiled floor.

One of the other men was washing his hands and saw Gene drop in the mirror. He turned around and approached the fallen man. Leaning over him, the man with the wet hands called to the other two men in the restroom. "Something's wrong with this guy. We need to get some help." One of the others said he would get someone and headed out the exit. After two minutes, no help came, and the other man fetched a security guard on the concourse who radioed for an ambulance. There was no sign of the first man who went for help.

* * *

Early Tuesday morning about the time that Mac was talking to Chief Whittaker about their new assignment, another homicide occurred in Northwest. Dominic Bonfiglio was fifty-four years old but in tremendous shape. Although he worked for a K Street lobbying firm, he made it a point to jog each morning whatever the weather. Other than his salt and pepper hair, he looked twenty years younger than his actual age.

Following his daily routine, at six a.m. on Tuesday morning, Bonfiglio left his Tudor-style detached home in the Cathedral Heights area of Northwest D.C., about two blocks west of the National Cathedral campus. After stretching on his front steps, Bonfiglio turned left and continued east, crossing Wisconsin and Massachusetts Avenues near their junction, using the traffic signals to cross the consistently busy thoroughfares. Once past

Massachusetts, he followed the south boundary of the Washington National Cathedral, which he liked to see in the foggy light of early morning. The perimeter of the Cathedral was bounded by eighty-year-old scarlet oaks.

When he reached the southeast corner of the Cathedral property, he normally turned north to traverse the east side of the church campus. Today he leaned against one of the oaks momentarily and bent his knee to shake out some stiffness and resumed running. Like most runners, Bonfiglio ran in the streets, rather than on the sidewalks. Pavement in the streets was smoother and avoided the trip hazard of concrete sidewalk slabs pushed up by roots of the oaks.

Once he turned north on 34th Street along the east side of the Cathedral, the street had no traffic, and he was looking at the back side of Washington's most Gothic structure. He didn't hear the nearly silent electric-powered vehicle accelerating as it closed in on him.

The white car hit him at a speed of around thirty-five miles per hour, squarely in the back of his thighs, which propelled the back of his head into the windshield. He was then flipped into a car parked at the curb, hurling his head into the post between the windshield and front door. By the time he hit the ground, the white car was well down the street and turning toward Rock Creek Park. When Bonfiglio was spotted bleeding in the street against the parked car, his heart had given out.

CHAPTER FIFTEEN

AT THE SAME TIME Maggie was traversing the tunnel between the two CIA buildings on Wednesday morning, Kurt Bardak was waiting on the third level of the underground parking garage beneath the New Headquarters Building on the south side of the Langley campus. He was leaning against his red Camaro convertible, smoking a cigarette.

He had worked for Ground Support ever since he had lost his baseball scholarship and bombed out of Brown University. After that, he had gotten in some bar fights and developed a short arrest record. Bardak never understood what had attracted the CIA to him but was grateful they showed up out of nowhere and offered him a career path, particularly since he had no options on the horizon. He had been with the Special Operations Group now for twelve years.

The doors of the nearby elevator opened. A blond-haired man stepped off the elevator and headed toward Bardak, who threw down his cigarette and rubbed it out with the toe of his shoe.

Kurt Bardak had worked for this man both in Afghanistan and at Langley. At least until his former supervisor had transferred over to the Political Action Group about five years ago. They had become good friends while working together in Afghanistan. Kurt always called him "Boss."

Bardak knew he had crossed several lines in the time he had known the Boss. He had always done whatever the Boss requested of him without question. When the Boss had come to him six months ago with a request to kill an individual at a ski resort in New Hampshire, Bardak assumed it was CIA business and asked for no details. He knew that the CIA did not officially operate within the U.S. and suspected this was being done *sub rosa* for that reason.

Bardak was provided with a syringe of succinylcholine and was told how to use it. He was provided with a picture of his target and details of his trip itinerary. He was paid $5,000 up front and an additional $10,000 when the job was completed.

Today, the Boss walked up to him, doing that sniff thing he frequently did with his nose. He gave Bardak a 9 x 12 envelope containing $15,000 in cash. Ten was the balance for the ballpark job and five was for a new one. The envelope also contained a syringe filled with succinylcholine, along with a photo and details on his next victim's schedule over the next several days.

Bardak asked, "Boss, we have a deadline on this one?"

"Within a week would be good. This one's a lobbyist."

Bardak nodded, and they shook hands. The Boss sniffed again and returned to the elevator with no further conversation.

*   *   *

Toward midafternoon, the same person who Bardak called *the Boss* made another trip to the parking garage under the CIA's New Headquarters Building. This time he met with Marian Benedict, who had also worked for him during his time in Ground Support.

He nodded to her and handed her a regular business envelope containing $20,000. She didn't look inside the envelope. She just slipped it in her shoulder bag.

He sniffed, bunching up his nose. "Good job on the two matters this week. Might have another one coming up for you shortly."

CHAPTER SIXTEEN

OLIVER AND I DECIDED to next interview Michael Fitzgerald, the partner involved in the law firm's downsizing most likely to carry a grudge. We had been given the address where he had hung out a shingle for his solo practice. It was on Harrison Street NW, just off Wisconsin Avenue near the D.C./Maryland line.

It took us about a half hour to get from the Charter Building to Fitzgerald's new office. We found a parking space and proceeded to the fourth floor. It appeared to be a small office suite with a reception area, a modest-sized conference room, and a lawyer office.

We identified ourselves to his receptionist, who also appeared to serve as Fitzgerald's secretary, and asked to speak with him. She was a pleasant-looking lady of around forty-five, dressed conservatively with a small strand of pearls.

She advised us that Mr. Fitzgerald was in court at the D.C. Superior Court. "His hearing should be about finished. He told me that, since he didn't have any appointments the rest of this afternoon, he planned to head home after court."

Oliver asked if we could have his home address. She seemed a little hesitant, but ended up giving us the address in Chevy Chase. Even though it was across the D.C. line, we regularly interviewed people in both Maryland and Virginia because the majority of people who worked in D.C. lived in the suburbs surrounding the District. We also asked for his home telephone number, which she gave to us, as it was a listed number.

Once in Maryland, we headed north on Wisconsin Avenue, which ran past the Chevy Chase Country Club. About four blocks past the golf course, we turned right on Leland Street and found his house number. It was a red brick Colonial with white shutters, a well-landscaped yard, and white columns on the semi-circular front porch.

We rang the bell. The door was answered by a blonde lady in her mid-fifties. Oliver introduced us both, and we showed her our credentials. She responded that her name was Audrey Fitzgerald.

"Ma'am," Oliver said, "we're here to speak with Michael Fitzgerald, whom I assume is your husband?"

"That's correct. He phoned a little while ago and said he was headed home from court. He should be here shortly. What's this about?"

Oliver continued, "You may have heard that Weldon Van Damm died under suspicious circumstances."

"Oh, yes, I did. I'm not surprised. He was such a jerk. You want to come in and wait for Mike?"

"Thank you. That would be nice."

She led us to a formal living room, which most older houses have but are used little. "Please sit down where you'd like. Would you like some iced tea? I only have sweet tea made."

I said, "That would be great." She headed for the kitchen. I took a wingback chair, and Oliver sat on the end of a love seat.

She came back a few minutes later with a small tray holding three tall glasses of sweet tea, which were already sweating from the ice. "I make my tea the same way my grandmother did. I melt the sugar first in water over a flame and then add the tea."

I tasted mine and smiled. "Tastes just like my mother's also."

"So, why do you want to talk to Mike? He left the firm six months ago."

I responded, "We're talking to a number of current and former partners to see if anyone can help us determine who had a reason to do in Mr. Van Damm."

"Well, that could be a long list. Mike won't like me saying this, but Weldon treated him shabbily. With no notice whatsoever, Weldon canned a bunch of partners and associates. We were caught totally off-guard. That was a really tough day."

"I'm sure it was very upsetting."

"That was about the worst day we've ever had. And we've been married for thirty-five years."

I asked, "What was your husband's reaction to the termination?"

"He was crushed. He had a very good stable of clients at his old firm, which he helped found. And we made a very good living. Then Gideon & McCaffery lured him away with a good salary and bonus package. He had been a partner with the firm for eight years and then gets fired with no notice. It totally sucked."

"Did your husband ever threaten suit or other action against Mr. Van Damm or the firm?"

"Two things. First, he had to sign a waiver, or he wouldn't get his ninety days' severance pay. Second, you don't know Mike. He's like a duck. He gets through adversity like a duck lets a thunderstorm roll off its feathers. He's a survivor. Wait . . . I hear him pulling in. Let me get him, so you can talk with him directly." She headed back to the kitchen, where the door from the garage apparently connected.

We could hear a brief whispered conversation coming from the kitchen. Then Michael Fitzgerald entered the living room with his wife behind him. He introduced himself, as did we, and showed him our credentials.

As Fitzgerald sat in the other wingback chair, he initiated the conversation. "I understand you're investigating Van Damm's death."

"Yes," I said. "We're talking to different people, past and present, who worked at Gideon and McCaffery to see who might have had a grudge against Mr. Van Damm."

"Well, that's not going to be a short list. He treated people poorly. I think it was his general nature. And that was even before the purge."

"Mr. Fitzgerald, in recent history, did he have any conflicts with people at the firm—or even outside the firm—that were contentious or hostile?"

"Inside the firm," he replied, "the biggest group of people were the ones, like me, who got fired so he could raise the profits per partner with no regard to how that act—the firing—would impact the ten individuals who were unceremoniously canned."

"How did your firing affect you personally?"

"Not well. I'm fifty-eight years old. Who's going to hire me at my age after being canned for under-producing at the Gideon firm? It wasn't like I had a big nest egg to fall back on.

"I signed the waiver because I needed the ninety days of severance pay, which I thought was downright stingy for a partner who had been there for eight years. Van Damm was a damned Scrooge. He had always been a shithead.

"Not only was I kicked out of my office, Van Damm had the IT guy cut off access to my computer files. Those files related to my clients. They were only with the firm because I brought them there. I had to get each client to sign a letter directing the firm to transfer their files to me, which meant I had to go to each and every one and explain why I'd been so shabbily fired.

"What's more, I had to tap into my retirement account to fund opening an office and to carry us until I built up enough billings to support us. Plus, I had to pay taxes on the money I took out of my IRA."

Fitzgerald shook his head slowly. "That's just the financial side of it. Candidly, I was pretty pissed. After I got done ranting and raving to Audrey about what had happened, I downed two-thirds of a bottle of eighteen-year-old Glenlivet single malt. The good stuff. Before I crashed that night, I told Audrey that I'd start dealing with this mess the next day. Think my exact words were, 'Tomorrow's another day, Scarlett.'"

Audrey smiled. "Exactly those words, Rhett."

I asked, "Did you have to make any changes to your lifestyle?"

He replied with a grimace. "I said we would have to figure out what to cut back on. But we never did. We lived on money borrowed from my retirement account."

Audrey added, "We told the girls about the situation and assured them there would be no changes."

I frowned. "The girls?"

"Our daughters, Erin and Shea. Erin had finished nursing school at George Washington University and taken post-graduate classes to be certified as a CRNA—that's a nurse anesthetist. Shea is a junior at Georgetown, majoring in foreign service. They both still live with us."

"Where does your daughter Erin work?"

"GW Hospital. Why do you ask?"

"Just curious."

I turned back to Mike Fitzgerald. "Did Mr. Van Damm have clients or anyone else who basically hated his guts or had a major grudge against him?"

He thought for a second and then looked at me. "Not that I know of but, on the other hand, I was not close to him. Professionally or personally. I can tell you that not many people at the firm liked the man. He was not pleasant. I don't think any of the attorneys could be considered a friend of his."

"Was he close to any of his clients? Or other people outside the firm?"

"Again, I just don't know."

After thanking them both, we climbed in my Jeep and headed for the office. Oliver said, "I noticed you picked up on the older daughter's occupation. I gather you connected the dots where Doc Vaughan told us one of the most common uses of the 'sux' chemical is by anesthetists."

I smiled. "Very perceptive, my dear Watson."

Oliver took out his notebook. "I'll add her to the list of people we need to speak with."

*   *   *

We had just finished meeting with the Fitzgeralds when Beverly Gray called my cell. She said Chief Whittaker would like an update on our case. Timing is everything. We told her we would be back in the office in about twenty-five minutes. Once there, Oliver grabbed a copy of our to-do list, and we headed up to the fifth floor.

Beverly sent us in as soon as we arrived. Chief Whittaker seemed to be in a good mood. "So, what've you got so far?" Not a man for small pleasantries.

As usual, I took the lead. "We've interviewed a number of people. I'll run through the list in a minute. So far, no obvious suspects. Time of death around nine p.m. on Monday. The M.E. is not certain on cause of death but suspects an injection of a muscle relaxant called 'sux' for short. Actual name is succinylcholine. Problem is the chemical dissipates quickly and is mirrored by the same potassium naturally released by the muscles after death."

"So, she's not certain?"

"No. Nothing cleanly provable at trial."

Whittaker nodded that he understood.

I resumed. "Van Damm apparently led a purge of ten attorneys, five partners and five associates, about six months ago."

"Why?"

"Mainly to increase profits per partner for those who survived the cut. The ten were the least productive in terms of dollars generated or otherwise not cutting it. We interviewed the other two partners who were in on the downsizing.

"One of the fired partners was financially devastated and had to borrow from his retirement account to open a solo practice. He was late fifties and too old to get hired at another firm.

"We just interviewed him and his wife both. She's more hostile than her husband. He seems to have moved on, but it was a pretty difficult situation for them. They have two daughters. One in college at Georgetown, and one who is a nurse anesthetist at GW Medical Center. That may be significant because Doc Vaughan, the M.E. on this case, says a common use of sux is by anesthetists. The daughter is on our list."

Oliver handed Whittaker a copy of the list that we had put together yesterday afternoon. He looked it over, while continuing to listen to me.

"We searched Van Damm's house this morning. Got all of his phone numbers. Pamela Chenire in IT is assembling all incoming and outgoing calls on his cell, desk phone, and home phone along with the identity of the party on the other end. For the last thirty days.

"From the search, we also got all the financial records we could find. Brady Pollard's financial person is reviewing them for anything of interest."

Oliver added, "We also got Van Damm's will and power of attorney. His two children from his first marriage are both grown, and are the sole beneficiaries of his will. Their names are on the list. Need to see where they were on Monday evening. Also, a Whitney Van Damm had the power to make financial and medical decisions for him if he became incapacitated. We're going to track her down, too."

Whittaker said, "I can help you a little there. I met her years ago. She was Weldon Van Damm's first wife. Was it an old will?"

"No," Oliver replied. "He made a new will after the divorce from his second wife about seven years ago."

"Van Damm and his first wife must still have been in contact. I assume she is the mother of the two kids who inherit," Whittaker said as he reviewed the list. "What about the closed-circuit video?"

I answered. "Lots of cameras around the building, but none in their law office or their dedicated elevator. We've got our intern, Kit Cardona, reviewing all of the video footage to cull it down for whoever we're going to show it to. We pulled video from five to midnight, but are only currently looking at eight to ten—one hour either side of the TOD.

"We also have to talk to the cleaning crew that came on duty around eight on Monday evening. We're going to talk to the supervisor and then catch the entire crew when they come on duty."

"Okay, Detectives, sounds like you have it under control—even if you don't seem to have made any progress solving it yet."

"Early stages, sir," I responded. He gave a backhand wave to send us out of his office.

CHAPTER SEVENTEEN

ABOUT TEN MINUTES LATER, my cellphone rang.

"Mac, it's Courtney Vaughan at the M.E.'s office."

She didn't call me very often. "Hey, Doc, what's up?"

"Mac, something's come up that I want to show you. It may be related to your case, although I'm not sure. If I'm right, it may be important. Can you come over?"

"We'll be right there." I told Oliver what Doc Vaughan had said. We headed to the Medical Examiner's office in Southwest.

* * *

Once we were settled in Courtney Vaughan's office, I asked, "What you got, Doc?"

She had a computer file open on her desktop. "This may sound strange, but I have an idea running through my head.

"Yesterday morning, we got a body of a man who died during the Nationals baseball game on Monday evening. The guy's body was discovered in a restroom on the gallery deck. No obvious cause of death. He apparently collapsed while using a urinal. An ambulance was called, and he was transported to the ER at Howard

University Hospital where he was pronounced DOA. No obvious cause of death.

"The hospital sent his body to us yesterday. I finally got an opportunity to look at him this afternoon, more than twenty-four hours after time of death.

"I think everyone along the chain of care assumed a heart attack, but none of the usual chemical releases showed up supporting that. From what's in his file, apparently no history of cardiac problems. Age forty-three. Had his two sons with him at the game.

"I did a full autopsy. No sign of heart disease. It appears he died of asphyxiation. I only found one unusual thing. Come with me."

She led us to the morgue. "You won't even need to gown up. This will take thirty seconds." She pulled the drawer holding the body of Eugene Rollins and eased back the cover drape. She handed me a pair of latex gloves. "Give me a hand rolling him on his side," which I did.

Then she pointed to a small red spot in his left buttock. We both leaned close.

She added, "Looks just like the puncture we found on Van Damm's neck. Very fine gauge needle. We ran a prelim tox screen. Again, all we got back was potassium, which could be naturally released by the muscles following death.

"Or it could be another injection of succinylcholine, as I suspected with Van Damm. But I can't prove it because too much time had passed after whatever was injected on Monday night. But no other chemicals, say more long-lasting chemicals, show up in the toxicology report. Other than the elevated potassium levels.

"I again got the chief toxicologist to run an expedited tox screen, specifically looking for succinylcholine. I explained my concern that it may be related to the earlier injection case on which I had requested an expedited tox screen. The toxicologist called me when the analysis was completed and told me that too much time had passed—the best he could say was that *there was a possibility— but not a certainty*. Not enough for court."

I asked, "Other than the injection site, do you see any other possible connection between the two cases?"

"That's your job. I'm just passing on what may only be my intuition. I could be wrong, but I'm kind of suspicious. I doubt it was the same person as the two homicides occurred miles apart within about thirty minutes." Oliver made a note in his small journal.

"Anything else?"

"Nope," she replied with a single shake of her head.

"Okay," I said, "send us whatever you've got. Other than EMTs, there probably haven't been any law enforcement types looking into this yet." A statement, not a question.

Doc Vaughan: "That would be my assumption also. Oh, by the way, I have a solid time of death for you: 8:09 p.m. Monday."

"You sound awfully certain on that."

"Using my Sherlock Holmesian skills, I took the time of the 911 call and subtracted ten minutes. Also, there are probably some witnesses from the restroom and the security guard who assisted."

"Thanks for the heads up, Doc. We'll let you know what we come up with."

*   *   *

When we got back to MPD, Oliver checked the system and found no report on Eugene Rollins, meaning no MPD interaction with his death. He called Beverly Gray and asked for a quick audience with Chief Whittaker, who was available, so we went up to the fifth floor for the second time today.

She sent us in. The Chief was standing. "Long time, no see. What's going on?"

Oliver took the lead this time. "After we met with you earlier, we got a call from Dr. Vaughan at the M.E.'s office asking us to come over. She showed us the body of a guy named Eugene Rollins who died in a restroom at Nationals Park on Monday evening. Apparently collapsed while using a urinal. Help was summoned and an ambulance called. Guy was DOA in the ER at Howard University Hospital."

Whittaker said, "Okay . . . so why's this of relevance to us?"

Oliver nodded. "Neither the hospital nor Doc Vaughan could determine a cause of death. But her autopsy discovered a pinprick in his butt cheek. Tox report shows nothing except potassium, which, as we discussed regarding Van Damm, is released by the muscles after death. If the chemical Doc suspected was injected into Van Damm . . . this 'sux' . . . was also injected into this Rollins guy at the Nationals game, there may—or may not—be a connection."

"A lot of ifs and suppositions on the M.E.'s part," Whittaker commented.

"Agreed," Oliver said. "But, if she's right, it's pretty strange to have two deaths on the same evening in the District where the chemical disappears fast. We don't know of a connection between Rollins and Van Damm. But it probably warrants a little time checking it out. We could use a couple extra bodies on this angle, if you've got someone available. We already have plenty on our to-do list."

I added, "And this could be time-sensitive finding witnesses from the ballpark and preserving closed-circuit video, as well as trying to find a connection to Van Damm's case."

Whittaker puffed out his lips as he thought and then nodded. "I'll send Rae Davis and Jerry Faircloth over to see you. You guys open a new case for Rollins and hang on to it, but have them work it to see if there's a connection. If not, you can pass it off to them."

Oliver raised a finger. "Also, Chief, as we told you, we interviewed Michael Fitzgerald this afternoon. He was the partner hit hardest by the purge at the law firm. One of his daughters is an anesthetist at GW Medical Center. Doc Vaughan says anesthetists have ready access to this 'sux.' She is now on our interview list."

"Keep me updated," the Chief added and pointed toward his door.

*   *   *

Oliver opened a bare bones case file on Eugene Rollins, while I reviewed our to-do list. Davis and Faircloth showed up a few minutes later. Oliver told them to grab a chair, and they each snagged one from an empty desk nearby and pulled them up to our desks.

Faircloth said, "The Chief said you needed our assistance, Ollie." Oliver ignored him. Oliver has always hated the nickname *Ollie* and refuses to acknowledge anyone who uses the sobriquet.

While Rae Davis had been a detective for about ten years, Jerry Faircloth had only been promoted to detective three years ago and had never worked a case with Oliver. He apparently didn't know the unwritten rule about Oliver Shaw.

Rae did, however, and said, "How can we help you, *Oliver*? We just wrapped one up and are at your disposal. At least, according to the Chief."

"We caught a homicide that occurred on Monday evening," Oliver began. "Attorney named Weldon Van Damm. The M.E. is Doc Vaughan. She thinks, but can't prove, that he was injected with a chemical known as 'sux.' What is significant is that this sux releases potassium, which dissipates in the body pretty quickly and doesn't leave a trace.

"That brings us to your part of this mission. Also on Monday evening, a man named Eugene Rollins dropped dead in the restroom at the Nationals game. He was rushed to Howard University Hospital but was DOA. By the time Dr. Vaughan caught this second autopsy today, she couldn't determine a cause of death other than asphyxiation, which can be caused by an over-dose of sux. During the autopsy she found a small injection mark on the left side of his butt. Again, she suspects, but can't prove, that it was sux. The M.E. says that, if he was injected with this chemical, he probably had a short period of shakes or spasms before dropping dead."

"Here's what we need you to follow up on," I interjected. "If the cases are related, we need to get the closed-circuit footage of people entering and exiting that restroom. Time of death is right around 8:09 p.m. So, probably an hour either side of that time. Security at Nationals Park can identify the restroom. They were promptly called in and called 911 for an ambulance. That foot-age could be our best shot at identifying the person who injected him, if that was the case. The security people probably have names of people who were in the restroom and tried to help. Get driver's license photos to compare to the video footage and give us a recap."

"We also need to see if Rollins had any connection to Van Damm," Oliver added. "We're looking for a thread tying them together. That probably involves interviewing his wife as well."

"If Rollins ties in with Van Damm somehow," I said, "then this case will merge with ours. If not, then it will spin off into a separate case for the two of you. Appreciate the help. We've got alligators chewing the seat out of our pants."

They took what information we had on Rollins and headed out.

CHAPTER EIGHTEEN

THE PERSON IN CHARGE of the Financial Analysis Section of the CIA's Political Action Group was Vincent Morehead. He had previously served for fifteen years with the Special Operations Group, dealing primarily with paramilitary black ops and other CIA covert agencies. No one in the Political Action Group fully understood why someone from the Special Operations Group received a rare lateral promotion from the Ground Support side to the PAG. The two sides of the Special Activities Division normally didn't interface, until Morehead was recalled from Afghanistan about five years earlier and promoted to Chief of the Financial Analysis Section of the PAG.

He brought with him a military mindset after years of commanding former Delta Force and other special ops personnel. Morehead was not much for following rules himself, but expected his directives to be followed without question. He was not much on personality and had not endeared himself as a manager since taking over the unit.

Vincent Morehead was 5'9" tall but seemed taller due to his perpetually erect posture. Some called it stiff-necked. He was fit due to regular exercise. He wore nice suits but, more often than not, they came from Jos. A. Bank clothiers and not a custom tailor.

His blond hair and round wire rim glasses gave him the appearance of a German officer from the World War II era, an observation spoken quietly behind his back from time to time. Morehead was referred to generally as "Chief," which he seemed to prefer over being called by his name.

On Wednesday, Morehead had called a meeting in Conference Room A next to his office. Present were Tarik Aziz, Allain Bouchard, Mikhail Dobrev, Zou Yoang, and Maggie Hampton. Upon entering the room, the Chief sniffed, crunching up his nose like someone had farted. He started off by telling them that the Financial Analysis Section had been tasked with obtaining access to medical records in their various assigned countries of interest.

"We're not going after a specific individual's medical records. At least, not yet. We want to find the back door into these countries' medical records, even if we don't know the doctors or hospitals that specific individuals use.

"We don't know where the weak links are. And they certainly will vary from country to country, perhaps even city to city."

Mikhail Dobrev asked, "Since each of our countries is likely to have a much less organized medical system than ours, how do we start looking for weak spots?"

"We're going to start by looking for weak spots in the American healthcare system," Morehead replied. "And then see if there is a counterpart weakness in your assigned countries."

Maggie replied, "We have HIPAA. I doubt other countries have a comparable records confidentiality law. So . . . it may be harder to find those holes in the American record systems than it will be elsewhere."

"Exactly," the Chief answered. "If we can find holes in our medical record systems, the working theory is that it will be even easier to penetrate medical records at the same contact point elsewhere."

"Aren't we going to run afoul of HIPAA laws?" Maggie asked.

"No, because we're not looking for a specific person's medical data here in the States. We are looking for a way to access that information. A flaw in a system's protections."

Tarik Aziz added, "Seems like this is more a project for the cyber boys and girls."

"It will be eventually," Morehead said, "but first I want the five of you to put your heads together and come up with a list of all the possible repositories of medical records. Once we have that list, it may become more obvious where the weak sisters are.

"I've got a conference call on another matter. I'll be back in thirty minutes. Give me your first cut at a list of targets." Without saying another word, Morehead sniffed again and left through the door that connected to his office.

They looked at each other, uncertain how exactly to proceed. Allain Bouchard spoke first. "Someone needs to be our scribe."

Maggie jumped on that. "Well, don't expect it to be me, just because I'm the only female here."

Based on the others' expressions, that was exactly what they were all thinking. Tarik Aziz noted, "Mikhail prepares the best lists and reports, despite having grown up with the Cyrillic alphabet."

The entire group nodded, except Dobrev himself, who said, "So it looks like I've been elected the foreman of this little jury." He opened his CIA-issued laptop. "Let's make a list of likely medical records repositories."

"Based on our limited knowledge," Zou Yoang added, "we should probably annotate the list as to which ones will likely be the most protected or not." The group agreed.

Each tossed out various possibilities, and others would add thoughts as to the pros and cons of likely security. In twenty minutes, they had assembled their list. Mikhail started reorganizing the list of targets in a more ranked fashion. The final listing read as follows:

Medical Data Repository / Likely Strength of Security

Medicare / Medicaid
Probably very strong

Hospitals
Chains probably strong, but multiple facilities
Independents probably have weaker security

Doctors
*Multiple target points, unless connected to hospital data
    system*
Stand-alone doctors probably weakest on records security

Stand-alone clinics—Doc-in-the-Box
Those not connected to hospitals are probably more accessible

Emergency medical services
Those connected to hospitals, probably very secure
*Municipal EMS probably connected to Fire Depts. and may
    be weaker*

Health insurance companies
Probably strong
*Look for smaller regional health care companies or
    state-sponsored health care, as opposed to large national
    companies*
Self-insured companies probably weaker

Life insurance companies
Probably less strong, since health data only collected on intake

Annuity companies
About the same as life insurance companies

Viatical insurance companies
Companies that buy life insurance from living people at a discount
Again, probably only gather data on intake
May also cross-access to life insurance medical record

Pharmacies
National chains probably have strong security
Mom and Pop independents may be weaker

Online pharmacies
Unsure
Often connected with big health insurance companies
Probably stronger

*   *   *

Dobrev sent the list to a nearby printer. He fetched it and made copies for Morehead and the rest of the group.

Chief Morehead returned to the conference room in exactly thirty minutes, as he was wont to do. Dobrev gave him the group's list. Morehead read the list carefully and asked, "So, who's the weakest and, at the same time, likely to be an option we can focus on in your target areas if we find a back door here?"

Maggie replied, "I seriously doubt they sell life insurance in the Middle East."

Dobrev nodded. "Not sure about that either in the Eastern Bloc or the Russian Republics. It just has never come up."

"What about health insurance companies?" Morehead asked.

Allain said, "France and Germany have state-run healthcare. So, they aren't likely to have health insurance."

Maggie held up a finger. "Israel also."

Zou Yoang added, "China, too. Not sure about India or Southeast Asia."

Vincent Morehead ran his finger down the list again. "The most likely categories will be the doctors and pharmacies. Probably the most universal targets, although the smaller the groupings, the more work it will be to track down medical records, if we don't know which doctor or pharmacy a specific individual uses."

"We need someone to research which of these entities even exist in our countries," Tarik said.

Morehead added, "I'll put the cyber guys on it, as well as seeing which ones are susceptible to having their health data breached." He gently tapped the list with the bottom of his fist. He turned and left without another word.

The five of them looked at each other without a word. Maggie said, "Guess we're dismissed."

CHAPTER NINETEEN

OLIVER AND I DECIDED next to follow up on Michael Fitzgerald's daughter, Erin, who was an anesthetist. Not wanting to forewarn her that we were coming to see her, I instead looked up the number for the GW Hospital operating rooms. After identifying myself to the lady who answered, I said that I understood Erin Fitzgerald was working, which the lady confirmed. I asked when her shift ended and was told around three o'clock. I thanked her and said I would contact Erin later.

Oliver and I discussed what to pursue until then. We decided to check with our trusty intern, Kit Cardona. I texted her: ANY PROGRESS ON THE VIDEOS? Like most Generation Z's, she texted right back: AM DONE. JUST GOT IN OFFICE. WILL COME UP.

Not two minutes later, Kit was standing by our desks. She grabbed a chair from a neighboring desk and sat down.

"Well?" I asked.

She gave us each an Excel spreadsheet. "Tell us what we have," I said.

"Across the top, I've listed all of the cameras. Down the left side, I've broken the video down into ten-minute segments from eighty thirty to ten on Monday evening. In the intersecting boxes, I've indicated whether a male or female appears on that camera. If the box says male twice, that means there were two men who appeared during that time segment, and so on. If the box is empty, the camera caught no one during that block of time. This will save time reviewing the entire video for each camera. As you directed, I did not look at the video before eight thirty or after ten."

"The next step," Oliver said, "will be to show these videos to someone at the law firm to see if they can identify the people in each segment."

"Who do we get to do that?" I asked.

Oliver suggested, "Why not start with the office manager, Cornelia Cox?"

"Kit, with the narrowing of the portions of video to be viewed, roughly how long will it take to show these clips to someone?" I asked.

"If the person knows most of the people, we can probably do it in under two hours."

"Are you available to help us run the videos and annotate the chart?" I asked.

"Sure, I can do that."

"Flip you, Oliver, to see who has to sit through the viewing with Kit?"

"I always lose these tosses with you," he said with a grimace as I dug out a quarter and flipped it in the air.

Oliver called "Tails." It landed on my desk heads up. With a pucker of frustration in his left cheek, Oliver said, "I knew it."

Oliver picked up his phone and called the office manager's direct line. "Ms. Cox, this is Detective Oliver Shaw with MPD. We've culled down some of the closed-circuit video from the building's cameras on Monday night and need someone to help us identify people. Who would be the best candidate to help us?"

"That would probably be me," she responded. "I'll also bring in our HR person. Do you want to do it here or at your office?"

"We can do either," Oliver said. "We'll need a large-screen television connected to a computer so that we can insert USB drives."

"We can do that here. And maybe grab other people, if needed. When do you want to do it and how long will it take?"

"Hold on a second," Oliver said and put his hand over the mouthpiece. "Kit, can you go now?" She nodded in the affirmative. Oliver resumed, "Ms. Cox, we can come over now, if that works for you?"

Ms. Cox agreed. Oliver and Kit gathered up their charts and the envelope of thumb drives. After he called for a car from the motor pool, they went down to get an unmarked and headed over to the law firm.

*　　*　　*

I now had about two hours to fill before trying to catch Erin Fitzgerald getting off her shift at GW Hospital. I called Potomac Office Cleaners and got a number for Maria Valdez, the head of the cleaning crew at Gideon and McCaffery. When she answered, I explained that we needed to talk to her and her crew about Monday evening to see if they'd noticed anything. We arranged to meet tomorrow evening—she'd assemble them all in a conference room at the law firm so we could ask about what they observed on Monday. She told me the entire crew would be there except Tatyana Williams, who had called in sick on Tuesday and was still out today. She gave me the only contact information she had for Tatyana Williams, which was a cellphone number. I made notes to pass this to Oliver for his journal.

Then I called Lyle Barber, the interim managing partner, and explained that we would need a list of Mr. Van Damm's clients and his primary contacts at those clients. He said he would get the list put together and email it to me. More notes for Oliver.

I checked my watch and saw that I had time for one more outreach before heading to GW Hospital. I was surprised to find Whitney Van Damm's phone number was listed and rang her up.

When she answered, I identified myself. "Ms. Van Damm, my partner and I are investigating Weldon Van Damm's death. Would it be possible for us to come visit with you tomorrow morning?"

"Certainly. I was expecting to hear from someone." We agreed to meet at nine the following morning. She gave me her address on 31st Street NW. I put another note on Oliver's desk about meeting with Mrs. Van Damm tomorrow morning.

*   *   *

It had started raining about two this afternoon. Good thing I'd brought my raincoat based on the weather forecast. I grabbed it and my notepad and headed across the street to the Judiciary Square Metro station. I got on the Yellow Line and rode it to the Foggy Bottom station in Northwest D.C. It was still raining when I got off the subway.

The GW Hospital was across the street from the Metro station. It was about two forty-five when I found the main desk in the surgery center. I presented my credentials and asked to speak with Erin Fitzgerald when she came off shift. As instructed, I took a seat in the waiting area.

After about ten minutes, a young lady in blue scrubs and a blue hair covering approached me. "Are you Detective Burke?"

I rose. "Yes, I am. Are you Erin Fitzgerald?" She nodded.

"I'm with MPD. We're investigating the death of Weldon Van Damm."

"I just got off shift," she said. "Can I change into street clothes and then we can talk?"

"Sure."

"Okay. Meet me in the cafeteria in about ten minutes." She pointed the direction I should go and then walked off.

I found the cafeteria, got a cup of coffee, and found a table. In a few minutes, I saw her in the line getting a Diet Coke. She looked a lot different in jeans and a loose shirt. She had a full head of curly red hair. She spotted me and came over and sat down. She had a nice spray of freckles across her nose. She definitely looked Irish.

"So, what's this about? My mom and dad texted that you'd talked to them."

"That's correct. I assume you know who Weldon Van Damm was?"

"Oh, yeah. He's the asshole who ruined my father's life. A colossal jerk."

I paused, somewhat taken aback by her directness. "Tell me what you know about him."

"My father was never a big fan of his. But they had made my dad a partner at Gideon and McCaffery about eight years ago and, apparently, it was a pretty good deal financially. We lived well. Had a nice house. My parents put me through GW. My sister is going to Georgetown. Neither was cheap."

"What happened after your father was terminated?"

"There was a lot of shouting and yelling. That never happens at our house. My father is the calmest person you'll ever meet. He also doesn't drink much, but he did that night."

"What did your father say that day?"

"He cussed the hell out of Van Damm, something else my dad seldom does. He said they cut him loose with only three months of pay and escorted him out of the office. He was humiliated. My mother was cussing at Van Damm nonstop."

"How did you and your sister take it all?"

"We both were crying. It was so sad. It was like the whole family had been destroyed. My sister was worried that she would have to drop out of Georgetown. My parents assured her that she would not have to drop out. Plus, we both could continue to live at home. We were all mad as hell."

"Were any of you mad enough to harm Mr. Van Damm?"

"Hah! That night probably all of us could have formed a posse and beaten the shit out of him."

"Anybody do anything to pursue that thought?"

She shook her head back and forth slowly. "By the next morning, we had all calmed down a lot. My dad is a survivor. He had figured out how to move forward. I think he was going to borrow against his retirement account and open his own office. The more I think about that, I don't know what he's going to do when he retires. He's almost sixty. I'm not sure what he'll do when he has to hang it up."

"Do you know anyone else who had a grudge against Weldon Van Damm?"

"No, but I'm sure there are plenty of them."

"Do you know what succinylcholine is?"

She looked surprised at the question. "That's out of left field. Why are you asking me that?"

"Answer the question."

"Yes, I know what sux is. We use it all the time."

"For what?"

"Sometimes when we're intubating patients, we have to relax the airway and administer a small dose to relax the throat muscles."

"So, you have access to it?"

"Sure, when we draw meds for a procedure, we usually get a small hypodermic of sux when we draw the other meds."

"Is it dangerous to the patients?"

"Not in the very small doses we use. Why do you ask?"

"Just something we're checking out . . . So, do you have any idea who would want to kill Weldon Van Damm?"

"No. But I suspect he deserved it."

I told her we were done. She got up and left. I spent a few minutes making notes of her responses, then headed out to the Foggy Bottom Metro station. It was still raining, so I donned my raincoat again. I rode the Yellow Line back to Judiciary Square and walked over to MPD headquarters.

CHAPTER TWENTY

OLIVER AND KIT were at our desks when I got back. "What did you get from the videos?" I asked.

Kit handed me another copy of her spreadsheet. This version had her handwritten annotations in the boxes. Oliver held an upturned palm toward Kit, yielding the floor to her.

She turned to me and using a pencil started pointing to the notes in the boxes. "In short, the office manager and HR person were able to identify many of the people. We then went through the same exercise with Lt. Johnson and one of the other security people to show them the video pictures where we still did not have names. That gave us coverage on most of the time slots. We still have a few open boxes, particularly in the tighter time frame from 8:45 to 9:30."

"Did they identify anyone who shouldn't have been there?" I asked.

Oliver responded. "Other than the unidentified people, it seems everyone is accounted for—either as an employee of the law firm or one of the offices on the other floors. At least we have names and offices for all of the identified people."

"What about the ones who they couldn't identify?"

"We got screen grabs on all of those people and printed them out," Kit said as she handed me a manila envelope. I undid the clasp and poured the pictures out.

There were six pictures. Two were men in suits who apparently got on the elevator on floor seven. Two more were women in cleaning uniforms with a cleaning cart who appeared to get on the elevator at floor four. The last two were of a blonde woman in a blue suit. The first was of her coming out of the stairwell at the parking level. The second appeared to be the same woman leaving the parking garage in a white compact car, but the photo did not show her face clearly and also did not catch the license plate.

Passing those two photos to them, I asked, "Do you think these last two pictures are the same person?" They both looked closely at both pictures. Kit raised her right shoulder in a half-shrug.

Oliver said, "Can't tell for sure. But at least we got a clear profile shot by the stairwell. She's coming out of the stairwell at 9:14. Didn't take the elevator. By the way, Lt. Johnson confirmed that there are no cameras in the stairwell. That car exited the garage about two minutes after this woman went by the camera near the garage elevators."

I looked at those two pictures again. "Kind of looks like a young lawyer to me."

"Nobody seemed to know who she is," Oliver responded.

"Let's make more copies of this picture to show people. We can run it by the cleaning crew tomorrow night."

Kit went off to make more copies of that picture.

*   *   *

I then brought Oliver up to speed on my interview with Erin Fitzgerald and gave him my notes. After hearing my recap of my conversation with the anesthetist, Oliver asked, "Overall impression?"

I shrugged. "At the time her father was fired by Van Damm, the entire family was mightily pissed, as you might expect. But, as she described him, her father was an even-keeled guy and eventually borrowed against his retirement account to fund his new solo practice and cover their bills.

"She was curious as to why I was asking about sux. She admitted to using it in small doses in connection with intubation and anesthesia. Bottom line is she still thinks Van Damm was a Class-A asshole, but my gut tells me she didn't do it. It was six months after the purge. Her alibi was that she was home with her parents on Monday night. While we thought we might have a connection with the sux, I'm not sure it links her.

"Guess we need to continue scratching away. We've got the cleaning crew scheduled for tomorrow evening. Also, I talked briefly to Whitney Van Damm, his ex-wife. We're scheduled to meet with her at nine in the morning. She lives in Northwest."

A thought occurred to me, and I pulled out a copy of Van Damm's will. "I don't know why we didn't focus on it when we first reviewed the will, but his ex-wife is also listed as his Personal Representative. That's like his executor. So, she may have a handle on his financial status. Our meeting with her could be educational."

"Speaking of which," Oliver said, "we should check with Brady's financial person to see what they've come up with."

Oliver lifted his desk phone and made the call. "Hey, Brady, Oliver Shaw here. Has your financial person looked at Van Damm's financial records?" Oliver listened for a few seconds and then said, "Okay. Can you ask her to come see us around eleven tomorrow morning? We'll be back from an interview by then. Thanks."

"Brady's financial person now has a name," Oliver said. "Simone Reese. She's charted out Van Damm's financial info, but she's gone for today."

*   *   *

We both just sat thinking for a minute. Oliver raised a finger and said, "I've got an idea." Without explaining what it was, he dialed our intern's extension. She was still in her cubicle.

"Kit, Oliver here. Can you do some research on NCIC for us?" A pause. "Here's what I'm thinking. The M.E. suspects that succinylcholine might have been involved in the two homicides we're looking at." He spelled it for her. "It's commonly called sux. Spelled s-u-x. See what you can turn up. Thanks."

Oliver shrugged. "Since Erin Fitzgerald didn't pan out, I'm wondering where the sux came from," he said. "May turn out to be nothing, but it's a small hole to be checked out."

*   *   *

It had stopped raining when we got out to the parking area and climbed in my Jeep. The pavement still glistened.

CHAPTER TWENTY-ONE

I DROPPED OLIVER OFF at his house around five p.m. and told him I'd be back to pick them up about six for dinner. Then I headed home, where I found Maggie's Speedster on the other side of the garage.

Mags was sitting in the living room with a glass of pinot noir. I dug a bourbon glass out into which I added a generous pour of Woodford Reserve bourbon over a large, square ice cube.

I joined Mags in the living room. She looked up and gave me a nice smile. "Are we on for dinner with the Shaws?"

I said, "Yep. We have a six thirty reservation at Pascal Manales. Pick them up about six."

"Oh, good. I love that place. We haven't been there in quite a while."

"I agree. Oysters and barbeque shrimp, here we come."

She smiled again. "What are you wearing?"

"Probably a linen jacket over jeans. Have to wear the coat per MPD policy."

She finished her wine and went upstairs to change. When I downed my whiskey, I followed. I really hated carrying my Glock 17 when I wasn't on duty, but MPD had its rules.

We went down to the garage, and I opened the passenger door for Mags, as I always did. My father taught me that when I first started dating, and he was serving as our chauffeur. Mags seemed to appreciate it.

When we pulled up in front of the Shaw home, they came out the front door before I could even honk. Jewell and Oliver were a tall couple. By unspoken rule, Mags climbed out of the front passenger seat and got in back where Jewell joined her. Mags and Jewell gave each other a hug.

Oliver took his usual position in the front passenger seat. I observed, "Just like old married couples. Men in front, women in back."

Mags responded, "Just another reason why part of that adage is no longer applicable to some of us." I glanced at her in the rearview mirror. The Shaws didn't know officially that we were divorced.

We took a right on Florida Avenue NE and continued into Northwest D.C. At 7th Street, we turned right and continued north past Howard University. A few blocks past the university, we pulled in the small semicircular entry drive for Pascal's. We exited the Jeep, and the valet took our vehicle to their private lot.

Pascal's restaurant is referred to as Pascal Manales by locals who have visited the 100-year-old restaurant of that name in New Orleans, because the menu is basically identical. The backstory is that the owner of our local eatery, Pascal Bougain, had once worked as a cook at Pascal Manales in The Big Easy, where the chefs were called by the less-pretentious name of "cooks."

By the mid-1990s, Pascal Bougain had become a favorite cook, in part due to his first name. He worked there for sixteen years before deciding to return to his native D.C. and open his own restaurant and, when he did, Pascal got the family members' permission to use the same menu at his new restaurant. Since 1996, Pascal's has served diners in a former neighborhood grocery store on 7th Street NW in Washington.

We ordered our drinks and said we were going to have oysters first. The bartender directed us to a chest-high bar topped in black marble. Standing only. No seats or stools in the raw oyster bar area.

Our drinks were served by the bartender. Three of us each ordered a dozen raw oysters. Jewell ordered a half dozen Oysters Bienville and a half dozen Oysters Rockefeller.

While we sipped our drinks, our shucker would grab an oyster from its cold bath and insert a short-bladed shucking knife into the bivalve. With a quarter-turn of his forearm, the top of the shell popped off. The shucking knife then went under the oyster to loosen it from the shell, and it was placed on a plate with twelve depressions perfect for holding a dozen shells.

In front of us sat a small dish of fresh horseradish, another of ketchup, a bottle of Tabasco, and a small basket of saltines. We promptly had at it, and the oysters were all consumed in about the same five minutes it took to finish our drinks.

With the precision timing of one of Mussolini's trains, our waitress escorted us to our table. She waited for our drink orders. Maggie suggested that she and I share a bottle of Villa Maria Sauvignon Blanc from New Zealand. Oliver and Jewell ordered another bottle of the same.

We didn't need menus. We were all there for the house specialty: barbeque jumbo shrimp. When our wine arrived and was poured, we ordered three dozen barbeque shrimp to share. The waitress smiled an acknowledgement that we had selected well.

Maggie toasted everyone and clinked glasses. Then she turned to Jewell and asked what she had going on at work. She had a way of focusing conversations away from herself.

Jewell was in the audit section of her accounting firm, which had thirty-five accountants plus support staff. "My latest glamorous project is an audit for an insurance company that has to make a quarterly filing with the SEC."

Maggie followed up. "Why do insurance companies have to file with the SEC? I thought that was only for companies that sell stocks."

Jewell took a sip of her wine. "This is really an excellent wine. Have you had it before?"

Maggie nodded. "We started drinking it years ago after meeting the couple who actually grow the grapes in New Zealand."

Jewell said, "To answer your question, this company doesn't sell stock or insurance. It buys life insurance policies at a discount. The reason they have to file with the SEC is because of how they raise their money to fund the purchases of the life insurance policies."

My eyes scrunched down a bit, my standard reaction when I wasn't following something. "What am I not understanding here? An insurance company buys life insurance policies?"

"Yeah," Jewell said, "they don't sell life insurance. Instead, they buy larger life insurance policies held by individuals at a discount from the face value. They're basically gambling that the person will eventually die, and the company will make a profit when the face amount of the life policy pays out. In the meantime, my client takes over paying the premiums on the life insurance."

"So, they're gambling that they will come out ahead. What if the insured person lives forever?" I asked.

"Then my client likely will lose money on that one. They play the numbers game. They buy a lot of policies, particularly from older people who are retired and see no purpose in continuing to pay for life insurance. I guess the odds are that retired people die sooner than the rest of the population."

Oliver added, "You've probably seen some of the TV ads that some of the big companies run, selling the idea as a way to raise more money for retirement."

Maggie turned back to Jewell. "So, if your client doesn't sell stock, how do they raise the money to buy the life insurance from people?"

"That's why they have to file with the SEC. They set up funds, which are basically limited partnerships. They raise a lot of money doing that. The investors basically get a nearly guaranteed annual return and, when that fund collects on some of the life insurance policies it holds, it puts half the proceeds back in the fund to buy more policies and pays the other half to the investors. The SEC considers that an 'investment vehicle' akin to buying stock," Jewell said using air quotes. "That's why the government regulates them."

Maggie's financial background was turning the numbers over in her head. "Do they buy all kinds of life insurance?"

"Oh no, they only buy policies of $100,000 and up. It would be a big headache to manage ongoing payments on a lot of smaller policies. Probably not worth the headache."

"Huh," Maggie said and took a sip of her wine. "Do they get health information on the insured person before buying the policy?"

"While that doesn't fall under our audit responsibilities, I'm sure they must. They probably have actuaries who review the health information and make an educated guess as to whether the insured person will expire before the policy does."

Just then our waitress showed up with a large metal platter with the three-dozen jumbo shrimp, which she placed in the middle of the table. Her assistant placed a baguette on the edge of each of our plates, while the waitress tied a long white bib around the neck of each of us. "We recommend scooching your chairs close to the table to avoid splatters on your clothes. Enjoy!"

We each grabbed a jumbo shrimp, which were four to six inches long, all with their heads and legs. The first step is to tear off the head. Per tradition at Pascal's, we sucked out the heads and tossed them in two empty bowls the servers had put on the table, and then peeled the shells off the spicy shrimp. I tore a piece of bread off my baguette and dipped it in the broth on the platter.

"You know," I said, "Mags and I have eaten at the original Pascal Manales in New Orleans. The first time, I assumed that barbeque shrimp meant that they had been grilled. But, no. They are sautéed in a wonderful sauce of spices—garlic, Worcestershire sauce, Tabasco, Chablis, and a lot of margarine. They very definitely do not use butter."

Oliver commented, "Whatever they use, this is always the best tasting shrimp I've ever eaten."

When the discard bowls were full and the platter was empty, we all leaned back in our chairs and sighed. No one had room for any of Pascal's excellent desserts.

After settling our bill with a generous tip, we headed for the front door. The valet brought my Jeep around, and we climbed aboard, each occupying the same seats as we had on the ride over.

Once we'd dropped the Shaws off at their house, Mags and I drove home, put the vehicle in the garage, and headed into the kitchen. "How about a nightcap on the deck?" I asked Maggie.

"Perfect idea. I think an appropriate beverage would be Grand Marnier, neat."

"I agree. Two coming up."

Maggie settled into an iron chair on the deck. I brought out two balloon snifters with a healthy pour of the orange liqueur. I held up my glass. "Here's to a perfect evening."

"Indeed." She swirled the heavy cousin to cognac and inhaled the aroma before taking a sip and savoring it on her tongue. She put her hand on top of mine and gave it a gentle squeeze.

CHAPTER TWENTY-TWO

On Thursday morning, I picked up Oliver at his house at eight thirty. He was standing on his porch, ready to roll. I could tell by his posture that he was eager to begin the third day of our case. So much for television shows saying homicides had to be solved in the first forty-eight hours.

We headed toward Northwest D.C. Just after we passed the Old Stone House, which had been built when Maryland was still a colony, we turned north on 31st Street NW and found the address that Whitney Van Damm had provided.

We found a space on the street and got out to admire the classical four-story apartment building. It was an attractive beige-colored structure in a large U-configuration with a red barrel-tiled roof. The landscaping was traditional and well maintained. The entry to the building was set at the back of the wide front walkway through the courtyard.

Entering, we were greeted by a uniformed doorman behind a counter. We identified ourselves and asked for directions to Mrs. Van Damm's unit. She lived on the first floor in the southeast corner of the building, so she had classic double-hung windows on three sides that appeared to be 8' tall.

Mrs. Van Damm answered the doorbell. She was a slim woman of about 5'8" with a short bob haircut in a nice multi-shaded gray color. Smiling, she said, "I'm Whitney Van Damm. I assume you're the MPD detectives who wanted to speak with me. Please come in, gentlemen."

Her unit had 10' high ceilings and appeared to contain several rooms. It was tastefully decorated with traditional furniture and colors, except one wall of her living room was covered in mauve-colored grass cloth, which accented some of the upholstery in the room.

Mrs. Van Damm said she was about to pour herself some coffee and asked us to join her, to which we agreed. She gestured us over to a small coffee urn atop a marble-topped buffet and invited us to doctor our coffees as we wished. The china cups came with saucers, which I certainly didn't see much anymore.

She led us to a comfortable sitting area in one corner of the living room with windows on both walls. She sat on a love seat and waved us to two upholstered wingback chairs with a small table in between to hold our coffees.

After a sip of her coffee, she looked at us both and said, "How can I help you?"

I started off. "Mrs. Van Damm—"

She interrupted me. "Not to be rude. I know I'm sixty years old and considerably older than both of you, but I'd be more comfortable if you would call me Whitney. My full name is just so formal sounding. Okay?"

With a bow of my head, I replied, "Certainly, Whitney. We appreciate the courtesy and your time. We are investigating the death of Weldon Van Damm. I'm led to believe that you are his ex-wife—is that correct?"

"Yes. I am. We met when I was an underclassman at Yale and he was in law school there. We got married after he graduated and took a job with his former law firm here in D.C. We got divorced in 2010 after twenty-seven years of marriage."

Oliver joined the conversation. "We understand you have two children—is that correct?"

She nodded. "Yes, Billy was born in 1986. Aurelia in 1989."

Oliver continued, "Are they local here in D.C.?"

She kind of semi-shrugged and tilted her head a little to the left. "Billy is here. He works for a lobbying group on K Street. He's still single. Aurelia is married and lives in Philadelphia. She has two young children."

"Were either of them in town on Monday evening?"

She threw her head back. "Hah. You can't believe that either of them would murder their own father. They have always loved Weldon. He was a good father. Less attentive to the kids while he was married to his second wife. And then renewed his time spent with the kids after divorcing her, although they were both in the early stages of their adulthood by then."

"You didn't answer the question," Oliver said. "Were your children in D.C. on Monday evening?"

"Billy was in town. He lives here. Aurelia was with her family in Philly. I assume you have to ask that question because they are Weldon's sole heirs?"

"Yes. How do you know that your children are Mr. Van Damm's heirs?"

"Very simple. One: logic. Two: I'm the executor of his will and have a copy of it. Three: he told me so." She picked up her coffee and took a sip. "Ugh. Mine has gone cold. I'm going to warm it up. Please help yourselves to more." She went to the coffee urn and topped hers off.

After she had resumed her seat, I asked, "You must have maintained a good relationship with him, even after the divorce?"

"Let me give you a little insight into Weldon Van Damm," she said. "At his core, he was a good and honest man. But he was a driven man. He always wanted to make a lot of money, which he was successful at doing. We lived very well.

"But as a person, he let his fixation on making money mar most of his business and professional relationships. I can candidly say that he seldom had any real friends. Even going back as far as law school. He was driven to succeed and expected the same from nearly everyone around him.

"Except me. He let me be me. He always accepted me as I am. Which is one of the greatest gifts a spouse can give you."

I followed up. "It just seems unusual for a man to name his ex-wife as his executor. Especially after he has remarried."

She gave me a knowing smile. "Even better than that is the fact that I was his executor even while he was married to Patsy. That's his second wife. They were only married for three years. And he made a new will after they divorced and again named me as executor."

I asked, "Who were his beneficiaries during his second marriage?"

"Patsy was to get half and the kids were to split the other half."

I added, "He must have trusted you through it all."

She set down her coffee cup. "It goes back to what I was telling you about his friends. Or the absence of friends. He always trusted me and knew that I would honor his wishes.

"Our divorce was very amicable. We had plenty of money, and he agreed to split everything. He also gave me a fairly generous alimony arrangement, so I never had any resentment on account of money. He also gave me enough to buy this unit which, even eleven years ago, cost nearly a million dollars.

"His second wife was twenty years younger than him. That's fifteen years younger than me. She was a newer model. Quite attractive. I always thought she was just arm candy. I think he figured out fairly early that, in his world, he didn't need that. He may have smartened up that his clients' wives were not comfortable with the younger bride giving their own husbands some ideas. In the end, all Weldon got out of that marriage was a very high-end kitchen in his house on Riggs Street, if you've seen it?"

I smiled. "I noticed that when we checked out his house. I made that assumption when I noticed he apparently didn't do much cooking."

"How about no cooking at all? He was totally helpless in the kitchen, other than making some very fine cocktails."

I decided it was time to talk substance. "Do you have any idea who would want to see him dead?"

She pressed her lips forward while she thought. "Other than pushing people too hard and not being very likeable, I really don't. While we didn't talk a lot, we would have dinner now and then. Since he had no other confidants, he used those occasions to generally update me on his world. Sometimes we discussed his finances and investments. Sometimes we discussed his clients. Sometimes we just talked about the progress of our children. Basically, we remained friends. But he never mentioned feeling threatened by anyone."

Oliver added, "In going through his files, we noticed that he apparently invested a lot in his clients' companies."

"Oh, yes. If he thought his client's business had serious potential, he would invest in the company. Usually, it paid off well for him."

"Did he ever have arguments or disputes with any of his clients?" Oliver probed.

"Not that he mentioned to me."

I asked, "How were his overall finances?"

"He made very good money from the law firm. And from his investments in his clients' businesses."

I scrolled down my cellphone looking for a list of his investments. "From a preliminary list of his investments, it looks like he invested multiple times in Portland Life Solutions. Did he ever talk about that company?"

"Yes. Several times. He set that company up some years ago. It's local, I think. It's one of those companies that buy life insurance policies from older people."

"It must have made good money. He kept investing in it."

"Yes, I think so. Weldon was kind of proud that he set it up similar to real estate partnerships that he had set up previously."

I asked for a clarification of what that meant.

She said, "As I understand it, real estate groups set up funds to buy or build new properties, like apartment complexes. That way they don't have to finance through commercial lenders and pay interest. The money comes from the investors in the fund or partnership."

Oliver asked, "How does it work for the investors? How do they get money from the investment?"

"Again," she said, "this is kind of secondhand from tidbits he told me over time. I think the investors get a nearly guaranteed return on the money they invest. The fund then buys life insurance policies and takes over paying the premiums. I think they pay the people somewhere between 15 and 35 percent of the face value of the policy.

"Then, when the person dies, the fund collects on the life insurance policy. If I remember correctly, half the policy proceeds go back into the fund to buy more life insurance policies. The other half gets split among the investors."

I scratched my head to visualize my puzzlement. "So why did he keep investing in Portland?"

She held up her palms. "I think they kept opening up new funds to buy more policies. Weldon didn't need the distributions from the earlier funds, so he just rolled them over into the new funds."

"You said he was sixty-five years old. Did he carry life insurance on himself?"

"Oh, yes. As part of our divorce settlement, he took out a two-million-dollar life policy with the kids as the beneficiaries."

I followed up. "Did he still have that life insurance?"

Whitney frowned. "No, after his divorce from Patsy, he sold the policy to Portland. He asked me if it was okay since it had been part of our settlement. He got 35 percent of the face value, which is the high end of what they pay. So, he got $700,000, which he promptly rolled back into more funds. I'm sure it's still sitting there."

Oliver got addresses and contact information regarding both children. Then we thanked her for her time and departed.

CHAPTER TWENTY-THREE

WHEN WE GOT BACK to headquarters, it was about ten fifteen. Rae Davis and Jerry Faircloth were at their desks. Oliver and I approached them and asked if they had made any progress.

Faircloth looked at us and, as if to make amends, focused on Oliver Shaw and said, "Oliver, we may have a picture of the doer." Oliver looked at Rae Davis and gave a small nod to acknowledge that she had apparently educated Jerry Faircloth on the proper form of address for him. She gave him a half smile in return.

I said, "Tell us what you've got."

Faircloth replied, "First thing, we went to Nationals Park and tracked down the security officer who responded on Monday night to the situation in the restroom on the gallery deck. His name is Irv Beecher. Turned out he was on duty yesterday because the Nationals had a doubleheader against the Milwaukee Brewers.

"First, he showed us the restroom where Eugene Rollins died. Then he told us that he had talked to the other men in the restroom and gotten their names and contact information. One of them said Rollins said something like, 'Hey, watch it,' shortly before heading over to the urinals. There was another guy with a Nats cap near Rollins when he said that. Apparently, nothing further was said between them."

Rae Davis pushed her glasses on top of her head and took over the story. "Not long after that, Rollins collapsed at the urinal. Apparently dropped straight to the floor after bouncing his forehead off the urinal. Not a very dignified way to go." She added, "But one of the witnesses was washing his hands at the sink and happened to look in the mirror when Rollins started to shake, just before he dropped to the floor.

"The witnesses said someone said, 'This guy passed out,' or 'This guy is dead,' or something like that. The witnesses didn't precisely agree on what was said or by whom.

"One of the men volunteered to get some help and headed out of the restroom. The consensus seems to be that this guy was Caucasian and wearing a Nationals baseball cap. After a minute or so, nobody came back, so another guy went out and found Security Officer Beecher and led him back to the restroom. Beecher quickly called 911 and asked for an ambulance."

About to get to the good part of the story, Faircloth jumped back in to resume the narration. "Beecher then took us down to the security office under the stands and pulled a copy of his report from their files and made us a copy. It pretty much says what we just told you and has a list of the names and contact info for the people in the restroom, except for the guy who left to get help but didn't come back.

"Then we asked to see the closed-circuit video from the gallery deck outside that restroom. They have a good digital system in color. We have ten minutes of video on either side of eight p.m. We also got screen grab stills of those going in and those leaving."

Jerry pulled an envelope of eight by ten color photos. Jerry pointed at the bottom right corner of the photos. "Each of these has a date and time stamp. He pointed to one of the photos. "We are pretty sure this is Eugene Rollins going into the john. And we think this guy next to him is the person who followed him in. As you can see, he is white and wearing a Nationals cap."

"Well, that's the back side of those two men," Oliver said. "Do we have one of the guy leaving the restroom?"

Faircloth nodded. "Yep. It's this picture here. Per the time stamps, no one else left until the second guy who came out to get the security guard. There's no picture of Rollins exiting the restroom for obvious reasons."

I couldn't resist. "Brilliant."

Rae Davis rolled her eyes at me. Kind of an unspoken communication that said, *See what I put up with?* I suppressed a grin.

Faircloth resumed the tale. "We got an enlargement of this picture to get a better look at this guy's face. As you can see, the top half of his face is kind of shadowed by the bill of his cap." It was a clear shot, except for the part from the eyes upward.

Rae said, "So we sat down with the guy running their video system and asked him to try to track this guy from that point forward. Since we had a precise time to work with, he checked the cameras in both directions on that level. We quickly found him, although he had apparently ditched his cap. Here's that picture." She pointed to another enlargement.

"How can you be sure it's the same guy?" Oliver asked.

"Mainly by comparing the clothes. Both guys had on a Nationals jersey over khaki pants. Both guys had on blue running shoes. It helped that there were not a lot of people on that concourse at that particular time. So, we followed him from camera to camera and printed pictures each time." She pointed out those photos. "We followed him until he went out of one of the exit gates. Unfortunately, none of the cameras in the parking lot caught him getting in a car, which would have been a big help in getting an identification. But we have a pretty good set of facial photos. Plus, leaving in the third or fourth inning kind of cinches it."

I said, "Great work, guys. We'll have to see if our sometimes friends at the Bureau can run him through their facial recognition system. We'll do the same with the woman we caught leaving the law office building."

Jerry Faircloth added, "Once we had the names and addresses of the other men in the restroom, we got copies of their driver's licenses so we could compare their pictures. Clearly, none of them were the guy we've focused on here. Also, only the guy who fetched the security guard came out, and he returned with the guard. I don't think any of them are the person responsible."

"We also got their video guy to burn us copies of the closed-circuit tapes," Rae added as she handed us an envelope containing several thumb drives.

*   *   *

We paused for a minute and looked at the pictures. "Moving on," I said to Rae and Jerry. "Anything tying Rollins to Weldon Van Damm?"

Rae Davis responded. "Before we went to Nationals Park, we called the M.E.'s office and found that they had Rollins' wallet. We asked them to text us copies of his driver's license and his emergency contact card.

"Once we had finished at Nationals Park, we called Rollins' wife. Her name is Teresa. She was home, so we drove straight there. They live in Rosecroft Village in Oxon Hill, which is in Prince Georges County, just across the line from Southeast D.C."

"Near Rosecroft Raceway, I assume?" asked Oliver.

Rae nodded. "Not far at all. It's a medium-priced townhome development. She's a fortyish mother of two early teenage boys. Still very much in shock."

Faircloth pulled out his notes. "Eugene Rollins was forty-three years old. He went by Gene. No health problems. He was a civil engineer with a medium-sized engineering firm in Temple Hills. Mrs. Rollins seemed to respond best to Rae, so she took the lead in talking with her."

I turned to Rae Davis and extended an upturned palm, giving her the floor. Rae said, "She had no idea of anyone who would want to do her husband harm. She said he was an easygoing guy. Typical engineer.

"She also said she had never heard of Van Damm or the law firm of Gideon and McCaffery. She said they had never hired a lawyer for anything. Their house closings were done by a title insurance company recommended by the realtor.

"They've been married about fifteen years. Until about five months ago she worked as a project coordinator for a large construction company that built apartment complexes. She said the bottom dropped out of that market, and her employer had to cut back, so they laid some people off, including her.

"She said her income roughly equaled her husband's, so they had to get by on half of what they'd been making before. Both of their sons are in a private school. In the end, they sold their house and bought the small townhouse in Rosecroft Village, which was about half the price. While that cut their overhead on the mortgage payments, they didn't have much equity in the house they had to sell.

"In the end, they decided to sell their life insurance policy on Gene Rollins."

"Wait . . . sorry to interrupt," I said, "but our case also involved the sale of life insurance policies. How big was Rollins' policy?"

"His wife said it was a half-million-dollar policy that her husband took out fourteen years ago when their first son was born. Gene was only twenty-nine years old at that time and got it dirt cheap. They sold it to one of those companies that advertises about buying life insurance policies. They got $100,000 and got rid of the premiums. She said it pretty much replaced a year's worth of her lost income."

The wrinkles on my forehead moved up. "Huh," I said. "Did you find out who bought it?"

"No, but I'll call her and find out. I'll let you know."

"Thanks, guys, good job," I said. "Appreciate you jumping on it."

CHAPTER TWENTY-FOUR

As soon as we got back to our desks, Oliver said, "As Sherlock Holmes would say: 'Huh.' That was progress." I knew exactly what he meant.

I saw a number of heads turning down the row of desks and looked to see what was drawing their attention—a very attractive lady with shoulder-length blonde hair. She was thirty-ish and about 5'10" although her heels made her seem even taller. I had to agree with the unspoken sentiment of my colleagues.

The lady walked up to us and introduced herself. "I'm Simone Reese, from Brady Pollard's shop." The financial person previously unnamed. If I weren't semi-divorced and semi-married, I definitely could've been semi-interested.

We both stood and introduced ourselves. I slid a chair over from a neighboring desk. Seemed like the gentlemanly thing to do.

She got right to it. "So, you want a rough breakdown on Weldon Van Damm's financial situation?"

We both nodded and managed to keep our tongues from hanging out of our mouths or drooling. We know how to be professional, when necessary.

Oliver and I sat down after she had taken the chair I provided. I asked, "So, what do you have so far?"

She handed us each a typed summary of several pages stapled together. She also had a copy in front of her.

"Short version is that the man was quite wealthy. I'll give you the CliffsNotes version."

I interrupted. "You may not know it, but I went to the University of Nebraska. CliffsNotes was started in Lincoln by a guy named Cliff who worked in the university bookstore."

She looked at me for a second. "Wow. Thanks for that factoid."

Was that a put-down?

She returned to her notes and began again. "First, let's start with his law firm of Gideon & McCaffery. The partners of the firm each own a percentage of the stock of the firm, but the original five partners each had 20 percent of the stock when the firm was founded. As partners left the firm either by death, retirement, or otherwise, that partner's shares of stock were split among the remaining partners based on the percentage of the stock they each held.

"As best I can tell from Van Damm's financial statements, he held 28 percent of the law firm's stock at his death. Based on his financial statements over recent years, he estimated that stock to be worth about $800,000.

"In addition, he made $900,000 to $1,100,000 per year over the last several years. I got those figures from his federal tax returns, which Brady's people gathered during the search of his residence.

"His most recent bank statement from Wells Fargo says he has $178,000 in cash in his checking account.

"Also, he and his firm made maximum annual contributions to his 401(k) retirement account, which is managed by Charles Schwab. His most recent IRA statement said he has $8.2 million in that account.

"His row house on Riggs Street is free and clear. The Tax Assessor has it valued for property taxes at $1,600,000. That's probably low.

"Then there's a bunch of privately held companies in which he owned a portion of the stock. It is hard to value stock in companies that are not publicly traded. On his personal financial statements, he showed these stocks to be worth about a combined total of $1,500,000. I figure that number is lower than reality as part of playing the estate planning game.

"But then comes the big Mama Jama. It's a company called Portland Life Solutions, which appears to be a viatical company that buys life insurance policies. He is a limited partner in twelve different Portland funds. Those appear to be funds that Portland created to raise money to buy the life insurance policies. His percentage ownership in each of those funds appears to be about 15 percent.

"On his financial statements and tax returns, he valued his Portland partnership interests at . . ." She paused. "Get this . . . $8.7 million."

My eyes went wide, and Oliver said, "Holy cow!"

She said, "Yeah. That was my reaction, too."

I asked, "So, how does that give someone a motive to murder him?"

She nodded. "Who inherits?"

"His two grown children," Oliver said. "Guess we're going to have to look closer at them."

Her eyebrows went up to their limit. As if she were a mind reader, she said, "Huh." Out of the corner of my eye, I saw Oliver glance at me while he gave me a one-sided smile.

Simone said, "Conventional logic is always to follow the money. I have a gut feeling that we should look deeper at the Portland funds. Don't really know why. Just a feeling."

"Okay," I replied. "Would you chase that rabbit and let us know what you turn up?"

"Even though that is a mixed metaphor?"

I was becoming intimidated by this lady. "Can I ask how you got into this game?"

She smiled. "I'm a CPA by training. In fact," she addressed Oliver, "I worked for six years at the same firm where your wife works. Jewell and I were both in the audit department. She was there before me, and we didn't run into each other much. But I kind of knew her."

"Surely you could have made a lot more money in private accounting," Oliver said.

"Sure, but I was bored to death. I saw a placement notice for this job and interviewed. The variety sounded like a lot more fun. So, I up and quit the accounting firm. Plus, I inherited a good chunk of money around the same time. Go figure. Here I am."

"Well, we're kind of stuck," I said. "No obvious suspects are cropping up. Follow the thread you are sensing on the Portland funds and see if you can weave something together that will help us."

She smiled. "At least that metaphor is not mixed." She stood and returned the chair to the neighboring desk. "And I knew the history of CliffsNotes anyway. Who could get through college literature classes without them?" And she walked out of the room with an even larger group of detectives watching her exit than those who had caught her entrance. I had a sense that she knew it and was eating up the attention.

Oliver looked at me with a serene smile similar to *Buddha*. "Well, I thought I was going to have to fetch the defibrillator from the hallway."

"What?"

He had kind of a smirk on his face. "She had your number from the start. I could hear your heart beating from over here."

"Hah. Just proves that I'm not dead yet."

"Uh-huh." And he leaned back and smiled again.

CHAPTER TWENTY-FIVE

I FELT THE NEED to change the subject. "So, what do we do next? Seems the first thing is to get someone going on the facial recognition of the lady from the parking garage and the guy at the ballpark."

"Want to go through channels and try the Bureau? Or use Frisco?" Oliver asked.

The FBI was always a hassle and sometimes not very cooperative. Depended on whether they needed you at the time.

Frisco was one of the guys we work out with at Buster's gym. He was a 5'5" fireplug of a guy with lots of muscle and tattoos on his black skin. My first encounter with Frisco at the gym came sometime after I had bought my first fixer-upper near Oliver's house in Northeast D.C.

Oliver and I had resumed our workouts together at a nearby pig iron gym in a recycled mom-and-pop grocery store that had been closed for years. Oliver had been a regular there before I moved back to the States.

The folks who worked out there were mostly African American and reflected the neighborhood where the gym was located on 21st Street NE in the shadow of the Robert F. Kennedy Stadium. It was not a big gym and, while it had a few weight machines, it was primarily free weights. Neither of us was bulky like most weight lifters. We just wanted to stay in shape without the torture of running.

Oliver and I usually rode there together. We both had to sign in on a clipboard and pay ten dollars each visit. I just signed in as Willy, which is what the regulars called me. I was welcomed as a friend of Oliver's. Different people would bring in a CD to play while they worked out. The other lifters offered open critiques of the music, so the owner would know whether to ever bring that particular CD back again.

After I had become a semi-regular with Oliver, I took in a CD by David Sanborn, the saxophonist. It was much mellower than the rock and hip-hop normally brought in and didn't seem to go with the crowd of sweaty weight lifters but, surprisingly, they actually liked it. I think it was just the change of pace.

One of the regulars whom everyone called Frisco said to me, "You sure you aren't part Black?"

I smiled back and said, "Well, my father's middle name is Washington." Which is actually true.

That drew a fair number of laughs, and Frisco said I now had to sign in as Willy Washington. Which I did after that.

Frisco became a casual friend. Over time, Oliver and I learned that he was a hacker of some considerable talent, and he would occasionally help us out on a case.

Frisco never told anyone his entire name. Or whether he was self-employed or working for some government organization, although I doubted the latter. A lot of times in D.C., it could be both.

*   *   *

"Frisco," was my immediate response to Oliver's question about whether to use the Bureau. No paperwork. No bureaucracy. We just traded favors from time to time.

Oliver pulled his personal cell and dialed Frisco's number. "Hey, Frisco, Oliver here. Got something where we need your assistance . . . Yeah. Got a couple video screen grabs and need some facial recognition." He listened some more. "Sure, we can be there in about thirty minutes. Thanks, man."

"He can give us an immediate audience," Oliver announced. "At his place."

*   *   *

We packed up copies of our screen grab pictures and the thumb drives with the original closed-circuit footage and headed to my Jeep. We drove over to 24th Street NE where Frisco owns a non-descript two-story building near Anacostia Park. It was a brick building that had last been painted two or three decades ago. Based on the very faded sign above the ground floor, it had once been an appliance repair store. It had an old-looking garage door on the left side, again with peeling paint, which Frisco used to store his equally nondescript 1999 Impala. The Chevy had sun-bleached blue paint covering the entire body.

We suspected, but never asked, that Frisco made some very good money doing whatever it was that he did. The blandness of his building was intentional. He didn't want to attract any attention. Ever.

We parked just outside the sole entry door on the right side of his building. The door appeared rusty and deteriorated—although that was just cosmetic. The door was solid metal. There was no window in the door. Oliver pressed the buzzer.

Frisco could see us via a hidden camera above the doorframe and pressed the button that released the lock. We entered and faced a narrow stairway directly in front of us. The building felt like it was airtight.

In reality, it was probably one of the most secure structures in the District. Frisco had installed redundant security systems to protect what was surely a large investment in the computers and servers on the second floor.

We climbed the stairs covered with threadbare carpet, pressed another buzzer, and waited for Frisco to release the automatic door lock. Once we entered, there he stood in faded blue jeans and a black pocket T-shirt stretched taut across his chest and biceps. We shook hands—which involved bent arms, hooked thumbs, and leaning in to each other with a single pat on the other's back. While he was a little unusual, he was actually a nice guy.

The room we had entered looked like a Best Buy on steroids. There were 60" flat-screen televisions hanging on the walls. Frisco was an avid football fan with season tickets to the Washington Commanders—previously known as the Washington Football Team—and, before that, the Washington Redskins. He never missed a home game.

There was also a wall-mounted set of twelve smaller flat screens that showed the views from his security cameras. The room was neat as a pin, whatever that phrase means, with computers and servers organized around the perimeter of the room on tables. He had obviously upgraded the electrical service in the building as there were outlets everywhere. Every piece of equipment was also protected by a surge protector and battery backup. I suspected that he also had generator backup in his garage in case of a loss of power. His kitchen and living quarters occupied the rear of this floor.

"So, what can I do to help you?" he asked.

We explained that we had two homicides and told him the background of each. Oliver showed him the two screen grabs of the lady at the Charter Building. He then showed Frisco the multiple screen grabs of the man from the baseball park.

"We have no idea who these two people are," Oliver said. "But right now, they're our prime suspects. We've also got the actual closed-circuit footage that these screen grabs came from. Can you run some facial recognition magic for us?"

Frisco nodded. "Let's give it a try." He sat at one of his computers with a 19" screen and started pecking away on his keyboard. We stood over his shoulders, which we knew from prior experience he didn't mind.

"Since we're in D.C., the best facial recognition database is at Homeland Security."

I asked, "You can get in there?"

He nodded as he continued to pound away on his keyboard. "Yep. They think I'm one of their own." He paused and smiled as he looked at me. "Who knows? Maybe I am." Another enigmatic smile.

I replied, "And I don't need to know."

"You are correct." He turned back to his screen and almost immediately said, "I'm in. Now let's feed in our pictures. Let's start with the lady. That will be the tougher one as we only have a single profile shot and the picture through the windshield when she exited the garage." He fed in the shots from the thumb drives from the Charter Building because they had better definition than the screen grabs.

Talking to his computer screen, Frisco said, "Okay, baby, let's see what you can do." Then we waited as his screen showed only the rotating circle signaling that the computer was searching.

After about sixty seconds, Frisco said, "It's taking longer because we don't have much in the way of images to feed it. Plus, I have to say she looks like a whole lot of women of that age, which makes the pool of people to search much larger."

Eventually, his computer gave a single ping. "That means we have a hit," he said. But the spinning wheel came back up on the screen.

"Uh-oh," Frisco said. "That means it probably has a hit, but is deciding whether the identity can be released to us."

"What's that mean?" I asked.

"It probably means the system figured out who she is, but her identity may be protected."

"Protected?"

"Yeah, like maybe one of those dark operations, which officially do not exist."

Then his computer beeped again. Up came a single line of text: *"This information is not available."*

"That confirms it," Frisco said. "She's in the system, but some part of the government has decided that there is to be no record of her."

Oliver said, "Damn. Can you run the guy from the ballpark?"

Frisco nodded and used the thumb drives to feed in the multiple pictures of the guy, both those with the ball cap on and those without. Again, the whirling circle told us that the system was searching. This time it only had to think for about fifteen seconds before we got a ping.

"He's in the system," Frisco said. "Better input made the search easier." Then we got the whirling circle again. "Not good," said Frisco. "We may have another one who is protected."

Sure enough. We promptly got the same, *"This information is not available."*

"There you go," Frisco said as he turned and looked at both of us. "Same story. Sorry, guys, but this is the best recognition system available. Not even Interpol has anything better."

We thanked Frisco and told him we owed him. We repeated the handshake process and headed downstairs.

*   *   *

After we were in the Jeep, I shook my head. "Damn. Those were our best leads."

Oliver looked as downhearted as I felt. He shook his head once and said, "On a different subject, I'm kind of hungry. Since we're in the neighborhood, how about swinging by Sadie's?"

"Sure," I agreed and drove the five blocks to Sadie's grocery store and kitchen.

Oliver and I generally worked out at Buster's gym around seven in the morning on days when we were on the later shift at MPD. On those days, we followed our workouts with an improvised breakfast. We went to a nearby house where a fifty-something African-American lady named Sadie ran a small neighborhood grocery store in the front room of her little house. The shelves were an odd assortment with a limited inventory.

Sadie had an opening cut into the wall between the main room / grocery store and her kitchen. She also did cooking for takeout. We would step up to the window and order our food. Oliver's breakfast usually consisted of a dozen gizzards sprinkled with hot sauce, and I normally had her drop two hot dogs into the deep fryer at the same time. We then would sit outside on the edge of her low front porch to enjoy our gourmet breakfast.

Oliver had been a regular at Sadie's before I moved to D.C. He had grown up nearby and attended Howard University on a

ROTC scholarship, much the same as I had done at the University of Nebraska. Sadie considered him to be almost family.

When we went inside today, Sadie was standing behind the opening to her kitchen. Oliver asked, "Sadie, I know we're a little late, but you got anything cooking?"

Sadie smiled. "I've got some wings that are asking to be thrown in the fryer." We both agreed and asked for a dozen each with hot sauce sprinkled on top, and we each got a Diet Coke. Once our food was in hand, we sat on the edge of Sadie's front porch and ate in silence as we thought.

I started to slowly roll my neck in kind of a figure eight.

"What?" Oliver asked.

I leaned over and stared at the stunted grass in Sadie's postage stamp-sized front yard. I mumbled, "What are we missing?"

Oliver responded, "Yeah, I know. Do we have two homicides that are related or not? Do we have two doers that are related or not?"

"I sense there are threads floating around. But we can't even snag them, much less tie them together."

Oliver remained quiet. We headed back to the office.

CHAPTER TWENTY-SIX

BETWEEN PROJECTS, Maggie Hampton went to the cafeteria for lunch. She got chicken salad in a wrap and a Coke.

In looking for a seat she spotted Lindsey Brown, with whom she had worked on various projects. Lindsey was thirty-something and a little pudgy. They had always gotten along well the several times they worked together. Maggie headed over to the table where Lindsey was sitting. "Saving seats or can I join you?"

Lindsey looked up from the book she was reading and smiled. "Absolutely. How are you, stranger?"

Maggie pulled out a chair and set her plate and drink on the table. "You still doing IT, or what the Chief calls *cyber*?"

"Oh, yeah. Nothing exciting at the moment, but the world will need us more than the alpha types carrying guns."

Maggie bit into her wrap. "Our group worked on something that will be coming your way."

"Good. Hope it's something challenging."

"May or may not be," Maggie said. "Something about trying to penetrate medical records on companies here to see if the same tactic would work overseas."

Lindsey raised her face up from her plate of chicken Parmesan. "Actually, we did something like that for Morehead several months ago. He had us look for holes at insurance companies and stand-alone physicians and pharmacies. Nothing too corporate or government. They probably had big IT departments and major fire walls."

Maggie's brow wrinkled a little. She was wondering why Morehead had them compile a similar list yesterday. He'd apparently already given some thought and focus on where to search. "Find any glaring holes that I should worry about as a consumer?"

"Nah. Some private doctors were pretty sloppy and out of date. The small pharmacies had pretty good systems, probably packages they bought off the shelf from a software company. Life insurance companies were leakier than you would expect. Small viatical insurance companies were fairly easy to penetrate."

Although knowing the answer, Maggie asked, "And what are those?"

"You're not a prospect. They're companies that buy up life insurance policies from retired people."

"Huh. The only life insurance I have is the same policy we all get as part of our benefits package."

"I guess they only buy from older people. Or folks who have large premiums they can no longer afford."

Maggie swallowed another bite of chicken salad. "What kind of info were you guys able to access?"

"Just about everything. People they bought policies from. The health records on those owners. Even got the list of people who owned the investment fund, if it was structured that way."

"Their records must not be very secure. Is that something we could use in other countries to dig out info?"

Lindsey shrugged once. "Guess it depends on whether there is such a business wherever you're looking. My gut feel is that probably only Western countries would have life insurance. Maybe not even all of them. I never heard any more about it. You know the Chief. You seldom hear back on whether any of your work is used."

The topic then changed to the latest in Lindsey's dating life. She was dating a nice guy who worked at Housing and Urban Development.

CHAPTER TWENTY-SEVEN

ON THE WAY BACK, I called Beverly Gray to see if Chief Whittaker was available. "He just got back from a meeting upstairs. His calendar is open for the next half hour."

"We're en route. We'll be there in fifteen minutes."

We went straight to his office on the fifth floor. Without a word, Beverly waved us toward his door. I knocked once and was beckoned to enter with his usual "Come." We entered. The Chief was wearing a tan two-piece suit with a blue button-down shirt and yellow tie. Rather sporty for him.

I said, "Got an update for you, Chief. We're making progress." He gestured us to the seats in front of his desk.

Chief Whittaker said, "I've only got fifteen minutes, but I'm getting questions upstairs about the Van Damm case."

I started off. "First, Rae Davis and Jerry Faircloth helped us out a lot."

The Chief replied, "Good, glad to hear it. I've always thought Rae Davis is a good detective." Noticeably absent was a similar accolade for Jerry Faircloth. The Chief was no fool.

"They interviewed the security guard at Nationals Park and, because the M.E. gave us a precise time of death at eight o'clock

Monday evening, they were able to get pictures of the likely doer immediately after Eugene Rollins dropped dead." Oliver handed the Chief the photos.

"Any luck identifying him?" the Chief asked.

"That's the interesting part of our report. We got the photos run through Homeland Security's facial recognition program."

"How'd you do that so quickly?" Chief Whittaker asked with a true look of puzzlement on his face.

"You really don't want to know," I replied. His eyes narrowed for a second. Then he said, "This is why I love you guys. You get the job done. Go ahead," he said, turning his hand to me. Made me wonder if I had adopted that gesture from him.

"Well, the good news is that the facial recognition software got a hit on this guy. The bad news is that the system refused to give us any information on him."

"What does that mean?" Chief Whittaker was clearly frustrated.

"It was explained to us that this probably means that this guy is part of some black ops part of the government and that his identity has been concealed on purpose."

"Holy shit," Whittaker exclaimed. "We now have a dead engineer at a baseball game and it's part of a Jason Bourne conspiracy?"

Oliver joined in. "That was our reaction as well. And especially frustrating because we have clear pictures of the person who likely killed Eugene Rollins."

The Chief then asked, "Is there anything that connects the Rollins case with Van Damm?"

I said, "Not at first glance, but there are two things percolating in my mind that might tie them together. First, Rollins had recently sold his life insurance policy because of some financial setbacks due to his wife losing her job. Rae Davis is following up to see who he sold it to. No answer yet.

"Van Damm also sold his $2 million life policy to reinvest the money elsewhere. I don't know if there is a thread there or not, but we're looking at it. His ex-wife told us he reinvested the $700,000 he got from the sale of his life insurance in Portland Life Solutions. Van Damm had a large stake in Portland, which is a viatical company that buys life insurance policies.

"We had Simone Reese in Brady Pollard's shop look at Van Damm's financial status." Chief Whittaker got a small smile on his face that told me he had probably also met the lovely Ms. Reese. "She said Van Damm's total investment in Portland was worth around $8.7 million."

Whittaker's eyebrows went up.

"Yes, sir."

Now the Chief's entire forehead inched up. "Holy cow."

"Yeah. But we're still working on those threads."

The Chief focused on me. "You said there were two things that might tie them together. What's the second?"

I smiled as I played my hold card. "We also ran the lady from the Charter Building through the facial recognition system. Again, we got a hit. And, again, we were denied any identifying information. We were told this likely means that the mystery lady probably also had her identity concealed by the government, perhaps because she is also part of some black operation."

Whittaker frowned. "How do we find out if these two are from the same operation?"

"We don't know, sir. But we're working on it."

Whittaker shook his head left and right in slow motion. "I can't believe we have photos of the people who likely committed these two murders but no way to identify them. You two have made major progress here, but we're a long way from the finish line."

I said, "Yes, sir. But we're making steady progress."

The Chief said, "I can see that. I'm glad you two guys are on this." With that he waved us toward the door, and we left.

CHAPTER TWENTY-EIGHT

ON THE WAY BACK to our desks, Rae Davis flagged us down. "I talked to Mrs. Rollins again. She said they sold her husband's life insurance policy to Portland Life Solutions. Does that help?"

"It might," I said. "That name keeps cropping up. Thanks, Rae."

As we were hanging our suit coats over our chairs, Oliver said to me, "So, you told the Chief that there are two possible ways to connect the Rollins and Van Damm cases. The sale of life insurance policies and whether there was a connection between our unidentified suspects. When did that occur to you?"

"An epiphany on the spot. I was trying to identify similar threads in both cases, and that was the only thing I could come up with."

Oliver said, "I wonder what Pamela Chenire has come up with on Van Damm's phones."

"Call her and see. We can go down to their shop right now, if she's available."

When Oliver called, Pamela said she was in her cubicle and that she had a fairly comprehensive list of all of Van Damm's calls. Oliver asked her to print two copies for us and said we'd come down to see her.

We didn't put our coats back on for this internal excursion and took the stairs down to the third floor. Pamela actually seemed glad to see us. I suspected she didn't get many visitors.

"So," I asked, "did you get what you needed to talk to his service providers?"

"I did. I had three different providers to work with. First, on his desk phone, they had direct inward dialing so people could call him without going through the firm's switchboard or receptionist. Brady had talked to the law firm's IT person, and he printed out a list of the phone numbers Van Damm called or who called him over the past thirty days. The IT person also said the firm's phone service provider was AT&T.

"The list from the firm's IT person only had phone numbers in and out. No information who was on the other end of those calls. I contacted my source at AT&T's office here in the District. He has helped me in the past without requiring a formal subpoena. In return I sometimes do favors for him.

"The first thing I did was go over the outgoing calls from Mr. Van Damm's desk phone. I worked backwards starting with midnight on Monday. Here's a list of all of Van Damm's outgoing calls from that phone in reverse chronological order.

"As you can see, there are no outgoing calls after 8:47 p.m. on Monday evening. The last number he called is for an internal number at a company called Portland Life Solutions. It was not their main line. Without that company's internal directory, I couldn't identify the actual recipient of that call. Since it was close to the time of death, I decided to take a chance. So, I called that number. It was answered by a man who identified himself as Parker Winston. I said that I had the wrong number, apologized, and hung up.

"Then I looked at Portland's website and determined that Parker Winston is the CEO of that company, as well as one of the original founders. Before I got out of the website, I noticed that Weldon Van Damm was also listed as a founder. Small world, huh?"

I smiled. "Great work, Pamela. We'll make a detective out of you yet."

She absolutely beamed.

I told her, "That company keeps coming up in our conversations with people. I would dearly like to know what was said during that conversation. Can you get that for us too?"

"Hardly. Wish I could."

Then I pointed at her list. "Per the information you've assembled, it appears that call lasted from 8:47 to 8:55. Am I reading that correctly?" She nodded. I said, "So, an eight-minute call shortly before he was killed."

Pamela said, "Because it was apparently his last call, I went through the list and highlighted in yellow the other times when Mr. Van Damm called that number. There were five other calls in the previous thirty days. Total of six calls altogether."

I read off the dates she had highlighted: "April 5, back to March 21." I turned to Oliver. "Maybe we should chart those on a monthly calendar page or pages and see what coincides with those calls." Oliver made another entry in his notebook.

"Let's look at the other calls on those dates," I suggested to Pamela.

"I'm ahead of you," she said. "I highlighted those in blue."

All three of us looked at the entries on the list highlighted in blue in reverse order. I said, "There doesn't appear to be a recurrence of any other calls on those dates."

"And they all occurred during the workday," Pamela said. "They may well be calls with clients or other attorneys."

"Anything else notable on the list of incoming calls to his desk phone?"

"Not that I noticed. And we were able to identify everyone on that list of incoming calls."

"Okay," I said, "let's look at the incoming calls to his desk phone." She passed us each another list of calls. There were fewer incoming than outgoing calls.

"Again," Pamela explained, "I have highlighted three incoming calls from that same number. Based on the duration of the outgoing calls, some of these may have been return calls after Mr. Van Damm left a voicemail for Mr. Winston on the other end. Otherwise, nothing stands out on the incoming list."

"What's next?" Oliver asked.

She said, "Let's do the easiest one. His house landline."

"Why is that the easiest?" Oliver asked.

She gave us a new list that combined both incoming and outgoing columns for the house phone. There was nothing in either column. She saw our puzzled looks and smiled. "He never uses that phone at all. It is apparently there solely to serve his alarm system."

"And finally," Pamela said, "his cellphone. He uses it less than his office phone. Actually, probably uses it a lot less than most people do. I have charted his cell calls in a different manner because there are fewer of them." She gave us each a schedule of the cell calls. "I have two vertical columns. The left column is for outgoing calls that Mr. Van Damm made. The right column is for incoming calls. Then I have blocked rows putting the calls in boxes by each day in reverse chrono order from Monday, April 5."

We looked at her new chart. Again, she had indicated who was the recipient of his calls or, in the case of incoming calls, who made the calls to him.

She said, "Verizon is his cellular provider. I have a good contact there also, and they provided additional help beyond what I could get on my own from the phone's call history and list of contacts. Verizon helped me identify who the calls went to or came from."

She noted, "There were not a lot of recurring calls. There were three calls to or from Parker Winston. Those were on April 1, March 29, and March 28."

Oliver said, "I'll add those to the calendar of the calls."

We thanked Pamela for her help and took the stairs back up to the fourth floor. As we walked, Oliver observed, "It looks like we need to talk to Parker Winston at Portland." I agreed.

CHAPTER TWENTY-NINE

OLIVER AND I DISCUSSED whether to set up an appointment to see Parker Winston. Normally, we prefer to arrive unannounced—giving people no time to contemplate their responses in advance. But this person was the CEO of a substantial company. He wouldn't be sitting around waiting for people like us to drop in.

It occurred to me that we needed more preparation before just showing up and asking what Van Damm had been calling him about. I looked up Simone Reese's extension. Oliver asked, "Who you calling?"

"Simone Reese."

Oliver said, "Uh-huh. What for?" Kind of a knowing semi-smile on this face.

"I want to see if she has come up with something that will make it look like we know more than we actually do." I rang her extension. She answered. "Hey, Simone, this is Mac Burke. We have checked all calls in and out of Van Damm's phones over the past thirty days. He called or received calls from the CEO at Portland Life Solutions six times over the past month. Guy's name is Parker Winston.

"In fact, he was on the phone with Winston just minutes before he was murdered on Monday evening. I can't just ask him what they have been talking about, particularly over the last ten days of his life."

She responded, "So what can I do to help you?"

"Have you come up with anything on Portland that smells wrong? Something that would cause Van Damm to be calling him repeatedly?"

There was a short pause. "Well, I've come across something that may be of interest. I'm not sure yet."

"Like what?"

"I've been looking at his quarterly and annual statements from Portland. You remember I told you that Van Damm was invested in all twelve of Portland's Funds?"

"Yes. Guess that's logical. We've found out that he's listed as a founder of Portland. I suspect he set up the company. Hang on a sec."

Oliver had been following my side of the conversation and I asked, "Did we get his client list from the law firm?"

As usual, Oliver was already a step ahead of me. He was searching through his emails. "Yeah. Here it is. Came in from the new managing partner. I've got it on my screen. Yes, here it is. Portland Life Solutions has been a client of his since 2003. Eighteen years. And, get this, his main client contact is one Parker Winston."

Back to the phone with Simone Reese. "Don't know if you heard Oliver, but it looks like Van Damm set up Portland in 2003." I paused. "That reminds me of something. His ex-wife told us that he was proud of how he set up the funding on this company. Not a typical sale of stock to raise capital. Instead, he set up funds similar to limited real estate partnerships."

Simone came back on the line. "That makes sense. He was invested in twelve Portland funds and got quarterly payments equal to 8 percent of his investment annually, which is a pretty good return. Then he got additional payments when each fund collected on the policies it had purchased."

"Was there something that would cause Van Damm to be calling the Portland CEO?"

"There were some ups and downs based on when policy payouts came in," she said.

"Can you chart those to see if anything particular stands out?"

"Sure. I can have that for you in a couple hours. Maybe sooner."

"Great," I said. "We're going to try to get a meeting with the CEO of Portland."

"You probably should get on his calendar. Based on my experience in the audit world, those people really don't like spur-of-the-moment meetings. They are very controlled people who insist on preparation."

"Good point. Get back to me as soon as you can. We'll try to set it up for tomorrow. Thanks." And I hung up.

*   *   *

I turned toward Oliver. "Simone says we need to make an appointment to get in to see Winston. Goes against my grain, but I guess we should, especially since tomorrow is Friday." He started looking for a phone number for Portland. Once he found it, he slipped it to me on a Post-it note.

I dialed and asked Parker Winston's executive assistant. I got a refined-sounding lady on the line who said her name was Ermine Bell.

"Yes, ma'am. This is Detective McDermott Burke with the Metropolitan Police Department. My partner and I need to see

Mr. Winston." As expected, she asked what this was about, which is why we don't normally call in advance.

"It concerns the death of Weldon Van Damm."

She said, "Oh, yes. We were very saddened to hear of his passing. He has been our attorney for a long time. I'm sorry, but Mr. Winston is currently in meetings. I'm sure he will want to talk to you. Can you meet with him at two tomorrow afternoon?"

"That would be fine. We'll see you then. Thank you."

"We're on for two tomorrow afternoon," I told Oliver.

*   *   *

After she was off the phone, Ermine Bell rapped lightly on Parker Winston's door and stuck her head in. "Got a minute?"

"Sure. Come on in, Ermine."

She closed the door behind her but didn't sit. Instead, she stood directly in front of Winston's desk. "I just had a call from a Detective Burke with the Metropolitan Police Department. He said they wanted to see you in connection with Weldon Van Damm's death."

"Oh? Did he give you any more specifics?"

"No, sir. I told him you were tied up in meetings today, but I could schedule him in at two tomorrow. I've put it on your Outlook calendar."

Winston appreciated her running interference for him, as any good executive assistant should do. "Okay, that's fine. I guess we'll see them tomorrow afternoon. Thanks, Ermine." She went back to her work area outside his office, closing the door behind her.

*   *   *

Parker Winston picked up his phone and dialed the extension for his corporate counsel. Pinckney Rutledge answered after a single ring, having seen Winston's name on his phone screen.

"Yes, Mr. Winston. How can I help you?" Even though he had served as Portland's in-house corporate counsel for fifteen years, he had always referred to the CEO as "Mr. Winston" out of proper courtesy. Winston had never told Rutledge to call him anything else.

"Come see me in about fifteen minutes," Winston said. Then he hung up—commonplace etiquette from the boss.

At the appointed time, Rutledge put on his suit coat and buttoned the middle button. He grabbed a legal pad and marched five doors down to Winston's office. He told Ms. Bell that Mr. Winston had asked him to stop by, knocked once, and entered after he heard, "Come in," from inside.

"Have a seat, Pinckney." Winston had always called him Pinckney, ever since he was hired out of law school at Georgetown. Rutledge sat as commanded.

"Want to bounce something off you," Winston said.

"Yes, sir?"

"This is not something we want notes on or any other kind of record." Rutledge put his yellow legal pad down on the front edge of Winston's desk and put his pen back in his shirt pocket to show compliance.

"As you know, Weldon Van Damm died on Monday evening. Apparently, under suspicious circumstances. He helped me found Portland, and he came up with the funding scheme we use, which avoids paying interest on the capital we use to operate. And we also don't have to account to shareholders. All of which has given us a step up over our competitors in what has become an aggressive industry. It wasn't that way in the early days, but it certainly has been over the last ten years."

Rutledge listened obediently, even though he was intimately familiar with the funding model, having reviewed the documents each time a new fund was set up.

"Weldon has always been a true believer in our business model. He is around a 15 percent investor in all twelve of our funds, which makes—or made—him one of our biggest investors. He always closely monitored our progress, as he had such a big stake in the company."

"Yes, sir."

"Here's the touchy part we need to discuss. About two or three months ago, Weldon started noticing that Funds Five and Six were returning far more than the other funds. At first, he and I both thought it might be an aberration, but those two funds continued to exceed the performance of the other ten funds."

Rutledge leaned forward and raised a finger. "He was complaining about receiving bigger payouts in those two funds? About getting more money? I would think complaints would come in when a fund underperforms, rather than overperforms."

"One would think. But you have to understand Weldon Van Damm completely. I've known the man for over twenty years. He's done our legal work for eighteen years. I've served on boards with him. I've played golf with him.

"While his people skills definitely left something to be desired, there was no question about his integrity and honesty. That's why, when he raised these questions, I became concerned. If there is a scandal related to one or two of our funds, it could potentially wipe us out as a business. It could even hurt the industry as a whole.

"I've asked Chuck Deason to look into those two funds and compare them to the others. I figured the CFO was the best person to ask. I'm supposed to hear back from him on Monday."

Rutledge leaned forward, staring directly into Winston's eyes. "Do you think there's anything wrong with those two funds?"

Winston shook his head. "No, I don't. I have no idea why those two funds are outperforming the others. My feeling is that it is just an aberration. That there may be more deaths in any given fund from time to time.

"That brings us to the point of this conversation. We've got to figure out what to tell the police—or, better put—what not to tell them at this point."

"We're talking about walking a fine line," Rutledge said. "You can't lie to them. That would be obstruction of justice. On the other hand, a carefully steered conversation might avoid areas where we are concerned."

"Thank heavens, my conversations with Van Damm were all verbal. Nothing in writing. No texts. No emails."

"That's good," said Rutledge. "Did you put anything in writing to Chuck Deason?"

"Definitely not. That conversation was private and verbal—just like this one."

"Do you want me to sit in on your meeting with the detectives?" Rutledge asked

Winston shook his head. "No, that might convey a different impression than we want to give."

*   *   *

What Parker Winston had not told his corporate counsel was that he had told one other person about Van Damm's inquiries about

Funds Five and Six. That person held 12 percent of those two funds but was not invested in any of the other funds. Vincent Morehead. Now he had to wonder.

Winston thought back to his early contacts with Morehead. They had met at Eastwood Country Club where they were both members. The two of them had played golf together several times as part of a foursome.

After one round of golf in 2016, Winston and Morehead were having drinks in the 19th Hole at the club. Morehead asked about Winston's business. At the time, the company was slow in raising funds for Portland Fund Five, so Winston was eager to discuss the investment opportunity with a new prospect. Morehead seemed very interested. Later that day, Winston emailed the prospectus on Fund Five to Morehead.

Morehead called Winston the next day and said he would invest $500,000 in Portland Fund Five, and asked if Winston could bring the necessary paperwork to the Eastwood Club the next day after work. Morehead said he would bring a personal check on one of his accounts, but was too tied up to get a certified check or get the funds wired. Because he seriously needed this investment, Winston said that wasn't a problem and clearance of his check could be verified promptly.

Because of the hurried nature of the investment, Winston had Morehead fill out the investor qualification sheet by hand. Morehead largely skipped the various questions or wrote "classified" on them, explaining to Winston that he held a classified position with the government and couldn't disclose what he did for a living. Because he needed the investment, Winston said that was fine and put the investment documents through without the standard approval process.

When Portland Fund Six opened in 2017, Winston asked Morehead if he wanted to invest again. Morehead said he would invest another $500,000 in Fund Six. Again, Winston never asked the source of the funds. He also never pursued what Morehead did for a living. His need for investors overrode the usual investment protocols.

Winston now wondered whether the urgency of getting those investments left blind spots in his knowledge about Vincent Morehead. And there was really no one with whom he could discuss the issue.

CHAPTER THIRTY

SOMETHING WAS NAGGING at the back of my mind, but I couldn't put my finger on it. I picked up the phone and dialed Brady Pollard.

"Brady, Mac Burke here. Can we come down and look at your photos from the Van Damm crime scene? I'm not sure what I'm looking for, but thought the pictures might help my befuddled mind . . . Great, we'll be right down."

Again, sans jackets, we took the stairs to the third floor. Brady had already laid out the Van Damm crime scene photos on a conference table and asked, "What's rambling through your crazy Irish mind?" Oliver glanced at me, equally uncertain as to what we were doing.

"I'm really not sure myself," I said as all three of us started looking over the photos. I picked up two pictures and set them side by side. The first one had Van Damm facedown on his desk. The second was the exact same angle, but after Van Damm's body had been removed.

"Brady," I said, "he apparently was looking at something in the newspaper. Do you still have that paper here in your shop?"

"I'm pretty sure we do. We bagged and tagged it, but I don't think it's gone down to the evidence storeroom yet. Let me check." He got up and left the room.

About three minutes later, he returned carrying a standard MPD evidence bag. "Voilà, ask and ye shall receive," he said, laying the oversized bag on the table in front of me. I signed the attached chain of custody receipt and opened the bag.

I pulled out part of Monday's edition of the *Washington Post*. "Brady, this doesn't appear to be the complete copy of the *Post*."

"That's right," Brady responded. "This is the part that was on his desktop. We found the rest in his wastebasket. Which we also bagged and tagged."

"Was it folded just like this or did it get refolded to put in the evidence bag?"

Brady picked up one of the photos showing the newspaper after the body had been removed from the desk. He said, "Actually, it looks to be folded just the same as we found it."

I slid the paper over in front of Oliver and me. The quarter page we were looking at contained a number of obituaries. "Can we get a photocopy of this part of the page? I'm not sure how this figures in, but one of these names might matter later." Brady took the newspaper to a nearby copier and made us two copies.

I told him that he could return everything to his case file. "There may not be anything significant here, but I had to scratch that itch. Appreciate it." We headed back upstairs.

We both looked over the obituaries. None of them rang a bell for either of us. Oliver said, "What's percolating in your mind?"

"I'm truly not sure. But why did he have a list of obits on his desk that particular evening?" Perhaps another thread. Perhaps not.

CHAPTER THIRTY-ONE

WE SAT AT OUR desks for a little bit without saying anything. "Feels like we're finally making progress," Oliver said. "May not be any closer to suspects, but that should take shape once we find a motive."

"Feels like we're getting more of the big picture. I'm still not certain where it's headed," I said. My phone interrupted and I answered: "Mac Burke."

"Mac, Simone Reese. Think I might have something for you and Oliver. Can you come down?" I told her we would be right there, and we headed down the stairs to the third floor.

After getting directions to Simone's office, we knocked on her door. She opened the door. While it was not a big office, she had managed to make government furniture look presentable.

We sat in her guest chairs. She had some charts on her desk that she spun around so they faced us. "What I've done is ignored the quarterly 8 percent returns and only focused on the payouts coming from collections on life insurance policies.

"Half of the policy proceeds get distributed to the investors once a month based on their percentage of that fund. That is what this chart shows. The reason I had access to all of this information is that Van Damm had invested in all twelve funds, ever since the company was founded. He had kept all of the statements over the years."

Oliver tapped the chart. "Looks like there are ups and downs on the insurance payments over time."

She replied, "That's exactly right and what you would expect. Not everyone dies on a predictable schedule. So, there are some clumps of collections and also some periods where there are no or very few collections."

"Have you come up with an 'aha' moment here?"

Simone smiled and pointed to Funds Five and Six. "Starting in December of last year or January of this year, these two funds seemed to hit a bigger string of insurance collections. Unlike the other ten, Funds Five and Six collected on a larger-than-normal number of policies from the first of the year through March. There's no report yet on April, but that might warrant looking at also."

"Anything that indicates something unusual is going on?" I asked.

"Nothing I can clearly point to, but it seems like something of a red flag that warrants a further look."

"Do the records we have show us the names of the people who were insured by the policies that Portland bought?" I asked.

"Nothing at all. I'm not surprised by that. Those names and the amount of life insurance on each of them probably are listed only in the company's records. There's nothing specific in the monthly reports."

"If we can't identify who died, can we identify the investors in those two funds who benefited?" I asked.

Simone thought for a minute. "Not in the reports we have. They'd be in Portland's records."

I pondered for a second. "Without getting a subpoena . . . which I would think Portland would resist and for which I also would anticipate having a hard time getting a sustainable subpoena . . . is there any other way to find out who the investors are?"

She seemed to focus her eyes toward the ceiling and, after a pause, she said, "You know, there may be a way. I did see copies of periodic SEC filings by Portland in Van Damm's files. They're usually boilerplate and most people don't even read or save them."

"Would those include the names of those who were invested in the funds?"

She shook her head. "I'm not sure. But, you know, back from my days doing audits, I think companies using partnerships have to report anyone holding 5 percent or more of a limited partnership. I think that should be a public record. Let me see what I can dig up online through SEC's records. Probably get you an answer by early morning."

"Great. We're talking with the CEO of Portland tomorrow afternoon. I'm thinking that you may have a better bullshit detector on this one than we do. Are you available to go with us if Brady clears it?"

"Sure. That would break the monotony of sitting in this box. What time?"

"I'll clear it with Brady. We'll leave here about one o'clock. Either way, we'll see you in the morning with the identities of the investors in Funds Five and Six. Let us know what you find."

"Will do. I'll bring copies of this chart in case you need them. You may want it for the meeting with the CEO."

Oliver and I headed over to Brady Pollard's office. He approved of Simone accompanying us the next day. Oliver texted Simone to confirm that she was cleared to go.

*   *   *

Back at our desks, I asked Oliver, "We don't have time to make another trip to see Frisco before meeting with the cleaning crew. Can you call him and set up an early meeting tomorrow?"

"Sure, what are you thinking we need to see next?"

"It would seem the most direct route to what we need would be through Portland's own records."

"Like what, specifically?" Oliver asked.

"Like who the investors are in all of the Portland Funds and who sold policies to Portland. And who had died over the past six months."

Oliver picked up his cellphone. Frisco's answer was, "I see who this is, but I'm busy right now. Can we meet early tomorrow?"

"Sure. What time?"

Frisco replied, "Seven thirty?"

"We'll be there," Oliver said.

CHAPTER THIRTY-TWO

ON OUR WAY to meet the cleaning crew, I suggested we stop by DCity Smokehouse. Once we'd had our fill of rib tips, hushpuppies, and Brussels sprouts, we were ready for our next interview. I made sure to grab some rib tips and grits to go for later, and after stopping to stoke up a Marlboro by the Jeep, we were off.

*   *   *

We got to the Charter Building and parked in their underground garage. We met Maria Valdez in the lobby on the 12th floor, and she led us to a conference room off the reception area.

Maria introduced us to the eight people assembled around the table, all of whom wore dark gray uniforms with the logo of Potomac Office Cleaners on their shirts. Three men and five women. Maria explained that this was the same crew that cleaned the offices on Monday night, except for Tatyana Williams, who was still out sick.

I explained that we were trying to identify whoever was on the 12th floor on Monday evening. Maria Valdez explained that they came on duty around eight p.m. that evening. Two of the men and two of the women cleaned on the 11th floor, and the other four, along with Maria herself, cleaned the 12th floor. Tatyana Williams also cleaned on the 11th floor.

I passed around a legal pad and asked everyone to print their name and cell number, in case we had further questions later. I asked them to also indicate what part of the office they personally cleaned on Monday. The pad made its way around the table.

Once it got back to Oliver, I asked who cleaned Mr. Van Damm's office. Maria said that she normally did that office herself, but only if Mr. Van Damm wasn't there. She had a key to his office that she kept on her personal key ring.

"But I don't clean his office on the nights when he's in there working late. I got everyone started on their assigned areas, and then I went to his office around eight thirty or a quarter to nine. I could hear him on the phone. He was talking kind of loudly, so I didn't even knock."

I asked, "Did you see anyone else around his office?"

"No, it was pretty quiet in that corner of the floor on Monday night."

I looked at the rest of the crew. "Did any of you see anybody near Mr. Van Damm's office on Monday night?" Nobody said anything. Most of them were shaking their heads in the negative. I suspected they were probably all a little anxious dealing with police detectives.

I followed up with, "Did any of you see someone on either floor who wasn't a regular employee of the law firm?" Again, all of them shook their heads, although they all seemed to be maintaining eye contact.

I pulled out two copies of the picture of the woman caught by the camera in the parking garage and passed one down each side of the table. "Using the closed-circuit cameras, we identified most of the people who came in and out of the office on Monday evening. Nobody seemed to know who this lady is. Did any of you see her on Monday?" Again, each of them shook their heads in the negative as the pictures made their rounds.

Oliver and I exchanged glances. Neither of us had further questions, so I thanked them all for talking to us and told them they could go on with their duties. They rose and headed out.

Maria Valdez was the last to leave. I held up a hand. "Ms. Valdez, you gave me a phone number for Tatyana Williams. We'll need to speak with her also. You don't happen to have an address for her, do you?"

"I might. Let me check my cell." She pulled a phone from her uniform pocket. After poking a number of buttons, she said, "Yes, I do." She held the phone up to show us the screen.

"Can you forward that contact to Detective Shaw's cell number?" She did, and we thanked her and headed back to the parking garage.

As we rode the elevator, Oliver said, "She lives in Southeast. Want to swing by on the way home?"

"Why not? Let's close out this day."

*   *   *

Tatyana Williams lived in a garden apartment building not far from Alabama Avenue in Southeast D.C. We didn't call in advance and just rang her bell when we found her unit. A Black woman in her thirties answered, and we identified ourselves and showed our credentials.

Oliver asked, "Are you Tatyana Williams?"

"No. I'm her roommate. She's in her room. She's kind of sick."

"We only need to speak with her for a few minutes. Could you ask her if she could come to the door?"

The roommate nodded and headed back into the apartment. In a couple minutes a woman came to the door wearing pajamas and a chenille bathrobe. She said, "I'm Tatyana."

Oliver said, "Tatyana Williams?" She nodded. "Maria Valdez told us how to contact you. You may have heard there was a death at the law firm of Gideon & McCaffery on Monday evening."

"We have a few questions you can help us with. On Monday, which floor were you cleaning on?"

"I'm always assigned to clean on the 11th floor."

"Were you on the 12th floor at all that night?"

She shook her head no and then said, "No. I never left the 11th floor."

Oliver followed up. "Did you see anyone in the law office that night that wasn't regularly there?"

"No, I didn't."

Oliver pulled out the picture of the woman and passed it to her. "Ms. Williams, do you recognize this lady?"

She squinted at the picture and then held it up to better catch the light coming out of the apartment. Then she looked at it again. She looked at Oliver and said, "You know what? I don't know who she is, but I do think I saw her that night. I think I saw her come down the curved staircase from 12 and walk straight to the stairway door. I didn't think much of it at the time—she was dressed like all those young women lawyers. I remember wondering why she didn't take the elevator instead of the stairs."

"Do you remember what time that was?"

"Probably a little after nine or so."

"Had you ever seen her before?"

"Nope. I don't think so."

"Thank you for your assistance." Oliver concluded the interview. "You've been very helpful. Have a good night." She gently closed the door behind us.

Once back inside the car, I said, "Hot damn. Did we just get a real clue?"

"Seems so," Oliver said with a smile on his face. "And we thought we weren't making any progress. We'll have to give this more thought in the morning."

I dropped Oliver at his house on Holbrook. "I'll pick you up about seven for our visit to Frisco," I said, noting that he headed to his front door with just a touch of a spring in his step.

CHAPTER THIRTY-THREE

WHEN I PULLED into the garage, Maggie's car was in its usual place. I heard the engine of the Speedster ticking—it was still cooling off, so she hadn't been home very long.

I grabbed the take-out bag from the back seat and headed up the steps to the deck. I heard the television on in the living room. Peeking around the corner, I saw that she was watching *The Rachel Maddow Show* on MSNBC.

"Hey," I said.

"Hey."

"Have you eaten? I've got some takeout."

She looked over her shoulder. "Oh yeah? From where?"

"Ribs and grits from DCity Smokehouse."

Her eyes got wider. "No kidding? I'd kill for that right now."

"We'll have to reheat it. Oliver and I ate there earlier, and I got some extra for the larder."

By then she was up and moving to the kitchen. "I can do that part. You want some, too?"

"Just a little of each."

She opened the container of grits, stuck a spoon in, and tasted. "Oh, I love jalapeño and cheese grits."

"The ribs are not slouchy either."

As Mags nuked the food, I got a Tecate from the fridge and asked, "You want a beer also?"

She nodded. "A Mexican beer sounds good."

In a matter of minutes, we were eating at the coffee table and watching Rachel Maddow. Between bites, she asked, "What did you have to do this evening?"

"We interviewed the cleaning crew at the law firm. Came up with nada. But we caught a break."

"How so?"

I smiled. "Well, one member of the cleaning crew has been out sick for the past couple days, so we went by her apartment in Southeast to see if she had anything for us. Oliver did the questioning and, at first, it looked like another dry hole. But . . ."

Maggie talked around a bit of a rib. "Must be good if you're playing the suspense card. Out with it."

"We showed her a picture of a woman who left the building shortly after the time of death. We haven't been able to identify her. But this last cleaning person remembered seeing her leave the office shortly after our deceased had expired."

"No shit? A real live clue?"

"My words, exactly."

Mags ran her tongue around the outside of her upper gum. She seemed to be chasing a lost morsel of rib meat. "Any idea who the mystery lady is?"

"Not a clue. But we finally have a place to start."

"You got a picture?"

"Yeah." I set my beer on the coffee table and reached over for my suit jacket, which was draped over the end of the sofa. I handed the picture to Mags.

She looked at it for a bit. "Kind of looks like every blonde young lawyer in the city."

"Afraid so. But we have a face."

Mags laid the picture on the coffee table and went back to her food. When the food was gone, I took the plates and the leftovers back to the kitchen.

When I came back in the living room, Mags was looking at the picture again. I said, "Do you know her?"

Mags slowly shook her head. "She looks like twenty or more thirty-somethings I know or have met."

"Yeah, being a decent-looking person of a certain age is not as helpful as scars or tattoos."

"Well, good luck. That's progress." She leaned over and gave me a nice kiss. "And thanks for dinner. Better than I would have whipped up."

CHAPTER THIRTY-FOUR

As PROMISED, I pulled across the end of Oliver's driveway at seven o'clock Friday morning. He greeted me with a big smile.

"You know," I said, "I have a feeling that today we are going to make real progress on this case."

"Why so?"

"Just a premonition," I replied.

"Well, I hope you're right."

"I certainly hope so. I didn't get coffee or any breakfast."

Oliver raised his eyebrows. "Does that mean you're going to be grumpy today?"

"No," I said. "It simply means we've absolutely got to get breakfast after meeting with Frisco." Oliver gave an understanding nod.

We headed to Frisco's building on 24th Street NE. I parked in front of the door as before. We rang the bell, and Frisco buzzed us in. We climbed to the second floor and repeated the process.

Frisco greeted us both with his standard thumb shake and half hug. "Thanks for coming early, guys. I've got a lot going on later. But to show you that I have some limited social skills, I've made a pot of coffee."

I smiled at him and said in the manner of a priest, "Bless you, my son." He led us to his small kitchen, where his Mr. Coffee had finished brewing. He had a short stack of Styrofoam cups sitting next to it. Frisco already had his coffee in an old heavy ceramic cup with a chip missing on the rim—looked like a castoff from an old-time truck stop.

We then moved to Frisco's work area, and he pulled a wheeled desk chair in front of what I'd always thought of as his primary computer. We pulled up two other chairs to form a close triangle.

Frisco said, "How can I be of assistance to D.C.'s finest this morning?"

I started us off. "One of the names that keeps coming up in our case is Portland Life Solutions. It's one of those companies that buys up life insurance policies and then takes over the payments. When the insured tosses off the mortal coil—"

He interrupted me. "You know, part of the reason I like you guys is the fancy way you sometimes use the King's English."

I nodded an acknowledgement and continued. "So, when the life insurance policy is collected, Portland gets the money. Portland has twelve different funds that are like partnerships. The investors are like partners in one of the funds. The money raised from the investors is used to buy the insurance policies. When the policy pays out, half the proceeds go back into each of the funds to buy more policies and the other half gets distributed to the investors based on their percentage share of the fund."

Frisco nodded. "Okay, what do you want from me?"

"We need three things—if you can do it. First, we need the names of the investors in each of the twelve funds. Second, we need the names of the people who sold their life insurance to Portland in each of the funds. And, third, we need to know which of the former insurance policy owners have met their untimely demise over the last six months or so, up to the current date."

Frisco repeated, "*Untimely demise*—that's exactly what I'm talking about. Let me see about getting into Portland's files." He starting playing his keyboard like a Steinway grand piano. We just sat back and enjoyed our coffee, which was actually quite good.

After about a minute, Frisco said, "These guys need to invest more in their IT department. Some kid in middle school could get into this system. Let's see what we've got here." He continued typing on the keyboard.

"Okay, here are the investors in the twelve funds. I'll print them out for you." After hitting PRINT, he got up from his chair and went over to the printer. He came back and handed one stack to Oliver and one to me. Looking at Oliver, he said, "You've got Funds One through Six." Turning to me he added, "And you've got the investors in Funds Seven through Twelve."

Then he started typing again. After a minute, he looked up and said getting lists of the insurance policies purchased by each fund and the person named on each of the policies was also easy. "I can get you more than six months with the push of a button. How far back do you want me to go?"

Oliver suggested going back to when Funds Five and Six were started and coming forward to the present date. I agreed. Frisco nodded and started printing again. In about five minutes, he headed back to the printer again. He brought all of the paper and a stapler to Oliver and said, "There's multiple pages on each fund. I'd recommend stapling them together." Oliver took the stapler and started separating the lists.

After he had assembled each fund, he passed it to me. I went straight to Five and Six. "Nothing in Five, that I see. Wait. Rollins is in Fund Six. No sign of Van Damm in either of them."

Oliver started working backward from Twelve. "Aha," he said, "Van Damm is in Fund Eight."

While we were looking through those lists, Frisco was back on the keyboard. "Well, well, life gets easier and easier. Their accounting system has a separate journal account for each fund entitled 'Policy Payouts,' which lists the date the policy was purchased, face value of the policy, amount paid to owner, date of death if deceased, date of payment by the life insurance company, specific distribution of proceeds to the fund, and the individual investors. That should about cover the rest of your requests. I'll print these for the same window of time."

Within four minutes we had another set of sheets holding the key data we needed. We assembled the printouts carefully in a pocket folder in order to preserve everything in the correct order.

I said, "Frisco, you are amazing. Sure you don't want a low-paying job with MPD?"

He gave me a sardonic smile and said, "I'll pass."

"I understand completely. But this is another incomparable bit of assistance you have given us, and we sincerely appreciate it." He bowed his head in acknowledgement.

We all stood and repeated our standard handshake and back-slap. I bowed my head to him and said, "Thank you." He nodded back.

We took our pocket folder of new information and got in the Jeep. I suggested we get some drive-thru food so that we would have the privacy of the Jeep to continue reviewing what we had just received.

*   *   *

I knew there was drive-thru service at McDonald's on New York Avenue NE just around the corner from North Capitol Street, so we headed there. Oliver continued looking over the papers while I drove.

At McDonald's, we pulled up to the order speakers.

"What do you want?" I asked Oliver.

"I need to see the board."

"They haven't changed the menu in twenty years. What do you usually get?"

Oliver looked at me. "I hardly ever eat at McDonald's. Let me look at the board."

I gave in. I turned to the speaker and said I would have a large black coffee and a sausage, egg, and cheese McGriddle. Then I turned to Oliver. He said he'd have the same.

After we had received our food and pulled into a parking space, we got settled with our coffee and breakfast sandwiches. Then Oliver handed me the investor lists for Portland Funds Five and Six.

I compared the lists. Both lists appeared to be the same, except for a few very small investors. Basically, the lists were as follows:

JP Morgan Chase - 20%
Harvard Perpetual Trust - 20%
Clarkson Family Trust - 18%
Weldon Van Damm - 15%
Vincent Morehead - 12%
Parker Winston - 10%
Miscellaneous - 5%
Total: 100%

I read the list to Oliver. "I assume JP Morgan, Harvard Trust, and, probably, the Clarkson Trust are what we hear referred to as institutional investors. We've been told Van Damm was invested in all the Portland Funds. I would suspect Parker Winston is also. That leaves Vincent Morehead who holds a 12 percent stake. Is he in the other ten funds?"

Oliver picked up the rest of the investor summaries and went through them. He was shaking his head as he went along. When he got to the end of the stack, Oliver looked at me. "Nope, Vincent Morehead is only invested in those two funds."

"Huh," I said. "I wonder if that's significant or not."

"Don't know," Oliver replied. "But it is another factoid for the mix. When we get back to the office, let's try to find out who he is."

CHAPTER THIRTY-FIVE

WHEN WE GOT BACK to headquarters, we stopped by the third floor and knocked on Simone Reese's door. When she invited us in, I asked if she had made any progress on identifying the investors in Portland's various funds. She pointed us to the two chairs in front of her desk.

She'd gone with a more professional look today, wearing a navy suit with skirt over a cream-colored blouse and a single strand of modest-sized pearls. It set off her blonde hair and definitely made a statement. While Oliver and I had both worn some of our nicer suits, we looked like humble government servants by comparison.

Simone jumped right into business by handing us each a stapled set of papers with one page for each of the funds. "The SEC reports produced the information I had anticipated," she said. "Here are lists of all investors in the twelve funds Portland shows as of their last filing about six months ago."

Oliver remained quiet as we reviewed each of the lists of investors. When we were done, we looked back at Simone. "So, these are all of the investors?" I asked.

"All of them holding a 5 percent or greater share of each of the funds."

"Did you glean any pearls from your research?" I asked.

She looked at her own copy of the printouts. "Well," she said, "in general, half of the money invested in each fund came from large players. Among the individual people with money in the funds, both Weldon Van Damm and Parker Winston were the only individuals with investments in all twelve funds. Combined, the two of them represented about 25 percent of the total investments in each fund.

"There were individuals invested in the 10 percent range in some of the funds. There was one person who invested in both Funds Five and Six. His name is Vincent Morehead."

Oliver asked, "Could you get any information on him?"

"I had just begun working on that. Other than the address listed on SEC forms, I haven't found much. And that was just a post office box in Fairfax County."

Oliver again. "Any suggestions how we get more information on him?"

"I'm cogitating on it."

I couldn't resist. "Do people really say *cogitating* anymore?"

Her reply was, "Only when I'm dealing with detectives likely to grasp the symbolism of an arcane term like that."

"We're going to leave about one o'clock," I said. "Portland's office is in Tysons Corner over in Fairfax County. We'll grab you on the way to the car. Can you bring another set of what you've put together on the Portland funds and the list of investors? I'm not sure we're going to show our cards at this meeting, but it would be good to have them handy."

"Sure."

"And if you can keep digging on this Morehead guy," I added, "you can brief us on the way over. Good work." We headed up to our desks on the fourth floor.

*   *   *

As soon as we got back to our desks, Oliver said, "The names she got from the SEC filings matched what Frisco got for us to a T."

"Right," I agreed. "And if it ever becomes relevant, we can say we acquired that information from public records. No need to reveal our initial source."

He acknowledged the wisdom of that step with a solemn nod. "You realize Morehead's only a person of interest at this point. At best, we have only a very tangential connection between Morehead and our two decedents. And absolutely nothing connecting him to the actual murders."

"Yeah. But it's all we've come up with so far. We're still looking for a thread to start weaving something with." Oliver gave me a kind of a look best described as a puckered right cheek. Not sure what it meant, but I'm pretty sure that I felt the same way.

We didn't really have anything to update the Chief about, so we put that off until after our meeting with Parker Winston at Portland this afternoon.

Oliver suggested that we look at the lists of life insurance policies that had been paid out over the past six months to see if there was a discernible trend. We agreed to focus initially on the policies collected by Funds Five and Six, only because those had stood out to Simone Reese. Of course, she didn't know that we had obtained this information through Frisco.

Oliver said, "You know, if something pans out on this thread, we will need to come up with another way of explaining how we got this information."

"The only common threads we have at this point are that Van Damm and Rollins both sold their life insurance to Portland and that the M.E. thinks, but can't prove, that both were injected with the same chemical." I paused. "An added wrinkle with our developing theory is that we think Van Damm may have been injected by the mystery woman and Rollins by the guy at the ballpark. If we're right, different doers also complicate our scenario."

Oliver pointed out, "And we have no known connection between the two of them or between either of them and Vincent Morehead."

"Yeah," I said. "It's not coming together yet. But at least we have rabbits to chase. Let's see where they lead us."

Oliver suggested, "Let's work backward with the deaths of people whose life insurance policies were held by Funds Five and Six." We pulled the lists that Frisco had printed for us.

"Hmm," Oliver noted, "the most recent death is Dominic Bonfiglio on Tuesday of this week. Let's see what we can find on that one." He was working his keyboard. After some navigating through MPD's files, Oliver got a one-sided smile that told me he had found something. Oliver would probably not be a very good poker player.

He hit some more keys and said, "I've just forwarded you a hit-and-run report on the death of Dominic Bonfiglio." We both read the report on our screens.

I said, "It looks like he died early Tuesday morning while out jogging by the National Cathedral. At about the same time we were getting word of Van Damm's death. So that means we had three deaths in the space of about twelve hours on Monday evening and Tuesday morning."

"And Rollins and Bonfiglio had both sold their life insurance to Portland's Funds Five and Six. Too many coincidences piling up?" Oliver asked.

"Maybe. But Van Damm hadn't sold his policy to either of those funds. Tell me again which fund held his policy?"

Oliver was already ahead of me. While I was still speaking, he had been flipping through the lists of policies held by Portland that Frisco had given us. "Here it is. Van Damm sold his two-million-dollar policy to Portland Fund Eight. And Morehead wasn't invested in that fund. That's another hole in our developing theory."

I held up a finger, "What if Van Damm's death was not to collect on his policy?"

"Whatcha mean?" Oliver replied.

"What if, for the sake of discussion, Van Damm had kicked over a hornet's nest? Say . . . with Funds Five and Six? It took Simone next to no time to see something was off about those two funds. If Van Damm was monitoring all of the funds closely, maybe he saw it also."

Oliver said, "His ex-wife said he was proud of the structure he set up for Portland. And . . . he invested a lot of money in all of Portland's funds."

"Plus," I said, "his ex-wife also said he was scrupulously honest. Oh, and she also said he rolled back into one of the funds the $700,000 he got from selling his two-million-dollar policy to Portland. No pun intended, but he was very *invested* in Portland in a personal sense."

"If your budding theory is correct," Oliver said, "that might explain the multiple calls between Vann Damm and Winston over the past several weeks."

"Sounds like fodder for our conversation with Parker Winston this afternoon. We have to decide how to play that card."

"Meaning?" Oliver had a querulous look on his face, sensing I was contemplating one of my schemes to play a witness.

"Maybe we should let Winston know that we're aware of the calls and see what he volunteers. In other words, does Winston bring up the subject of the unusual performance of these two funds as the topic of his conversations with Van Damm?"

"And, if not," Oliver added, "why is he hiding it?"

"My thought exactly. If we think he's hiding something, we may want to keep our cards hidden for now. If he opens up about Five and Six, maybe we play along and see what we can learn."

Oliver pursed his lips in thought. "What about Vincent Morehead? Do we play that card ourselves?"

"I'm not sure. I think that's one we probably play by ear."

*   *   *

Continuing to work backward, we then reviewed the list of all life insurance policies held by Funds Five and Six where the insureds had died over the past six months. I pointed out that we couldn't let it slip to either Simone Reese or Parker Winston that we had this information.

"Until we get another source for these names," I continued, "we probably need to do all of the investigative legwork ourselves so there is no trail of us following something before we should have had this information." A silent double nod from Oliver. He knew what I meant.

Oliver said, "This afternoon, we can mention Rollins because we got that from his widow. But we probably can't mention Bonfiglio until we've developed another source for his name. Or any of these others." He pointed to the list we had gotten from Frisco.

"And how do we do that?" I asked.

Oliver smiled. "The easy way is to ask Winston for that information. Who knows? He might give it to us."

"I kind of doubt it."

"Yeah. Me too, but let's see."

Over the past six months, Funds Five and Six had collected, or were about to collect, life insurance proceeds totaling over $9,000,000.

Insured	Date of Death	Age	Policy Limit	Status
Bonfiglio, Dominic	April 4	54	1,000,000	Claim filed
Rollins, Eugene	April 3	43	500,000	Claim filed
Coleman, Claudia	March 31	78	500,000	Pd April 5
Stuber, Arthur	March 12	71	300,000	Pd April 9
Garcia, Miguel	March 3	39	1,000,000	Pd March 20
Vernon, Robert	February 26	58	500,000	Pd March 15
Lawson, Beulah	February 15	63	250,000	Pd February 27
Miller, Patrick	January 30	49	500,000	Pd February 24
Reinemann, Perry	February 27	55	1,000,000	Pd February 12
McDonald, Hugh	January 15	59	250,000	Pd February 2
Pritchard, Andre	December 28	60	1,250,000	Pd January 20
Kearns, Samuel	December 11	70	500,000	Pd December 23
Hieber, Edgar	November 15	75	750,000	Pd December 2
Ritzen, Conrad	October 30	51	1,000,000	Pd November 16
Dudley, Stuart	October 2	47	500,000	Pd October 20
Total:			9,800,000	

"I wonder how that compares with the money received by the other ten funds over the same period of time?" I asked.

Oliver pulled his calculator from his desk drawer. "Well, let's just see." He started adding up the figures for the other funds. As he finished each of the funds, he would announce the total. I kept a running tally on a new sheet of paper. It took about ten minutes for Oliver to run all of the calculations. Then he looked at me and said, "So, what's the spread?"

I read from my list. "The low is $2,750,000 and the high is $4,900,000."

Oliver said, "So, Funds Five and Six combined were approximately two to three times higher than the rest. But, if we consider that these are two funds and divide the total in half, the sums average only at the top end of the range."

"Does that kind of blow our theory?" I asked.

Oliver tilted his head to the right and gave a small shrug. "I don't know what it tells us. But I'm wondering if it pokes something of a hole in our working theory."

I thought the same thing. "Huh," I said. "I still think there's something to this thread."

"Maybe our conversation with Parker Winston this afternoon will help us clarify our focus," Oliver added.

Maybe, I thought. But I wasn't holding my breath.

* * *

We sat there for a minute staring at our lists. I asked, "What's next, my good Watson?"

He replied, "My suggestion would be to start this project like any high school student would start a term paper. Let's go to Google and run these names and see what turns up."

I dug a quarter out of my pocket. Oliver rolled his eyes. "What now?" he asked.

"Heads you start at the top of the list, and tails I start at the top. Loser starts at the bottom." I flipped and it came up tails.

"Of course," Oliver said. "Can you remember the last time that I ever won a coin toss?"

"Nope."

CHAPTER THIRTY-SIX

BASED ON THE FLIP, I started with Claudia Coleman, aged seventy-eight. Google came up with twenty-eight hits in the D.C. area. But since I had lucked out and gotten the most recent dates of death, I found an obituary for her in a weekend edition of the *Post*.

We had learned over time that obits were no longer free. Newspapers charged to run obituaries and, in a *sub rosa* conspiracy with funeral homes, the print media had found another means of bolstering their sagging revenues: people of means were generally the only ones whose families would run an homage to their recently departed.

And, lo and behold, Claudia Coleman's family had run a three-paragraph obit on her. No picture, which I assumed costs extra. She was a retired schoolteacher with three children and ten grandchildren. Her husband of forty-two years had passed away thirteen years earlier. She had died in a hospice facility after a long battle with cancer. Scratch her off our list. I reported the result to Oliver.

* * *

At the bottom of the list, Oliver had drawn Stuart Dudley, age forty-seven. He had died on October 2nd. Turns out that he had a fairly common name to search, and Oliver had to narrow the search to the D.C. area. Oliver found an obituary on Dudley. He had been a colorectal surgeon at GW Hospital. He was divorced, no children. He had died while on a skiing trip to New Hampshire.

That led Oliver to a small newspaper article in the *Manchester Guardian*. Apparently, Dudley had died of unknown causes while on a ski vacation with his girlfriend at Crotched Mountain Ski Resort. It was not an accident while on the slopes. The article said it was assumed that he had a heart attack.

Oliver tracked down the county in which the ski resort was located and then searched for the medical examiner for that county. He found a phone number and called. After identifying himself as a detective from the Metropolitan Police Department in Washington, D.C., he asked to be connected with someone who could discuss their record on a death that occurred on October 2nd.

He was transferred to another extension. "This is Dr. Jeffrey Greene."

Oliver identified himself and then said, "Dr. Greene, we are investigating a series of deaths where our medical examiner here in D.C. has not been able to determine a precise cause of death. She believes, but can't prove, that there was a potential injection of succinylcholine in some of the decedents.

"It has come to our attention that a colorectal surgeon from D.C. named Stuart Dudley may have a potential similarity to some of our other decedents. We're curious what your office uncovered in connection with Dr. Dudley."

After making a call back to MPD headquarters to verify Oliver Shaw was actually a detective there, Greene called back and resumed their conversation. "Detective Shaw, I have pulled our autopsy file on Dr. Stuart Dudley. We couldn't reach a precise determination on cause of death. We found no cardiac or pulmonary disease. Generally, he appeared in decent health. It looked to me as if he died as a result of asphyxiation, although I couldn't determine what caused it. I finalized the autopsy myself."

Oliver asked, "Did you get any personal information on Dr. Dudley? Also, the newspaper article said he was with a girlfriend. Any chance you have a name and contact information for her?"

Dr. Greene responded with several bits of information. "According to what we have in the file, he was forty-seven years old. Most of the personal information we obtained was from Ms. Marie Osborne, who apparently had been vacationing here with Dr. Dudley." He gave Oliver a phone number, email address, and mailing address for Ms. Osborne.

Oliver followed up. "How soon did you get the body after death? And was there a tox screen? What we're looking for is succinylcholine or abnormal amounts of other chemicals, natural or otherwise."

Greene replied: "We received the body the same evening he died. As I recall, while I did the autopsy the next morning, one of our interns was working the evening shift when the body came in. Let me look here . . . Yes, I thought so. The intern pulled the labs and sent them out that same evening for a complete tox screen."

"Did the tox screen show sux in his system?"

"Sort of. It did show the chemical compositions that would comprise that drug, although not in a large enough quantity to make us consider it a cause of death. Remember, that is a chemical that is very rapidly absorbed by the body and normally does not show up on a tox screen."

Oliver inquired, "Were there other drugs in his system?"

Dr. Greene paused a moment as he reviewed the toxicology report. "No. No other drugs were evident in his system, other than aspirin. Overall, he appeared to be a fairly healthy middle-aged male."

Oliver concluded the call. "Thanks, Dr. Greene. We really appreciate your help. Is there a phone number that is best for reaching you in case we have further questions?" Greene gave him his cellphone number. "Thanks again, Doc."

*   *   *

Oliver hung up and gave me the update. I suggested that he call the girlfriend, which he did. After identifying himself and why we were calling, Oliver asked if she recalled anything unusual occurring shortly before Dr. Greene had died on October 2nd.

Marie Osborne said, "We had gone to Crotched Mountain Ski Resort because neither of us was a very good skier. It was kind of a place for near beginners. The slopes are not very challenging.

"The night Stuart died, we had dinner in the lodge, although it looks something like a converted bowling alley from the 1970s. After dinner we were having a drink in the Onset Pub, which is the bar in the lodge.

"Stuart struck up a conversation with another gentleman at the bar and they chatted a bit. Turns out they were both Washington Redskins fans, and neither of them were pleased by the Washington Football Team, which, as I guess you know also, was the temporary name for the team before they changed it to the Commanders.

"I excused myself to go to the restroom. When I got back, the other fellow was gone. Stuart was still sitting on his barstool but had started shaking badly. I asked him if he was okay but, before he could answer, he passed out. I helped the bartender transfer him to an armchair, and the bartender called for an ambulance."

Oliver asked, "Could you describe the other man at the bar?"

"Sure, he was a white guy, probably in his forties. Don't know his height, as he was sitting down."

Oliver followed up, "What about hair color or eye color?"

She said he had sandy-colored hair, cut fairly short. She couldn't remember his eye color.

"What about his clothes? Remember anything about what he was wearing?"

She said, "Um . . . not really. It's been six months. But, even back then, I don't recall what his clothes were like. At a ski resort, everybody is pretty much wearing sweaters."

Oliver asked, "Do you think you could recognize him, if you saw him again?"

"Gosh. I'm not sure, but I could try."

"Where do you work?"

She replied that she was a manager in the clerk's office at the D.C. Superior Court.

Oliver replied, "Heck, you're just across the street from our headquarters. Could we run over and show you an array of pictures?"

"Sure, my office is on the second floor. Can you come over now? I've got a meeting to go to in about an hour."

*   *   *

We quickly assembled a six-pack of photos, one of which was the best shot we had from the Nationals ballpark, and we headed across 4th Street NW. Following Marie Osborne's directions, we quickly found her on the second floor. She invited us into her small office.

As soon as introductions were made, Marie Osborne asked, "Is Stuart's death now considered a homicide?" She seemed surprised at that possibility.

"Oh no," Oliver replied. "His name just came up on a list of people, a number of whom had a similar life insurance situation." He didn't give her any details about the viatical setup, and she didn't push further.

We changed the subject by pulling out our envelope with photographs of six males, all roughly in their forties and with sandy-colored or light brown hair. We spread them on her desk in a single row and didn't interrupt her while she looked at them.

She took her time and picked up each picture and then returned them to her desk when she moved on to the next one. We didn't tell her, but the fifth photograph was our suspect from the ballpark.

After she had given all six photos a good review, she looked at Oliver and said, "You know, it has been six months since I saw the man in a lounge in New Hampshire. I can't be 100 percent certain. But . . . I'm kind of certain that it is this guy." She pointed to the fifth photograph.

Oliver asked, "Did you ever catch his name?"

She said, "I'm sure his first name came up, but I can't recall it."

I asked, "Do you think he was also a guest at the lodge?"

"I hadn't thought about it," she said. "One way or the other."

Oliver asked and found out there was no other information she could provide us about the man at the New Hampshire bar. We thanked her and headed back to the headquarters building.

Once we were outside the courthouse, Oliver said, "Huh, that is more than a mere coincidence. As soon as we get back, I'll call that ski lodge and ask for a list of all their guests on October 2nd."

This was the first time we had connected two of our decedents, other than different people having sold their life insurance to Portland Life Solutions. We both felt that something was finally coming together.

*   *   *

We had fifteen names on our list. We had tracked down two and ended with one viable hit. We also had Dominic Bonfiglio, about whom we needed further follow-up. We had eliminated Claudia Coleman. That left us eleven more names to research.

But we didn't have time right then. "We'll have to complete this research later," I said. "We need to head to Northern Virginia to talk to Parker Winston."

"Let's lock this up," Oliver said. "Don't want this information lying around until it's official." He picked up all of our copies and locked them in our file cabinet before we left to meet Simone and hit the road.

CHAPTER THIRTY-SEVEN

We rang Simone Reese and asked her to meet us in the parking lot. She was waiting by the exit doors when we got downstairs. We walked to my Jeep.

Simone asked, "Is this an antique or something?"

My reply was, "More of a classic, I'd guess you'd say."

She looked at me askance. "You're serious?"

"Indeed. This is a 1991 Jeep Grand Wagoneer. The last year this model was made after a run of approximately thirty years. They were always a mechanical nightmare. Back then, Jeep liked to brag that it never made any mechanical modifications to the Grand Wagoneer over the three decades. In short, the engine was early 1960s technology. I've even heard it was a Nash engine from the 1950s."

"Was that necessarily bad? And what is a Nash?"

"Forget the Nash part. That was a line of autos that went out of business in the 1950s. The point is it gets less than ten miles per gallon. That's the reason you hardly see any on the road."

"So why do you keep it?" she asked.

"Because, at my core, I'm a very stubborn person. I won't be broken by crummy engineering."

"So, was the wood paneling original?" Simone asked. "And what about this rose-gray color?"

"The wood paneling is fake but, yes, it was original to the vehicle. The rose-gray paint job was my doing. Never seen it on any other Jeep, regardless of model."

She rubbed a finger on the paint. "Where'd you come up with this color?"

"It's the color of a foal from a cross between a chestnut mare and a bay stallion. It's a unique color in nature."

"Huh," was all she said and climbed in the back seat.

*   *   *

"Why is Portland Life Solutions located in Tysons Corner?" Simone asked.

I shrugged. "I have no idea. Most of the bigger corporations are located in Fairfax County. Particularly the companies that support the Defense Department. That's where most of the high-rise office buildings are located. There aren't any in D.C. In the early 1900s, Congress passed height restrictions to preserve D.C.'s character."

*   *   *

We took the GW Parkway northwest following the Potomac River to where it ended at the I-495 Beltway. We then headed south. Tysons Corner was located between McLean and Vienna, Virginia, where a lot of high-rise office buildings had cropped up. We exited onto Dolly Madison Avenue and drove a few blocks east until we reached the office tower in which Portland Life Solutions was located.

A directory informed us that Portland was on the 13th floor. Oliver noted, "Apparently this builder wasn't superstitious about the number 13." When we got off the elevator, the facing wall held signs indicating that Portland's offices were to our right.

I told the receptionist in Portland's lobby that we had an appointment with Parker Winston. She announced us, and shortly, Ermine Bell entered the lobby and introduced herself to us as Mr. Winston's executive assistant. She then led us back to his corner office. She knocked once on his door and led us in. "Mr. Winston, Detectives Burke and Shaw and Ms. Reese are here from MPD."

Winston rose from behind his glass-topped desk, which was totally clear other than his phone and a twin set of computer monitors. Winston was about 5'9" tall and wore a navy-blue suit, which nicely covered his somewhat pudgy form. He came around the desk and introduced himself as he shook our hands. Oliver and I presented our credentials and introduced Simone Reese as a CPA from our financial analysis unit. In reality, there wasn't such a unit, but it sounded good for our current purposes.

Introducing Simone caused Winston a slight raise of his eyebrows. I wasn't sure if that was because of her title and credentials or her striking appearance. I suspected the former, which was my intent in bringing her along.

Winston waved us over to a seating area and asked if we would like anything to drink. We declined and he motioned Ms. Bell to depart.

I took the lead. "Mr. Winston, as I explained to Ms. Bell yesterday, we are investigating the death of Weldon Van Damm."

"Yes, we were saddened to hear of his loss. Weldon was a personal friend, as well as our lawyer. He helped me set up this company and has been an ardent investor since we started our operations."

"So I understand," I said, being intentionally ambiguous. "We have been told that he helped create the format for raising capital through the twelve funds Portland uses to acquire life insurance policies."

I saw his eyes widen slightly at my acknowledgement that we knew about the twelve funds. Probably more detail than he'd anticipated we'd know about his company.

"Yes. Weldon suggested that, rather than raising capital through a typical stock offering, we use a partnership format similar to real estate ventures. In the end, it has worked very smoothly for us and allowed us to raise money through a number of institutional investors rather than large numbers of stockholders."

"But you also have a number of individual investors; isn't that correct?" My further revelation that we had been doing our homework.

Again, his eyes widened. Another person who would likely not be a good poker player. "Yes, that is true also. Both myself and Weldon personally invested in all twelve funds."

"Any other individuals?" I could see him lean back somewhat as he contemplated his response.

"A few. Here and there . . . How does this relate to Weldon Van Damm's death?" Attempting to change the subject.

"That, we are not exactly certain about. Do you know of anyone who would have a reason to want to see Mr. Van Damm dead?" Letting him think his feint was working.

"Not at all. Weldon could be brusque. He was very direct. Always very goal-oriented."

I nodded. "We've heard that. We checked Mr. Van Damm's phone records and saw that he was on the telephone with you just minutes before he was killed." I let that hang. His eyes widened again. The hits just kept on coming for him.

Winston's brow wrinkled. "I talked to Weldon regularly. When did he die?"

"Monday evening, around nine p.m."

"Well, yes, I think I did talk to him on Monday night." Not volunteering anything.

"What did you discuss?"

He paused for a few seconds. I figured he was trying to figure out how candid he had to be. "Uh, I think he was voicing concerns about the number of policy claims that were coming up in some of the funds."

"Which funds in particular?" *Keep it short and sweet. Keep it coming.*

"Uh, let's see. I think he thought more claims than usual were cropping up in some of the funds." Again, avoiding naming the funds.

"Which funds in particular?" There it was again. I saw a slight bead of perspiration on his upper lip, which he apparently sensed because he drew his index finger across his lip. It probably didn't help that Oliver had pulled out his notebook and was jotting something down.

Winston apparently decided to give in somewhat, not realizing that it would only lead to more questions. He said, "I believe it was Funds Five and Six."

I followed up. "Just those two funds?"

"Yes, I think so." Still not volunteering anything extra.

"What was Van Damm concerned about?"

"Well, he followed all of the funds closely. He had made a lot of money from our funds over the years and kept track of them all. He said it appeared that proceeds from those two funds were far higher than the others."

"Wouldn't that be a benefit to him and all the other investors?"

Winston nodded. "Of course, that's our business model. But Weldon was concerned that there was something unusual about those two funds."

"Meaning what?"

"He wondered if there was something going on that was amiss. I told him it was probably just an aberration. Those occur from time to time in all of the funds. I told him that I would have our CFO check it out and let him know."

"Who's your CFO?"

"Charles Deason." Oliver made a note of the name. I gave Winston time to watch Oliver write the name down.

"Has he given you his report yet?"

Winston shook his head. "No. He's supposed to get it to me on Monday."

"Can we see a copy of it when it's prepared?"

"Well, it's really proprietary information but, given the significance of it to your investigation, I can agree to give you a copy if you agree to keep it confidential for now."

I nodded and said, "We can agree to that. Now, back to my earlier question about other individuals who are invested in Funds Five and Six."

He looked surprised that he hadn't dodged my probe into the investors. "We consider the identities of the investors as confidential."

I pursed my lips in a disappointed face. "Well, those names cannot be that confidential if Portland has to list them in your SEC filings." Winston looked at Simone Reese, correctly surmising that she had dug out that information.

"So, who is Vincent Morehead? He's listed as a 12 percent investor in both Funds Five and Six." Winston seemed concerned by the turn in our conversation. He acted hesitant to answer.

I repeated, "Who is he?"

"He is an investor whom I met through my golf club—Eastwood Country Club over in Vienna."

"Do you know him well?"

Winston shrugged slightly. "I've played golf with him several times over the years. That's how we met."

"What does he do for a living?"

Winston said, "I don't really know."

Simone Reese spoke up, which jarred Winston. "Don't you have to qualify your investors?" Winston looked at her as if he'd been caught in a clear lie.

"Of course. We are required to verify that investors are qualified and have resources to handle the level of investment."

Simone probed further. "Don't investors have to fill out an investment qualification sheet?"

"Certainly."

"Can we see Mr. Morehead's qualification sheet?" she asked.

Winston said, "I would have to believe that is information that we're required to keep confidential. I'd have to check with our general counsel."

I picked the thread back up. "This could be important information for our investigation. We can get a subpoena, if necessary, but would appreciate your cooperation."

"Let me check with our general counsel first," Winston replied.

"Can you call him now and ask?" I pressed. My thought was to break his rhythm.

In response, Winston rose from his chair and headed to his desk. He sat down and picked up his desk phone and pressed three buttons. "Pinckney: Got a question for you. I'm meeting with some detectives from MPD, and they're asking to see the qualification sheet on one of our investors. Is that something I can let them see?" After listening for about a minute, Winston said, "Okay, I'll tell them that. Thanks."

Parker Winston returned to his chair near where we were sitting. "Our general counsel, Pinckney Rutledge, says we assure our investors that their financial information is confidential. He said, however, that if you were to provide us with a subpoena, we could give you the investor qualification sheet, subject to MPD's agreement to keep the material confidential in your files unless ordered otherwise by a court."

Without any authority to say so, I again agreed to that condition and told Winston we would have a subpoena delivered this afternoon. I could tell he was surprised that we could act that fast.

I asked Oliver to call the Chief's office and make the arrangements. He nodded and stepped out of the office to make the call to Beverly Gray to get the subpoena prepared and emailed to Parker Winston's office today. She told him she would get it done posthaste. Her actual word. No judge's signature was required for a subpoena.

Oliver rejoined us in Winston's office and gave me a nod that it was taken care of. While he had been out of the room, I asked Winston if we could have some water. He passed the request on to his executive assistant. She returned with a tray of glasses with ice and water, just after Oliver had come back into the room.

Once we were settled again, I asked, "Do you know where Mr. Morehead lives?"

Winston looked at me somewhat earnestly. "I think he once said that he lives in Vienna, somewhere south of the golf club. I've never been to his house. Why all the interest in Vince Morehead?"

"We're just being thorough. When a name comes up in connection with our investigations, we are obligated to see if they have a connection to the case or not. As often as not, it is a matter of eliminating someone whose name has come up."

I thought for a second, then said, "When our technical department checked Weldon Van Damm's phone histories, we saw that he had called you six times over the month preceding his death. What were those calls about?"

"That, I do not clearly recall. I know we played phone tag several times. I think there was only one other call of any duration. That was when Weldon was first starting to think there was something amiss with Funds Five and Six."

"Did you ever talk to anyone about Van Damm's concerns about Funds Five and Six?"

"Only when I asked our CFO to take a look at those two funds."

"Did you ever talk to Vincent Morehead about Van Damm's concerns with those funds?"

I saw Winston slowly inhale a larger breath than normal. He probably knew this was a critical moment when he had to decide whether to cross the line on obstruction of justice. Winston looked at Oliver who was busy transcribing my question, as he understood its significance as well.

Parker Winston ran his right hand from his eyebrows up through well-coifed gray hair. I could tell he had made a decision.

"Yes, I did. After that earlier call with Weldon, I was playing golf with Vince Morehead the next day, and I mentioned that Weldon had inquired about the aberration in collections from Funds Five and Six."

I asked, "What was his reaction?"

"Nothing. He asked if those funds were performing the same or differently from the other funds."

"What did you tell him?"

"I said I didn't know, but I was having it checked out."

"Anything further discussed with Morehead about this subject then or at any other time?"

"I called him after I heard that Weldon had died. He expressed surprise and remorse. He said that he knew Weldon was a good friend of mine."

"Okay. We're almost finished. We need a list of the people from whom Funds Five and Six bought life insurance policies over the past few years. And the details, like addresses, policy amounts, and claims collected by Portland."

Winston thought for a second. "Well, I guess that's proprietary information, but not necessarily confidential. We'll give you that information, subject to the same agreement that you will keep it confidential absent an order from a court."

"Agreed."

He picked up his phone and asked Ermine Bell to come in. When she did, he gave her the details of the list he needed. He then gestured to me to confirm that the details he had requested were what I wanted.

While Ms. Bell prepared the list, we sat and discussed how the viatical business worked and how they found people willing to sell their life insurance policies. As it turns out, most sellers contacted Portland based on television commercials and print ads. Portland mainly focused on the D.C. metropolitan area.

Ms. Bell returned with four copies of the list of original policy holders. She gave one to Mr. Winston, and he looked it over. After he nodded, she distributed the other three copies to Oliver, Simone, and me. She then returned to her office.

While we were wrapping up, Ms. Bell came back into Winston's office with a copy of the emailed subpoena and showed it to Parker

Winston. He read it over and nodded to her. "Make them copies of Mr. Morehead's qualification sheet. Make one for me also. Thanks." She came back with copies a few minutes later and distributed them. We then thanked Mr. Winston and Ms. Bell and shook their hands and headed back to my vehicle.

*   *   *

As soon as we got back to the Jeep, I reached in and cranked the engine and turned on the air conditioning. I made no move to get inside.

Simone looked at me in puzzlement, but Oliver knew what was up. I pulled out my box of Marlboros and lit one up.

Simone said, "Well, hell, if we're taking a smoke break . . ." She reached in her purse and pulled out a box of Virginia Slims. She shook one out, and I lit it with my lighter.

Simone looked at Oliver and said, "Is that a typical interview by Mac Burke?"

He gave a half chuckle. "Pretty much."

She said, "No shit? That was masterful." She gave me a head bob, to which I smiled.

Oliver said, "We got the list of the insureds, as well as Vincent Morehead's financial particulars. And we got him to admit the conversations with Van Damm were about Funds Five and Six. Finally, he was as nervous as a whore in church on Sunday when we started talking about Morehead. My opinion is that Mr. Winston knows—or at least suspects—that something is rotten in Denmark, as Shakespeare said, about those two funds and that Morehead is involved."

Simone added, "I'm no pro in this interrogation business, but I'd say that was a pretty good haul."

"You are correct, madam," I said. "Let's go back to the office." I flicked the ash off my smoke with my fingernail and put the butt in my box. She dropped hers and rubbed it out with toe of her shoe.

*   *   *

After the MPD detectives had left, Ermine Bell knocked on Parker Winston's door and stuck her head inside. "Anything else I can do for you, Mr. Winston?"

"No. Thanks again, Ermine. I'm going to call it a week shortly. Why don't you close up and head out yourself?"

She smiled. "Thanks. That would be nice. I'll see you on Monday." She closed his office door, shut down her computer, and locked her desk.

After about ten minutes, Parker Winston called the cell number he had for Vincent Morehead and left a short voicemail saying there were new developments and asking him to call.

By the time Morehead called back about forty-five minutes later, Winston had conjured several different scenarios that could put him personally in serious jeopardy. He had started to bite his fingernails, a habit he had given up before high school.

Winston answered Morehead's call with rushed speech. "Good, I had a visit this afternoon from two MPD detectives and a forensic CPA."

Morehead replied, "What did they want?"

"They're looking into Weldon Van Damm's death and asking questions about Funds Five and Six."

"Huh," Morehead said. "How are those two things related?"

Winston answered, "I don't know. But they seem to think there's a connection. Plus, they were asking for the names of insureds on the policies collected by those funds. They had also dug out the names of the investors in those two funds. They seemed to be focused on you."

"Why me?"

"That wasn't clear. But they did ask for your investor qualification sheet. Our in-house counsel said it was okay to provide them, as long as they kept it confidential."

Morehead said, "Well, tell you what. I have no idea what's going on. Let me know if you hear anything further. Thanks for calling, Parker."

After disconnecting, Parker Winston wasn't any calmer. He shook his head twice, compressed his lips, and closed his eyes, almost as if he were in prayer.

CHAPTER THIRTY-EIGHT

MOREHEAD ALSO SAT and analyzed the conversation. The police couldn't have put anything together, but they may be getting the scent. Probably time to close it down. But was Parker Winston a problem? He was clearly getting skittish.

Morehead didn't think he had a problem with the source of the succinylcholine. Serendipity had again helped him with that issue. About nine months earlier, he had been paired with Jay Willingham in a random-draw one-day club tournament at Eastwood Country Club in Northern Virginia where both were members. They were fairly evenly matched and played well together.

Over the course of the eighteen holes, Morehead got to know a little about Willingham, who was a large animal veterinarian. Morehead had only told the vet that he worked for the federal government but couldn't get into any details about what he did exactly, which seemed to make him even more interesting to the vet riding shotgun in the golf cart.

Morehead didn't realize that the vet noticed that his partner had a tic where he frequently lifted his nose, which pushed his cheeks up toward his glasses. It seemed to the vet as if Vince was smelling something foul.

After the round was completed, they adjourned to the 19th Hole for beers and lunch. Morehead learned that Jay Willingham had been a jockey in his youth who had literally outgrown what he thought would be his career in horse racing. The owner who had used him as a jockey for nearly five years took Willingham under his wing and, given his love of horses, encouraged Jay to go to college and veterinary school to become a horse doctor. The owner treated him like a son. His benefactor agreed to pay Jay's college and vet school expenses if he agreed to return to Northern Virginia to take care of horses and other large animals.

Jay told Vince that he had gone to Auburn University for both undergrad and veterinary school. After graduation he had returned to Virginia as promised and took a position with a large animal vet clinic in Leesburg and bought a house with his wife in Northern Virginia. He had joined Eastwood Country Club about twenty years earlier and became the owner of Marshall Veterinary Equine and Farm Clinic five years later after the old vet retired. He said he treated horses and cattle all over Northern Virginia and the general area around Washington.

Jay also told Vince that he was the on-call vet for both Rosecroft Raceway, which was a harness track in the Oxon Hill area of the Maryland suburbs south of D.C., and for Laurel Park Racetrack situated between D.C. and Baltimore. That eventually led to a discussion of occasionally having to put down an injured racehorse.

The vet explained that he would anesthetize them with a chemical called succinylcholine, commonly called sux, to relax their muscles and then give the horse a fairly large injection of pentobarbital in the jugular vein of their neck. The horse would then gently stop breathing without any evident pain within one to two minutes.

Vince asked, "What is sux?"

The vet replied, "That is the common name for the drug I mentioned before, succinylcholine."

Vincent Morehead sniffed with his nose, which pushed his cheeks up against his glasses. He said, "Well, that's a short education I won't run across every day."

But Morehead knew then that this chance discussion had pointed him to a source of sux he needed to execute his plans with respect to some of the people whose life insurance was held by Portland Life Solutions. Morehead believed that source would never be traced back to him.

*   *   *

What Morehead didn't know was that Dr. Jay Willingham, DVM, had contacted the Leesburg Police Department eight months earlier to report the break-in at the Marshall Veterinary Equine and Farm Clinic. A detective came to the clinic and took the report on the burglary. After gaining access to the clinic during the night, the burglar had pried open the locked drug cabinet and a number of drugs had been stolen.

After a crime scene tech dusted for prints, the detective asked Dr. Willingham's assistant to inventory the drug cabinet to determine what was missing. She gave the detective a list of the drugs taken: their entire stock of ivermectin, pentobarbital, and succinylcholine—also called "sux"—along with lesser quantities of other pharmaceuticals, mainly antibiotics.

Dr. Willingham explained to the detective that ivermectin was used to treat parasitic diseases—and was often referred to as a horse dewormer—and that this particular chemical had been a hot topic on the internet as a potential cure for Covid-19—a claim the Centers for Disease Control considered bunk—but some people were still searching for a cure other than the vaccines. Willingham told the investigating detective, "I suspect it was one of those damn anti-vaxxers."

No fingerprints were found, and the clinic did not have a security system or cameras. With nothing to pursue, the burglary report languished without further investigation. The Leesburg detective did, however, file a detailed standard report online with the National Crime Information Center, which maintains a computerized index of criminal justice information maintained by the FBI and is available to all law enforcement agencies nationwide.

CHAPTER THIRTY-NINE

ONCE WE WERE mounted up and headed back to headquarters, Oliver said, "I think we have enough developments that we should brief Chief Whittaker."

He pulled out his cell to call Corporal Beverly Gray. "Beverly, Oliver Shaw here. First, thanks for the expedite on that subpoena . . . Yeah, I know, but we really do appreciate your help when we need it. Second, we're making some real progress and thought we should brief the Chief . . . Yeah, we're headed back in from Tysons Corner. Should be there in forty-five minutes, considering the Friday afternoon traffic we're dealing with. Probably about a quarter to four before we get there . . . Appreciate it."

He looked at me. "You heard?"

I gave him kind of a dumb smile. "Of course, I was sitting right here the whole time. Hey, Simone, you want to sit in on the briefing of Chief Whittaker?"

"You bet. Face time with the brass on a Friday afternoon. Good finish to the week."

We survived the usual Friday afternoon exodus from our Nation's capital and got back to headquarters as predicted at about three fifty. All three of us went up to the fourth floor to make some copies to give Chief Whittaker.

We then took the elevator to the fifth floor and introduced Simone to Beverly Gray, who said, "You're a few minutes early, but I don't think he'll care. You're the last thing on his schedule today." She walked over to the Chief's door and knocked once. She opened the door and said, "Chief, Detectives Burke and Shaw are here along with Simone Reese from Brady Pollard's shop."

"Show them in, please. And no need for you to hang around. We're closed for business after I talk to these folks."

"Then I'll lock up and disappear."

The Chief pulled over a third chair in front of his desk. "Ms. Reese, good to see you again. I hear that you've been helping Mac and Oliver with their case."

Oliver said, "Indeed she has. She went with us to Portland Life Solutions this afternoon and participated in interviewing the CEO. She asked some questions that sparked some nervousness and ultimately led to us getting financial and background data on Vincent Morehead, who is one of the individual investors in Portland's Funds Five and Six."

Chief Whittaker said, "Good to hear." He looked at her. "More fun than crunching numbers in Brady's shop?"

Simone smiled. "Beats the hell out of my usual CPA drudgery."

The Chief replied, "Maybe you should consider becoming a detective."

Simone replied, "I'll definitely think about it."

The Chief looked at me. "So, Mac, bring me up to date on your progress."

"Yes, sir. I'll give you the highlights, and Oliver and Simone can jump in whenever they want. First, you've already seen the photographs of the two people we suspect are the murderers of Weldon Van Damm and Eugene Rollins, the guy killed at the ballpark." I laid copies of the photos in front of the Chief.

"One of the cleaning crew ladies saw the blonde lady leaving the law office shortly after Van Damm's death. We've also had a further confirmation related to the guy from the ballpark that Oliver tracked down."

Oliver took over. "We've been focused on Portland Funds Five and Six, which the CEO confirmed this afternoon had been the subject of calls between him and Van Damm over the past several weeks. The Portland CEO is named Parker Winston. He and Van Damm were on the phone Monday evening, just minutes before Van Damm was murdered. Winston confirmed they were discussing an unusual number of death claims in Portland's Funds Five and Six that had drawn Van Damm's attention."

Oliver paused to catch a breath. "Van Damm monitored all twelve funds and noticed that Five and Six had a spike in death claims over the last six months."

Oliver swallowed, out of his comfort zone, reporting to the Chief. "Simone sorted through Van Damm's investment records and came to the same conclusion in fairly short order. We then had her search for the names of the investors in those two funds. Simone found what we needed from Portland's most recent SEC filings." Oliver then passed the torch to Simone.

She picked it up and continued. "Based on the SEC filings, two-thirds of the investments in Funds Five and Six were basically large institutional investors and trusts. About one-third of the investors in Funds Five and Six were a combination of Weldon Van Damm, Parker Winston, and a third individual by the name of Vincent Morehead.

"Van Damm was a 15 percent investor in those two funds, as well as the ten other funds. Winston was a 10 percent investor in all twelve funds. Vincent Morehead was a 12 percent investor in Five and Six but was not an investor in any of the other funds."

I said, "When I asked Winston questions about Morehead, he claimed to have little knowledge about him, at which point Simone asked Winston about Morehead's investor qualifications sheet. Winston claimed that was confidential information. We pressed him for copies of it, and he said he had to talk to their corporate counsel. We pushed him on it, and he got on the phone with their in-house counsel."

"After talking to his corporate counsel," I continued, "Winston said they would produce Morehead's financial qualification sheet, if we subpoenaed it."

"I called Beverly," Oliver said, "and she got a subpoena prepared and emailed it to Portland."

Oliver raised a finger. "As they say in the infomercials," he said. "'Wait, there's more.' We tracked down one of the death claims in Fund Five. A colorectal surgeon from GW Hospital who died while on a ski trip in New Hampshire last fall. An obit led us to the local M.E. in New Hampshire who gave us the name of the woman who was with the doctor.

"Her name is Marie Osborne. She said they were having drinks at the bar at the ski lodge and were having a conversation with a sandy-haired man. She went to the restroom. When she came back the guy was gone, and Dr. Dudley was shaking violently at the bar. They called for an ambulance. The local M.E. could not determine a cause of death.

"Our own M.E., Courtney Vaughan, had told us that shakes are a side effect of injection of sux, the chemical which she suspects was involved in the deaths of both Van Damm and Rollins.

"So, Mac and I put together a six-pack of photos of sandy-haired men, including the suspect from the ballpark. We asked Ms. Osborne to look at the photos. Our suspect was the fifth in the line-up. We did nothing to influence her. After carefully considering all of the photos, she pointed to number five and said she was fairly certain that was the man from the bar."

I rejoined the narrative. "Dr. Dudley had sold his life insurance policy of $500,000 to either Fund Five or Fund Six, as had Rollins. So, we continued to home in on those two funds. Plus, we now have the male suspect likely connected to two deaths related to those funds."

The Chief asked, "Didn't you tell me Van Damm also sold a two-million-dollar life insurance policy to Portland?"

Oliver answered, "Yes, Chief. But he sold his policy to Fund Eight. We have a working suspicion that Van Damm's death was not related to collecting on his life insurance. It's our tentative premise at this point, but his death may be related to his raising a question about the larger-than-usual death claims in Funds Five and Six."

"We have no connection at this point," I added, "between our two suspected doers and Portland. What we do have is a connection between Vincent Morehead and the two funds. Now, if only we find a thread between him and our two suspects, things would start to get serious."

"Chief," I said, "I'd like to have Simone use her CPA and audit skills to scrutinize whatever she can find on Morehead. Not just his investment qualification sheet, but other sources as well. We need to get this done over the weekend, if possible."

"I'm available," Simone said.

The Chief said, "And I'll authorize the overtime." Simone smiled at that.

"While I haven't discussed this with Oliver, I think he and I need to pound through the list of decedents connected to Funds Five and Six over the past six months."

Oliver didn't look surprised. He knew when I got hold of a thread, I just kept pulling.

So did the Chief. "I think this also justifies overtime. But with the budgetary crisis, if you gentlemen would take comp time instead of overtime, it would help my numbers."

"Fine by me," I said.

Oliver added, "Me, too."

The Chief stood. "Really good progress, folks. Now, I think I'm going home to see if my wife still lives there. Have a productive weekend. Keep me posted."

* * *

With that, we headed back down to the fourth floor and locked our stuff up. I said, "Since we're all working this weekend, Oliver, I think we should introduce Simone to our favorite neighborhood bar."

He smiled. "Capital idea, guv." We both looked at Simone.

She smiled. "Indeed, a capital idea."

We headed down to the Jeep and made our way to Northeast D.C. Once we were headed east, Simone spoke from the back seat. "So, where is this secret place?"

I replied, "We can't let you know. In fact, we should probably ask you to wear a blindfold or, at least, make a double-secret vow not to disclose our destination to another member of MPD for fear they would taint its humble character."

I looked in the mirror. She smiled and crossed her heart and said, "Done."

Living with my Irish luck, I found a parking space in front of Burton's. As we entered the front doors, Shirley spotted us. Her eyebrows went up a hair at our inclusion of Simone, but Shirley asked, as usual, "Business or pleasure?"

And, as usual, Oliver and I simultaneously said, "Business." We're like twins in answering some questions. Shirley waved us to the booths. The last two of which were empty. We took the last booth for privacy.

Not knowing the proper etiquette for the situation, Simone slid into one side by herself. Oliver and I looked at each other, and I pulled a quarter from my pocket. Oliver said, "Oh no, not again."

I said, "Yep. Heads you get the wall and I get the outside on tails." I flipped the quarter and let it land on the table. It was heads.

"Wait," Oliver said. "That was a heads-you-win and tails-I-lose flip. Do it again. Heads I get the wall and tails I get outside." Having been caught, I flipped again. It was heads.

Oliver mumbled, "Of course," and slid in first. As soon as we were seated, Shirley was standing there, quietly waiting for our orders.

I told Simone, "This is Shirley, the lady who owns this fine establishment. She is patiently waiting for your beverage of choice."

Simone smiled at Shirley and said, "I would like a double Angels Envy on the rocks." Shirley nodded her approval.

Oliver said, "I would appreciate an ice-cold Yuengling."

Shirley turned to me.

"Please make mine Jack Single Barrel on the rocks." Shirley smiled and departed.

Given the lack of preparation time required for any of our drinks, they arrived rather expeditiously. We held our beverages up for an air toast, but no clinking of glasses.

"Was our outing as educational as you had hoped?" I asked Simone.

She nodded once. "It truly was. It was amazing watching you two work together and finesse your cards out ever so subtly. Poor Mr. Winston was fricking out of his league. I'm sure he went into the meeting thinking he could deal with a couple of bush league detectives."

"Guess he didn't know that we were called up to the pros a long time ago," Oliver said and pointed to Simone. "Your sense of timing on the investor qualification sheet was on the mark. It really threw him off."

"It was obvious that he was hedging and stalling on any information on Morehead," she said. "I had a definite feeling that he was hiding something there."

"What you don't know, Simone, is that Mac and I have worked together at MPD for thirteen years and before that when we were in the military at the same time."

"What did you both do in the military?" she asked.

"I was a Special Agent in the Air Force Office of Special Investigations," I said.

"And I was a Special Agent in the Army Criminal Investigation Division," Oliver added. "We were both in Qatar at the same time."

"So," Simone said, "what don't I understand about your working relationship?"

Oliver replied, "I'm the listener. Kind of like a horse whisperer. I listen for undertones that tell us as much as the spoken words. What I heard was exactly what you just said. Winston was holding back big-time on Morehead."

"There's more there than he wants us to see," I added. "I have a gut feeling that (a) he told Morehead more about Van Damm's concerns than he let on and (b) that he harbors suspicions that Morehead may be behind the mysteries related to the two funds. He has to wonder who is behind the increase in deaths and who is behind Van Damm's death and why."

Simone pushed the ice around in her drink with her finger. "Your jobs are far more challenging than the stuff I've done in my career, including MPD."

I put on my serious face. "Be careful digging on Morehead," I told Simone. "We have already determined that the two people in those pictures are not in any governmental facial recognition system, which we're told could well mean they work for some black ops agency of the government. If Morehead is connected to those people, he could also be connected to that arena."

"I have a suspicion," Oliver said, "that Winston will tell Morehead that we are focused on him. That could make Morehead a very nervous person right now. Mac is right, remember they now know your name and that you are working on the case. Be careful."

"You know what I would like to know about Morehead? What does he do for a living?" Simone said. "And where did he get the money he invested in Portland? And, something else, what has he been doing with the money he is getting out of Funds Five and Six?"

Shirley appeared with refills and a bowl of Hub's peanuts. Simone tried the peanuts and noted how good they were. I explained that they come from a family peanut farm in Virginia.

Then she turned to both of us and asked, "If I were to take Chief Whittaker up on his suggestion about applying to be a detective, what would be involved?"

Oliver responded first. "There'd be some testing," he said. "They might cut you some slack on the police academy requirement, given your education and experience, as well as your time working for MPD. I'm not sure what else would be involved."

"Do you guys have to shoot guns very often?"

"I've been an MPD detective for thirteen years and have never fired my pistol once in the line of duty," I said. "You probably wonder why we wear suit coats to this fine establishment. It's because MPD regulations require us to carry our weapons, even when we're off duty. I'm probably the worst shot on the entire force." Oliver just nodded in agreement.

Women being the more curious of the species, Simone looked at me and said, "Mac, how did you get the scar next to your left eye?" In all the years that I've known Oliver, he had never asked about my scar.

I gave her the same answer as I'd given to anyone else who ever asked. She seemed skeptical about my supposed sword fight with a pirate in the Caribbean. "Really?" she replied. Why is it women always say that when they don't believe something you've said to them? I didn't respond further.

We finished our drinks and took Simone back to the headquarters' parking lot where she'd left her vehicle, which turned out to be a navy-blue Cobra Mustang. She could see we were both drooling over the car.

"Not to worry, guys. It's not an original. It's a reproduction. But it makes a lot of noise and goes really fast."

She climbed out of the Jeep and jumped into her car. We just sat there for a minute with the windows down and listened to her fire it up. Just to show off, she laid some rubber as she peeled out. The engine gave off the throb of a dragster as she drove it out of the lot.

CHAPTER FORTY

As I DROVE Oliver home he said, "I sure hope we're pulling the right threads here. It seems to me it's the first time that we're getting some pieces to come together."

"I'm kind of feeling the same way."

After dropping Oliver at his house, I lingered at the curb to send Mags a text. HEADED HOME. THINKING ABOUT A PIE FROM PIZZA WALAY. INTERESTED?

She replied about ten seconds later. SOUNDS GOOD. HOME IN 15 MINS.

I called Pizza Walay and ordered a large thin crust with half pepperoni and pork—for me—and half everything but anchovies—for her. I headed back west on H Street to the pizza shop. After I got the pizza in the Jeep, the smell made me seriously hungry. I hadn't eaten lunch again.

When I pulled down the alley behind our row house, I saw Maggie's Speedster ahead of me about five car lengths. She had already activated the door opener on her side of the garage. I hit my garage remote before her door had come down completely. Not often we both end up in the garage at the same time.

I handed her the pizza box and gathered my coat and work file. I was rewarded with a smile and a *"Merci, monsieur."*

"Pizza is Italian, not French."

"There is some serious question whether pizza really comes from Italy," she replied.

Once inside, she pulled down two plates while I went to the fridge for beers. I looked at her. "Preference?"

"Got any Italian beer?"

"Let's see." I squatted down and pushed some cans around in the back of the bottom shelf. "Aha! We have three cans of Birra Moretti. No vouching for how old they are."

"That will be perfect."

We took the pizza box, plates, and three cans of beer to the breakfast table. We each snagged a slice of our preferred kind and popped a can of Birra. As usual, Mags clicked on the local news channel for background noise.

I quickly consumed all four of my slices. Proof of hunger. Mags ate three pieces and put her last slice in a Ziploc baggie. As she was putting it in the fridge, she must have read my mind when she said, "Hands off, buster."

She then came back to the table and poured half of the last beer into a glass and passed it to me. She took the can and proceeded to finish it off in three long gulps, followed by a small belch covered with the back of her left hand. She gave one of those little expressions that passes as an apology, without really being one.

"So, any progress on your case?" she asked. "And what was so exciting that made you forget about lunch?"

"Who said I forgot lunch?"

"Odds are, based on how you inhaled the pizza."

I explained the highlights of the case so far. "Actually, we have photos of the woman we think killed Van Damm, which you've already seen, and multiple photos of the guy we think killed the engineer at the ballpark. But we haven't been able to identify either one. Even after running them both through facial recognition software."

Mags said, "Lots of difference in the quality of facial recognition programs. Does MPD have a good system?"

"Actually, we don't have one at all. We usually sponge off the Bureau if they decide to like us that day."

"Did the Fibbies come up with anything?"

"No, we decided we didn't want to deal with the bureaucratic hassle. We used a source Oliver and I have developed over the years."

"What does that mean?"

"Not to go any further than here."

She nodded her agreement, which was enough between us, and I continued. "We've got a guy who can get us into a lot of systems."

"So, what facial recognition system did your 'guy' get you into?"

"DHS."

She was shocked. "Holy shit. Homeland Security?"

"Yep."

Mags made several different facial expressions that indicated she was reflecting on the fact that two DC detectives had access to Homeland Security's systems. All she said was, "Man."

"Yep."

"So, did you get any hits on either the woman or the man?"

"We got hits on both of them."

She said, "So who are they?"

"Don't know. While the system pinged indicating it had found a match both times, the system then came back with a single line message: 'This information is not available.' Same exact language both times."

"Huh," Mags said. "What does that mean?" I had a strong feeling she already knew the answer and was asking solely to protect her cover.

"We were told their identities are concealed by the government, probably because they have classified jobs of some sort."

"So, is that it? A dead end? Even using DHS's facial recognition software?"

I tilted my head to the side and raised my eyebrows. "Here we are with pictures of the people we strongly suspect of two murders, and we hit a stone wall because the government has decided no one should know who these people are. It is frustrating."

"So, where do you go from there?"

"We're not sure, but we are looking at other information that might tie us to someone who had a clearer motive for the two deaths. If that pans out, maybe we can find a way to connect that person to our two mystery guests."

She gave me a semi-smile of sympathy. "There's no such thing as a straight line from A to B sometimes."

"Amen, sister."

"Let me see the pictures, if you've got them with you."

I reached over to the pocket folder where I kept my work notes. Reaching inside, I pulled out two 5 x 7" manila envelopes. The first contained the two shots of the woman from the Charter Building. I passed those to Mags. "You've seen these two before."

Then I opened the second envelope and pulled out the fourteen pictures of the man at the ballpark. I passed them to her as well. As she slowly went through the second set of photos, I was monitoring her eyes closely for any sort of reaction—which I got almost instantly. Her eyes tightened just enough to show increased focus.

"Any idea who the ballpark guy is?" I asked as innocently as I could.

She paused just a couple seconds as she composed her response. "No, I don't think so. Just like the woman, he looks like a lot of people." She dropped it there and handed the pictures back to me.

I slid them back in their envelopes but left them lying on the table next to my folder.

"But we're actually making progress on our two homicides and may have even added a third to the mix."

"Serial killer?" she asked.

"No. Nothing like that. It's people dropping dead who are all connected to this viatical company, Portland Life Solutions, in one way or another. Most of them had sold their life insurance to Portland. We've narrowed down the mysterious passings to two of the twelve funds that Portland uses to finance the purchase of life insurance policies."

She appeared confused. "So, what made those two funds stand out?"

"Well, over the last six months, those two funds collected two to three times as much as any of the other ten funds. It looks like our first decedent, Van Damm, was causing a stir about it with the CEO of Portland, a guy named Parker Winston. We spent some real quality time interviewing him this afternoon."

Mags muted the television. "This might be worth listening to. I assume by 'quality time,' you mean you worked this guy over pretty well?"

I didn't deny it. "We're also pursuing another angle. Since the dead people appear to mostly have sold their life insurance to Portland's Funds Five and Six, we've tracked down who the investors are in those funds. Some are typical institutional investors. Some are founders and officers of Portland. Only one sizable individual investor appears. He gets 12 percent of the policy proceeds collected by Funds Five and Six. We're checking him out right now." After a brief pause, I added, "We're early stages trying to connect him to the two suspected doers. Nothing substantial yet.

Portland's CEO got a little squirrelly when asked about that investor."

"How so?"

"Like claiming he didn't know much about the guy, even though they've played golf together several times and belong to the same golf club. Claims he doesn't know what the guy does for a living or where he lives. Then he didn't want to give us the guy's investor qualification sheet, claiming it was confidential. So, we laid a subpoena on his ass for it before the afternoon was out. And now we have it. Brady Pollard's financial person is digging into it over the weekend."

"What's this guy's name?"

"Vincent Morehead."

For just a second, Mags' eyes went wide, but she quickly recovered her poker face. I didn't ask if she knew him because I sensed that would put her in the uncomfortable position of outright lying to me.

Always the master at instant deflection, Mags asked, "What are your next steps?"

"Oliver and I are working over the weekend to track down the details on fifteen people whose deaths put big money into those two funds over the past six months. We got those names today from Portland."

"How do you do that?" Mags asked, keeping the deflection going.

"Believe it or not, we start on Google. Then move on to obits. And then, if there is a hint of anything other than natural death, we start talking to medical examiners, family members, and police."

"Well, good luck reaching people over the weekend," she noted.

"Yeah, but we'll make some progress. It is truly amazing how many threads we can pull off of the internet."

I told Mags that I was going to get out of my suit and get comfortable. And I headed upstairs to do that. I suspected that she would look at the pictures again while I was gone. I knew better than to push.

When I got back to the living room, Mags stood up. "I'm bushed and have to go in early in the morning. Think I'll bunk down tonight in the guest room."

I said, "Okay," kind of softly. She leaned over and gave me a nice kiss on the lips as a consolation prize and headed upstairs. I guess Vincent Morehead just cost me a night of benefits.

I unmuted Stephen Colbert and watched the rest of his show before heading off to bed myself.

CHAPTER FORTY-ONE

Simone Reese lived in a six-story building with twenty-four two-bedroom units built in 1976. The reason Simone had purchased the condo years ago was that it came with a secure one-and-a-half-car garage.

Her purchase of the Cobra Mustang back when she was still with a private accounting firm led her to base her housing choices purely on whether the available options had a secure place to house her vehicle. She knew that she probably paid too much at the time but, with the passage of time, it had turned out to be a wise financial decision.

The first thing she did when she arrived home was shed her business suit, put on a pair of gray sweats, and get herself a glass of chardonnay from the bottle already open in her refrigerator. Next, she grabbed her laptop and sat down in the most comfortable armchair in her living room.

With her wine on the side table within easy reach, she opened her laptop on the ottoman in front of her. She picked up the investor qualification sheet on Vincent Morehead. She was still wired from what had perhaps been her most fulfilling day since joining MPD eight years earlier. She was going to put that energy to good use and not wait until the next morning to start her review.

Since she lived alone, she had long ago developed the habit of talking to herself when working at home. "Okay, let's see what we've got here." She made a quick review of Morehead's sheet.

The first thing she noticed was that he listed his home address as "classified" with no physical address provided. Under occupation, he listed GS-15, and under job title he wrote "classified" again. On the line for salary, he put "classified" one more time, which she thought was foolish.

She picked up her laptop and opened Google and searched for GS-15 salary. She quickly found that the salary for a GS-15 in the D.C. area is currently $144,128. She didn't bother to search back for the salary in 2016 when Morehead had signed the form.

Next, Simone picked up her folder on Funds Five and Six. It took her seconds to confirm that Morehead had initially invested $500,000 in each of those funds in 2016 and 2017. Out loud she said, "So, where did you come up with a million dollars on a salary of less than $150,000 per year?" Her brow wrinkled as she thought about how to answer her own question.

She had no information as to how much Morehead had received from the two funds since his initial investments. She picked up her white lined pad and made a note for further follow-up on that topic.

Under the entry on the qualification sheet for "liquid assets," he listed $800,000 but provided no details. Under the line for real property, he listed $600,000, presumably for his house.

Otherwise, he listed no additional assets. Based on her time as an auditor in the private sector, she thought that this had to be the sketchiest investor qualification form conceivable. She didn't know for certain but thought it probably did not meet whatever standards there were for investments of this magnitude.

"Bottom line," she said, "this is a piece of garbage. How could he be qualified to participate in these funds?" She made a further note on her pad.

"And," she added, "how could Portland ever let this pass muster?" She made a further note and said, "Maybe Portland needed the money to complete those funds."

Totally frustrated, she decided to go back to basics. She picked up her laptop again and searched Google for Vincent Morehead. There were a number of hits but, in the end, she eliminated all but one as just being someone else with the same name.

And she wasn't even sure that last entry was her Vincent Morehead, but had a gut feel that it was. The article was from April of 2016 and appeared in the U.K. edition of *The Guardian*. The brief article read as follows:

KANDAHAR, AFGHANISTAN. *Based on three sources,* The Guardian *has received verified reports that $3 million designated for support of Afghanistan resettlement programs has gone missing. The senior U.S. official in charge of the program, Vincent Morehead, refused comment. Reports establish that an investigation is ongoing. It is believed that the CIA is in charge of this program.*

Simone texted the article to both Mac Burke and Oliver Shaw with a note attached saying, *"Only entry on Google re Morehead. Investor qualification sheet is garbage. More tomorrow."*

She finished her wine. No longer as fired up as she was earlier, she said to herself, "As Scarlet O'Hara said, 'Tomorrow is another day.'" With that, she turned off the lights and went to bed.

CHAPTER FORTY-TWO

MAGGIE WOKE UP on Saturday at five a.m. She had not slept well. She knew that she would have a restless night, as her mind would keep turning over Vincent Morehead's possible involvement in McDermott's case. Not to mention the photographs of two people she knew she had seen at the New Headquarters Building. She had slept in the guest room so that McDermott wouldn't see her agitated state during the night and ask questions.

She retrieved her laptop from its carrying case. She never took it to work because they were absolutely forbidden to do Agency work on their personal computers, no matter how secure they thought them to be.

Maggie duplicated the search on Google that Simone Reese had done the previous evening. Again, Google came up with the same list of hits in response to the search for Vincent Morehead. And, again, Maggie narrowed the search down to the same small article from *The Guardian* in April of 2016.

She had heard that Morehead had worked for the Special Operations Group prior to being transferred to the Political Action Group some years earlier. It had never dawned on her that such an internal transfer was actually a very rare occurrence.

Over her years of working for the Agency, pondering facts in semi-paranoid thought patterns had become somewhat second nature. After reading the Afghanistan article, she wondered if Morehead had been transferred out of Special Operations to the Political Action Group as some sort of cover-up or burying of his questionable past. "Hmm," was all she said. She printed a copy of the article.

She showered and dressed in casual clothes before leaving the house around five forty-five, just before McDermott had risen for the day. She took her computer bag with her.

Mac wouldn't hear her Speedster purr down the alley. She didn't know what she was going to do at Langley but had to avoid another encounter with McDermott until she had organized things in her own mind. In fact, she didn't get past the end of their alley. She just sat there with the engine running.

She thought back to the gray-haired man who had recruited her to work for the CIA when she was finishing her MBA at Wharton. She had later learned that his real name was Harrison Jones III. He had taken an interest in her career and become something of her personal rabbi over the years. He held some undefined executive position not far from the director's office on the seventh floor.

Maggie had now been at the Agency for fifteen years. Over that time, Jones and she would meet for lunch a couple times a year or when some conundrum was confronting her. They still met occasionally even after he had retired from the Agency ten years earlier, after serving with the CIA for thirty-four years. He had to be in his late seventies by now.

It was far too early to call Harrison Jones. She decided to kill time with a long breakfast. She wanted to go to Ted's Bulletin, one of the best places for breakfast in the District, but they didn't open until seven a.m.

She decided to just go for an early morning drive. She cruised down to Constitution Avenue and took a slow roll down the length of the north side of The Mall. As she passed the East Building of the National Gallery of Art, she thought of the large mobile by Alexander Calder, how she enjoyed sitting and just watching it move. After passing the Washington Monument on her left, she then took the circle around the Lincoln Memorial and she headed north. She got on Rock Creek Drive and followed it through the City's most famous park to the National Zoological Park, which was also not yet open for visitors.

She parked at the zoo for a while and thought about the two people in the pictures. She didn't know their names but was sure they worked on the other side of the third floor in the New Headquarters Building at Langley. How was she to get their names, she wondered? For some reason, she thought the guy was named Curt something. No clue on the woman's name.

Eventually, Maggie drove back toward downtown. She turned left to 14th Street. Given the early hour, she nabbed a parking space almost in front of Ted's Bulletin. She only had ten minutes to wait before they opened.

When Maggie saw a lady unlock the front door, she headed inside Ted's. She was their first customer of the day. The hostess told her to take any table she wanted, and she made her way to a two-top by one of the front windows.

A server approached her. "An early good morning to you!"

Maggie looked up at her and smiled. "I could use a large cup of coffee, cream, and, if you have it, turbinado sugar."

The waitress set down a menu and said, "Coming right up." Maggie thought the woman was a touch too cheery for this early in the morning but admired her spirit.

The coffee arrived promptly with a small pitcher of half-and-half, as well as several packets of turbinado sugar. Maggie said, "Bless you. I'll need my first cup before thinking about food."

"No problem. I'll come back in a while to refill your cup and get your order."

Maggie assembled her coffee as she liked it, perused the menu, and made her selection. As promised, the server returned with a pot of hot coffee and refilled her cup. She ordered the Ted's Hash, which was pastrami, eggs, and potatoes with wheat toast.

As she was the first customer of the day, her order came out promptly with another refill on the coffee and a new pitcher of cream and more sugar packets. Maggie thought the hash was excellent, and her spirits brightened a bit.

After stalling as long as she thought appropriate, Maggie put cash on the check and left the waitress a ten-dollar tip. She went outside and did some window-shopping at nearby shops and then returned to her car about eight o'clock. She pulled out the copy of the article from *The Guardian* and read it again.

Instead of going straight to work, Maggie diverted to the Library of Congress. Computer bag over her shoulder, she headed to the large circular reading room, which was several stories high with exposed alcoves on each of the several floors. She made her way to the circulation desk at the center of the massive room and approached a librarian. She asked how to access their newspaper collection and was told that the library had about sixty years' worth of newspapers digitalized and that it was all available online.

To which Maggie responded, "Duh. So, I came in for nothing?"

The librarian smiled nicely. "I see you have your computer with you. Now you can do your research right here in the largest library in the world." Maggie returned the lady's smile. The librarian gave her the access password for the library's digital system and waved her toward the seating area.

Maggie looked around and found her way to one of the alcoves on the second floor where she set up shop overlooking the circular reading room. Once in the system, she narrowed her search to a time frame starting with April of 2016 and searched for Afghanistan, missing funds, relocation project, and Vincent Morehead. The search came back with several hits, which she culled down to the ones that appeared to her to be the most on topic.

She didn't have the ability to print anything here, so she took a picture with her cellphone of the two articles that looked most on point.

The *New York Times* ran the following on April 20, 2016:

KANDAHAR, AFGHANISTAN. *Reports continue that a U.S.-funded program to assist the Afghan government relocate people displaced by conflict with the Taliban rebels has been terminated following suspected corruption. A large amount of American funding disappeared and, despite investigative efforts, has not been recovered. While no official announcement has been made, all U.S. officials connected to the program have been recalled to the United States and the local offices have been closed.*

The *Washington Post* reported on May 1, 2016:

Nothing further has been heard about a reportedly terminated program in Afghanistan to help relocate refugees. The American-funded relocation program was rumored to have been closed down after the financing for the project was thought to have been embezzled by local Afghan officials.

Maggie then packed up her computer and walked back to her car.

* * *

Once inside her car, she said to herself, "What are you doing here, Maggie Hampton? It can't be good for your career." She rested her head on the steering wheel and closed her eyes.

Having made a decision, she sat back up and pulled up the contacts on her cellphone and rang Harrison Jones. He answered on the second ring. "Harrison Jones here."

"Mr. Jones, this is Maggie Hampton. Sorry to bother you so early on a Saturday morning."

Jones replied, "You wouldn't have called if it wasn't important. How can I help you?"

"I need your advice on something that is very sensitive."

Jones said, "In that case, you better come to my house. You were here before. Remember how to get here?"

"Yes, sir, I do. When would be a good time?"

"How about right now? I'll put some coffee on."

"Thank you, sir. I'll be there in about twenty minutes."

CHAPTER FORTY-THREE

HARRISON JONES LIVED in the Woodley Park area, just west of Rock Creek Park. He had bought the house in 1976 when he joined the Agency, using family money to buy the stately three-story Victorian. He and his wife of forty years had enjoyed the house, until she had passed away five years ago.

Maggie pulled up the driveway and parked in a pullout level with his front porch. When she rang the doorbell, Jones answered.

"Maggie, good to see you," he said. "Please come in."

"Thank you for seeing me, Mr. Jones, on no notice."

Maggie had long considered Harrison Jones as something of a surrogate father. Hers had died in Afghanistan about twenty years earlier.

He led her to the kitchen and over to the counter where the coffee maker sat. He had set out cream in a small white pitcher and a bowl with turbinado sugar. "You remembered how I like my coffee," she observed.

He smiled. "It's the little things in life." After they each had prepared their coffee, he led her to the kitchen table. When they were seated, he asked, "How can I be of help?"

Maggie pressed her lips together and began. "This may be totally out of line and, if it is, please say so and kick me out of here."

"I'm sure that won't be necessary."

"As I've explained a little bit in the past, I still live with my ex-husband, McDermott Burke, when I'm in town. Even though we've been divorced for three years, we actually get along very well." She saw his small smile, acknowledging the unusual arrangement.

"McDermott is a homicide detective for the Metropolitan Police Department. He is currently the lead investigator on a series of homicides of people with a common thread that they had each sold their life insurance policies to a viatical company."

"I'm familiar with the term," he said.

"Well, as the investigation has gone on, they have obtained pictures of two people, a man and a woman, who are their primary suspects in three of the homicides. McDermott showed me their pictures at different times over the course of this week. The thing is, Mr. Jones, I think I have seen both of these people at the New Headquarters Building. I believe they both work in the Special Operations Group. I have no idea what they do or what part of the Ground Support operation they are in. For some reason, I believe the man's first name is Curt."

Jones asked, "Do you have copies of these photos?"

"Yes, I do." She pulled her cellphone out of her pocket and pulled up her photo directory. "Without McDermott knowing, I took a cellphone picture of each photo." She pulled up the two photos and handed the phone to Jones.

He looked at the pictures and widened each by spreading his fingers on the screen. "Hmm, I believe I know who both of these people are. As I recall, the woman's name is Marian Benedict. The man's name, I'm sure, is Kurt Bardak. Kurt with a *K*."

Maggie resumed, "Here's the hitch with these two. MPD has run these pictures through the facial recognition software of Homeland Security, which came back with pings indicating that matches had been found and then a delayed response saying no record could be provided. McDermott was told that could mean that they are in the facial recognition system, but disclosure of their identity is blocked. He was also told that could be because they work black ops or some classified position for some government agency."

Jones said, "CIA puts such a block on most of its people, especially field agents and Ground Support people."

"I have seen them in the building at one time or another. The problem is that MPD cannot come up with any identification of these two. They also cannot find any motive for either of them to be involved in these murders. And that's where this gets real problematic."

"Uh-oh. What's next?" he asked.

"Do you know who Vincent Morehead is?"

"Yes, I've run across him several times over my thirty-four years at the Agency. How does he factor into this saga?" Jones asked.

"Well, you know he is my ultimate boss in the Political Action Group?"

He nodded. "Saw that wrinkle coming."

"Wait, it gets worse. But first, I have to give you some background on this viatical company, Portland Life Solutions. They have been in business about eighteen years, and they set up funds to raise capital to buy the life insurance policies. Over the years, they have set up twelve of these funds.

"Each of these funds works kind of like a real estate limited partnership. The investors put in the money and get a guaranteed return of 8 percent."

"Not bad," Jones commented.

"Yeah, but here's the kicker. When Portland collects on a life insurance policy in one of their funds, half the proceeds go back into the fund to buy more policies. The other half of the insurance proceeds are split among the investors in accordance with their percentage interest in that fund." She paused to take a sip of her coffee, which had now gone cold.

Jones asked, "So, where does Vincent Morehead fit into this scenario?"

"He's a 12 percent investor in two of the twelve funds."

Jones anticipated where this was going. "Which two funds?"

"Five and Six."

"And which funds hold the policies on the people who are being murdered?"

"Five and Six."

Jones asked the question to which everyone wanted the answer: "And how much has Morehead received from these two funds?"

"MPD doesn't know the answer yet."

Jones pondered for a moment. "How much did Morehead invest in these funds?"

"A million dollars combined."

Jones shook his head. "On a government salary?"

"Exactly. That's what got me digging. First, I found this article from *The Guardian* in April of 2016." She showed him the print-out of the article.

Although it wasn't very long, he took his time reading it, thinking back to that time frame.

Maggie resumed, "Then, this morning, I did some more research through the Library of Congress newspaper collection and found two more articles on the same subject from around that period. I took some screen shots." After she passed her phone to him, Jones again took his time reading them both.

"Now, the big question," Maggie said, "was Vincent Morehead involved, and did the Agency move him from the Special Operations

Group to the Political Action Group as part of a cover-up? I think it happened about the same time as all of this broke in 2016."

Jones leaned back in his kitchen chair and slowly shook his head. "You'd have made an excellent detective, Maggie."

She leaned forward. "And the answer is?"

"'Yes,' is the simple answer. The Agency called me back to look into it. We could never prove anything specifically. But we had serious doubts about him. In general, many people didn't like Morehead, but he was effective at his job until this mess in Afghanistan."

"I guess that's why there are no more news accounts after the three I've shown you."

"I'm sure that's the case."

Maggie leaned forward again. "But wait, there's more."

"Oh no."

Maggie half-smiled. "Oh yes. Morehead pulled in several of us in my group recently and asked us to generically determine which businesses in our assigned parts of the world were most susceptible to having their medical records hacked. We came up with a list and concluded that life insurance companies and viatical companies were probably the weakest sisters. He said he would take that to his 'cyber' people, as he calls them.

"I didn't think anything further about it until one day I was having lunch in the cafeteria and ran into an old acquaintance who works in the 'cyber' department. She asked what we'd been up to lately in my area, and I told her about the groupthink on hacking vulnerabilities. She said that was strange, because Morehead had asked her group to look at life insurance and viatical companies for the same vulnerabilities six or seven months earlier.

"According to what McDermott told me, the murders started about six months ago. He also told me that the names of the people who sold their life insurance policies to Portland were highly confidential. I surmised they could be obtained only by hacking."

Jones put his elbows on the table and said softly, "Wow. That is a lot to take in."

"You see why I wanted to get your input on this. I can't disclose anything I know about other Agency people. Not to my ex-husband or anyone else. On the other hand, I think something needs to be done."

"I agree. Let's discuss what might help MPD without revealing the Agency's fingerprints."

He sat without saying anything for two to three minutes. Maggie knew how to honor silence when wiser people were thinking.

Finally, Jones held up one finger. "Let's start with Marian Benedict and Kurt Bardak. Surely, they have driver's licenses, probably in Virginia. Maybe a confidential source with a burner phone could tell MPD to pull the licenses for those two names. But don't send it to your ex-husband. That would be too obvious."

Maggie nodded. "Then MPD would have their identities and could take it from there."

Jones nodded. "No need to go further on that point. I'd leave it there, at least for now."

She raised one finger herself. "I would think MPD is going to have to connect the two of them to Morehead. Is there a connection there?"

"Oh, yes. They both worked for Vincent at different times. I don't know how close he was to Marian Benedict, but I recall that he worked with Kurt Bardak closely a number of times. They may have even been friends."

Maggie pressed her lips together. "I don't see any way to tip that information without revealing the Agency's handiwork."

"I agree," said Jones. "MPD will need to extract that connection from Benedict or Bardak. That way we stay clear of it."

"*Wow*, as you said earlier," Maggie acknowledged.

Jones rose. "Let's leave it there for now. If it gets more complicated where we need to do something else from behind the curtain, we'll have to talk again."

He walked her to the front door. "Thanks for coming to see me, Maggie. The old brain gets rusty from lack of use, and a discussion like this gets the blood pumping again. Is that a mixed metaphor?"

"Probably," Maggie said and gave him a kiss on the cheek and left.

Once she was back on the street, she felt she at least had a plan. As her father had always said, "A bad plan is better than no plan." She agreed. On the way home, she stopped at a no-name convenience store and bought a prepaid cellphone.

CHAPTER FORTY-FOUR

My mind must have worked overtime while I slept on Friday night, because I woke with a definite idea of something we needed to do promptly. It was only six thirty, but I could not hold off any longer. I called Oliver.

"What's burning, Mac? You never call this early unless your hair is on fire about something."

"I had a subconscious epiphany overnight. We're doing something all wrong."

"What's that?" a sleepy Oliver mumbled.

"We are looking at the dead people," I said.

Oliver grumbled, "That's what we do, Mac. It's called homicide, which usually involves a dead person."

"No, no," I said. "In order to catch the doers, we need to be watching the insured people who are still living."

"I see where you're going. One wrinkle is that we don't have the names of the people who sold their policies to Funds Five and Six who are still living. Another is that you're talking about surveilling one or more people in hopes of nabbing a doer. We don't have the manpower to staff that exercise."

"Okay," I said, "let's press Frisco to get us the names of the living insureds in those two funds. Maybe he would discuss it on the phone and then email the lists to us."

"I doubt it. That would violate two serious security protocols that he has adhered to for a long time."

"How about I give it a try and see if I can persuade him. If not, I'll see if we can see him early this morning."

Oliver asked, "You going to call him now?"

"Yeah. He claims that he never sleeps."

I couldn't see it but was certain that Oliver was shaking his head in the negative. "I sure hope you don't burn our very valuable bridge to a tremendous asset."

"I'll call you back and let you know."

*   *   *

Frisco answered after only one ring. "I see who's calling. It's usually your sidekick. No names or details on this call."

"Need to see you as soon as we can. New wrinkle."

"Okay. Be here in thirty minutes." He hung up.

I called Oliver. "You were right. Got to be there in thirty minutes. I'm headed to a speed shower and pick you up in fifteen."

"Okay."

*   *   *

When I got down to the garage at a quarter to seven, I noted that the Speedster was already gone. I headed to Oliver's house and was pulling in front of his driveway when he came outside. I was in jeans and a long-sleeve blue denim shirt with a tan jacket. Oliver wore khakis and a red canvas shirt covered by a bone-colored linen coat.

We were only a couple of minutes late arriving at Frisco's building. We rang the buzzer and were told to come on up. Frisco met us at the door. "Must be important," he said. We did the usual thumb-handshake and single slap on the back.

I said, "Had a thought overnight. I'm worried that more people may be exposed and, at the same time, it might provide us a way to catch the doers in our case."

Frisco said, "Well, come on in and let's see what we can do." He led us to his main computer. I told him we wanted to see lists of the people who were still living but had their life insurance policies owned by Portland Funds Five and Six. "Hang on," he said and started typing on his keyboard. "This is starting to get familiar."

In five minutes, he had printed out two lists showing the life insurance policies still held by those two funds, including the face amount of each. We thanked him, did the usual thumb shake and backslap, and headed out.

Once we were in the Jeep, Oliver looked at the lists. "Each list has a single $1,000,000 policy. One list has a single $500,000 policy. All the other policies were in the $250,000 to $300,000 range."

The Dunkin' Donuts on New York Avenue NE was the nearest location with a drive-thru window. It was not very far from Frisco's building. Without asking Oliver, I pulled up to the speaker and ordered a dozen assorted donuts and a box of their reasonably good coffee. We picked up the goodies at the window and headed for the office. We got there around seven thirty.

As we were parking, the navy-blue Cobra pulled in and parked next to us. Simone Reese climbed out wearing tight blue jeans and a loose beige sweatshirt. Her boots made her look even taller.

We said good morning to Simone and headed into the office. She said, "Oh, good, you brought donuts to make this an official cop exercise." We let the security guard at the side door take his pick of the donuts and headed up to the fourth floor.

*   *   *

We grabbed Styrofoam cups from the coffee station and took the donuts and box of coffee to our desks. We put the coffee on a neighboring desk and fixed our cups. We put the donuts on the corner of Oliver's desk. We didn't dare leave them by the coffee machine, what with cops hanging around.

Simone pulled a chair over and asked if we'd read the article she had sent us.

"That may answer the question where Morehead got the money to invest in Portland. Hard to prove, but a good theory for now," Oliver said.

Simone seemed irritated. She said, "That snake's investor qualification sheet was truly garbage. Everything was marked classified, right down to his home address and salary. But he did say he was a GS-15. I went online and found that the current salary for that rating in the D.C. area is around $143,000 per year. Unless he inherited a bunch of money in 2016, it is pretty suspicious. Also, I'll check land records this morning in Northern Virginia and see if I can locate his house."

I said, "Good work."

While she was looking through the box of donuts, she asked what we were doing today. Oliver took a bite of a maple frosted donut. Then he said, "Originally, today was to be devoted to digging out information on the remaining eleven policy claims from Funds Five and Six over the past six months."

Simone looked up. "Originally? Is there a new game plan?"

"Mac had an epiphany overnight," Oliver said. "He thinks we need to be watching some of the remaining higher-end insureds in case they are targets."

I added, "It occurred to me that it may be the fastest way to connect the doers to our case."

Simone looked somewhat surprised. "Isn't that kind of dangerous for the people who are the insureds?"

"No more so than they probably already are," I said. "We might even be able to prevent someone else from being killed."

"That sounds like a lot of logistics will be involved." She plucked a chocolate cake donut with chocolate icing out of the box.

"We've only begun to talk about that," I said. "First, we need to focus on the three people we think are the most likely candidates to be targeted."

She looked up from tearing apart her donut. "You already have their names? We didn't get that list from Portland."

"Yes, we do."

"How?" she asked.

I said, "Don't ask. We'll backstop it with a subpoena on Monday."

She shook her head, but I could tell she liked seeing behind the curtain at how things really worked. She finished off her donut and refilled her coffee. "I'm going to retreat to my office and see what I can do to unravel the mysterious Vincent Morehead. Will let you know if I find anything else."

* * *

Now that she was gone, we each picked up the lists that Frisco had printed for us. The top three persons of interest were as follows:

Insured	Address	Age	Policy Limit
Joshua Levine	1215 Bragg Rd Vienna, VA	62	$1,000,000
Bradley Ford	2306 Woodley Ct NW Washington, D.C.	59	$1,000,000
Mildred Bronson	156 Chain Bridge Rd #1200 Fairfax, VA	68	$500,000

"I'll take numbers one and three," I said to Oliver. "You take number two."

"No coin flip?"

"I'm feeling magnanimous because you picked up the donuts."

"But I didn't."

"Yeah, I know." I bobbed my eyebrows twice and gave Oliver a good friend smile. Kind of like Groucho Marx.

*   *   *

I started with a LinkedIn search on Joshua Levine. He is a Senior Group Manager at Perigrintec, a defense contractor specializing in modular training systems. His corporate office is in McLean, Virginia. He lists a spouse and three children, two of whom are in college and one in high school. He has a degree in mechanical engineering from Virginia Tech in 1981.

I also found Mildred Bronson on both LinkedIn and Google. She is a recently retired attorney, now working as an adjunct professor of law at the Antonin Scalia School of Law at George Mason University in Arlington, Virginia. She appeared to have grown children. No husband was mentioned. Presumably divorced or deceased. Graduated from Georgetown University's Law Center in 1978.

Oliver's research on Bradley Ford was relatively quick also. Ford is a senior partner in a consulting firm on Connecticut Avenue NW, which probably means he is a lobbyist. He had been a wrestler at Ohio State and graduated with a degree in management in 1987. Married, with two children in college.

After we had exchanged this information, Oliver said, "So what do we do with this? Two of them are in Northern Virginia and one in Northwest D.C."

"I think we're going to have to run this whole new approach by Chief Whittaker, and I don't know if it should wait until Monday."

CHAPTER FORTY-FIVE

Maggie had long had a negative instinct about Vincent Morehead. Maybe she just didn't like him because of his sniffing. Her gut told her not to trust him. That feeling was reinforced with what Harrison Jones had just revealed.

After she got home, Maggie wanted to do more to help McDermott close his case on Vincent Morehead. She would send the anonymous text to Oliver Shaw about looking up Marian Benedict and Kurt Bardak with the Virginia DMV. That would give them a better place to start.

As she thought about it, Maggie had another idea that she was fairly sure her rabbi would reject. She felt he would say this was something that MPD should handle on its own. But she knew from her many conversations with McDermott over the years that the courts now required a search warrant before putting a tracker on a suspect's vehicle.

McDermott and Oliver may not need the help she was contemplating. If so—then no harm, no foul. But, if it turned out the help was needed, she would have it in place. "Well," she said to herself, "I guess you've made a decision. Let's get on with it."

Now that she had all three names, Maggie went on the Virginia DMV website and found a way to determine what vehicles

Benedict, Bardak, and Morehead owned. It took a little while, but she finally was able to determine the vehicles that each owned: Benedict had a white 2019 Prius; Morehead had a silver 2016 Range Rover; and Bardak had three vehicles: a red 2020 Camaro convertible, a gray 2014 Ford F-150 pickup, and a black 2012 Harley-Davidson motorcycle. She also got license tag numbers for each of the vehicles, making notes on a single sheet of paper. No way to hack a sheet of paper.

Her next step was to go online and get pictures of each of those vehicles so that she could spot them more easily later. These she printed out and trimmed with scissors so they would easily fit in her pocket.

She couldn't ask the tech shop at work for tracking devices, so she had to go back online again. She found five suppliers in the D.C. metro area that stocked tracking devices and found a magnetic model that looked like it would be a quick installation under surreptitious circumstances.

"Now," she said to herself, "you're going to need a nondescript vehicle." Her 1959 Porsche Speedster was too well known. It also attracted attention. Although she had never used them, she recalled a company called Rent-a-Wreck. She looked them up on her computer and found they had two offices in the D.C. area. She called the one in Prince Georges County, Maryland, not too far across the boundary of Southeast D.C.

She told the young man who answered that she needed some simple transportation for three days and needed it to be affordable. He told her they had a blue 2017 Chevy Impala for $39.95 per day. They also had a silver 2015 Ford Taurus for $34.95 per day. She took the Taurus and gave him the name of Sarah Addams, one of her alternative identities for which she had a driver's license and a MasterCard.

Maggie then called for a taxi to take her to the address in Maryland for the Rent-a-Wreck office. While she waited for the cab, she pulled out her Glock 19 from its hiding place in the guest bedroom. The Agency had given her the 9mm automatic upon completion of her training at Camp Peary at the start of her career with the CIA. She checked that the magazine was fully loaded and that there was also a bullet in the pipe. Other than practicing periodically at the firing range in the second basement under the Old Headquarters Building, she had never fired the weapon in the course of her work.

She put the small Glock in the waistband holster and dropped it in her shoulder bag. She put her Sarah Addams driver's license and credit card in her wallet to replace her actual license and card.

She was waiting on the front steps of the Morris Place row house when the taxi pulled up a few minutes later. She gave the driver the address for the Rent-a-Wreck store in Prince Georges County and was dropped off there about twenty-five minutes later. She paid the cabbie in cash with a modest tip so as to not be memorable.

At the counter was a man in his twenties, who remembered her call when she gave him her name. "Yes, Ms. Addams, we have the Taurus ready for you. I'll just need a driver's license and credit card," which she gave him. She also accepted the extra $10 per day for insurance coverage so that she didn't have to produce her own auto insurance card.

Five minutes later she was on her way to Eagle Eye Tracking in Falls Church, Virginia. Maggie crossed the Woodrow Wilson Bridge over the Potomac and angled northwest. It took her about forty minutes to find the tracking store.

She put on a pair of nonprescription clear-lensed glasses and tucked her hair under a blue baseball cap to alter her appearance in case of cameras. A young man, probably no more than nineteen years old, offered to help her. She explained that she needed to look at GPS tracking devices for automobiles. He took her to a glass-encased counter and explained the models available and how each worked.

In the end, she narrowed her choice down to a Hawkeye model, which was small in size with magnetic attachment. It had a battery life of thirty days. The salesman explained how to download the app to monitor the device. He explained that the app could be run at the same time on both a smartphone and a computer. He said the app was capable of handling five devices at the same time and showed them simultaneously on a GPS map of an area up to twenty miles in diameter.

The devices were actually reasonably priced. Maggie bought five of them plus the application software. The total bill was only $243. She paid cash and took her purchases with her and locked them in the trunk, along with her cap and false glasses.

She then headed back to Northeast D.C. and found a parking space on the street about a block and a half from their row house on Morris Place. She disarmed the alarm with her cellphone and entered the front door. She let out a big sigh of relief. She hadn't done a clandestine assignment in some time.

CHAPTER FORTY-SIX

IT DAWNED ON ME that I had not checked my email since before we had left for Portland Life Solutions the prior afternoon. I opened my email, and saw that Oliver and I had received an email from our intern Kit Cardona, regarding her search of NCIC—the National Crime Information Center—for sux.

I told Oliver to check his email also as I clicked open the message from Kit. She had found no homicides tied to sux but had found a reference to succinylcholine tied to a burglary at a vet clinic in Loudon County, Virginia, about eight months earlier. A number of drugs had been stolen during a night-time burglary, including sux. A copy of the report was attached.

Oliver finished reading the report. He made a note of the name of both the detective and the vet. He got on the internet and found a phone number for the Marshall Veterinary Equine and Farm Clinic and called the number.

Although it was a Saturday, the clinic was open for business. Oliver identified himself and asked to speak to Dr. Jay Willingham. The receptionist said that he had just walked in from the stables out back and asked Oliver to hold.

After about a minute, the vet answered. "This is Jay Willingham."

Oliver said, "Thanks for taking my call, Dr. Willingham. This is Oliver Shaw. I'm a detective with the Metropolitan Police Department in D.C. My partner and I are investigating a homicide that may have involved the use of succinylcholine. We saw an NCIC report that said a number of drugs had been stolen from your vet clinic about eight months ago."

Willingham replied, "Yes, that's correct. One of the drugs stolen was sux. The burglary was never solved. We thought it was probably someone trying to get ivermectin, the horse dewormer, that some people thought was a cure for Covid. Which was absolute bunk, but there you have it."

Oliver followed up. "Had you talked to anyone about having sux in your clinic's pharmacy prior to the burglary?"

"No, I don't think so. Wait. I may have mentioned it once to a golf partner during a member tournament at Eastwood Country Club about a month earlier. I'd never met the fellow before. I'm not sure I can remember his name."

Oliver asked, "Can you please try to remember his name? It could be important."

The vet said, "Sure. Let me see. I remember he worked for the federal government but couldn't tell me anything about his job. We did get to talking about my having to occasionally put horses down, and it may have come up as part of that discussion. I'm just not sure of his name. I think it was Vinnie or Vince. Something like that. Can't remember his last name."

"And he was a member of your golf club?"

"Yes, it was a one-day member tournament at Eastwood."

Oliver concluded, "Thanks for your help, Dr. Willingham. Can I get your cell number in case I need to follow up further with you?" The vet gave Oliver his cell number, and they ended the call.

Before briefing Mac on the call, Oliver grabbed his ever-present notebook and started reviewing his notes from the prior day's meeting at Portland. "Aha. I thought so. Parker Winston told us he met Vincent Morehead at Eastwood County Club. This vet says he played golf about nine months ago with another member at that club, and they discussed that the vet used sux as part of putting down horses. A guy named Vinnie or Vince. A month later, his clinic's pharmacy was robbed of a number of drugs, including sux. Thin, but another thread."

CHAPTER FORTY-SEVEN

AROUND NINE O'CLOCK, Oliver's cell pinged notifying him of an incoming text message. As most of us will do, he picked up his cell and glanced at the portion of the text showing on his screen. That obviously piqued his curiosity, so he unlocked his phone and read the whole text.

I noticed that he was frowning and then kind of smiling. "What?" I asked.

He said, "I'm not sure if this is what I think it is but, if it is, we may have a new best friend." He handed me his phone. The text screen said the following:

CHECK VA DRIVER'S LICENSES FOR MARIAN BENEDICT
AND KURT BARDAK.
MIGHT HELP. A FRIEND.

I handed the cell back to Oliver. "Forward it to me and make a note of the number. Try calling it back."

He did and said, "No answer. Probably a burner." Even though it was a Saturday, he tried to reach someone at the Virginia Department of Motor Vehicles. "No answer there either."

"We worked a case two years ago with the Virginia Highway Patrol," I said. "Who was that guy we dealt with?"

"Oh, yeah," Oliver said as he started scanning through his phone's contacts. "It was Lieutenant Schwartz or something like that . . . Here it is, Verne Schwartzel." He hit the cell number for Schwartzel. I waited.

Oliver said, "Verne, Oliver Shaw at MPD here. Sorry to bother you on a Saturday. You doing okay? . . . Well, congratulations! That's great news."

Oliver continued, "I'll get right to the point. Mac Burke and I are working three related homicides. We've got photos of a woman and a man who we're fairly sure are our doers, but not even Homeland Security's facial recognition can ID them for us. We just got an anonymous tip to check Virginia driver's licenses for two specific people. Any chance you've got a connection that can get us copies on a Saturday?" He listened while Schwartzel replied.

"Great! The names are Marian Benedict and Kurt Bardak." He spelled them both. "Can you get them sent to my email? Yeah, that's still my email address. Verne, I can't tell you how much I appreciate it. And congrats again on the promotion."

Oliver hung up. "Verne's been promoted to Captain. Better yet, he has a personal friend at DMV who he thinks can get them for us. Now, all we have to do is wait." We each grabbed one of the remaining donuts and smiled.

For whatever reason, it took longer than we hoped. But, about thirty-five minutes later, Oliver's computer pinged. He smiled and opened up his email. Before saying anything, he forwarded it to my email, which I opened.

And what to our wondering eyes should appear? Two driver's licenses with photos matching our prime suspects. Oliver was already busy printing copies.

Both of them lived in Fairfax County. Benedict in Arlington and Bardak in Falls Church.

I said, "Bardak is likely involved in at least two of our cases, and Benedict in one. Flip you to see who researches whom. Heads you get Bardak; tails I get him."

I flipped a quarter and let it land on the desk. It came up heads. Oliver said, "Holy cowabunga, dude. Did I just win a flip?"

"Not sure there was a winner or loser on that one, but I'll concede that you got the more interesting alternative."

*   *   *

Per her driver's license, Marian Benedict was thirty-four years old and apparently lived in a high-rise apartment building just west of Arlington, Virginia. Having her birth date and address helped narrow down my search.

I turned to Google to start. There wasn't a lot about her. I discovered that she had once been in the Army but left after eight years. At some point, she had apparently had some specialized training at Ft. Bragg in North Carolina, which is the home of the Army's Special Forces. I could find nothing on her employment after she left the Army.

Next, I searched Fairfax County's property tax assessment records. That search revealed that she apparently owned a condominium on the 16th floor in a building with an Arlington address, although it was actually in Fairfax County. The assessed value was $210,000. Title was in her name alone.

Then I tried Facebook. She had entries from ages sixteen through twenty-six but nothing after that. She had graduated from a private high school in Fairfax County in 2005. No sign that she went to college. She enlisted in the Army after high school and had posted a number of entries up until she was transferred to Ft. Bragg and then nothing else other than a couple of vacations with her parents and siblings.

I also ran her name through NCIC. There were no hits on her in the database. Long and short of it was that I didn't find much on her, which I conveyed to Oliver.

* * *

Contrary to my prediction about Kurt Bardak being the more interesting of the two, Oliver found even less on him than I did on Benedict. Kurt Bardak was forty-three years old, born in Brooklyn, New York. The only information gleaned from Google was that he went to Brown University on a baseball scholarship. Brown is in Providence, Rhode Island. He was apparently a pitcher of some promise but had lost his scholarship due to poor grades and dropped out of college. He had no presence on Facebook or other social media sites that Oliver could find.

The County property tax records showed that his house in Falls Church was currently assessed at $480,000. A little digging in the land records showed that he had purchased it for $260,000 in 2004. Title to the house was in the name of Kurt and Elaine Bardak.

Oliver found nothing about Bardak's employment history after he dropped out of Brown. He also ran Bardak through the NCIC and got two ancient hits for bar fights shortly after he dropped out of college. No jail time. Just fines.

When Oliver gave me his results, we agreed that we were either poor researchers or there just wasn't much about these two people in the public domain. We sat and pondered that for a minute.

I said, "I think we should call Chief Whittaker about both identifying Benedict and Bardak as a result of our tip and then getting no traction on either of them. We can also run the idea of watching the three top living insureds by him."

Oliver nodded. "I agree. No coin flip. This needs to come from you."

CHAPTER FORTY-EIGHT

It was now a little after eleven on Saturday morning. I looked up Chief Whittaker's cellphone number in my contacts. We had long been given to understand that calls should only be made to that number when it was really important that we talk to him.

After two rings, he answered, "George Whittaker."

"Chief, Mac Burke here. Oliver and I need your input on a couple of items that have come up this morning."

"Go ahead. I know you wouldn't call if it wasn't important."

"Yes, sir. The big news is that we've identified our two suspected doers. Oliver got an anonymous tip this morning suggesting that we should check Virginia driver's licenses on Marian Benedict and Kurt Bardak."

"No idea who the tip came from?"

"No, sir. Oliver had a connection with Captain Verne Schwartzel at the Virginia Highway Patrol. Schwartzel has a friend who works for the Virginia DMV, and that person got us copies of the licenses. There is no doubt that they are the people in our pictures."

The Chief said, "Well, that's good news."

"Yes and no," was my response. "We know their names and where they live, but after some serious digging, we can't find anything else about them. Or anything tying them to Vincent

Morehead. Both of them live in Fairfax County. And we're stuck on tracking them further at the moment."

"Was there something else?" the Chief asked.

"Yes, sir. Overnight I had a thought that we are somewhat thin on connecting these two people to the three murders we believe they were involved with: Van Damm, Rollins at the ballpark, and Dr. Dudley at the New Hampshire ski resort.

"And we have no connection between them and Morehead. As of now we have no motive for Benedict and Bardak. We have a good line on a financial motive for Morehead.

"We still have eleven decedents who sold their life insurance policies to Portland Funds Five and Six. That's in addition to Rollins and Dudley. I don't know if we told you about Dominic Bonfiglio, who was killed in a hit-and-run near the National Cathedral the morning after Van Damm died?"

"I don't recall that one," the Chief replied.

"We need to look into Bonfiglio and eleven others who died over the last six months. They all had sold their policies to Portland. My concern is that we may not luck into another possible identification like we got on Bardak from the ski resort where Dr. Dudley died.

"My epiphany overnight was that we are only focusing on those who are deceased."

"Duh," Oliver said clearly in the background.

The Chief said, "Tell Oliver I heard that."

I said to Oliver, "The Chief says he heard that." Oliver laughed.

"Chief, I'm putting you on the speaker, so I don't have to repeat all of this for Oliver later."

"Okay."

I resumed, "So, here's what I'm thinking. First, there are a number of living people whose life insurance policies are held by Funds

Five and Six. Their lives may be at risk. We may be making a mistake in assuming that whoever is behind this string of murders has quit. We haven't even finished checking out the other twelve deaths tied to these funds.

"Second, these two doers may be used again if further murders are planned. Third, we now know who the remaining policies were issued to."

The Chief interrupted. "How did you get those names?"

"You don't want to know. We'll backstop it with a subpoena to Portland on Monday."

"Okay."

I resumed my narrative. "Chief, there are only three people with large policies in the remaining group. Two are for $1,000,000 and one is for $500,000. If whoever is behind this, say Morehead, feels the pressure closing in and wants to score one or two big hits, I think it will be among these three people. Two of them are in Fairfax County and one is in Northwest."

"So, what are you thinking?" the Chief asked.

"I'm not certain. I can come up with a couple of scenarios. One is to surveil our two suspected doers. That might even lead to determining where they work, which could possibly give us a connection to Morehead also.

"Second, we need to notify the individuals that they are at risk and ask if they will let us cover them."

The Chief said, "Oh, I'm sure they'll love that. They'll say we're using them as bait. They'll probably also climb all over Portland, which in turn will climb all over us. Plus, sooner or later, the press will get wind of this, and it will all blow up, possibly in our faces."

"Chief, I don't disagree with what you just said. But there could also be a big backfire if one of these folks is murdered, and it is later discovered that we were concerned for their safety but did nothing."

"Yeah, I see that," the Chief said. "It's kind of a no-win situation for both MPD and the individuals you're talking about. Plus, we would have to coordinate with Fairfax County."

I said, "Yeah, I know."

The Chief said, "Let me bounce something off of you and Oliver. I came through the academy in the dark ages with Leon Handley. He was with MPD for about ten years, before transferring to the Fairfax County Police Department and working his way up the food chain there. He eventually got himself appointed Police Chief about eight years ago. What do you think about trying to coordinate a meeting with him to discuss this further and maybe coordinate something?"

Oliver said, "It might help solve the obvious manpower and jurisdictional problems."

"Yeah," the Chief said. "Let me call Leon and see if I can set something up for Monday. In the meantime, I suggest that the two of you chase down those other twelve cases and see if you can generate anything else tying this case together."

"Will do, Chief," I replied. "Sorry to interrupt whatever you were doing."

He replied, "Some jobs just don't have regular business hours. Ours is one of them." Then he hung up.

*   *   *

I picked up my desk phone and dialed Simone Reese and asked her to come up to see us. Then I looked at Oliver and said, "We've got to do something to connect Morehead to Benedict and Bardak."

A couple minutes later, Simone arrived and pulled up an extra chair. She looked in the donut box and saw one lonely raspberry-filled donut. She looked up at us. I said, "Take it. We've eaten more this morning than the normal cop allotment."

She grabbed the donut first, then said, "I found where Vincent Morehead lives on Abbottsford Drive in the Spring Lake area of Fairfax County. He bought the house in 2016. According to the County's land records, it is titled in Morehead's name alone. Using the documentary stamp taxes on the deed, I calculated that he paid $625,000 for the house. The mortgage was for $475,000. So, he put $150,000 down when he bought the house.

"Somewhere along the line, I heard he belonged to the Eastwood Golf Club. I think that came up in the interview with Parker Winston. Anyway, Morehead's house is about a mile from that golf club.

"So, in the same general time frame he was investing $500,000 each in Portland's Funds Five and Six, he also put a down payment of $150,000 on his house and joined a golf club. I have no idea as to the source of those funds."

"Good work," I said. "Now, we've had some further developments and need some further assistance from you. First, the big news is that we got an anonymous tip this morning telling us to look at Virginia driver's licenses for Marian Benedict and Kurt Bardak. We got copies of their licenses and guess who they are."

Simone said, "The two people in the pictures?"

"Exactly. We now have their names and addresses. But we have been unable to pick up much on either of them through Google, Facebook, and public records. There was nothing on either of them on NCIC, except some old arrests on Bardak."

Simone asked, "So, what do we need to find out on these two people?"

"I don't know how we do it," I said, "but a good start would be finding out where they work. I have a gut feeling that may be how we find a thread to tie them to Morehead. Also, we need to find out where they bank. If we can look at their bank accounts, we can see if they deposited money around the same time as the murders."

I thought for a second. "You know, if we could also find out where Morehead works and where he banks, that may also give us a way of tying them all together."

"You know," she said, "I have a friend who works for the IRS. Supposedly, everything including tax returns is confidential. I wonder if I could get my friend to just look at their returns to see who their W-2 lists as their employer and if their refunds were direct deposited to a bank and, if so, what bank?"

"Do you really think you can get that information?"

"Let me cogitate on it. Give me those names, birth dates, and addresses. I'll see what I can do."

"If you pull that off, we could try to trace the money, which might be the best way to connect them to Morehead. We'll keep our fingers crossed."

CHAPTER FORTY-NINE

SIMONE REESE HAD known Cole Benjamin for about nine years. They first met when they were on opposing sides of an IRS audit during her last year in private accounting practice. Benjamin was an agent for the Internal Revenue Service. In the end, that audit was resolved in favor of her client. She wondered at the time whether Cole Benjamin had cut her client a break because he had a crush on her. A few weeks later, he called to ask her out for dinner. She agreed.

They dated a few times, but nothing came of it. Eventually, it just tapered off, and she thought that he had moved on. He would still telephone her every few months just to talk. She always kept it light and never slammed the door on him.

After wrestling with her conscience, she decided to contact him. He had always initiated the telephone conversations, and she knew a call from her would give him encouragement.

It was Saturday afternoon. She called him. "Hey, Cole, it's Simone Reese."

"Hey, Simone. Good to hear from you. What's up?"

"Well, as you know, I've been at MPD for some time now. I'm helping investigate three related homicides."

"Wow. That's wild. Not your everyday situation for a CPA."

She nodded even though he couldn't see her. "Yeah. I'm even thinking of applying to become a detective."

"That's really impressive."

"I need to pick your brain on something," Simone said. "We've got three suspects identified in our homicides. We need to tie them together. Our best way to do that is through their bank accounts, but we don't know where they bank."

Cole said, "Okay . . . what is it you want from me?"

"Does the IRS have banking details on people?"

Cole paused and then said, "Only if they get tax refunds by direct deposit or make quarterly estimates by auto deposit. And some people who owe taxes have the payments withdrawn from their bank account."

Simone was now at the pivotal point. "I know tax returns are confidential. But, for investigative purposes, can the IRS assist the police with non-confidential information? Like bank account information?

"What if the source was never revealed, just like we treat confidential informants? We never have to reveal confidential sources."

Cole Benjamin didn't say anything for ten to fifteen seconds. Simone sensed the wise move was to remain silent and let him process their discussion. He said, "How crucial is this information to solving your murders, in reality?"

"Cole, we're stuck. We have photographs of two people who committed these homicides. We've managed to identify the people in the photos. But we can't connect them to the third person whom we're sure is behind these murders and perhaps a series of more homicides. We think that third person is paying the other two to commit these murders. We need to track any money flowing from the third person to the others. We just need to know where to start looking."

Again, there was another pause of several seconds. Then Cole said, "There might not even be anything there, even if I were to look." Simone took this as a positive sign.

She asked, "Could you at least look and let me know?"

Cole Benjamin said nothing for another five seconds. Then he said, "Let me do a preliminary look, then I'll call you."

"Cole, that's great! If you can check, what we need is the name of their bank, bank account number, and the name of their employer."

He said, "What the hell am I doing here? I must be nuts. You absolutely need to keep my name out of everything. No reports. My name appears nowhere. Agreed?"

"Absolutely."

"Okay, give me the names."

Simone gave him the names, birth dates, and addresses of Marion Benedict, Kurt Bardak, and Vincent Morehead. Cole said, "Give me an hour to see what I can find. I'll call you back."

"Thanks, Cole, I really appreciate it."

*   *   *

Thirty minutes later Cole Benjamin called Simone Reese on her cellphone. "I've got something, but we can't discuss it over the phone."

She had anticipated that. "How about we meet for a drink?"

"Sure. Where are you?"

"I'm at MPD headquarters downtown. How about we meet at The Pursuit on H Street?" She knew it wasn't very far from where he lived. He agreed.

Simone called and made a reservation, knowing they had just opened at three that afternoon. She locked up her office and made the drive in fifteen minutes. When she got inside, Simone asked for a booth with a view of the front door.

Cole Benjamin arrived a few minutes later and walked up to her. "Saw your Cobra outside, drawing a crowd as usual."

She smiled. "It does that. Sit down."

Just then a waitress brought her a glass of white wine and looked at Cole. He said, "I'll take the same, please."

Simone said, "I didn't have lunch, so I ordered a cheese and charcuterie board. This is on me. I really appreciate your help."

He kind of half-smiled. "I hope it helps you." He handed her a printout listing all three people and their banks with account numbers. He added, "Got nothing for you on employers. All three simply said 'United States of America.' That's what we see a lot here in our Nation's Capital."

"Oh, Cole, this is great. It should be a major help with the investigation."

Just then, the charcuterie board and Cole's wine arrived. They both dug in and moved on to catching up with each other. Simone was dying to get back to headquarters but knew the minimum she could do would be to spend a little time with Cole as a way of thanking him. After two more glasses of wine each, they had polished off the charcuterie board. Simone paid the bill, and they headed outside.

He walked her to the Cobra, which, as usual, had a couple of admirers standing next to it. She thanked him again and gave him a kiss on the cheek. She went around the car and hopped over the door into the driver's seat. She fired up the engine, which drew even more comments. She let the car growl as she headed back to work.

CHAPTER FIFTY

"Per the Chief, we need to track down the remainder of the deaths from Funds Five and Six," I said to Oliver once we were back by ourselves.

"As I recall, I lost that flip and drew the bottom half of the list. Although I must admit that Dr. Dudley turned out to be productive."

"I've still got some follow-up on Dominic Bonfiglio, the hit-and-run victim. We've already dealt with Eugene Rollins and Claudia Coleman on my part of the list."

Oliver picked up his copy of the list. "Of the policies with larger dollar amounts, that leaves you with Miguel Garcia. I've got Perry Reinemann, Andre Pritchard, and Conrad Ritzen."

Looking at the list I said, "After Bonfiglio, I'm going to move on to Miguel Garcia, as he's the only $1,000,000 policy on my part of the list."

Oliver nodded. "Using that logic, I'll hit Andre Pritchard who was a $1,250,000 policy and then Reinemann and Ritzen, who are both $1,000,000 policies. All of the others on our lists are much smaller amounts."

*   *   *

Starting with Dominic Bonfiglio, age fifty-four, whom we had looked at briefly, I again pulled up the hit-and-run report and reread it. The reporting officer was Patrolman Andrew Bauman. I looked him up in the MPD's online directory and called his cellphone.

He answered on the third ring. "Andy Bauman."

I said, "Patrolman Bauman, this is Detective Mac Burke. My partner and I are taking a look at what we think are related murders. One of them is Dominic Bonfiglio, which was a hit-and-run you investigated."

"Yeah," he answered. "I remember that one. This past Tuesday morning. How can I help you?"

"Well, I'd like to pick your brain about the case. What is your status?" I asked.

"We're just coming off shift. Not too far from headquarters. After I report in to the duty sergeant, I'm available."

"Great. Come up to the fourth floor. My partner is Oliver Shaw, and we're working a number of these recent cases. I drew Bonfiglio. Once you get to the fourth floor, we're near the back. I'm the good-looking guy."

"Yeah, right. See you in thirty."

I turned to Oliver. "The reporting officer on Bonfiglio is going to come by in about half an hour." Oliver nodded and went back to working on his computer.

* * *

Just then Simone Reese showed up carrying three sheets of paper. She grabbed a chair and pulled it up to our desks, wearing a smile.

"Okay," I said, "what's up?"

"I worked my source, whom I absolutely cannot reveal. I have bank account numbers for Morehead, Bardak, and Benedict.

Nothing on employers. All three showed the United States of America as their employer on their W-2s."

"Holy shit. How did you get that?"

"I can't tell you. For real." She was emphatic.

"Major accomplishment, Simone," I said. "Well done. This could be a shot at tying the three of them together. Or maybe just connecting Benedict and Bardak to Morehead. This is the next step. Now the question is how we can get into their bank accounts without subpoenas or search warrants."

Simone looked perplexed. "I'm not sure how we can do that either without a first-rate hacker."

Oliver chanced a quick glance at me, but said nothing.

Simone asked, "What can I do next to help the cause?"

"It will sound a little like grunt work," Oliver said, "but there is one loose end that we have yet to run to ground."

"Okay. Hit me."

Oliver explained. "The son of our first decedent is William Van Damm. Goes by Billy, according to his mother. He lives in the District." Oliver checked his notes from our interview of Whitney Van Damm. "Young Mr. Van Damm works for a lobbying group on K Street and is single. He's around thirty-five years old. His mother said Billy was in D.C. on Monday when his father was killed."

Simone made some notes. "What do you want me to dig up on him?"

Oliver replied, "I'd start with a credit check. See if he's heavily in debt. Any lawsuits. That sort of thing. Where does he live? Own or rent? General reputation. Billy and his sister stand to inherit many millions from Weldon Van Damm. We don't think he's a likely suspect, but we can't ignore him. Any defense attorney would chew us up if we overlooked the obvious beneficiaries of Van Damm's death."

She said, "You mentioned a sister. Want me to check her out as well?"

"For thoroughness' sake, yeah," Oliver said. "We ought to check her out also." Again, he referred to his notes. "Her name is Aurelia Van Damm Perkins, age thirty-two. She's married and lives in Philadelphia and has two young children. Don't have anything else on her. She was not in D.C. on Monday, according to her mother. Probably should also take a look at her husband, whose name I didn't get."

Simone took more notes. "Not sure this will tax my skills, but I'll get right on it."

Oliver smiled, which she took as her cue to head back to her own office.

* * *

Not more than two minutes later, Patrolman Andrew Bauman walked up to us carrying a pocket folder with an MPD case number on the outside. He was a good-looking twenty-something with bright red hair. His uniform was wrinkled after a day of riding the District in a cruiser. He stuck his hand out to me and said, "I'm Andy Bauman. How can I help you?"

I pointed to Oliver and said, "This is my partner, Oliver Shaw. I'm Mac Burke." He also shook Oliver's hand. I waved him to the chair Simone had left next to our desks.

"Andy, we're investigating what we believe are a series of related homicides. Your hit-and-run victim, Dominic Bonfiglio, is one of the people we think might be connected to our case. We've both read your report but wanted to see what other information you might have picked up that would help us ferret out whether it actually is tied to our cases. Tell us what you came up with that might not have made it to the formal report."

"Sure, whatever I can do to help. As the report says, we got a call from Dispatch at 6:24 on Tuesday morning to check out a hit-and-run on 34th Street NW next to the Cathedral. We got on scene about four minutes later and found a small group of people gathered around a body lying next to a parked car.

"My partner is Dan Blackmon. He's a former EMT. He checked Bonfiglio for a pulse and found none but called for an ambulance anyway. There was blood on the car he was lying next to. It appeared that a car had hit him, and he was slammed into the parked car.

"My partner found a small pocket inside the waistband of Bonfiglio's running shorts that had his driver's license and a key, presumably to his house."

I asked to see his driver's license, which Bauman located and handed to me.

Bauman continued, "We asked the six or so people standing around if anyone had seen anything. One lady"—he paused and checked his field notes—"name of Paula Jenkins, said she had been walking her dog up the street at the next corner when she heard a thump. Not loud enough to be a crash, but just enough sound to draw her attention.

"She said that a few seconds later a white car came past her going pretty fast and turned right and headed toward Rock Creek Park. Jenkins said the car was really quiet, like an electric car. She did notice that it was a blonde woman driving but did not get a license number or make of the car."

I asked, "Any chance she could identify the woman if we gave her a photo lineup?"

"I don't think so," Bauman replied. "I asked if she could give me any more details on the woman. Only additional piece of information she provided was that she was white and maybe in her thirties. I've got Paula Jenkins' contact information in the file." He patted the folder and opened it again to find his notes. He then gave us Jenkins' phone number and address, which Oliver jotted down in his notebook.

I followed up. "Anything else at all that might help us?"

Bauman said, "After the ambulance cleared the scene and all the other people there turned out to be dry wells in terms of information, my partner and I went up to Macomb Street NW and turned toward Rock Creek Park. We were looking for any buildings with cameras. There is a convenience store about one block east of 34th Street.

"We went in and talked to the owner." He again checked his notes. "Fellow by the name of Kim John. Think he's Korean or something. Fairly heavy accent. He told us that he had a camera facing the parking area in front of his building. We figured the time of the hit-and-run to be around six fifteen a.m., give or take a little, so we asked if he could show us the video from six to seven that morning. It showed quite a bit of traffic, including some white cars but nothing we could identify. We asked him if he could make us a copy of that hour's worth of the video, which he put on a USB flash drive."

"You still have that thumb drive?" I asked.

"Oh, yeah. It's in the file." He looked in the file and pulled out a silver thumb drive on which he had written the name of the store, the owner, and the time frame covered. He handed it to me.

I said, "We'll have the tech guys downstairs take a close look at this and see if they can pull anything we can use. This could be helpful in identifying the vehicle. Did you check back along the streets leading up to the scene of the hit-and-run for other cameras?"

"No. We didn't think of that. You think it could be helpful?"

I nodded. "It might be. Different angle might give us another shot of the car and maybe a brief glance at the driver. Maybe the license plate."

"Huh," Bauman said. "Since I'm still in uniform, I'll go check out a cruiser and check the neighborhood right now. My partner's already gone home. His son had a baseball game that he had to go to."

"Andy, that would be great. If you get anything, be sure to date it and put the other information we'll need for a chain of custody. Definitely worth a shot."

We gave him our cards with our cellphone numbers and told him to call us either way, whether he was successful or not. Oliver made a copy of Bonfiglio's driver's license and returned the original to Bauman, who put it back in his file.

Oliver crossed the fingers on his right hand and said, "Here's hoping. We need something to better tie Benedict into our case. She's a possible for Bonfiglio."

* * *

Chief Whittaker called me around four o'clock that afternoon. I put him on the speaker and told him that Oliver and I were at our desks.

The Chief said, "I called Leon Handley, the Police Chief over in Fairfax County. I explained the situation to him, and he agreed we should meet to discuss how to handle this going forward. We're set up to meet with him at his office in Fairfax at two on Monday. He's going to have his Chief of Detectives there also. I plan on going with you to this meeting because of my personal connection with Leon."

"That's great, Chief. Thanks for arranging that for us," I said. "We have a couple updates for you also. First, we have the bank account information on our suspected doers, Bardak and Benedict, as well as on Vincent Morehead."

The Chief interrupted, "How did you get that?"

"Simone Reese has a confidential informant who provided that information."

"No kidding? Good for her. Any idea who her source is?"

"No, sir. And she's very adamant that her source has to remain confidential. But she feels that this source is very reliable."

After a pause, Chief Whittaker said, "Okay. So how do we get a look inside those accounts?"

"We're working on that now," I said. "We'll keep you posted. Also, we talked to the patrolman who investigated the Dominic Bonfiglio hit-and-run on Tuesday morning. Turns out that there was a witness who saw a blonde woman driving a white car leaving the scene seconds after Bonfiglio was hit. Patrolman's name is Andy Bauman. He also tracked down a convenience store camera a couple blocks away and got a copy of their video coverage. We've got possession of that now. Nothing conclusive on the video per the patrolman."

"But he's now checking for more video on the streets leading up to the hit-and-run site," Oliver added. "He's doing that right now."

"Well," the Chief said, "tell Patrolman Bauman that if he needs backup on overtime for this to let you know, and I'll authorize it myself."

"Thanks, Chief," said Oliver.

"We're going to keep pounding on the other eleven people who died in the last six months while their life insurance policies were held by Portland Funds Five and Six," I said. "We'll probably be here a couple more hours and then call it a day."

"Listen, guys," the Chief said, "I really appreciate your dedication." And he hung up. An attaboy goes a long way.

CHAPTER FIFTY-ONE

WHILE I HAD BEEN working on Bonfiglio, Oliver had been focused on Andre Pritchard, who had sold his $1,250,000 life insurance policy to Portland Fund Six. Pritchard was sixty years old at the time of his death on December 28th.

After a basic Google search, he found that Pritchard was the managing partner of two boutique hotels in Northwest D.C. He was a founding partner in the entities that owned the two hotels. He was married and had three children. He lived on Beecher Street NW in Georgetown. Oliver also found a news article on Pritchard's death in the *Washington Post* from December 29th:

WASHINGTON, D.C. – *Local hotelier Andre Pritchard was found dead in Glover Archibald Park last night. It appeared that he died of a heart attack while walking to his Georgetown home from the Bon Homme Hotel on Foxhall Road. Pritchard was co-owner and general manager of the prestigious hotel. He had resided in Northwest D.C. since he moved here 17 years ago to build the high-end hotel.*

Next, Oliver searched MPD's files for any hits on Andre Pritchard. The only entry was a brief follow-up to his death as described in the *Post* article. A 911 call came in at 8:34 p.m. of a body of a man down in Glover Archibald Park. Dispatch sent both a cruiser and an EMT unit. The medical technicians determined Pritchard dead at the scene. Neither they nor the responding patrolmen saw any signs of violence that called for further action. Pritchard was transported to the D.C. Medical Examiner's office.

As the M.E.'s office is open 24/7 year-round because death never takes a holiday, Oliver called over to see if someone could pull up the file for him. An intern on duty got the name and date and said he would pull the file and call Oliver back.

Five minutes later, the intern called back. "Detective Shaw, this is Josh Brownlaw again from the M.E.'s office. I've got the file on Andre Pritchard, date of death December 28th. It lists cause of death as uncertain. The notes say it was probably a myocardial infarction, aka heart attack."

Oliver asked if the file had information on next of kin. The intern took a second and came back with the name of Pritchard's wife and a phone number.

Oliver then asked, "Who was the examiner who did the autopsy?"

Brownlaw responded, "Dr. Brian West signed off."

"Is he still around today?"

Brownlaw said, "He's not around at all. He left the office early this year. I don't know where he went."

Oliver asked him to forward the file to Courtney Vaughan's computer so that she could look at it on Monday.

*　　*　　*

Oliver called Michelle Pritchard and, when she answered, said, "Mrs. Pritchard, I'm Detective Oliver Shaw with the Metropolitan

Police Department. I'm a homicide detective, and my partner and I are looking at a number of deaths over the past six months. May I ask you a few questions about your husband's death?"

She responded, "How do I know you are who you say you are?"

"Well, you can call back to the MPD main number and ask them to connect you with Detective Oliver Shaw."

She said, "Okay, I'll do that right now." And she apparently did because Oliver's phone rang less than two minutes after they had hung up.

"Detective Oliver Shaw here."

Michelle Pritchard said, "Okay, I feel more comfortable talking now. Yes, go ahead and ask your questions about Andre's death."

"The Medical Examiner's report said his death looked like a heart attack. Did he have a history of heart problems?"

Michelle Pritchard paused, then said, "Not really. He was a little overweight, but generally in good shape. He was only sixty years old. He walked to and from work every day, weather permitting. He only had a physical once a year, but his cholesterol was good. His blood pressure was also good. He basically took no medicines. I was very surprised that he would just drop over dead on the way home from work."

"Was he under unusual stress at the time?"

"The hotel business is always stressful," she said, "but the Bon Homme and his other hotel had both been fairly full since before Thanksgiving. They were doing fine."

"Anyone who would want to see him injured or gone?"

"No. He was in the hospitality business and, by nature, he had a fairly cheerful disposition. He had no enemies that I knew of."

"Did he have any life insurance?"

"He used to have a big policy for over a million dollars, but he sold it to one of those companies that buy up life insurance policies. I think he got around $350,000 for it. At the time, he needed the money for the start-up of his second hotel."

"Okay, ma'am. Thanks for your help. Let me give you my phone number and email in case you think of anything else. Thanks for your help."

Then he sent a text to Courtney Vaughan at the M.E.'s office to take a look at the Pritchard autopsy file and give him a call back. He gave her the date of death, as well as the name, and told her the file had been forwarded to her computer.

*　　*　　*

Oliver updated me on another death that was a candidate for the pool we were investigating. He said, "We have a healthy guy who dies walking home from the hotel he ran on Foxhall Road. He died crossing Glover Archibald Park in Northwest around eight thirty in the evening of December 28th."

I noted, "Probably dark at the time. Maybe cold also."

"His wife says he was in good shape and health. No cholesterol or cardiac problems. The M.E. said cause of death was uncertain but probably a heart attack. The Assistant Medical Examiner who did the autopsy is no longer there. I've had the autopsy file forwarded to Courtney Vaughan's computer and sent her a text to take a further look at it."

"So, no witnesses or obvious connections to our suspects?"

Oliver shook his head. "Nothing yet."

I suggested that he contact the IT department and see if they could access the city's video cams for Glover Archibald Park. He rang Carter Enright's extension and, as anticipated late on a Saturday afternoon, got voicemail. He left a message saying we needed video footage from the park from about five to ten p.m. on December 28. He sent a text to Enright saying the same.

"Had enough fun for today?" I asked him. When Oliver nodded in the affirmative, I packed up the most recent papers to study further at home, and we headed out. We stopped on the third floor to check on Simone Reese, but she had already left as well.

In the Jeep, Oliver asked, "How are we going to get those bank records?"

"Do you think Frisco can get them?"

"Probably, but how are we going to back that up later for evidentiary purposes?"

I said, "I'm not sure."

I dropped Oliver at his house and headed home.

CHAPTER FIFTY-TWO

As I drove down the alley behind my row house on Morris Place, I used my phone to disarm the alarm on the garage and house. When the icon came up, it showed that the alarm was already disarmed, which meant Mags was in residence.

I pulled into my side of the garage, grabbed my file, and got out. Her Porsche Speedster was already on the left side of the garage. The engine was not making that clicking sound it generates when it cools down, so it had been home for a while.

Mags was standing in the kitchen unpacking small cartons from a plastic delivery bag. "Good timing," she said. "I just got delivery from Tsim Yung." Our favorite Chinese restaurant in Northeast D.C.

"Absolutely perfect," I said as I gave her a hug. "All I've had to eat today were two or three donuts." She just shook her head slowly, almost like my mother did when I disappointed her as a child.

She set the assorted boxes of Chinese food on the breakfast table, along with two sets of chopsticks. I went to the refrigerator and pulled out a bottle of soy sauce. Before closing the door, I asked her what she wanted to drink. "Any cold white wine," was the reply.

There was a chilled bottle of chardonnay in the door. I pulled the cork and put the bottle on the table.

We used the chopsticks to scoop food from the four boxes onto our plates. We had an unwritten rule, established long ago, that no Western utensils could be used in eating Chinese food. As usual, I gave my steamed white rice a heavy dose of soy sauce. I poured the wine, and we dug in.

We said almost nothing for the next five minutes as we devoured the food, except a few satisfied "um-hmms." Mags has always been more proficient with chopsticks than I am and cleared her plate first. She poured more wine and leaned back in her chair.

Mags asked, "Did you have a productive day?"

"Actually, yes," I said, "we did. Oliver got a tip on the two doers. We were able to get their names from the Virginia DMV."

"Well, that's progress."

"Kind of. We have their names and addresses, but still don't know how to connect them. We managed to get their bank account numbers, as well as that of our prime suspect."

Mags looked somewhat surprised. She asked, "How did you do that?"

"Confidential informant. In fact, I don't even know his or her name. Our financial investigator had a source. But even they couldn't get the employer of any of them. All three were listed as employed by the United States of America, which was not very helpful."

"What good does the bank account information do you?"

"If we could get into all three bank accounts, we might be able to find a thread to connect them to each other. Our hope is to find withdrawals and deposits that correlate to the dates of death over the past six months."

She asked, "Can't you subpoena the bank records?"

"We don't have enough probable cause to get a sustainable search warrant yet. Basically, we have to connect these three together, but we don't have enough information to do that yet. We're hoping the bank statements will help."

"Well, good luck with that."

"Yeah, we'll find a way. Don't know what it is yet, but we'll find something."

Mags moved to the living room and turned on the television. I cleaned up the kitchen. All four boxes of Chinese had some food left in them, so they all went in the fridge. The glasses and plates went in the dishwasher. Cleanup accomplished.

While Mags was surfing for something to watch, I had leaned back and fallen asleep. I was beat. Next thing I knew it was about three a.m., and I was sprawled across the sofa. The television was off, and only one small lamp remained lit in the living room.

I got up and went to bed. Mags was asleep on her side. I shed my clothes and climbed in bed wearing only my boxer shorts and almost instantly was back asleep.

CHAPTER FIFTY-THREE

YESTERDAY OLIVER AND I had discussed two things on the way home. First, we agreed to not start early on Sunday. The plan was for me to pick him up about nine thirty.

Second, we decided to press Frisco again to help us get into the bank accounts for Benedict, Bardak, and Morehead. Oliver had called him from the Jeep, and they agreed to meet at ten in the morning.

Mags woke me up on Sunday morning in the great way that some couples start the day. Afterwards, we showered together and made love a second time. We were still in bathrobes when we went downstairs and made coffee. I suggested making waffles and bacon. She agreed.

I dug out my square cast iron skillet and started the bacon. I then plugged in my aged waffle maker that produced the same kind of waffles as you get at Waffle House. The thin kind, not the thick Belgian waffles. I flipped the bacon and stopped for a coffee break.

I filled my cup and joined Mags at the breakfast table. Violating our no questions before coffee rule, I asked her, "What do you have on tap for today?"

"I have to go in to work for a while. Probably be done by noon. What about you?"

"Oliver and I have to finish going through the remainder of the people who died in the last six months. We have nine left to do."

I got up and checked the waffle iron. The light had gone out. It was ready to do its job. I grabbed the box of Bisquick and mixed the batter, poured it into the waffle iron, and closed the lid. I pulled the bacon and put it on a paper towel–covered plate to drain.

The waffle was now done. Using a fork, I pulled it from the waffle iron and put it on a plate and then refilled the waffle iron with the rest of the batter. Mags took half the waffle, put butter and strawberry preserves on it, and added two rashers of bacon to her plate and dug in. I did the same but used natural Vermont maple syrup instead of preserves. Overall, a successful Sunday breakfast.

"When we're finished," I said, "I'm going to put on some Sunday work clothes and pick up Oliver."

*   *   *

Maggie was the first one ready to roll. When she got down to the garage, she lowered the top on her Speedster as the temperature was already in the seventies.

She headed west down the alley, drove a couple blocks, and then pulled to the curb. She called her mentor. It rang twice, and he answered, "Harrison Jones here. I see it is you calling again, Maggie. Do we need to meet again?"

"Yes, sir. We do. Further developments to discuss."

"Come on over. I've already got the coffee going," he said and hung up.

She pulled out and headed to his house in the Woodley Park area. She parked in the same place on the side of his driveway. Jones opened the front door as she walked up the front steps. "Come on in." He again escorted her to the kitchen and told her to fix her cup.

She joined him at the kitchen table and sat down with a sigh. He raised his eyebrows.

"Per our discussion, the MPD detectives got a short text from a burner phone. It was two sentences long and simply gave them the two names and told them to check with the Virginia DMV."

Jones asked, "That didn't go to your ex-husband, did it?"

"No. It went to his partner, Oliver Shaw. They apparently had a contact at the Virginia DMV and got copies of their driver's licenses in no time, which gave them addresses and birth dates, as well. They searched online, including social media and other sources, and came up with no current information on either of them. McDermott and his partner were looking for the identity of their employers but found nothing."

"So, what did they do next that led to our meeting this morning?"

"They apparently have another source who got them bank account information on both Benedict and Bardak, as well as Morehead. That source could only identify the employer as the United States of America, based on their W-2s. Which leads me to believe that their source is at the IRS."

"I assume that leads us to what you want to discuss."

"Yes, sir. As you know, the Agency trained me to penetrate banking systems on targets. I am fairly positive that I could get them the six months of bank statements that they need."

Jones pursed his lips for a second. "What would that give them to help their case?"

"They're looking for withdrawals of funds by Morehead and deposits by Benedict and Bardak that correlate to the dates of the murders. They think it finally gives them a way to connect Benedict and Bardak to Morehead."

"But that doesn't sound like a very strong link," Jones said. "And, certainly, does not tie them together through their connection at Special Operations."

"Agreed," Maggie said. "I don't think we can give them a direct answer on the common employer between the three of them. They'll have to extract that from Benedict or Bardak, once they have enough to put pressure on them."

Jones thought for a few moments. "Can't they just subpoena the bank records?"

"They don't have enough at this point to subpoena bank records on Benedict and Bardak. And certainly nothing to connect them to Morehead, who is the one person with a motive for pursuing these homicides. If I give them the bank statements, they can later rely on a confidential informant to support a subpoena. Kind of like closing the barn door after the horse is out."

Jones again paused, even closing his eyes while he thought. Maggie remained silent. Jones took a deep breath and said, "I'm not sure I like it."

Maggie prepared herself to be disappointed.

"But," he continued, "I sure as hell don't condone what I think these Agency people are doing. It is literally murder to make money. If you give them the bank statements, I think the MPD has to take it from there. We cannot get in the business of turning on our own, regardless of how despicable these people are. You good with that?"

"Yes, sir. I took a photo of the list of bank accounts last night when Mac was asleep. It shouldn't take long, although I will need to use the Agency's software to grab this information."

"Can you use someone else's login to avoid a direct digital trail back to you?"

Maggie nodded.

Jones rose, indicating that the meeting was over, and escorted Maggie to the front door. "Be careful. You're dancing on a tightrope without a net."

"Yeah, that's exactly how this feels. Thanks for the advice." She squeezed his shoulder as she left and headed to her office at Langley.

CHAPTER FIFTY-FOUR

WHEN I PULLED UP in front of Oliver's house, he came out the front door dressed in khakis and a blue golf shirt covered by a casual tan jacket. Once he strapped in, we headed over to Frisco's building.

We pressed the buzzer on the door of Frisco's two-story building. He could see us through his camera, but didn't say anything this time and just pressed the buzzer that released the door lock. We went in and climbed the stairs.

He was waiting for us at his interior door. We did our usual greeting. I said to Frisco, "We really appreciate you seeing us so many times on short notice. This has been an unusual case for us. People we cannot identify and then a growing number of suspected murders. You have been a big help."

Frisco smiled. "What can the world of digital science do to assist with your case today?"

"We've got three bank account numbers," Oliver said, "and need to get the last six months of statements."

Frisco smiled. "Is that all? I thought you might have something kind of difficult for me. Come on."

We all marched over to his main computer. Oliver gave him the list of names and bank accounts, and Frisco started typing on his keyboard while humming what sounded like a Beethoven overture.

"Can you work your magic and hum classical music at the same time?" Oliver asked.

"You guys need to come up with tougher requests," Frisco said.

Marian Benedict's account was at PNC Bank. Frisco accessed their system and quickly had her account information on his screen. She had a current balance of $42,312. He printed out the last six monthly statements. Then he asked, "You also want the debits and credits since the last monthly statement?"

"Yes," Oliver said. "We've had three homicides just this week."

Frisco printed out another sheet on Benedict's account.

"Okay," Frisco said, "next up is Mr. Bardak whose account is at Bank of America." He typed a little longer than he had with Benedict's bank. Frisco said, "Bardak was more careful with his password, but it still wasn't all that difficult to break." He again printed six months of statements and a summary of the current month's activity.

After retrieving the Bardak printouts for us, he picked up our list and started typing in Vincent Morehead's information. His account was at BB&T Bank. He again took more time typing.

"Hah," Frisco said, "this guy is even better than the last one. His password is twenty figures with caps and lower case, numbers intermixed with symbols. A very secure password by most standards, but not against my software." And up popped his account. Morehead's current balance was $16,589.

"That's kind of disappointing and surprising at the same time," I said.

"Be patient, grasshopper," Frisco said. "Let me print off the six months of statements and the current activity."

He then said, "There are a number of coded transfers to other accounts at three different banks. Let's see where those accounts are." He did some more typing. "Well, well," he said. "One account in Grand Cayman, one in the Bahamas, and one on the Isle of Wight."

"Huh," I said. "A tad unusual for your average GS-15."

"Yep," Frisco agreed. "Let me get into those accounts as well. I'll start with the bank in Grand Cayman." After some more typing, he said, "This bank's security is better than the American banks. But I'm making progress. At one time or another, I've been inside all three of these banks."

He kept working away on his keyboard. Finally, he said to the computer screen, "There you are." At which point, his screen lit up with a statement of Morehead's account, although his name did not appear anywhere.

Oliver asked, "How do we know it is Morehead's account? His name's not on it."

"Standard for a numbered account," Frisco said. "Five will get you ten that it is his numbered account. This one shows a balance of $346,709. It acts like a savings account. There are primarily only deposits going in. Very few withdrawals. They don't send out monthly statements like American banks. You check your balance only online. I'll print you the last six months of activity up to today." Which he did, and gave us the printouts.

He did the same thing with the Bahamas and Isle of Wight banks. Both were also numbered accounts. The Bahamas account had a current balance of $476,888. The Isle of Wight account had a balance of $809,589. Altogether, he had over $1.5 million in the offshore accounts.

"How can we show those accounts belong to Vincent Morehead?" Oliver asked.

"It's logic," Frisco said. "Money goes from his BB&T account. Any money coming out of the offshore accounts largely goes back to the same BB&T account, which is not a very sophisticated system. But he also occasionally transfers money between the three offshore accounts. To answer your question, Oliver, is the money originates with Morehead and never goes anywhere other than back to him."

"Huh," Oliver said. "You're right. It's really not very sophisticated."

We thanked Frisco profusely again and left.

* * *

Unknown to Oliver and Mac, Frisco fancied himself as the Robin Hood of hackers. He had been orphaned at age six when his parents drowned in the Potomac River following a multi-car collision on the 14th Street Bridge, now known as the George Mason Memorial Bridge.

When he was placed in the hands of Children and Family Services, Frisco was totally nonverbal and thought to be autistic. He could not even tell the lady from the Agency his actual name—his parents had always just called him "Son." The CFS agent gave him a sheet of paper and a pencil and asked him to write his name. He just shrugged, as he truly didn't know.

When the agent went to bring in the proposed foster parents, Frisco stared at a poster on the wall of the Golden Gate Bridge with San Francisco in block letters below the picture. Wanting to give the lady something, he slowly copied the letters FRISCO on the paper. When the agent returned with the prospective foster parents, she asked him if that was his name. He smiled and nodded, happy that he had been able to help the agent.

He was placed with a childless couple who had volunteered as foster parents. Due to his lack of speech, they decided to home-school him. His foster mother was an elementary school teacher. His foster father was a computer programming consultant who worked from home.

The foster parents quickly determined that he could do math at a second- or third-grade level and could read at the same level, even though he appeared to be only five or six years old because he was small. Once his foster father showed him how to do arithmetic problems on the computer, it was apparent that Frisco had a natural ability to understand how computers worked.

With the help of a speech pathologist, the foster parents eventually helped him learn to speak. Not well enough to attend regular school classes, but sufficient to communicate. They also learned that Frisco was not autistic, but rather was something of a mathematical savant.

Within three years, Frisco was not only using a computer as well as most adults, but his foster father had also taught him how to write software to address specific topics and assignments. Frisco's foster parents had given him his first computer when he was eight. Unknown to his foster father, by age nine Frisco was visiting websites on hacking.

By age twelve, Frisco was a very competent hacker and started piercing different systems just for the challenge. With his love of the story of Robin Hood, Frisco decided to use his hacking skills to help others. Things like changing grades at schools or helping aspiring high school seniors to get into quality universities or get them financial aid.

He even set up a bank account online. When he moved money out of bank accounts or businesses, Frisco put 20 percent into his bank account and moved the rest to benefit others. He got great pleasure from helping people. He became a significant supporter of Gallaudet University, which had been founded in 1864 to help deaf, blind, and mute students, although the school had no idea that its benefactor was a teenage hacker. He closely monitored the university's applications and requests for financial aid. He steered funds to those he found most deserving.

CHAPTER FIFTY-FIVE

NOT TWENTY MINUTES later, Maggie Hampton sat at an unassigned desk on the third floor of the Central Intelligence Agency's New Headquarters Building. There was almost no one there at this time on a Sunday morning.

Over the years, she had acquired the passwords of most of her colleagues and now put them to use in pulling up the bank accounts of Benedict, Bardak, and Morehead. She used a different password to open each of the accounts.

She printed copies of the last six months' statements on all three accounts. She also printed out the current month's activity on each of the accounts, making a separate set of the printouts for herself to study further.

She took one set and put it in an 8.5 x 11" manila envelope, making sure none of her fingerprints or saliva was on either the envelope or the copies. Using her left hand to disguise her handwriting, she printed *Detective Oliver Shaw, MPD* on the front and slipped it in her large shoulder bag.

Maggie retrieved her car from the underground parking garage. She had put the top up when she had arrived and left it up now. She found a parking garage near Judiciary Square and left her car on the third level. Walking down to the ground level, she pulled on a floppy wide-brimmed hat and sunglasses to conceal her features from any cameras around.

Then she walked to where she could see two taxis parked near the Superior Court building, waiting for fares. Maggie had a straight visual shot down the street to the MPD headquarters. She had put on clear latex gloves.

Maggie paper clipped a $20 bill to the envelope and had two $50 bills in her other hand. After a few minutes, a teenager on a skateboard came along the sidewalk. She waved him down and he stopped.

Maggie held up a $50 bill and said to the skateboarder, "Take this envelope to the first cab in line and tell the driver to drop it at the front desk at MPD headquarters down the street a block and tell him the $20 is his to keep. Don't tell him anything else. Nothing. I'll give you $50 now and another $50 after the cabbie delivers the envelope."

The kid asked, "For real?"

She replied, "For real." She gave him the first $50 bill and the envelope. The teenager skated down to the first cab and rapped on the passenger window, which the cabbie lowered. Maggie saw the kid hand him the envelope and say a few words to him and then turn around to come back to her. She watched the cabbie pull up in front of MPD headquarters and hop out of his taxi and walk through the front door carrying the envelope. He came back out without the envelope, got in his cab, and left. Maggie gave the kid the other $50 bill. He said, "Thanks," and skated off.

Maggie wandered around the block and eventually ended up at the parking garage. She left her hat and sunglasses on while she paid her parking fee and headed home.

CHAPTER FIFTY-SIX

WE GOT TO HEADQUARTERS a little before eleven o'clock. When we got to our desks, a manila envelope was lying on Oliver's desk. He looked at it for a second, picked up his phone, and punched in the digits for the front desk.

Oliver listened for a second and then said, "Hey, Sergeant Jackson, this is Detective Oliver Shaw. I just got in and there's a manila envelope on my desk. Did that come in through you?"

"Yes, sir. About twenty minutes ago. A cabbie came and dropped it off. Said some kid had given it to him to deliver here. We made a copy of his taxi operator's license in case you need to contact him. I also got his cellphone number."

"Give me his name and number." Oliver also asked who had handled the envelope.

"As far as I know, the cabbie, the kid who gave it to him, me, and Corporal Brown, who I asked to take it up to your desk. Probably has all of those prints on it."

Oliver thanked him and dialed the cabbie's cellphone number. The phone was answered by the cabbie. "Ernie Johnson here."

"Mr. Johnson, this is Detective Oliver Shaw with MPD. Did you just deliver a manila envelope to the front desk at MPD headquarters?"

"Yes, I did. I was in the queue at Judiciary Square when some teenager on a skateboard came up on the passenger side of my cab and knocked on my window. He handed me the envelope with a $20 bill clipped to it and asked me to deliver it to the front desk at MPD, which I did. It was only about a block away."

Oliver asked, "Did you see who gave the envelope to the kid?"

"No, sir, I didn't."

"Okay, thanks for your help, Mr. Johnson."

Oliver put on a pair of latex gloves and opened the envelope. He slid the contents onto his desk without touching them. He pulled a large Ziploc baggie from his desk drawer and slipped the envelope into it. He said to me, "Mac, there's probably no point in worrying about prints, but let's be careful just in case."

"Agreed," I said. "What's on the papers you got?"

Still wearing his gloves, Oliver flipped through the pages. When he got to the end he said, "It's the same six months of bank statements we just got from Frisco. Without the numbered account info."

"Huh. You think it's from the same C.I. who sent you the text about checking Virginia DMV?"

"Or maybe Simone Reese's confidential informant." Oliver picked up the papers with his gloved hands and went to the copier. He made two copies and returned to his desk. He put the originals in the same baggie as the envelope.

We both looked at the bank statements. Exactly the same as what Frisco had printed for us, without the printouts from the numbered accounts. It seemed to me that we had another friend out there trying to help us.

I dialed Simone's internal number. When she answered, I asked her if she could come up. "We've got a development that we'd like you to look at."

"Which set do we show her?" I asked Oliver.

He didn't hesitate. "The complete set we got from Frisco, including the numbered accounts. We can say it came in the envelope."

I took the Frisco set to the copier and made two copies, while Oliver put the other set in a new manila envelope. Not long after, Simone came down the aisle and pulled a chair over to our desks.

"Before we get to the late-breaking news," I said, "did you find anything on Van Damm's children?"

She shook her head. "Nothing too surprising. The son, Billy Van Damm, works for a consulting firm on K Street NW. He's been there around twelve years. Apparently, it's a lobbying firm. Probably makes pretty good money. He's single, as best I can tell, and owns a condo in Northwest. Looks like he still owes about $90,000 on his mortgage. I checked NCIC and got no hits. Credit check came up clean also.

"I also checked out the sister, Aurelia Van Damm Perkins of Philadelphia. A stay-at-home mom with two small kids. Husband is Ralph Perkins, who is a partner with a major law firm in Philly. They own a house in the Rittenhouse Square area. No mortgage. Looks like the husband inherited it from his family—the husband has family money. No NCIC hits on either of them. No adverse credit reports. Overall, I'd say there's nothing directly pointing to either of the children having a reason to kill their father."

"Okay," I said. "That's what we suspected. Now, let's move on to the latest news. We received an anonymous envelope this morning with six months of bank statements for the accounts of Marian Benedict, Kurt Bardak, and Vincent Morehead. Here's your copy of the set.

"But there's something especially interesting on Morehead's set. It appears he has three numbered offshore accounts. One each in Grand Cayman, the Bahamas, and the Isle of Wight."

Simone's eyes were wide. "How do you know that's where the numbered accounts are located?"

"We contacted a special CI of ours to look at the transfers shown on Morehead's statements at BB&T. Our CI told us that is where those banks are located. The last pages attached to Morehead's bank statements include the activity in the numbered accounts over the last six months."

She leaned back in her chair as she looked at those pages. After flipping through those sheets, she said, "Holy cow, he has about $1.5 million in the numbered accounts."

"Yeah," I said. "Doing pretty well on a GS-15's salary of $143,000 a year."

"No kidding. What do you want me to do with this?"

"First thing," Oliver said, "we need you to chart out the dates of death of all the claims coming out of Funds Five and Six over the last six or seven months. Then add to that chart how much money was paid to Morehead some period later from those claims. That's one chart."

Oliver continued, "The second chart is to try linking Benedict and Bardak to Morehead through his withdrawal of funds and their deposits of funds. And tie those to the dates of the deaths. See if there is a pattern that can be discerned."

Simone had been taking detailed notes. "Now, this is more in my skill set. Let me get cracking on this right away. But I've got one big question."

"What's that?"

"Who is the source for this information?"

"We truly don't know," Oliver said. "Would your source have access to this kind of information?"

"I seriously doubt it. Not in their wheelhouse, I don't believe." She stood up. "I'll get on this right away. How long will you be here today?"

"Probably until well into the afternoon," I said.

"If I haven't contacted you," Simone said, "call me before you leave."

"Will do," I said.

*   *   *

Oliver's cellphone rang less than a minute later. He answered and listened. "Thanks, Doc, for calling back. Let me put you on the speaker so Mac can hear at the same time." Oliver pushed the speaker button.

"Well, Oliver, I got your text from yesterday. I was out jogging this morning and went by the office to look at the file on Andre Pritchard that you had sent to my computer."

"What can you tell us?" Oliver asked.

"Well, the cause of death was probably uncertain," she said. "The doctor who signed off on the autopsy was Brian West. He had only been with us for about six months. He was let go shortly after this autopsy. Candidly, his work was shoddy. His gratuitous comment about cause of death probably being a heart attack had no basis given the enzymes were not typical for a myocardial infarction. He just made an assumption."

I asked, "Can you give us a better guess as to cause of death?"

"Sorry, Mac, but I really can't. Too much time has passed and the workup in the file is insufficient. Best I can say is that you should keep this one in the open category."

"It keeps Pritchard on our list of possible homicides," I said.

* * *

Then I got a call from Patrolman Andy Bauman. He said he had scoured the area south and west of the hit-and-run scene. He found three places with cameras and got their video footage for the hour preceding the death. He was bringing in the additional footage. I told him we would be at headquarters for at least a couple of hours.

I updated Oliver and said, "Tomorrow let's get Carter Enright's shop working on looking for white cars on Bauman's four videos. We also ought to have them compare the cars to the one that left Van Damm's office shortly after his death. Maybe we'll get a hit."

Oliver said, "I'm making a note to check with Virginia DMV in the morning to see what kind of cars Benedict and Bardak drive. We never know."

CHAPTER FIFTY-SEVEN

USING OUR STRATEGY to focus on the top dollar claims first, I was just about to start my research on Miguel Garcia, my remaining big dollar claim. His policy had been for $1 million.

At that moment, I saw Patrolman Andy Bauman walking down the aisle toward our desks. He was not in uniform.

"Tell us what you got," I said.

"I got video from three stores, two convenience places, and a service station. All three were cooperative. Each gave me a thumb drive with an hour's worth of video preceding the time of the hit-and-run on Tuesday morning. I haven't reviewed any of them."

"That's okay," I said. "We'll have the IT people look at them, plus the one you gave us yesterday. We really appreciate your follow-up. Chief Whittaker said he'd sign off on your overtime, if you need help."

"I should be fine," Andy said. "If I need help, I'll just drop his name. Thanks."

I handed the new videos to Oliver, who added them to the earlier one in his desk drawer. "I'll notify Carter Enright that we need someone to scan these for us, looking for a white car—and get them down to him in the morning."

* * *

I went back to researching Miguel Garcia. He was thirty-nine years old. My Google search came up with scads of hits as it was a fairly common name. I eliminated all but three as just being the same name but not our Miguel Garcia. The rest told me that he was a curator at the Smithsonian Museum of Natural History.

Then I searched the web page for the Museum of Natural History and found his biographical entry. He was the son of immigrants who migrated to California from Mexico City in the 1950s. His father had become a success in developing special effects for the movies. I gathered that the father was wealthy.

Miguel went to USC but studied history rather than filmmaking. After obtaining a master's degree in history, Miguel had landed a position at the Smithsonian. He had been there for the past fourteen years. He and his wife owned a row house not too far from mine in Northeast. The biography indicated that he had passed away unexpectedly at age thirty-nine.

I found nothing on him in NCIC. In MPD's system, I located a 911 call on March 4th from a gym in Northeast. It was called in at 7:14 a.m. An ambulance was dispatched, and he was taken to Howard University Medical Center and pronounced dead on arrival. He was then transferred to the M.E.'s office in Southwest D.C.

Hoping to catch her before she left her office, I called Courtney Vaughan's cellphone. She answered, "Mac Burke. Twice on a Sunday morning when I'm supposed to be off duty."

"Yeah, sorry about that, Doc. But I just came across another one that doesn't have much of an explanation."

"Well, Mac, if you had called sixty seconds later, I would have been back out jogging with my cell turned off. What have you got? I'm at my desk and can pull it up."

I said, "Name is Miguel Garcia. Died on March 4th."

I could hear her typing on her keyboard. She said, "Yes, I've got his autopsy file pulled up. Let's see what we've got. I didn't do this exam. It was done by Archie Peck, another assistant here at our shop. He does excellent work. Give me a second to review the report."

I waited and made some notes from my research. Dr. Vaughan came back on the line. "This is another one classified as 'uncertain.' Dr. Peck found him to be a healthy thirty-nine-year-old male. No sign of heart disease or other ailments.

"Tox screen showed meds to control cholesterol and a baby aspirin. No indication of illegal substance usage. Otherwise, very fit. Dr. Peck doesn't mention any of our mysterious pinpricks that we've been discussing recently. It could be that he missed it, if there was an injection site."

I asked, "Is he still in your cooler?"

"No," she replied, "he was released to his wife two days after arriving here. A note said that she planned to have him sent to California to be buried in a family plot." She gave me the wife's name and contact information. I thanked her and told her to enjoy her run.

*　*　*

I grabbed my coffee cup and asked Oliver if he wanted a refill. He handed me his cup. When I returned to my desk, I called Miguel Garcia's widow.

She answered, "This is Margie."

I said, "This is Detective McDermott Burke from the Metropolitan Police Department. I'm trying to reach Marguerite Garcia."

"That's me. I go by Margie. How can I help you?"

"Ma'am, first thing, my condolences about the loss of your husband last month."

She said, "Thank you. What is this about?"

"My partner and I are looking into several deaths with no real explanation or cause, and your husband's name has come up on our list. Do you have any idea of the cause of his death?"

"Wow. This is out of the clear blue. I'm still grieving over the loss of Mickey."

"Mickey?"

"Yeah. Miguel had gone by Mickey since grade school. We met in high school in Los Angeles and became high school sweethearts. Then we both went to USC and got married after he graduated the first time from college. What part of MPD are you with?"

"My partner and I are with the Homicide division."

She asked, "Are you saying Mickey was murdered?"

"We don't know for sure. We haven't come to any firm conclusions yet. We're just trying to see if there is a connection between several unexplained deaths."

"Okay. What do you need from me?"

"Again, do you have any feeling about what caused your husband's death?"

"No, I don't. Mickey worked out three times a week. He ran once or twice a week. Got annual checkups. Other than his cholesterol being a little high, he was very healthy."

"Did he have any enemies?"

"Hah. No way. Mickey was everyone's friend. Everybody liked him."

"We understand you had him sent to California for burial."

"Yes. Both our families are still in Los Angeles. We were the only ones who had ever moved away, mainly because of Mickey's job at the Smithsonian. His father is nearing retirement. Mine also. It just seemed appropriate to bury him in the family plot out there."

"May I ask what you do for a living?"

"I work at the Commerce Department on the census. I've been there about eight years."

"Interesting job in these times."

"No kidding."

"Did your husband have life insurance?"

"He had a couple small policies. Each about $100,000. When we were younger, he took out a million-dollar policy to protect me, but we agreed to sell it to get a down payment when we decided to buy a house."

"Okay. That pretty well covers it. Thanks for talking to me."

"If you find out there was foul play in Mickey's death, will you let me know?"

"Yes, ma'am, we certainly will. Thanks again."

CHAPTER FIFTY-EIGHT

OLIVER HAD MOVED ON to Perry Reinemann, who died on January 27th at age fifty-five. He had sold his $1,000,000 life insurance policy to Portland Fund Five.

Oliver's research disclosed that Reinemann was a dealer in high-end books and documents. His office was located in Georgetown. He also found an internet story about Reinemann's wife and two minor children being killed in a five-car pileup on the GW Parkway in 2019. Not long after that tragedy, he had sold his life insurance policy to Portland.

As the Fates would have it, Perry Reinemann was also killed in an automobile accident, although his was in West Virginia. He was traveling to Charleston, the state capital. The report said he was on his way to negotiate the acquisition of a private library of a prominent coal mine owner who had passed away months earlier.

The West Virginia State Police had concluded that it was a one-car accident on U.S. 60 west of Lewisburg where Reinemann had let his passenger-side wheels get onto the shoulder and then over-corrected to get back on the pavement. He then over-corrected again and went across the shoulder and off an unprotected embankment. Reinemann's car rolled two or three times until it settled after falling about thirty feet. The name of the investigating officer was given.

Oliver looked online for the West Virginia State Police main number. He identified himself and asked to be connected to Officer Nelly Bruce. He was transferred to the regional State Police office in Beckley.

When Oliver asked to speak to Nelly Bruce, he was told the officer was out on patrol. Oliver explained that he was a detective with the Metropolitan Police Department in Washington, D.C., and needed to talk to Officer Bruce about a fatal accident he investigated about two and a half months ago. "Please ask him to call me when he gets a chance," he requested and left his cellphone number. He then updated Mac on what he had found out about Perry Reinemann.

*   *   *

Oliver and I discussed whether we were ready to further update Chief Whittaker. "My thought," I said, "is that we wait until we see what Simone comes up with after looking at the bank records. Maybe she can develop a thread that finally ties these three together."

"Good point," Oliver agreed, at which point his cellphone rang. He answered, "Detective Oliver Shaw. I have you on speaker."

"Yes, sir. This is Officer Nelly Bruce with the West Virginia State Police. I was just getting off my lunch break when I got a call from my station to call you about an accident I investigated."

"Thanks for calling back. My partner and I are investigating a series of homicides over the past six months that seem to be connected. One of the people on our list is Perry Reinemann who died in a crash in West Virginia, which I believe you investigated."

"Yeah, I remember that one. About two months ago. As best I could tell, it was a one-car accident. Apparently lost control on a mountainous stretch of U.S. 60 near Lewisburg, went down an embankment, and rolled over."

Oliver asked, "Any witnesses?"

"Not at the time I did the investigation and wrote my report. Strange thing is I got a call about two days later from a local who claimed to see an older model F-150 seeming to try to recover control and get back in his lane not too far past where Mr. Reinemann went over the edge of the road. The caller didn't have enough details for me to do anything with that information. Hang on a sec. Let me fire up my in-car laptop and pull up my notes of that call."

There was a pause during which they heard some typing on a keyboard. Then Officer Bruce came back on the line. "Yeah, here it is. The caller was a guy named Leonard Tufts from Lewisburg." Then he read off the phone number for Tufts. "He was certain that the driver was a white male. He also said that the truck was a faded black Ford F-150 that looked like it had been ridden hard. Nothing else in my notes."

"Thanks for that additional information," Oliver said. "I'll follow up on it to see if it fits with our case. I'll let you know if we find a connection to what we're investigating."

After the call with the State Police Officer, Oliver dialed the number for Tufts.

"This is Lenny."

"This is Detective Oliver Shaw with the Metropolitan Police Department in Washington, D.C. Is this Mr. Leonard Tufts?"

"That's me, but I go by Lenny, not Leonard. Don't know what my parents were thinking giving me that name. What can I do for you?"

"Mr. Tufts, my partner and I are investigating a series of homicides. One of the possible names on our list is Perry Reinemann who ran off the road on Highway 60 near Lewisburg in late January. There were no witnesses to the accident according to the State Police Officer I just talked to. He gave me your name and said you may have seen something near the site of the accident."

"Yes, sir. I called the State Police after I read an article in the local paper. Apparently, the guy went off the road near where I saw that pickup trying to get back into his own lane, which was a good thing because he was coming at me in my lane. Acted kind of out of control."

"Do you remember anything about the driver?" Oliver asked.

"Like I told the State Officer, he was a white guy. I think he had sandy-colored hair, but that's all I remember about him."

"What about the truck? Any details on that?"

Tufts said, "It was an F-150. Looked to be about ten years old. Kind of beat up. Think it was originally black or some dark color."

Oliver said, "Since you were going in opposite directions, I don't suppose you caught anything about his license plate."

"Well, I looked in my outside mirror to make sure he got back in his lane. I saw that he had a plate that looked like a Virginia tag, but I couldn't swear to it."

"Did you see the accident where the car had run off the edge of the road?"

"Nope. Didn't realize there'd been an accident until I read about it in the paper."

Oliver thanked him and ended the call.

To Mac, he said, "I think we need to check vehicles on all three of them." He made another entry in his notebook.

CHAPTER FIFTY-NINE

SIMONE REESE CALLED Oliver to make sure they were still in the office. "Think I've got something for you," she said. "Just checking that you and Mac are still here. I'm coming up." Oliver told Mac that she was on her way upstairs.

"The bank records paid off," she said. "There's a pattern of payments coming in to Marian Benedict and Kurt Bardak shortly before and after the deaths." She gave them each a spreadsheet.

Insured	Date of Death	Morehead W'drawal	Benedict Deposit	Bardak Deposit	Morehead fr Portland
Dudley, Stuart	10/2	15,000 9/28		5,000 9/28 10,000 10/3	30,000 10/25
Ritzen, Conrad	10/30	15,000 10/25		5,000 10/27 9,500 11/3	60,000 11/21
Pritchard, Andre	12/28	8,000 12/24 14,000 12/27		5,000 12/27 10,000 12/30	75,000 1/25

Insured	Date of Death	Morehead W'drawal	Benedict Deposit	Bardak Deposit	Morehead fr Portland
Reinemann, Perry	1/27	7,000 1/20 15,000 1/26		5,000 1/22 9,000 1/29	60,000 2/17
Garcia, Miguel	3/4	15,000 2/28		5,000 3/1 10,000 3/6	60,000 3/25
Rollins, Eugene	4/3	30,000 3/30		5,000 3/30 8,500 4/5	30,000 (pending)
Van Damm, Weldon	4/3	" "	5,000 3/31 10,000 4/5		Not in Fund 5 or 6
Bonfiglio, Dominic	4/4	22,000 4/1	5,000 4/2 10,000 4/6		60,000 (pending)
Totals:		141,000	30,000	87,000	375,000

After taking a few minutes to review her chart, I said, "This shows a clear pattern between Morehead and the other two."

"I thought the same thing," Simone said.

Oliver added, "Now we need to establish that Benedict and Bardak were at the scene of each death attributed to them."

I had kind of an epiphany. I held up a finger and pulled up the MPD online directory and found the cellphone number for Pamela Chenire from the IT department. She answered on the first ring.

"Pamela," I said, "this is Mac Burke. Sorry to bother you on a Sunday afternoon, but I had an idea I wanted to run by you . . . Thanks. Let me put you on the speaker. I've got Oliver Shaw and Simone Reese here with me. We're still working on the same string of homicides as the last time we saw you. The list has grown to eight people that we think are connected."

"When we met," she said, "I thought it was just the one case. Van something."

"At that point it was, but it has grown as a result of one of the phone numbers you located for us. It came out of the number you found for the CEO of Portland Life Solutions.

"We've come up with three suspects. One we think is the person behind the whole thing. We have two others who we think probably committed the actual murders . . . Yeah, I know. Surprised us too."

Pamela Chenire said, "How can I help you?"

"First of all, is there a way to I.D. cellphone numbers that belong to our three people?"

"Probably," she said, "if they're using cells with a major service provider, rather than burners."

"Can you get specific cellphone numbers from the service providers?"

"Usually. They like to appear cooperative with the police."

"Can you also get a list of calls made and received for about the last six months?"

She said, "I can try. Depending on which providers they use, I'd say the odds are 50/50 that I can also get data back that far. Don't know for sure about going back six months, but certainly recent history."

"Okay," I said. "Now for the next question. You know how Google is always asking if they can use your location? I'm wondering if cellphones continuously monitor or store someone's geographical location."

"Actually, they do," Pamela said. "What I don't know is whether that geolocation information is stored and for how long. I'm also not certain whether it can be retrieved by the service providers. My best contacts are not in today, but I'll be able to reach them tomorrow."

I gave her the names and addresses for Morehead, Benedict, and Bardak. Then I decided to add the name of Parker Winston. I thanked her profusely.

Oliver looked at me. "What do you think we can get with that information?"

"Take Van Damm, for instance," I said. "We're very thin on evidence that Marian Benedict was at his office at the time of his murder. If her cellphone puts her there at the same time, our physical identification by the lady on the cleaning crew becomes backup rather than the primary evidence."

Oliver added, "If that works, we may get something putting Bardak at the scene of Perry Reinemann running off the embankment in West Virginia."

"Or," I said, "at the ballpark with Rollins. Or the park with Andre Pritchard."

"Or," Oliver added, "Benedict doing the hit-and-run on Bonfiglio."

"Is the case starting to come together?" Simone Reese asked.

"It feels like pieces are coming together," Oliver said.

CHAPTER SIXTY

OLIVER AND I DECIDED to call it a day and start early on Monday. I called Mags and told her I was headed home. She said that she was thinking about making spaghetti and asked if that sounded good. "Indeed," was my response. I told her I would be home in about thirty minutes.

When I got my Jeep tucked into the garage for the night, I went upstairs. Mags already had the sauce made and was dropping thin spaghetti noodles in the boiling water. After saying hello, she turned to run a wet hand over the crust of a loaf of Italian bread and laid it on the rack in the oven. "Dinner in about ten minutes," she announced.

"Perfect timing," I said.

Mags said, "I bought a bottle of Chianti. Why don't you open it up and pour us a starter?" When I handed her a glass of the wine, she said, "Grab the bread basket and saw up the loaf in the oven?" I carried the bread and wine bottle to the table while she was plating our spaghetti.

Following our usual pattern, we both dug in with nary another word being said. I cleaned my plate and went for seconds. She declined but poured herself some more wine.

When I got back to the table, Mags asked, "Is all your weekend work paying off?"

Of course, she asked her question while I had a mouth full of food, just like waiters do at restaurants. After I swallowed, I said, "It has been a very productive couple of days. We're focusing on Vincent Morehead as the conductor of this little orchestra."

I took a sip of wine and refilled my glass, as well as offering to top off hers. "We weren't sure how we were going to get a look inside their bank accounts but, lo and behold, our fairy godmother delivered us an anonymous envelope this morning with copies of six months of their bank statements. We turned those over to Simone Reese to compare to the dates of death we're looking at. And, voilà, she found that Morehead was paying his two helpers $5K right before and another $10K right after each of the murders."

Mags eyes went wide. "Wow."

I nodded. "Yeah."

She asked, "So, are you ready to arrest them?"

"We're close, but we need to tie up some threads. We're hopeful of pulling it together tomorrow. But we've got a new wrinkle."

Mags asked, "What's that?"

"There are three more people with large policies held by Funds Five and Six. I'm worried that they may be in danger until we get these three off the streets. We're meeting with the Fairfax County Police Chief tomorrow afternoon to discuss how to handle that problem. We'd be in a world of hurt if Morehead's crew killed one of them before we can get him and his helpers arrested."

"I can see that," Mags said.

"Tomorrow's going to be a big day," I said. "We might start rounding them up. I'm worried one or two of them might sense that we are getting close and run."

"How would they know?"

"We think the CEO of Portland has been talking to Morehead. We're not entirely sure why, but he told Morehead about Van Damm raising questions about all the death claims in those two funds. And, remember, those are the funds that Morehead has a big investment in. Something's off there, but I'm not sure what."

"So, who do you think is likely to run?" Mags asked.

"Mainly, Morehead. In digging deep in his bank account records, we found out that he has three offshore numbered accounts."

"What! How could you find that out?"

"Can't tell you. But we found out he has $1.5 million tucked away in accounts in Grand Cayman, the Bahamas, and the Isle of Wight."

Maggie's eyes went wide. "Where did that money come from?"

"Some of it is from the Portland death payoffs. But that doesn't account for it all. Based on our digging, it looks like he may have embezzled a bunch of money in Afghanistan while working for the CIA."

Her eyes got even wider when I mentioned the Agency, even though I had a suspicion that this was not totally new to her. *Leave it alone*, I said to myself.

She said, "So tomorrow may get tense."

"Yep. I think so. Got a feeling that Oliver and I will be earning our paychecks tomorrow."

Mags took her plate and glass to the sink. Knowing I would clean up, she said she was going to sleep in the guest room as she had to get up at zero-dark-thirty and head in to work. She gave me a nice kiss and headed upstairs.

I cleaned up the kitchen and loaded the dishwasher. I poured the last of the Chianti in my glass and went to watch the evening news.

CHAPTER SIXTY-ONE

ON MONDAY, Maggie was up and dressed for work by five thirty in the morning. She left without making coffee and got her Speedster out of the garage. The previous day, she had spotted a public parking garage about four blocks from where she had left the Taurus on Saturday.

She took a parking ticket from the machine to raise the mechanical arm, drove to the uppermost floor, and parked near the stairwell rather than the elevators.

Grabbing her shoulder bag, which still contained her Glock, Maggie walked down the stairs and headed toward the Taurus. When she got there, she retrieved the bag with the monitoring devices from the trunk.

She got to the CIA campus about six fifteen and pulled up to the south entry. Her security ID got her past the guard booth and into the parking garage beneath the New Headquarters Building. When she got to one of the three secondary security gates, Maggie waved her identification card in front of the smart reader, and the gate arm raised. She drove to the second level where she parked the Taurus in a slot that had a clear view of the three entry gates. Maggie scrunched down so that it appeared no one was in the car, although she could still see the gates. While

she waited, Maggie reviewed the pictures of the five vehicles she
was looking for.

*   *   *

Oliver and I had agreed to hit the office early on Monday morning. Mags had left home before I departed. When we got to headquarters, Oliver waited until he thought his contact at Virginia
DMV would be in and called. He asked for the vehicles registered
to Morehead, Benedict, and Bardak.

While he held the line, Oliver's contact gave him the list of vehicles and license plates. Benedict drove a two-year-old white Prius.
Bardak had both a red 2020 Camaro convertible and a gray
seven-year-old Ford F-150 pickup truck. He also had a black 2012
Harley-Davidson motorcycle model with a tapered tail fender, as
opposed to the usual curved rear fender. The DMV guy Oliver was
talking with was a Harley rider himself and pointed out that feature. Morehead had only one vehicle registered in his name: a silver 2016 Range Rover.

Oliver typed up a list of the vehicles and tag numbers. He then
went online and took screen shots of the same vehicles for use by
the IT department in reviewing the video footage we had acquired
over the weekend. He called Carter Enright, the head of the IT
department, and explained what we needed reviewed. We were
told to come on down to the third floor.

Enright met us in his conference room and introduced us to
Tony Walters, his video analyst. Oliver explained that we needed
a deeper look at the white car exiting from Van Damm's parking
garage, such as make and model. Possibly a better picture of the
driver.

He also told Walters that we needed to look at all white cars on the four thumb drives Patrolman Bauman had provided us on the Bonfiglio case, as well as the make of each of the white cars and any photo enhancements of the drivers. Finally, he told Walters that our prime suspect drives a white 2019 Prius. Just in case they were needed later, we also gave Tony Walters the photos of all vehicles owned by Benedict, Bardak, and Morehead. Walters gathered up the thumb drives and headed for his video lab. Oliver and I headed back to our desks.

*   *   *

I called Corporal Beverly Gray, Chief Whittaker's assistant, to arrange for a subpoena for the names and data on the living people whose life insurance policies were still held by Portland Funds Five and Six.

She got the information she needed for the subpoena and said she would get it served today. Then she said, "I was just about to call you. Chief Whittaker thinks it would be good to get together before going to meet with the Fairfax Police Chief this afternoon."

"When does he want to meet?"

"He's got an open half hour at ten this morning. That work?"

"We'll be there," I said.

CHAPTER SIXTY-TWO

WHILE SHE WAS watching the entry gates in the underground garage, Maggie activated all five trackers and downloaded the software on both her phone and laptop. She used a Sharpie to number the trackers one through five. Her plan was that number one would be Morehead. Number two would be Bardak's vehicle, whichever one he showed up in. Three would be Benedict's Prius.

Maggie knew that Morehead usually arrived early. His Range Rover pulled in the middle gate about seven fifteen on Monday morning. Because of his position in the Political Action Group, he had a designated parking space on Level One near the elevators.

The levels of an underground parking garage are numbered in reverse order of those seen in an above-ground garage. The first parking level is just below the two basement levels of the New Headquarters Building. Maggie was parked in an unassigned space on Level Two, the next level down. There are a total of six parking decks.

Maggie watched as Morehead parked and entered one of the elevators. She watched the numbers above the elevator and saw that it traveled past the two basement levels and then to the third floor above ground before stopping. She didn't hesitate. She grabbed tracker number one and got out of the Taurus. She hustled up the ramp to the first level and headed straight to the Range Rover. No one else was around and no cars were entering the garage. She knelt next to the rear passenger-side wheel well and attached the tracker to the metal just inside the fender.

She then took the stairs back to Level Two and returned to the Taurus. She checked her phone tracker app. Number one was flashing on the map of the D.C. metropolitan area, which she had downloaded as her background app. She verified that the app on her laptop was also showing tracker number one as flashing.

The parking garage started filling up in earnest about eight a.m. Still no sign of either Benedict's Prius or one of Bardak's vehicles. The second deck spaces where she was parked filled up first as they were unassigned. When cars parked on either side of the Taurus, Maggie pretended that she was talking on her cellphone so that the new drivers wouldn't think there was anything unusual about her sitting in her car. Once the second level filled up with cars, this ruse was no longer necessary.

About eight fifteen, she saw Benedict's Prius enter the left gate. Benedict drove past the Taurus moments later. Maggie lowered her window and listened to see if she could hear how far down Benedict had to go to find a parking space. Maggie thought it sounded like he parked on Level Three.

Maggie stayed put to wait until Kurt Bardak had entered and parked. She didn't want to be caught in the open. She maintained her focus on the gates.

About ten minutes later, a red Camaro convertible with the top up pulled up to the middle gate. Maggie could see the driver was Kurt Bardak. He drove past her and headed down to Level Three or Four based on the sound of his moderately loud exhaust pipes. Maggie thought it was a little touch of redneck.

She waited another ten minutes and then put trackers two and three in her jacket pocket and got out of the Taurus. She went down the stairs to the third level and looked around until she found the white Prius. She pulled the slip of paper from her pocket and checked the tag. Then she put tracker number three in the rear wheel well on the passenger side. She looked around Level Three but did not see the red Camaro.

Maggie headed back to the stairs and went down to Level Four. The Camaro was parked in a corner spot. Apparently trying to avoid door dings. Again, she checked the tag and attached tracker number two in the rear wheel well. She took the stairs back to the second level. She climbed in her rental car and checked her phone and laptop to make sure both of the new trackers were transmitting. She then locked her laptop and pistol in the trunk and headed upstairs. She would monitor the trackers on her cellphone.

CHAPTER SIXTY-THREE

PAMELA CHENIRE FROM our IT department came to our desks a short while later. She had located cellphone numbers for Marian Benedict and Kurt Bardak. She also found two registered cellphone numbers for Vincent Morehead, and another one for Parker Winston. She gave us a sheet with those numbers, which Oliver also jotted in his notebook.

She said, "I've only got part of what you asked for in terms of geolocation data. I was able to get ten days of geolocation on Benedict's and Bardak's phones." She gave us lists showing where those cellphones had been over the past ten days.

Benedict's cellphone was at Van Damm's office building on L Street NW from 8:15 to 9:20 p.m. on Monday when Weldon Van Damm died. Her phone then headed across the Potomac and returned to Benedict's condominium west of Arlington in Fairfax County.

Benedict's phone was also on 34th Street NW the next morning between 6:10 and 6:14 a.m. at the time of Dominic Bonfiglio's hit-and-run death. Her phone then crossed the Chain Bridge over the Potomac and followed Chain Bridge Road to the northwest. It eventually stopped at 1000 Colonial Farm Road in Langley where it remained for the rest of the workday.

I pulled up a street cross-reference app on my computer. That address was the headquarters for the Central Intelligence Agency. The specific location given appeared to be in the southernmost of two large buildings. A little more research told me that this structure was called the New Headquarters Building. Her phone went to the same location from roughly eight thirty to five on Wednesday through Friday.

I said, "Aha!"

Oliver looked up. "What?"

"I think we have finally established where Marian Benedict works. The CIA."

"No kidding?" Oliver asked. "What about Bardak?"

I looked at the geolocation data on Bardak's phone. It was at the Nationals ballpark on Monday evening, April 3rd. It was there from the start of the game until 7:43 p.m., which was shortly after Eugene Rollins died in the restroom. Bardak's phone then headed straight to his home in Falls Church. I told Oliver.

Then I checked Bardak's geolocation data during the workday for the entire week. On each day of the past week, Bardak's cellphone had been at the same address for the CIA's New Headquarters Building.

"Looks like Bardak works at the Agency also," I said.

"This is seriously helpful, Pamela," Oliver said. "It could tie these two people to three of our homicides."

Pamela Chenire blushed at the praise. Then she added, "Morehead's two phones apparently have the geolocation feature turned off. I got nothing on his. Winston's cell appears to travel back and forth between his home and office.

"The service providers on all five phones each gave me sixty days of call history, both in and out." She handed us printouts for each phone.

"Did you notice any calls between the different phones?" Oliver asked.

"Not yet. I brought this to you as soon as I got the information. I'll look over my copies and let you know what I find."

"Pamela," I asked, "do the service providers have more data on geolocation but are only willing to give out ten days?"

"That's what I'm guessing also," she said, "but I don't know for sure."

"You think it is the same situation with the call history?"

"I suspect so," she said. "Since I'm going to them without a subpoena, it's hard to press them for more. I don't want to wear out my welcome with my contacts. I'll call you if I find anything on calls between these phones." She headed back to her office.

Oliver referred to his notes. "You remember Simone telling us there was a British newspaper article about money disappearing in Afghanistan in 2016? And that Vincent Morehead's name was connected to the program, and the CIA apparently recalled everyone on the program to the States? I wonder if he works there also."

"So maybe the three of them work together?"

CHAPTER SIXTY-FOUR

OLIVER HAD BEEN working on the last of his big dollar policies: Conrad Ritzen, who had sold a $1,000,000 policy to Fund Six. He had died on October 30th at age fifty-one.

The research on Ritzen revealed that he was the Legislative Aide to Senator Alva Reckler of South Dakota. He had formerly been a State Representative in the South Dakota Legislature before becoming an aide to Senator Reckler thirteen years earlier. He was married with four school-age children.

The news account that Oliver located said that Ritzen had been robbed and severely beaten in the Senate underground garage on the day before Halloween. The incident fell within the jurisdiction of the Capitol Police.

Oliver called the main office for the Capitol Police, which is located near Union Station, and asked for assistance with the file on Ritzen's case. He was transferred to Sgt. Mary O'Brien.

When she answered, Oliver introduced himself. "Sgt. O'Brien, my partner and I are investigating a series of apparently related homicides over the past six months. One of the names on our list is Conrad Ritzen, who was an L.A. to Senator Reckler. According to what I've read so far, he was mugged in the Senate underground garage the day before Halloween."

"I remember that case very clearly," Sgt. O'Brien said. "He died a couple days after the beating. One of my officers did the investigation and reported to me."

"What was the investigating officer's name?"

"William Jefferson. We never came up with a motive or a suspect. We also couldn't find any closed-circuit videos of anyone with Mr. Ritzen. The case is still technically open, but we have no progress at this point."

"Sgt. O'Brien, do you have a file you could email to me?"

She got his email address and cell number and agreed to send him the file. He got her phone number also and told her he'd follow up after reviewing the file. Oliver then brought me up to speed on what he had learned about Conrad Ritzen.

*   *   *

It was about a quarter to ten when Pamela Chenire came up to see us again. "I've got some matches for you. Morehead called Bardak on March 2nd, March 30th, and April 6th. Morehead also called Benedict on March 30th, April 2nd, and twice on April 5th. Nothing before early March as we only got sixty days of call records. Could be more calls before that. No calls during February. No calls between Benedict and Bardak. All of the calls went from Morehead to Bardak and Benedict, not the other way around."

I asked, "What about Winston's phone?"

"Winston called Morehead on Tuesday, April 4th. Very brief call. Probably left a voicemail. Morehead called Winston on the same day for just under five minutes. Winston also called Morehead on the afternoon of this past Friday, April 7th. Again, a very short call, probably another voicemail message. Morehead called him back less than an hour later on that same day, and they talked for eight minutes." Oliver had taken detailed notes on these calls between Morehead and Winston.

"That last call," I said, "from Winston to Morehead, was not long after we left Winston's office at Portland."

Oliver flipped through his notebook. "He told us that he had called Morehead after hearing of Van Damm's death. Wonder if he told Morehead that the D.C. police were sniffing around Funds Five and Six."

We thanked Pamela and told her we had to go to a meeting upstairs in a few minutes, which she knew meant that we were meeting with Chief Whittaker. She smiled at each of us in turn.

CHAPTER SIXTY-FIVE

WE GOT TO Chief Whittaker's office on the fifth floor a few minutes early. Beverly Gray confirmed that she had sent a subpoena to Portland Life Solutions for a list of living people whose life insurance policies were currently held by Funds Five and Six. Then she knocked on the Chief's door and opened it. "Detectives Burke and Shaw are here to see you, Chief."

"Chief," we both said as we entered.

He pointed us to the chairs in front of his desk.

I took the lead. "Chief, a lot has happened since we last talked. First, we got the cellphone numbers for Benedict, Bardak, and Morehead. We also got the cellphone number for Parker Winston, the head of Portland Life Solutions. Pamela Chenire in IT got those for us."

"She's always been very good at digging out telephone data," the Chief said.

"Wait," I said. "It gets better. She got us geolocation data on the cellphones of Benedict and Bardak for the past ten days."

The Chief's eyebrows went up. "You can do that? What did that show?"

"Yep. Cellphones are apparently constantly tracking your whereabouts, unless you turn off your location feature, which

Morehead must have done on his two phones, as we got no location data on him."

"Huh. What did the locator show us about Benedict and Bardak?" the Chief asked.

"Like I said, Pamela only got ten days of location data, but that showed us some critical information. Benedict was at Van Damm's office last Monday evening when he was killed. She was also on 34th Street NW next to the National Cathedral at the same time on Tuesday morning when Dominic Bonfiglio was killed in a hit-and-run.

"You'll recall that the investigating patrolman, Andy Bauman, had one witness at the next corner who saw a car hurrying away from the scene. The witness said it was a white car with a blonde woman driving. Likely an electric car. Bauman went out yesterday and got three more videos from stores leading up to the hit-and-run site. We've got Tony Walters in the IT shop doing a deep dive on those videos, as well as a further look at the white car leaving Van Damm's parking garage shortly after he was injected."

"We also got the Virginia DMV to give us the vehicles owned by Benedict, Bardak, and Morehead," Oliver said. "Turns out Benedict drives a white Prius. Also, she's blonde."

I resumed. "Per her locator, she drove straight home to her condo near Arlington after Van Damm was killed. After the Bonfiglio hit-and-run the next morning, her phone tracked across the Potomac to the New Headquarters Building at the CIA."

"CIA?" Chief Whittaker's eyebrows crept halfway up his forehead.

"Yes. It stayed there all day on Tuesday. It was at the same building all day on Wednesday through Friday."

"What about Bardak?" the Chief asked.

"His phone shows he was at the Nationals ballpark Monday evening when Eugene Rollins was murdered in the restroom," I said. "Remember, we have multiple pictures of Bardak in the same part of the ballpark. His phone shows he left the game shortly after Rollins went down in the restroom. He then went home. He lives in Falls Church.

"His geolocation data also showed that he was at the same CIA building all day on Monday through Friday, which is a pretty good indicator that he works there also."

The Chief leaned back in his chair and locked his hands behind his head. "With the photographs, witnesses, and phone locators, are we getting close to arrests?"

"Wait. There's more," I said. "We still have to tie Benedict and Bardak to Morehead, who is the one with the clear financial motive. Remember the bank accounts that we had numbers for? Well, yesterday Oliver received an envelope by delivery containing six months of bank statements on all three accounts: Benedict, Bardak, and Morehead, including current activity since the last monthly statements."

The Chief asked, "Where did that come from?"

Oliver said, "A cab driver delivered it to the front desk yesterday morning. The sergeant on the desk got the cabbie's name and contact info. I called him right away. He said a kid on a skateboard gave it to him while he was in the queue at the D.C. courthouse down the street. No other idea who sent it. We handled it carefully and kept the originals in a sealed baggie."

"What did that tell us?" The Chief looked perplexed.

"We called Simone Reese, who was working yesterday on some other leads for us. She took the bank statements and put together a chart showing money flowing between Morehead and both

Bardak and Benedict. We had her match those transfers to our suspected homicides." I handed the Chief a copy of Simone's spreadsheet.

He read over the figures slowly, all the while pressing his lips forward as he absorbed each set of figures. He must have spent close to five minutes before he said anything. "First of all, there are eight names on this list. Where did they all come from?"

Oliver replied, "We kept looking into our list of deaths of people who had sold their life insurance policies to Portland Funds Five and Six. Other than Weldon Van Damm, all of those names came from that list and had causes of death that were suspicious or uncertain. When tied to these bank records, it appears Morehead paid $5,000 before their deaths and another $10,000 after. We think that is our link between the three of them and the deaths."

The Chief said, "I know I've said it before, but you guys are really good."

I held up a finger.

The Chief said, "I know. Wait. There's more. What now?"

"Morehead's account shows a current balance of only $16,000. We thought that looked off. We had another C.I. of ours look at the bank statements. He smelled something was off and did some digging. Turns out Morehead has three offshore numbered accounts where he hides his money. He has around $1,500,000 combined in numbered accounts in Grand Cayman, the Bahamas, and the Isle of Wight. Not bad for a GS-15."

Oliver added, "Plus, in 2016, he made a down payment of $150,000 on his house and invested $1,000,000 in Portland Funds Five and Six in 2016 and 2017."

The Chief shook his head. "Where'd the money come from?"

"Simone Reese did some internet digging," Oliver replied, "and the only thing she could find was that Morehead's name came up in a British newspaper article about $3,000,000 going missing from a refugee relocation program in Afghanistan in 2016. At the time, it was thought to be corruption by the Afghanis. Nothing else appeared about the missing money. It was a CIA program, and a Vincent Morehead was running the operation, who we believe is the same person we are looking at. The program was shut down, and all CIA personnel were recalled to the States."

Still shaking his head, the Chief said, "This gets stranger and stranger."

"No shit," I said. The Chief suppressed a chuckle.

Oliver said, "Pamela Chenire thinks the cellphone companies probably have more geolocation information than they gave us. We only got ten days' worth. She didn't want to press without a subpoena. Also, she only got sixty days' worth of calls on those phones. I think we should subpoena six or seven months of everything, both calls and geolocational data."

Chief Whittaker said, "I totally agree. Get with Corporal Gray and Pamela as soon as you leave here to find the quickest way to get that information from the cellphone companies."

"Got it," Oliver said. "That might give us more links that tie Benedict and Bardak to some of these other murders. For instance, Perry Reinemann went off the edge of a road in West Virginia. One witness saw an older dark F-150 shortly after that trying to get back in his lane not far from the scene of where Reinemann went over the edge. Virginia DMV says Bardak has an older gray F-150. Geolocation data may put him at the scene.

"Also, geolocation may help us nail Bardak on Andre Pritchard's death in Glover Archibald Park in late December when he was walking home from his hotel. We've also asked IT to look at the D.C.'s closed-circuit cameras around the park.

"And we've got Conrad Ritzen being mugged and killed in the Senate underground garage around Halloween.

The Chief had been following down Simone's list and must have seen all those related to money that had been paid to Bardak. He asked, "What about Miguel Garcia?"

"Died," I said, "with no obvious cause at the gym where he worked out here in the District. Geolocator info will likely put Bardak there also."

"And tell me again who Stuart Dudley was?" the Chief asked.

Oliver said, "The doctor who died in the bar at a ski lodge in New Hampshire. His girlfriend picked Bardak out of a photo six-pack as the guy talking to Dudley when she went to the restroom. He was dying when she came back."

The Chief took a pause. "Okay, let's talk about what we need to cover with the Fairfax Police Chief this afternoon."

"Originally," I said, "we were going to focus on the three people we think might be most at risk. These are people who sold their life insurance to Funds Five and Six. Two live in Northern Virginia and one in Northwest.

"In light of what we now have discovered about Benedict and Bardak, I think we need to broaden the discussion. We need to see Benedict's Prius to look for damage from the hit-and-run on Bonfiglio. We also need to look at Bardak's F-150 for signs he forced Perry Reinemann off the road in West Virginia.

"Also, I suspect that the weakest link among them is Benedict. Just a gut feeling. She's the least involved. We need to think about arresting her quietly and getting her to D.C. to put the pressure on her to see if she'll flip on Morehead."

"What about the three living people you're worried about?" the Chief asked.

"I think that's open for discussion at the meeting."

The Chief's face puckered. "No one's going to like that subject."

"Agreed," both Oliver and I said at the same time.

The Chief said, "I'm thinking we should arrest both of them. At the same time, I'm worried that those three people might still be at immediate risk. What if Morehead has someone else working for him?"

"That's why we need to discuss this with the Fairfax Police Chief. Something may be afoot already that we don't know about."

The Chief looked at me. "Mac, I agree with you. I'll get my driver to bring a Suburban around at one o'clock so that we can get to Fairfax in plenty of time. Meet me in the parking lot."

We left to meet with Beverly Gray and Pamela Chenire about subpoenas for the cellphone service providers. We urged them to get us the information as fast as possible.

CHAPTER SIXTY-SIX

AFTER MEETING WITH Chief Whittaker, Oliver and I discussed what information we needed to prepare for our meeting with the Fairfax County Police Department. We thought Simone's spreadsheet would provide a quick overview.

Then we prepared background sheets on Marian Benedict and Kurt Bardak. Each fact sheet included an enlarged color copy of their driver's licenses, their home addresses, their vehicles and license tags, online photos of similar vehicles, and their cellphone numbers. We also added a note that geolocation data from their cellphones led us to believe that both Benedict and Bardak worked at the Central Intelligence Agency and likely used the south entrance to the campus and parked in the underground garage below the New Headquarters Building.

Next, we got a copy of Vincent Morehead's license from the Virginia DMV. We prepared an information sheet on him as well, including his vehicle, license plate, home address, and his two cellphone numbers. We added our suspicion that he also worked at the CIA.

We then put together background sheets on the three people who we thought were still most at risk after selling their life insurance policies to Portland Funds Five and Six: Joshua Levine,

Bradley Ford, and Mildred Bronson. We got copies of driver's licenses from the Virginia DMV for Levine and Bronson. We also got a copy of Bradley Ford's driver's license from the D.C. DMV, as he lived in the District.

Each of these background sheets on Levine, Ford, and Bronson included the information we had gleaned from our research on their occupations, employers, home and work addresses, and family status. That information also included an enlarged copy of each person's driver's license photo.

* * *

Just as we were finishing assembling the information sheets for the Fairfax Police, I received a call from Parker Winston. He was clearly irritated and asked, "What is this new subpoena? What are you trying to do to my business?"

I put his call on the speaker, so Oliver could hear the conversation as well. "Mr. Winston, we are continuing our investigation."

He countered, "Why do you need the names on the policies held by Funds Five and Six? And why just those two funds?"

"As we discussed at your office on Friday, we are exploring whether there is a connection between some of the deaths that have occurred recently."

"Are you trying to ruin my business? If this gets out, not only will my company potentially be ruined by bad publicity, but the entire industry could be jeopardized."

"As we agreed in your office, we are keeping everything confidential. Nothing is going to get leaked from us. Have you told anyone that we are looking at the deaths in Funds Five and Six?"

He paused and almost stuttered. "No, of course not! Who would I tell? And why would I do such a thing?"

"Well," I said, "we certainly hope you keep it confidential as well. If you disclosed anything about our investigation, that could be considered obstruction of justice."

Winston almost gasped. "What? Are you accusing me of something?" He was huffing on the other end of the line.

"No, sir. But you definitely need to keep this under your hat. Otherwise, you could be jeopardizing our investigation."

Winston retreated somewhat. "Of course. I wouldn't do that. We want to cooperate fully with your investigation."

"Good. That's what we appreciate. This case is time sensitive. Please email me the information we requested as soon as we hang up. Will you do that? My email address is on my card."

"Yes. Of course. I'll take care of it right now."

"Thank you, Mr. Winston. We appreciate your cooperation." I paused. "By the way, if these deaths prove to be connected, do you have any idea who might be behind them? Or who would benefit from them the most?"

"No. Of course not," Winston said. "If I had such an idea, I would have told you on Friday."

"Thank you for your cooperation," I said. And hung up.

"There's one scared puppy," Oliver said. "Probably had to go change his underwear."

"Yeah. And he lied to us just now by saying he didn't tell anyone that we were looking at Funds Five and Six."

"Uh-huh. What else was his call to Morehead about on Friday after we left Portland's office?" Oliver said. "I think he suspects Morehead and was trying to warn him off."

"Let's hope that keeps Morehead away from going after our three anticipated targets."

* * *

Parker Winston paced around his office with the door closed. He felt like his world was closing in on him. He didn't know what to do.

Winston called Morehead's cell number and left a short voice-mail. "Call me. Got another subpoena."

Morehead did not check his voicemail messages until about two hours later.

CHAPTER SIXTY-SEVEN

My phone rang again about fifteen seconds later. I saw it was an internal call. I answered, "Detective Mac Burke."

"Hey, Detective. Tony Walters in IT. Think I've got something for you. Can you come down to my video lab?"

"Definitely. We'll be right there." Oliver and I headed down the stairs to the third floor.

Walters had apparently notified his boss that we were coming down. Carter Enright met us at the door and led us to Walters' lab. I asked, "What've you got for us, Tony?"

"It definitely saved time that you told me your suspect drives a white Prius. First, let's look at the video from the exit of the parking garage on L Street NW." He fired up the video. "I've slowed the video down and enhanced the resolution. First of all, as I expand the picture you can clearly see it is a white Prius. Second, I was also able to enhance the brief photo of the driver." He showed us on the screen and handed each of us a printout of the picture. It was a fairly clear profile shot of Marian Benedict.

"That's her, all right," Oliver said. "Good job."

Walters said, "Let's move on to the video the patrolman obtained that was taken on Macomb Street shortly after the hit-and-run on 34th Street. I think I've got the car again." He put in the thumb drive that Patrolman Andy Bauman had obtained on Tuesday. He fast-forwarded the video and then paused at a specific point on the time clock at the bottom. It was a photo of a white Prius passing in front of Kim John's convenience store approximately two minutes after Bonfiglio had been run over on 34th Street. He again gave us printouts of the screen grab, which also showed the time imprint.

Walters added, "I couldn't see the driver or license tag on this video. But I got lucky on one of the three thumb drives from the stores leading up to the hit-and-run scene." He pulled the prior video and inserted one of the other memory sticks Bauman had gotten. He again fast-forwarded to a precise spot on the time clock and paused the picture. It had an almost frontal picture of a white Prius. Walters moved the cursor deeper into the shot and refocused the picture on the license tag.

"Does that help?" Walters asked.

Oliver pulled out his notebook and flipped through several pages. Then he started comparing his notes to the screen. Oliver said, "That's Benedict's tag. Great work, Tony." Walters again printed us copies of the screen grab.

"One last thing for you," Walters said. He moved the cursor up to the windshield and refocused on the driver. Clear as if she were posing for a professional photograph, there sat Marian Benedict. Walters said, "It's such a clear shot because she's driving east toward the sunrise." Again, he printed copies for us.

Oliver sent Walters a photo of Kurt Bardak. "One of our other cases involves a suspected murder in Glover Archibald Park in Northwest. Victim was Andre Pritchard. He was murdered around 8:15 or 8:30 p.m. on December 28th." Walters was jotting some notes on the details.

Oliver continued, "We have bank records that we believe tie Kurt Bardak to Pritchard's murder in that park. Can you check

D.C.'s closed-circuit cameras before and after that time frame to see if you can put Bardak in or near the park?"

Oliver held up a finger. "Hold on. I've got a list of his three vehicles and tags. A Camaro convertible, an F-150 pickup, and a Harley." Oliver texted him a photo of the motorcycle.

We thanked both Walters and Enright and headed back to the fourth floor. Oliver said, "I'm thinking we should pick her up today. We have enough on her."

CHAPTER SIXTY-EIGHT

OLIVER AND I WERE waiting beside Chief Whittaker's black Suburban when he came out the side door of the headquarters building. He waved us to the back seat while he climbed in the front. After we were all in, the Chief turned to us and said, "Detectives Mac Burke and Oliver Shaw, this is Sgt. John Stilton," looking at his driver.

We both nodded at Sgt. Stilton. I said, "Hey." He gave me a small nod.

Chief Whittaker told Stilton, "Sergeant, we're headed to headquarters of the Fairfax County Police Department."

"Yes, sir. On our way."

As we drove, I told the Chief that we had more on Marian Benedict. "Tony Walters in IT verified that the car leaving Van Damm's office garage was a white Prius, same as the car she owns. He also enhanced the picture of the driver, and it is a clear profile shot of Benedict.

"Walters also looked at the convenience store videos Patrolman Bauman got us on the Bonfiglio hit-and-run. Again, he nailed her car both before and after the hit-and-run, including a shot of her license plate and a clear frontal photo of her driving."

"Why aren't we moving forward with an arrest warrant on her?" the Chief asked,

"Oliver and I had the same conversation after talking with Tony Walters," I said. "Also, I think we need to impound her car to look for evidence of the hit-and-run on Bonfiglio."

The Chief nodded. "After we talk to Leon Handley, let's get an arrest warrant cranked and an impound warrant, as well. Then after she gets home from work, we can get the Fairfax Police to assist with the arrest and delivery of her to our holding cells at headquarters. We can also arrange covering and towing of her car to our impound lot for analysis."

"We should keep it very quiet," I said. "Don't let her make any calls for a while. We need to roll up Bardak and Morehead before they get any kind of warning and try to split."

"Agreed," the Chief replied. He told me to call Beverly Gray and get the Benedict warrants signed by a judge and delivered to us by email while we were with the Fairfax County Police Chief, as well as arranging the impoundment of her car. I was on the phone with Corporal Gray for about ten minutes to give her all of the information she needed.

CHAPTER SIXTY-NINE

We got to the city of Fairfax and rolled up to the visitor parking in front of the headquarters building for the Fairfax County Police Department. The building was of newer construction with large windows separated by sandstone. The sign out front said it was the Fairfax County Public Safety Department. The parking lot had a number of navy-blue cruisers and SUVs with white lettering and tops. Their vehicles appeared to be almost new. The Fairfax County Police Department appeared to be better funded than ours.

Sgt. Stilton stayed with the vehicle. The rest of us went to the front desk and showed our credentials. Chief Whittaker said we had an appointment with Chief Handley. The desk sergeant called up and told us someone would be down shortly to take us up.

A forty-something lady with short black hair wearing a black skirt and starched white blouse exited one of the elevators and approached us. She walked up to Chief Whittaker and extended her hand. "I'm Britney Taylor, Chief Handley's administrative assistant. I assume you are Chief Inspector Whittaker?"

The Chief shook her hand. "Yes, I'm George Whittaker." He turned toward us. "These gentlemen are Detectives McDermott Burke and Oliver Shaw." We both shook hands with Ms. Taylor.

She said, "Please come with me." We rode an elevator to the fifth floor, where she escorted us to Chief Handley's corner office. "Chief Inspector Whittaker and Detectives Burke and Shaw are here for your meeting."

Chief Handley came around his desk with a big smile on his face. He was slender man, a little over six feet tall with gray hair at the temples. He wore a sharp-looking navy-blue uniform with the traditional four stars on both sides of his collar and a brass name tag above his right shirt pocket.

Handley gave Chief Whittaker a hearty handshake. "George. It's been way too long." His voice was sonorous with a touch of Southern accent reflecting his upbringing in the Commonwealth of Virginia. "I see you haven't been able to find honest work, either." He gave a deep chuckle.

George Whittaker smiled back as well. "Looks to me like you made the right move, getting out of MPD and moving on up. These are impressive quarters. And I noticed that your vehicles outside are all much newer than anything we have."

Handley said, "Comes with being in a county with a high per capita income level."

Whittaker nodded once. "Let me introduce you to my two best detectives. This fellow is McDermott Burke, commonly known as Mac. His better-looking partner is Oliver Shaw, commonly known as Oliver. They have been detectives with MPD for about fifteen years and each spent around ten years before that as special agents with Air Force OSI and Army CID."

Handley shook our hands and welcomed us. His voice was almost magical. It made me feel like greeting an old friend. Chief Handley turned to the other person in his office. "This is Woodrow Thomas, our Chief of Detectives. Woody is the best we have."

Thomas was dressed in a well-tailored suit in a light-gray summer weight fabric. Oliver and I both shook Thomas' hand as well.

Chief Handley motioned us to a buffet next to his glass-topped conference table. "Let's get some coffee and see what we can do to help you." We each got a cup of coffee and sat down. I noticed that Handley and Thomas sat on one side of the twelve-seat rectangular table. We took the opposite side with Chief Whittaker in the middle.

Handley turned to Woody Thomas and said, "Chief Whittaker and I went to the MPD academy at the same time in the late 1990s, so we've known each other for over twenty years. He's as upright an individual as you'll ever meet in law enforcement."

Chief Whittaker nodded in acknowledgement of the compliment. Handley held an open palm to Whittaker to give him the floor. There it was again, the open hand gesture that I had apparently learned from Whittaker. Maybe they taught it at the Police Academy back in the good old days.

Whittaker took the cue. "I'll summarize our situation and then let Mac and Oliver give you the details. Our case started one week ago today with the apparent murder of Weldon Van Damm, the managing partner of a medium-sized law firm in Northwest D.C. I put Mac and Oliver on the case when we got the call the next morning. Van Damm had been murdered on Monday evening, but his body was not discovered until the next morning when his secretary found him in his office. The medical examiner thinks he was injected with a chemical that quickly shuts down your breathing and can kill in a couple of minutes but dissipates quickly, leaving no traces. There were no witnesses and no obvious suspects.

"Mac and Oliver quickly eliminated some possible suspects but discovered that Van Damm had set up a corporation called

Portland Life Solutions, which buys up life insurance policies. You've probably seen the television commercials for similar companies.

"In the course of the investigation, they also found that Van Damm was heavily invested in Portland's funds used to raise the money to buy the life insurance policies. There were twelve of these funds.

"Each fund paid the investors half of the life insurance proceeds when the insured person died. Van Damm had 15 percent of all twelve funds. One of our key suspects, Vincent Morehead, owned 12 percent in Portland Funds Five and Six.

"Van Damm monitored the performance of these funds closely because he was so heavily invested. He noticed that Funds Five and Six had a sudden spike in collected life insurance proceeds over the past six months and talked to the head of Portland about it a couple of times. Van Damm sensed that something was wrong. Those two funds were collecting two or three times as much as the other ten funds.

"Van Damm was murdered shortly after the CEO of Portland had told Morehead that Van Damm was raising questions about the spike in death claims in Funds Five and Six. Remember, those were the only funds that Morehead was invested in.

"Mac and Oliver turned up a video of a white car exiting the office's underground garage shortly after Van Damm's murder. The video also yielded a profile shot of a blonde female driving the car. We tried facial recognition software but did not get a hit, but later got a tip to check the Virginia DMV and identified her as Marian Benedict. By using geolocation tracking on her cellphone, we have established that she apparently works at the CIA in the south building."

At this point, I was amazed at Chief Whittaker's recall from our briefings, as well as his omitting reference to our source on facial recognition. I thought Oliver probably had the same feeling.

Chief Whittaker continued, "The M.E. alerted Mac and Oliver to another death that appeared to also be an injection of that same chemical at a Nationals baseball game last Monday evening. Same day as Van Damm's death. That guy's name was . . ." He turned to Oliver, who said, "Eugene Rollins."

"Yeah," the Chief continued, "Rollins. We got several screen grabs from the ballpark's closed-circuit system showing a guy who left the restroom where Rollins was apparently injected. Again, no hit on facial recognition. But the same tip led us to identify him through Virginia DMV. His name is Kurt Bardak. Using cell-phone geolocation data, we have established that he works at the CIA also. In the same building as Marian Benedict.

"We found out that Rollins had sold his life insurance policy to Portland. We later found out it was either Fund Five or Six that bought the policy.

"Mac and Oliver then found out about a hit-and-run homicide near the National Cathedral on Tuesday morning, the day after the murders of Van Damm and Rollins. It was a jogger named . . ."

Oliver supplied, "Bonfiglio."

The Chief nodded. "We later found out that Bonfiglio had also sold his life insurance policy to Portland. Mac and Oliver then subpoenaed Portland's records on their death claims over the past six months. And Bonfiglio's name was on the list for either Fund Five or Six, so they checked closer on the hit-and-run.

"The investigating patrolman had a witness who saw a Caucasian blonde woman driving a white electric car seconds after the impact and tracked down convenience store videos that showed the white car and driver. It was the same woman from the Van Damm scene: Marian Benedict."

Whittaker had his audience in rapt attention. He could tell the story well. He said, "I've been talking enough. I'll let Mac take it from there." Chief Handley and Thomas turned to me.

I cleared my throat. "What we couldn't figure out was a motive for Benedict and Bardak to commit the three murders, although there was a common thread with the Portland Funds. So, our financial analyst got us the names of the investors in all of the Portland Funds from SEC filings. Particularly on Funds Five and Six.

"In addition to institutional investors, there were three individual investors in Funds Five and Six: Van Damm had 15 percent, Vincent Morehead had 12 percent, and Parker Winston had 10 percent. Winston is the CEO of Portland. Van Damm and Winston were in all twelve funds. Morehead was only in Funds Five and Six. Morehead was the person with a large financial motive, so we focused on him.

"Our financial analyst had a confidential informant who got us bank account numbers for Benedict, Bardak, and Morehead. A day later, we received an anonymous envelope with the last six months of bank statements for those accounts.

"By this time, Oliver and I had been digging on the other deaths coming out of Funds Five and Six. Some we eliminated as natural causes. Then we made a list of deaths that were suspicious or where the M.E. couldn't determine the cause. We gave that list to our financial analyst along with the bank statements and asked her to see if there was a pattern tying Morehead to Benedict and Bardak."

Oliver distributed copies of Simone Reese's chart to everyone. "As you can see," he said, "it appears that Morehead paid Benedict and Bardak $5,000 up front and another $10,000 after each murder. Altogether, it looks like these three have committed eight murders over the past six months. Three in the last week."

Oliver added, "We also have geolocation data on Benedict's and Bardak's cellphones. That shows Benedict at Van Damm's office last Monday evening and at the scene of the Bonfiglio hit-and-run on Tuesday morning. The geolocation data on Bardak's phone shows he was at the Nationals game last Monday evening and left just after Rollins went down."

I resumed the narrative. "We feel that we have sufficient cause to arrest all three of them. In fact, we're having a court-ordered arrest warrant issued this afternoon for Benedict. We're hoping to grab her after work today and also impound her car, which we're certain was used in the hit-and-run death of Bonfiglio.

"That's the first place where we'll need assistance from the Fairfax County Police Department. Benedict lives in a high-rise condo just west of Arlington, but inside the Fairfax County limits. We are hopeful that we can flip her on Morehead to strengthen our case on him."

CHAPTER SEVENTY

I TOOK A BREATH and continued. "The second place we could use help is with three people we think are in danger of being murdered. We subpoenaed the names of the still-living people who sold their life insurance policies to Funds Five and Six. There are three with large policies. Two live in Fairfax County, and one is in Northwest D.C. Other than our paranoia, we don't know for sure that Morehead and his helpers will be going after them, but certainly don't want someone else murdered on the eve of arresting these three.

"The two in Fairfax County are Joshua Levine, who lives in Vienna and works in McLean, and Mildred Bronson, who lives in Fairfax and works at the law school at George Mason University in Arlington." Oliver passed them the information sheets on Levine and Bronson. "As you can see," I said, "they are insured for $1,000,000 and $500,000, respectively.

"The third one is Bradley Ford, who lives in Northwest D.C. and works for a lobbying firm on Connecticut Avenue. He also sold Portland a $1,000,000 policy." Oliver distributed the fact sheet on Ford.

Chief Handley asked, "Have you notified these three about the danger?"

"We have debated that very question," Chief Whittaker said. "We figured they would go berserk and feel we are using them as bait. We also figured they would scream at Portland, and we already have Portland's CEO all over us about potentially ruining his business with bad press if anything leaks out."

"But if one of them gets killed and they weren't notified that you were concerned," Chief Handley said, "it will blow up really big-time."

"We came to the same conclusion. A no-win situation," Whittaker said.

"Amen," agreed Handley.

"If we get Benedict off the street this afternoon," I said, "that helps narrow the risk. We might need to monitor Bardak. He seems to be the one who has probably committed six of the murders. He may be Morehead's main 'go-to' guy. But there's another wrinkle."

"What?" asked Woody Thomas.

"As Chief Whittaker mentioned, we are pretty sure that both Benedict and Bardak work at the CIA. Probably Morehead also." Oliver passed them the information sheets on all three of them. "If we're right, they all probably have sophisticated training in surveillance detection. We certainly can't try to put a tail on them coming out of the New Headquarters Building at the CIA."

"Jeez," Chief Handley said. "Don't you have enough to pick up Bardak as well? Take him off the table also? That would seem to lower the risk to the three people who are potentially in danger."

"Leon," Chief Whittaker said, "I'm coming to the same conclusion. He's also more of a flight risk than Benedict, I would think, because he is so heavily involved. I think we need a warrant on Bardak as well."

"If they all work together at the Agency," I asked, "won't Morehead quickly get wind of something going down? He's the biggest flight risk of all. We know he has $1,500,000 in numbered offshore accounts."

Woody Thomas looked surprised. "How were you able to find that out?"

"Through a very trusted confidential informant," I said.

"Wow," Thomas replied.

Chief Whittaker said, "It seems clear that we need to scoop them all up at once. Obviously, the CIA isn't going to let us on their campus to arrest three people. We'll have to catch them after they're off campus."

"Agreed," Chief Handley added. He picked up a phone and asked Britney Taylor to come in. Handley waved her to a chair. "Ms. Taylor, we are going to need two arrest warrants for murder this afternoon."

Whittaker interrupted. "Chief Handley, let me make a suggestion. My assistant can get these additional warrants in no time. Let's have Ms. Taylor do the same here in Fairfax as a backstop in case there's a glitch at my end. Regardless of how and where we pick them up, we want them to end up in MPD's holding cells, rather than the jail here in Fairfax or even in D.C.'s jail for now. Let me get my assistant on the line and let Ms. Taylor listen in also so that we don't have to repeat the details. Let's get those warrants going, and then we can discuss the logistics of the arrests."

"Good plan," Chief Handley said and pushed the speakerphone over to Chief Whittaker, who dialed Beverly Gray's direct line.

When she answered, Whittaker said, "Corporal Gray, we're going to need two more emergency arrest warrants for murder naming Vincent Morehead and Kurt Bardak." He told her that Britney Taylor was Chief Handley's administrative assistant and that she would be seeking duplicate arrest warrants in Fairfax in case there was a complication. Gray and Taylor exchanged contact information, including cell numbers, then gathered the same information from everyone else present. Whittaker asked both women to email the warrants to everyone as soon as possible.

Beverly Gray concluded the call by telling Whittaker that an email copy of the arrest warrant for Marian Benedict had been delivered to Chief Handley's office within the last five minutes. It had also been sent by text and email to Whittaker, Burke, and Shaw. The Chief said he would forward it to his Fairfax counterparts. Oliver said, "Chief, I just sent it to them both plus Ms. Taylor."

CHAPTER SEVENTY-ONE

CHIEF HANDLEY SAID, "Let's move on to logistics. I guess we have to assume that all three of them are currently at work at the CIA. It's not realistic to assume we can spot them coming out of the south entrance after work."

Woody Thomas suggested, "We have cellphone numbers for them. Why not use Stingray to track them? The urgency would justify the use."

Handley looked at Chief Whittaker. "George, I know you guys also have Stingray. We've gotten some heat from the ACLU about tracking people with it, so we have adopted a policy to only use Stingray in emergencies. I think this qualifies."

"We have had the same experience," Whittaker said, "and have a similar policy on use of Stingray."

All five of the men at the table knew the ability of Stingray to locate specific cellphones. Stingray was originally developed by the U.S. government and the Harris Corporation to use in the wars against drugs and terrorism, but subsequently had been made available to federal law enforcement agencies and select police departments. The software and its capabilities were subject to an ironclad nondisclosure agreement. In short, the actual use of Stingray could not be disclosed, including to courts, even if that means the dropping of cases rather than disclosing its use.

Stingray is basically a cell tower simulator with a boosted signal. Cellphones automatically connect to the strongest cell tower signal. The cellphone user has no idea that Stingray has taken over the link to their phone and calls go through as usual. But Stingray can pinpoint the physical location of the cellphone so precisely that it can identify its exact placement to within six feet.

Woody Thomas said, "You know we can't use any location information we get in a trial, to the extent it would require us to disclose that we obtained that data through Stingray. Given the complication of tracking these three people as they come out of CIA's campus, I think the use is clearly justified, especially since we have three people whose lives are at risk."

"Agreed," Oliver said. "Let's plug in the cell numbers for Benedict and Bardak, as well as the two cellphones that Morehead uses. Can we get real-time data sent to all of our cells showing the location of all four of their phones?"

"I'm pretty sure we can," Thomas said. "Maybe even more people, but that widens the disclosure, which is a risk that we can't run."

"George, if you're agreed," Leon Handley said, "let's get this in place immediately. It's already past three. Some of them could be leaving the Agency before long."

"I agree," Whittaker said. "Can your technical people put it in place?"

Thomas picked up his cell and made a call. "Steve, can you come up to Chief Handley's office immediately? We're going to need to use Stingray. Bring your laptop." He hung up.

Within three minutes we were introduced to Steve Summerford, who was the technology guru for the Fairfax Police. He was forty-ish with a black beard.

He was quickly brought up to speed on the numbers we needed to locate and the five of us who were to receive the geolocation data in real time. It was amazing to watch Summerford fly through the process. You would have thought he did this every day.

In less than fifteen minutes from the time he had entered Handley's office, all five of us—six, if you counted Summerford—had maps on our screens showing the numbers one through four. All four numbers were thankfully still located at the New Headquarters Building at Langley. I didn't know about the others, but I breathed a sigh of relief.

Summerford told us that he had assigned number one to Benedict's phone and the number two to Bardak's phone. "I assigned three and four to Morehead's two phones," he said. "I didn't figure it mattered which one was which."

Chief Handley turned to Woody Thomas. "Let's get some unmarked cars to the residences of these three people. They won't need to be right on top of their homes, as we'll be able to warn them when our suspects are coming."

Thomas stepped out of the room to make the arrangements. He came back into Handley's office about five minutes later. "We've got two unmarkeds headed to each of the residences. One car at each location will have plainclothes detectives and the other will have uniformed officers. Everyone has been warned that these people may be dangerous, although we hope to catch them off guard."

* * *

I suggested to Chief Whittaker that we dispatch detectives to Benedict's residence to take her into immediate custody after the Fairfax Police made the arrest and drive her back to the holding cells at MPD headquarters.

He agreed and told me to call Detectives Rae Davis and Jerry Faircloth and tell them to get over there *posthaste*—his actual word, which I had also heard Corporal Gray use. I called Rae on her cellphone. "Rae, Mac Burke here. I'm with Chief Whittaker and Oliver at the office of Chief Leon Handley at the Fairfax County Police Department. We're getting ready to move in on arrests on the case you helped us with. Chief Whittaker told me to have you get over to the residence of Marian Benedict just west of Arlington in Fairfax County." I gave her the address.

I continued, "Oliver will send you and Jerry the D.C. arrest warrant. The Chief of Detectives here in Fairfax is Woody Thomas. He has already dispatched two unmarkeds to the same address. One car will have uniformed officers and the other plainclothes. I'll ask Chief Thomas to text you their names and cell numbers, so you can make contact when you get there.

"The Fairfax Police will make the arrest and immediately turn her over to you under our interlocal agreement. Take her straight to the holding cells at headquarters. Don't talk to her at all. Let her chill until we get back there to interrogate her. We hope she might flip on the guy behind this whole scheme. Let me know when you're in position and when you have her in custody. Thanks."

I then gave Woody Thomas the names and cell numbers of Rae Davis and Jerry Faircloth so he could forward contact information about the officers and detectives he would have at that scene.

While I had been talking to Rae Davis, Chief Whittaker was on the phone with Beverly Gray to get the tow truck en route to take Benedict's car back to MPD's impound lot. Whittaker then said, "The other two warrants for Morehead and Bardak are being sent to all five of us by text and email."

CHAPTER SEVENTY-TWO

WHEN VINCENT MOREHEAD finally checked his voicemail, he was not happy. He called Winston's cellphone. "What's happening?"

Parker Winston sounded frazzled. "Today we got another subpoena from MPD asking for all of the policies still held by Funds Five and Six. I called and complained that they were trying to ruin my business."

"Did they give you an explanation?"

"They just said they were continuing their investigation and pressured me to send the names on the policies we still hold."

Morehead just shook his head. It was about over, but now he was really worried about Parker Winston. "Tell you what. Let's meet at the club and discuss it. See you in the parking lot in about half an hour." And he hung up without waiting for a response.

Morehead then opened his safe, removed one of the loaded syringes, and put it in his pocket. Knowing that cellphones can be tracked, he put both of his cells in a desk drawer and locked it up. He then headed toward his vehicle in the parking garage.

* * *

Maggie Hampton had been on edge for most of the day. She hadn't gotten much of her regular work done, as she kept monitoring her tracking screen in her office.

Around four in the afternoon, she noticed movement on Morehead's car. She hadn't exactly figured out what to do with her implanted trackers. She decided to wait to see when the other two moved as well. She dug out her burner phone and sent Oliver a text: MOREHEAD LEAVING WORK. A FRIEND.

Over the past week, Maggie had quietly taken photos of the driver's licenses of Benedict, Bardak, and Morehead that McDermott had in the file he brought home each night. She checked Morehead's license, and it looked like he was headed home, based on the way the tracker was moving. She now kept her office door closed and was monitoring her tracking screen full-time.

*   *   *

At the conference table in Chief Handley's office, Oliver's cell pinged. He looked at the screen, and his eyebrows scrunched together. I knew that look and said, "What?"

Oliver told the group, "We originally identified Benedict and Bardak as a result of an anonymous tip from someone calling themself 'A Friend.'" He used air quotes. "I just got a text from the same person saying that Morehead was leaving work. And signed 'A Friend' again."

We all looked at our screens and saw that neither of the Stingray trackers for either of Morehead's cells was on the move.

"What's that mean?" Chief Whittaker asked.

Woody Thomas said, "Could mean that he's on the move without his phones."

"Why would he do that?" Chief Handley asked.

Woody replied, "Maybe he senses we're closing in on him and doesn't want to be tracked. If that's the case, Stingray won't help us with Morehead. As a belts and suspenders move, I put two unmarked cars about a block from either side of the south entrance. Maybe they can pick him up as he leaves the parking garage."

He picked up his cell and called one of the cars. "There's a silver Range Rover with a white male coming out of the CIA gate. Keep a loose tail on him. We no longer have a tracker on him. He may be headed to his residence in Spring Lake." Thomas told him the street that Morehead lived on. "I have two unmarked cars stationed near his house. If it looks like he's not going there, let me know."

* * *

After about four minutes, Woody Thomas' cell rang and he pressed the speaker button: "He must have left before we got the alert. No silver Range Rover has come out of the CIA's parking garage. What do you want us to do?"

Thomas said, "One of you stay there to wait and see if he comes out. The other one head at speed toward his residence address to see if he's headed home. Keep me posted."

Thomas turned to Oliver. "Can your source help us further?"

Oliver grabbed his cell and texted back to A Friend: WE'VE LOST HIM. DO YOU HAVE A WAY TO TRACK HIM?

* * *

Maggie read Oliver's text. Rule One: Never reply to texts on a burner. But she could tell something had gone wrong.

She jumped back to her tracker on Morehead's Range Rover. It still looked like it was headed to Morehead's house.

She sent Oliver a further text: APPEARS HEADED TO HIS
HOUSE.

*   *   *

Oliver read the text to the group. Woody Thomas contacted his
pursuit vehicle and the two cars near Morehead's home with the
update. They didn't know that Morehead had already passed the
logical turnoff to head toward his house and was headed toward
Eastwood Country Club.

*   *   *

At 4:50, Maggie's Hawkeye tracker number three showed movement. That was the tracker on Benedict's car.

Maggie watched it exit the CIA campus and appeared to be
headed toward Arlington. She checked Benedict's driver's license
and saw that she lived in the Arlington area. Maggie again assumed
that Benedict was headed home. She didn't send Oliver a text this
time, thinking it would be too obviously coming from inside the
CIA building.

*   *   *

In Chief Handley's office, Steve Summerford said, "We've got
movement on Stingray number one, which is Benedict. Appears
to be headed toward Arlington."

Woody Thomas said, "She lives near Arlington. We've got cars
waiting there for her. Also, MPD has someone en route."

Chief Whittaker added, "My detectives got there about ten minutes ago and have made contact with your officers and detectives."

Just then, Woody's cell rang. He listened briefly. "Okay. Stay there until we get an update. He may still be headed home."

"It appears that Morehead is not headed home," Woody announced. "At least, not yet."

About eight minutes later, Woody's cell rang again. He listened and said, "Good news, guys. And MPD has her? Great. Okay, I'll tell them that too."

Woody looked up. "Benedict is in custody and turned over to the MPD detectives on scene. They've already left for D.C. The tow truck is there also. The driver has put a tarp over the Prius and loaded it on a flatbed."

Chief Whittaker said, "One down."

CHAPTER SEVENTY-THREE

MOREHEAD PULLED INTO the parking lot of the Eastwood County Club. He spotted Winston's car and parked on the left side of him. He reached in the pocket of his sport coat and flicked off the protective cap from the needle. He had already decided that he did not want to get into Winston's car for fear of leaving any trace evidence.

He then walked around the back of his Range Rover and up to the driver's window. Winston lowered the window. Morehead sniffed and crunched up his cheeks. As Winston started to speak, Morehead jabbed him in the neck and depressed the plunger.

Winston blurted, "What the . . ." and faded off as he started to shake violently. Morehead gave him a push so that Winston was effectively lying across the console into the passenger seat, which made him less visible to passersby.

Morehead recapped the syringe and put it back in his coat pocket. He got back in his Range Rover and headed to a nearby Chick-fil-A. He went through the drive-thru to pick up some food and a drink and headed home. On the way, he dropped the spent syringe out the window.

* * *

Woody Thomas received a call from one of the cars he had stationed near Morehead's house. He put it on the speaker. "We've got Morehead in custody. He's in the backseat of the cruiser."

"Did he put up any resistance?" Thomas asked.

"None," the officer said. "He was carrying a Chick-fil-A bag and a Coke. He asked us what this was all about. We only told him that we had an arrest warrant for him."

"Perfect," said Thomas. "Per our interlocal agreement with MPD, take him to the holding cells at MPD's headquarters. Don't talk to him at all or let him call anyone. Got it?"

"Yessir. Will do. When we frisked him, he didn't have a cellphone or any weapons."

Chief Handley said, "Two down."

CHAPTER SEVENTY-FOUR

As there was only one more car to monitor, Maggie moved from her office down to the Taurus on the second parking deck. She had retrieved her laptop, Glock, baseball cap, and fake glasses from the trunk.

While she waited for Kurt Bardak to leave, she tinkered with the software on her phone to focus only on Hawkeye tracker number two. She also figured how to use the GPS feature on her phone to give her verbal directions over the speaker to follow Bardak once he was moving. As a backup, she also fired up her laptop and got it to focus solely on tracker number two.

At about four thirty, Bardak's car moved. Maggie heard his throaty exhaust coming up the ramp inside the garage. She scrunched down until he had passed her car on the second parking deck. Then she followed him out of the garage. She had noted that Bardak lived in Falls Church but, instead of heading south in that direction, he turned north on Colonial Farms Road around the western perimeter of the CIA campus.

As always in the D.C. area, evening rush-hour traffic was atrocious, which actually made it easier for Maggie to keep his red Camaro in sight. Bardak got on the GW Parkway and headed toward Arlington. Before he got there, he crossed the Potomac

River on the Francis Scott Key Bridge into Northwest D.C. When they were stuck at a red light with her two cars behind him, she sent Oliver another text: BARDAK HEADED TO NORTHWEST IN RED CAMARO. A FRIEND.

*   *   *

Back in Chief Handley's office, Steve Summerford had already alerted the group that Stingray Two was headed north and not toward his home in Falls Church. It showed that Bardak had just crossed the Key Bridge into Northwest D.C. For a moment, no one was sure what this meant.

I said, "We've been so focused on making the arrests, but Benedict is out of circulation. What if—going back to our earlier discussion about the three people at most risk—Bardak is pursuing another assignment which Morehead gave him earlier?"

Oliver grabbed the sheet on the table about Bradley Ford. "This guy Ford is the only one in Northwest."

I looked up the main phone number for Ford's firm on Connecticut Avenue. A receptionist answered, and I asked to speak with Bradley Ford. I identified myself as Mac Burke, but didn't tell her I was with MPD. The receptionist connected me with Ford's assistant.

I told his assistant that I was an old friend of Ford's from Ohio State and was hoping to catch him for a drink. She said he was tied up on the Hill working with the staff of a subcommittee of the House Armed Services Committee on details for the upcoming Defense budget.

"Darn," I said. "That sounds boring. Will he be tied up a long time?"

His assistant chuckled. "Boring is right, but it's what he does. They were supposed to start their meeting around five. I suspect he'll be there at least a couple of hours."

"Okay," I said. "I'll be in town a couple days. I'll try to connect with him tomorrow."

She said she would tell him in the morning.

"Ford is tied up with a subcommittee meeting on the Hill for at least a couple of hours," I said. "Chief, I say we boogie over to Northwest and, using Stingray, try to track Kurt Bardak down right now."

"Leon," Chief Whittaker said, "can you guys stay on tracking Bardak, and I'll get people moving to close in on him while we beat feet to get there ourselves?"

Chief Handley replied, "We'll be here, George, until this is wrapped up. Keep us posted. How about I offer you a chopper which can get you to the roof of either George Washington University Hospital or Georgetown's medical facility?"

Whittaker said, "Excellent. How quickly can you get the helicopter wound up?"

Woody Thomas held up a hand and finished talking on his cell. "They'll be on the roof in five minutes. I'll show you the way up there."

We shook hands with Chief Handley and Steve Summerford. Woody Thomas led us to the rooftop helipad. When the helicopter landed, Whittaker asked the pilot to put us on top of the GW Medical Center, which was the closest helipad to our last Stingray location.

While we were in the air, Chief Whittaker put out an all-points bulletin to stop and arrest Kurt Bardak for murder. He also gave them the latest geolocation we had from the Stingray system.

Oliver supplied a picture of Bardak and the description of his Camaro, both of which went out with the APB.

Whittaker also made arrangements for two cruisers to pick us up at the GW Hospital heliport. The Chief also called his driver and explained the change of plans and told him to return to headquarters.

CHAPTER SEVENTY-FIVE

MAGGIE WAS STAYING two cars behind Bardak as he negotiated rush-hour traffic toward Connecticut Avenue. He pulled into an underground parking garage at an office building which, unknown to her, was a half block from Bradley Ford's office. She pulled in right behind him and ended up parking three spaces from where he put the Camaro.

She put her hair under the baseball cap and put on her fake glasses. She stuffed her Glock into her shoulder bag. Knowing the tracker would no longer be of use, she put her phone away.

A steady flow of people were leaving work and retrieving their cars, so there was enough foot traffic that she wasn't noticeable tracking him. She was about twenty yards behind him and followed him to the staircase. Maggie stayed about one floor behind him until Bardak pushed open the door to Connecticut Avenue and stepped out onto the sidewalk. She accelerated and was out the door about fifteen feet behind him. She spotted him heading north.

Maggie chanced taking the time to send Oliver one more text. BARDAK ON FOOT AT 1705 CONNECTICUT AVE. A FRIEND.

She continued to follow Bardak up Connecticut Avenue.

* * *

A patrolman was waiting for us on GW Medical Center's helipad. He rushed us to an express elevator intended for incoming patients and got us to the ground floor faster than we could have run down the stairs. Two cruisers were waiting for us.

At that moment, we all got texts from Steve Summerford saying that Bardak was in the 1700 block of Connecticut. Then Oliver got the text saying Bardak was on foot at 1705 Connecticut. Chief Whittaker got in one cruiser, while Oliver and I took the other one. With full lights and sirens, we screamed through the rush-hour traffic a distance of six blocks.

Just as we spotted him and were hopping out of the cruisers, another patrol car screeched to a halt and a uniformed officer jumped out and tackled Bardak, who fought back. In the brief struggle, Bardak managed to get control of the officer's weapon.

* * *

Maggie saw Oliver and Mac jump out of an MPD cruiser. Mac was on the sidewalk side of the patrol car. She was now about twelve feet from Bardak and six feet behind Mac. At that moment, the tires of another police cruiser noisily smoked to a stop at the curb, and an MPD cop bailed out and tackled Bardak, knocking him to the concrete.

In seconds, Maggie saw Bardak punch the officer and grab the weapon from the cop's holster. Almost simultaneously, she reached in her shoulder bag and pulled out her Glock, while she saw Mac draw his weapon as well. Mac then shouted at Bardak, who turned to face Mac from his prone position on the sidewalk. Bardak started to raise his gun toward Mac.

Maggie knew that Mac was a very poor shot and instantly feared he would be hurt or killed. Wasting no time, Maggie put one shot into Bardak's right shoulder, causing him to drop the gun. The uniformed cops jumped on Bardak and quickly subdued him.

Maggie immediately did a 180 and walked away while casually putting her pistol back in her shoulder bag. She couldn't afford to be connected with any of this. She headed back to the garage, retrieved her rented Taurus, and drove toward home.

CHAPTER SEVENTY-SIX

I SAW IT HAPPENING almost in slow motion. There are moments in life when time slows down to a crawl. I was about six feet away from him and pulled my pistol while shouting at Bardak to drop the gun. From his position on the sidewalk, he saw me—and was raising the gun in my direction. I fired.

He was hit in the right shoulder and the two officers from the cruiser piled on him. He was cuffed and frisked. His cellphone and a hypodermic needle were bagged and handed to Oliver. An ambulance was called. Oliver placed him under arrest for murder. The ambulance took him to the GW Medical Center.

Before they departed, he was put in the custody of an officer who was given instructions to bring him to headquarters, if he was released. Otherwise, he was to be cuffed to his bed in the police unit at the med center and kept under close guard until he was released to our custody. The officer climbed into the ambulance to accompany Bardak to the hospital.

The Chief was standing next to Oliver and me. He said, "That beats the hell out of my normal day. Well done in every respect." He gave us each a pat on the shoulder and turned to call Chief Handley to let him know the outcome.

When he finished, we told him that we would do the initial interrogations and call him later. As Chief Whittaker stepped toward a cruiser to return to headquarters, his cellphone rang and he stopped to take the call. As he talked, he raised a finger to hold us up.

When he finished, he walked over to us, shaking his head. "That was Chief Handley again. They have another homicide that is probably part of our case. They've got a body in a car in the parking lot of Eastwood Country Club."

I saw Oliver's eyebrows click up a notch. The Chief said, "The I.D. on the body said it was Parker Winston."

I asked, "Homicide or suicide."

The Chief replied, "Not clear. But probably homicide."

Oliver said, "Both Morehead and Winston are members at that club. And Morehead lives about a mile from there."

The Chief looked at us. "More for you to solve. Where was Morehead when he went missing on us for a little while."

Oliver said, "Yes, sir. We'll get details from Woody Thomas and address Morehead's whereabouts during the short time we lost him this afternoon."

*   *   *

I stepped aside on Connecticut Avenue and, violating the social norms in our Nation's capital, I lit up a Marlboro while I sent a text to Mags: ALL 3 ARRESTED. HEADED TO INTERROGATIONS OF 2. ONE IN HOSPITAL. PROB HOME ABOUT 8:30.

She replied quickly. I'LL MAKE SOME DINNER. GLAD YOU WRAPPED IT UP.

CHAPTER SEVENTY-SEVEN

DUSK WAS SETTING when Oliver and I finally left MPD head-quarters after interrogating Benedict and Morehead and calling Chief Whittaker with a report. The dome of the Capitol was fully illuminated against the golden glow of the late evening sky. I lit a Marlboro, and Oliver and I quietly stood in the parking lot admiring the beauty of where we lived. We didn't say a word for a couple minutes and just savored the evening air.

"We earned our keep this week, partner," I finally said. It always feels like I stand an inch or two taller after the burden of a tough case is lifted off my shoulders.

All he said in reply was, "Yes, indeed."

I flicked the ash out on my cigarette and put the butt in the box. We climbed in the Jeep. After dropping Oliver at his house, I headed for home.

* * *

It was right at eight thirty when I pulled into my side of the garage. The Speedster was also in residence. I closed up the garage and went up the steps to the back door. Tonight, I was not carrying a work file.

When I went in, there was the aroma of dinner cooking, and Mags was standing at the kitchen counter pouring herself a glass of pinot noir. She set her glass down and gave me a giant hug and a long kiss full of emotion.

Looking deeply at my face, she asked, "You okay?"

I smiled. "Quite a day. My guardian angel was with me. I'm just glad to be home with you."

While I couldn't swear to it, I think she had a tear in her eye. To hide her emotions, she turned and took a sip of her wine. Then she turned around, leaned into me with another long hug, her head against my chest. I felt my heart swell for this woman.

Without breaking the embrace, I leaned back a little and smiled at her. "Mags, bless you for cooking dinner. I just realized that I didn't eat lunch today."

She returned my smile. Her eyes teared up again. "McDermott, you know I'm psychic."

I was truly contented and smiled. I felt embraced to be at home with Mags.

"How does pork tenderloin roasted with buttered Vidalia onion halves sound? Along with basmati rice."

"Absolutely on the mark. What can I do to help?" I asked.

Mags replied, "Set the table and pour yourself a drink. Dinner is about ten minutes away."

"I'm going to run upstairs and change. Be right back."

When I returned, she was slicing the pork tenderloin on a cutting board and plating our dinner. I grabbed cloth napkins and silverware and put them on the table. Then I poured myself a glass of the Willamette Valley pinot noir that Mags had opened.

On my way to the table, she handed me a full plate of food. "That one's yours. I gave you large helpings to save on steps later."

After she filled her plate, she joined me at the table. She saw that I hadn't started eating yet. "Why are you waiting?"

"I'm trying to be polite."

She shook her head. "Starving boys must be fed. Eat!"

And I dug in. Pork tenderloin is one of the ugliest pieces of meat when you buy it at the store but, after it is properly roasted, it is the leanest, most beautiful looking meat you can put on a plate. Also, one of the best-tasting. After I had eaten at least two bites of everything, I pronounced the meal to be absolute perfection. She bowed her head slightly in acknowledgement of the compliment.

"If I had known you could cook like this, I would have married you."

She got that dimple on the right side of her mouth. "As I recall, you did."

"Oh, yeah. Guess I did. How'd that work out?"

Mags smiled. "Actually, it's going better than either of us contemplated a few years ago."

My response was, "True statement, *mon ami*."

I leaned over and gave her a long kiss. "I still love you, woman. You are a true life partner in all the ways you watch over me."

Her forehead wrinkled a little as her eyes probed mine, trying to figure out what I was actually saying. Which was kind of my intention. I also can be a little mysterious on occasion.

Then we finished our dinner.

EPILOGUE

AFTER THE DUST SETTLED, a number of interesting developments occurred.

*   *   *

Marian Benedict waived her rights and flipped on Vincent Morehead. In recorded and written statements, she admitted that Morehead had hired her to kill Weldon Van Damm with succinylcholine and to kill Dominic Bonfiglio the next day in the hit-and-run.

She did not know the reason behind the murders. She also did not know anything about Kurt Bardak's involvement in other murders for Morehead.

In the end, Marian Benedict pleaded guilty to two counts of first-degree murder. She is currently serving thirty-five years to life. The District of Columbia does not have its own prison, so the Federal Bureau of Prisons assigned Marian Benedict to the Federal Detention Center in Philadelphia.

*   *   *

Kurt Bardak refused to cooperate in any manner. He was tried in the D.C. Superior Court, virtually across the street from MPD headquarters.

The cellphone geolocation records helped convict Bardak of the murders of Conrad Ritzen at the Senate underground garage, Andre Pritchard in Glover Archibald Park, Miguel Garcia at his gym, and Eugene Rollins at the Nationals ballpark.

The geolocation information also placed him at the murder scenes of Stuart Dudley at the ski resort in New Hampshire and being present when Perry Reinemann was forced off U.S.-60 in West Virginia, but neither of those states wanted to incur the cost of trying him after he had been convicted of the other four murders in the District of Columbia.

The closed-circuit video of Bardak at the Nationals ballpark was critical evidence at trial with respect to the murder of Eugene Rollins. D.C.'s closed-circuit cameras also captured Bardak and his tapered tail Harley at Glover Archibald Park at the time of Andre Pritchard's murder. The fact that he was carrying a hypodermic needle filled with succinylcholine at the time of arrest on Connecticut Avenue probably also contributed to his conviction. The jury in the Bardak trial was largely convinced by the bank records showing the payments from Morehead before and after each of the four murders. Bardak did not testify in his own defense.

The most convincing evidence against Bardak was the testimony of Vincent Morehead, which the jury found to be the clincher for conviction. Morehead testified that Bardak did not know why Morehead targeted these people. Bardak was just in it for the money.

Bardak was sentenced to fifty years to life. The Bureau of Prisons assigned him to the Federal Correctional Institution in Petersburg, Virginia.

* * *

Three things convinced Vincent Morehead to plead guilty to the eight counts of murder. First, the evidence against him was insurmountable. The second was the loss of his secret bank accounts. The third was the possibility of Virginia seeking the death penalty against him, while there was no death penalty in D.C.

Other than Parker Winston, none of the homicides occurred in Virginia. While the District of Columbia, New Hampshire, and West Virginia had all abolished capital punishment at the time of these eight murders, Virginia still had a death sentence on the books. The Virginia legislature had recently enacted a new law abolishing capital punishment effective on July 1st, which became effective after the date of all nine murders, leaving the death penalty still in play in Virginia.

The Virginia Commonwealth's prosecutor worked with the D.C. prosecutor to pressure Morehead into pleading guilty and testifying against Bardak in return for not prosecuting Morehead in Virginia for conspiracy to commit the eight murders, as well as the murder of Winston. In reality, Virginia was having difficulty putting together a solid case against Morehead on the murder of Parker Winston. All they really had in the way of evidence was a Chick-fil-A receipt from a nearby location, but the Virginia prosecutor played his role well and convinced Morehead and his attorney that Morehead faced the death penalty in Virginia.

A deal was struck with Morehead. He would be tried in the District of Columbia, plead guilty to all nine homicides, and the Commonwealth of Virginia would not pursue the conspiracy charge or a homicide charge for the murder of Winston. Per the agreement, Vincent Morehead pleaded guilty to all eight murders committed by Benedict and Bardak, including the death of Stuart

Dudley in New Hampshire and Perry Reinemann in West Virginia, as well as the murder of Parker Winston.

Another determining factor for Morehead was that the funds in his three offshore accounts disappeared. He ended up not even having money to pay a lawyer and was forced to use the D.C. Public Defender's office. It was never learned what happened to that money, although Mac and Oliver doubted anyone ever looked very hard.

Vincent Morehead was sentenced to life without the chance of parole. The Bureau of Prisons assigned him to the venerable United States Prison at Marion, Illinois, which is a medium security facility that has housed many notorious criminals over the decades.

* * *

Around the time that Morehead's offshore accounts had been drained, Gallaudet University received an anonymous gift of $1.2 million to enhance their program for nonverbal children and the training of therapists to specifically work with children with those conditions and issues related to autism. The generous donation received some limited coverage by the local media but quickly faded as there was no known benefactor on whom to focus.

* * *

Mac received a call from Pinckney Rutledge, the corporate counsel for Portland Life Solutions, requesting a meeting at MPD's offices. Chief Whittaker wanted to sit in on that meeting as well.

The meeting was held on the fifth floor of the MPD headquarters. In the conference room were Pinckney Rutledge and Samuel

Lynch, Chairman of the Board of Directors of Portland Life Solutions. For MPD, present were Chief Inspector George Whittaker and Detectives McDermott Burke and Oliver Shaw.

Samuel Lynch was a gentleman slightly over six feet tall with salt and pepper hair consistent with his apparent age of around sixty. He wore a bespoke charcoal-gray suit.

Lynch said that Portland had closely followed the trial of Kurt Bardak and the cases of Marian Benedict and Vincent Morehead. He said that they had also had extensive internal conversations about Parker Winston's involvement in the whole situation.

While claiming that Portland had no legal liability arising out of Morehead's actions, Lynch said that the Board felt that Winston had not made sure adequate safeguards were in place to prevent what happened. Portland had negotiated sizable settlements with Whitney Van Damm and the heirs of the other seven victims. Lynch said that Winston's widow had contributed a significant portion of his holdings in the company to help pay those settlements. Portland had made up the difference.

Chief Whittaker thanked them for bringing this matter to closure.

With that, Mr. Lynch stood up and shook hands with Whittaker, Burke, and Shaw, and left the room with Pinckney Rutledge in tow.

Chief Whittaker said, "Huh." Mac Burke said, "Yeah."

*   *   *

Simone Reese applied to become a detective with MPD. She was promptly accepted based on the strong recommendation of Chief Inspector George Whittaker. She did not have to go through the full course of Academy classes, but she received specialized training in the duties she would be performing as a detective.

She now works on the same floor as McDermott Burke and Oliver Shaw. Chief Whittaker partnered her with Detective Rae Davis.

*   *   *

Maggie Hampton was promoted to GS-15 and replaced Vincent Morehead as the head of the Financial Analysis Section of the Political Action Group at the CIA. She suspected, but didn't know for sure, that her mentor, Harrison Jones III, might have had a hand in her elevation.

*   *   *

MPD never figured who shot Kurt Bardak on the sidewalk on Connecticut Avenue. Mac's Glock uses 40 S&W ammo. Bardak was wounded with a 9mm bullet.

It was unknown to any others that Maggie was standing six feet behind Mac when Bardak started to raise the pistol. She and Mac fired simultaneously. All of the witnesses said they only heard one shot. Mac's bullet was never recovered. Only Maggie Hampton knows who actually fired the shot that wounded Bardak and probably saved Mac from being shot. Since she immediately turned and left the scene, neither Mac nor Oliver noticed her.

*   *   *

Maggie Hampton and McDermott Burke continue to live together as a happily divorced couple.

ACKNOWLEDGMENTS

One never knows whether the manuscript you are generating is well done or just drivel. Initially, I asked friends and family to review the manuscript. Ten people volunteered but, in the end, only two came through: my daughters Taylor Morris and Whitney Summerford stuck with it. I told them I did not want kudos, but rather criticism. That they gave me as I sent them ten chapters at a time. I changed the tone and characters in response to their comments and criticism. This story is better for their contributions.

Also, I must thank both my brother, Tom Spoonhour, a retired anesthesiologist, and my other daughter, Erin Spoonhour-Durrant, a CRNA—nurse anesthetist—for their input in what became the primary method used in the eight murders covered in this tale. How could I go wrong using a chemical as a murder weapon with the common name "sux"? David Ashley, DVM, lent me his veterinary expertise in treating racehorses, which provided an interesting part of the story.

This book would not have hit the shelves without the support of Bob Gussin and Patricia Gussin of Oceanview Publishing. They took a shot on a debut author and gave me encouragement and advice at so many turns. Lee Randall and Faith Matson of Oceanview were also critical in getting this book to the finish line.

Madeira James of Xuni.com built my website from scratch. Maddee is the best. See https://jamesspoonhour.com and join the newsletter list for a free short story on Frisco, the Robin Hood of Hackers, and periodic author ramblings.

BOOK CLUB DISCUSSION QUESTIONS

1. Would you consider selling your life insurance policy to a viatical company after reading this book?

2. Do you think that the methodical manner in which Mac Burke and Oliver Shaw pieced together multiple clues to solve this case is typical of the way detectives solve cases?

3. Do you think detectives regularly get help from non-official sources like the hacker Frisco?

4. Do you have any comments on the agreeable relationship between Mac and Oliver and their congenial relationship with the Chief and other departmental staff? Do you think that it's realistic? Idealistic? Refreshing?

5. What did you find to be the most interesting of the relationships in this story?

6. How did you feel about Maggie using her "employer's" resources in helping Mac and Oliver? Did you approve or disapprove? Were you worried about repercussions?

7. What were the turning points in this case that led to its solution?

8. Did you feel that the setting—the District of Columbia—was like a character in this book?

9. Some of the restaurants and bars in this book really exist in the District of Columbia and some do not. Did you recognize any of those that were real and did this contribute to the credibility of the story?

10. Did you feel justice was done at the end of the story?

11. Why do you think that Maggie Hampton and Mac Burke continue to live together three years after their amicable divorce?